TAYL

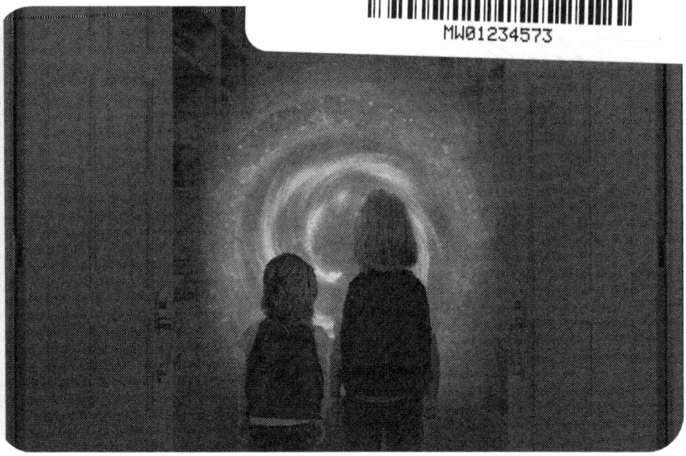

THE PORTAL IN THE PANTRY

BOOK 1

Illustrations by Taylor Gitonga

Educational Trainer Resources

www.edtrainerresources101.com

Publisher's Note: This is a work of fiction. Names, characters, places, and incidents are a product of the author's imagination. Locales and public names are sometimes used for atmospheric purposes. Any resemblance to actual people, living or dead, or to businesses, companies, events, institutions, or locales is completely coincidental.

Ordering Information: Special discounts are available on quantity purchases by corporations, associations, and others. For details, contact the publisher at the address above.

Educational Trainer Resources— First Edition

ISBN 978-1-7370125-7-3 (paperback)

ISBN 978-1-7370125-5-9 (e-book)

ISBN 978-1-7370125-6-6 (Hardback)

Printed in the United States of America

This book is dedicated to little me, a girl of twelve years old who wishes so deeply to follow in the footsteps of my favorite authors.

If you can see this somehow—which you probably can't—then I hope that this story is all that you have wished for and more.

Also, to you, the reader, thanks so much for taking a chance on me.

I truly appreciate you all and thank you in advance for reading my story.

CONTENTS

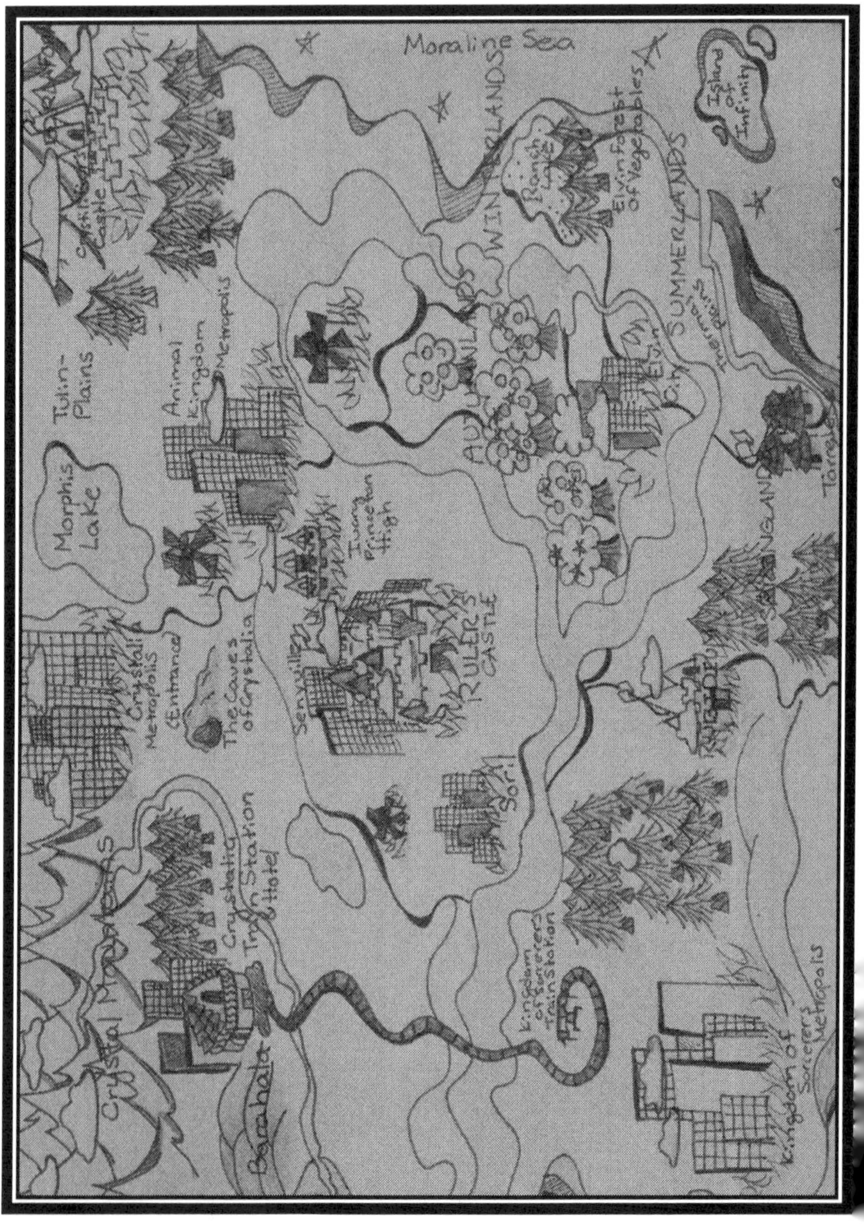
Moraline Sea
Island of Infinity
Elvin Forest of Vegetables
SUMMERLANDS
Tulin-Plains
Morphis Lake
Animal Kingdom Metropolis
Crystalia Metropolis
Entrance
The Caves of Crystalia
RULER'S CASTLE
Crystalia Train Station & Hotel
Kingdom of Sorcerers Train Station
Kingdom of Sorcerers Metropolis

Chapter 1
Disappearing

IN A FLASH OF WHITE, a great crack of lightning struck a lush, bright green clearing in the distance, transforming it into nothing more than a pile of charcoal, a stark contrast to the vibrancy of the swaying grass all around. The field had been ruined now, the stricken spot causing a dandelion to fall to the ground in silence.

It was so quiet, so unimportant, yet this sight caused the small animals in the grass to flee.

However, in the perspective of all the humans in the area, this was just a daily occurrence; nothing too bad would happen in this lightning storm if they were cautious.

"When's the storm ending?" asked Cassie's sister nonchalantly, nestling further into her dark blue blanket as she turned toward Cassie.

"I'm not sure," Cassie said back, handing her younger sister Katie a steaming bowl of freshly made spaghetti. She had just returned from a walk outside to retrieve the mail, her hair drenched with water from the pouring rain and her heart still beating hard from the sudden shock of hearing the deafening rumble of thunder.

She returned to the kitchen where she added, "But it's been over two hours, so it should end pretty soon. At least, I'm hopeful with the downfall that's happening right now."

"Thanks," Katie said as she received the big bowl of pasta cautiously into her hands, eyes still locked on the movie playing on the television screen.

In the light of the flat-screen TV and the lamps illuminating the comfy atmosphere around them, Cassie and Katie sat snuggled and cozy beneath their own two blankets, reposing on two of the three couches in their living room.

The house around them was still, all except for the vibrant figures moving quickly on screen and the fire dancing and crackling in the brick fireplace.

Occasionally, they would hear the sound of creaking steps upstairs, but that was probably their other sister Avery, pacing around her room or such.

That Friday night was one of the few in the year where the responsibilities of Cassie's parents would be placed upon her own young shoulders instead.

Almost every three months, their mother would go on a business trip where she would return home at the end of the weekend, usually late Sunday night or early Monday morning.

Her father would probably go along on the journey as well.

Due to their absence, fifteen-year-old Cassie had to oversee all the day-to-day responsibilities of her parents, which amounted to a lot more work than she had ever expected the first time this happened. To divide the work equally, she put herself in charge of cooking and taking her sisters to clubs by bike or by walking there together.

In contrast, Katie and Avery, her two younger sisters, would be responsible for cleaning the house whenever it was required and doing the things that they were responsible for—laundry, cleaning up their rooms, and the like.

Since it was summer, Cassie was relieved she didn't have to help her sister with math homework, which seemed much harder than she remembered it being for her in fifth grade. Free from the requirement to help Katie with her homework, at least she had a lot more time to relax. There was one downside though; Katie always had trouble with the concepts, which would result in Cassie having to stay up and help her in the late hours of the night, despite all the hard work she would have to do for her own classes as well.

So, her sleep schedule wasn't that good as a result. That was disappointing since whenever she lacked sleep, she couldn't do her own work to the best of her ability.

On the other hand, there was also Cassie's other sister to think about.

Avery had entered ninth grade alongside her the previous school year.

It had taken some time for Avery to become accustomed to being grades ahead of where she was supposed to be, surrounded by hundreds of kids three years older than herself.

But eventually, she was able to acclimatize. To her surprise, she had even managed to make a couple close friends. And for this, Cassie was really proud of her little sister.

After another hour of scrolling on her phone, Cassie stood from the couch and set her phone in her pocket. Standing about a foot from the fireplace, she took a large spray bottle full of water into her hands, spraying water on the flames and watching it shrink with each pull of the trigger. The fire had eventually diminished to piles of ash and chips of wood.

She retook her place on the couch again, observing the fire to make sure it didn't light again for a few seconds before rising once more.

Once the last of the fire was gone, she headed for the hardwood staircase leading upstairs, her large black pants that had stretched and now flopped all the way over her small feet causing her to slip and slide slightly on each foot. "'Night, Katie. Don't turn on the stove, and make sure to turn off the TV and the lights before you head to bed, all right?"

Katie didn't even make eye contact with her sister when she said, "'Night, Cassie."

Cassie was at the top of the stairs when she saw Avery in her room, sitting atop her bed and reading a book, despite it being rather late in the night at this point.

Didn't she ever have anything else she wanted to do?

"Hey, Avery," chirped Cassie, slipping her hand over her sister's smooth lavender bedroom walls until she reached a majestic painting with a bronze frame.

It appeared to be a detailed art piece displaying a gray marble statue of a regal princess-style poufy ball gown. "What's this painting?" she asked. It was an unusual thing to see in her sister's room all of a sudden. Where had she acquired this work of art?

"Just something from my book," Avery said hastily. It was obvious to Cassie that she was clearly being dismissive. "I thought it would be cool to paint it, so I did."

Cassie's face showed an expression of, *wow, just wow. My sister did this? Awesome!*

"It looks really nice," Cassie complimented. "In fact, not just *really nice*. Amazing!"

She hoped they had bonded there in that second.

She could swear Avery's eyes smiled at her, that there was even a little smile on her lips.

Cassie hoped they were enjoying some genuine sister time for a change.

This wasn't about school. Not about homework. It was all about who they were as girls and sisters, and Cassie was astonished and a little sad she had not realized her sister's ability.

But she didn't often get a chance to talk to Avery like this. Maybe now was the time.

She craved to continue talking to her sister, and perhaps now was the time for them to genuinely have that once-in-a-while conversation.

Her eyes looked up to the glass spheres casting light across her sister's ceiling.

Their spheres' strings held them high over their heads, some low enough to reach the lilac purple headrest of her bed.

A cylinder-shaped periwinkle purple lamp was standing atop each black nightstand on either side of her bed, the light they emitted illuminating the room in a faint purple hue.

"So, what're you reading?" she asked.

By the time Avery looked up to answer, Cassie was now sitting in the cloudy purple egg chair in the corner of her room.

"The new series Mom bought me," Avery said briefly. "It's the second book of the *Across the Universe* series."

The two sat in silence for a moment. It was already evident this conversation was going nowhere and was one-sided.

Avery looked back to her book after a few awkward seconds.

"How's—"

The loud flipping of a page stopped Cassie mid-sentence.

Her heart sank. When she had finally come to the realization her sister didn't wish to continue talking to her, Cassie rose from the chair and walked to her own room, leaving an unfazed Avery still sitting on her bed, immersed in her own private world.

Down the hall, Cassie entered a large space with a queen-sized bed with deep purple sheets and a light purple frame. Where her sister Avery had chosen a pale lavender as her bedroom's core color, Cassie's own walls had been painted completely dark purple, with everything in the room also painted in a deep purple hue. The only things not a shade of the color were her white nightstands, black desk, and white closet door.

She sat down in her rotating mauve chair, pulling out a large, black sketchbook from underneath her desk. Avery's work had inspired her. She was hoping to find some time to develop her own art a bit tonight, especially with all this free time she now had.

She played one of her music playlists on her phone as the sound of her scratching pencil reverberated in the empty room.

Checking the time on her phone after a while, it was already hours past midnight, and Cassie could feel her stomach grumbling incessantly.

Maybe I should eat some leftover pasta? It's been a bit over three hours since I ate something. Oh wait! I didn't even put the leftover pasta in the fridge!

She ran down the stairs, finding the kitchen completely deserted and dark.

When she flipped on the lights, she found a black pot still full of pasta, still resting there on the obsidian stove.

She approached the meal, seeing at least half of it still languishing in the pot.

She searched the cabinet for a plastic container large enough to fit the rest of the food into, pulling pulled out a ginormous container and setting it beside the pot on the black granite counter, starting to scoop the food into it.

Then she closed it off with a cover and stuffed it in the fridge.

Before Cassie could reach her room, Katie walked past her down the stairs, her steps echoing in the quiet of the night.

***

Without turning the lights on downstairs, Katie poured herself a glass of apple juice from a skinny carton and placed it back in the fridge.

She was heading back upstairs with the cup but veered off, seemingly having spotted the small green light emanating from their pantry. She stopped short, clearly observing it.

It seemed that while she was busy getting herself something to drink, Avery had come downstairs without her notice, evidently finding something rather peculiar in the pantry.

Katie most likely would've brushed off the sight if not for the green light reflecting into the space around them, and, from her perspective, if not for the way it swirled before Avery.

She was scared to approach the sight, but if Avery was able to, shouldn't she be as well?

"What's this?" Avery said. "Do *you* know?" she asked her sister.

Even though Avery had been observing it for several moments, it seemed as if she wasn't sure what this was either.

Her expression seemed to say, *Maybe, if I just…*

Avery stuck her hand into the portal, Katie jumping back as she did so, crying out, "Avery! Don't!"

What was Avery thinking? At this rate, her curiosity was bound to get the better of her. Katie had to do something before anything happened, but her feet struggled to move.

She knew she wasn't scared, but why couldn't she walk forward?

What if something bad ended up happening to Avery because she just stood here, rigid?

Anyway, why was she stuck like this?

From where she stood on the steps, she could only look on and witness as Avery peered closer into the portal, sticking her head into the source of the light.

Her grip loosened on the white doorframe of the pantry.

But just as Katie's feet finally managed to start moving, Avery's grip was lost.

And in a matter of seconds… Avery had disappeared!

The only noise reaching Katie's ears was the faint sound of her sister's screams.

Katie stood at the base of the steps in shock. The eeriness of the house and the acknowledgment of her older sister's absence were frightening.

She was painfully aware of everything that had just happened.

But where did Avery go? Where could she have disappeared to into that portal-looking thing Katie had just witnessed? This was like make believe—only it was real. It was scary, yet somehow, it seemed to be oddly exciting for Katie too.

She appeared confused and fuzzy-headed—and maybe even a little scared or intimidated—but even so, she approached the pantry, setting her glass down on the floor.

She was curious, inquisitive, like a cat naturally drawn toward a tunnel or a hole.

She still held tightly onto the doorframe, peering warily inside, unable to see anything but an endless void of black, throwing her head back, ready to retreat.

But not because it was scary…

…because it was *nothing.*

Just an endless void in which she could see no beginning, no end.

And if that was where Avery had disappeared to, then was she dead? If not, where had it taken her? Where had she been transported to, from this eerie void?

It was upsetting how terrified she was about this, and so she searched for guidance in Cassie, running into her room with a look of sheer panic on her face.

Cassie looked up immediately, removing her earbuds, saying, "Katie! What was that—"

"Cassie!" Katie screamed over her, tears welling in her glossy eyes. "Avery! She's *gone!*"

"Gone? What are you talking about, Katie?" Cassie immediately denied what Katie was saying, her dismissive tone too audible. It sounded as if she didn't care. But it was more that she had only just seen her sister, and she couldn't possibly be 'gone', could she?

"Avery's gone, Cassie! She's gone!"

Cassie's eyes widened and she tried to pull herself together somehow. Yet there was no sense of control now; she just wasn't herself.

"Well, how then? Where'd she go?"

"She disappeared into this green swirly portal thing.

But it was more like a swirling light—in the pantry."

Katie wiped her eyes, the heaviness of her emotions beginning to subside.

Cassie jumped from her seat as she charged for the door.

"Wait!" Katie shouted, grabbing her sister's arm before she could leave.

If the only other person with her—Cassie—wasn't going to be the voice of reason, it seemed *she* would have to be. "We can't just go in there! I don't even know where Avery went! For all we know, she might not be able to come back."

She let go of Cassie's arm with a sigh.

"We'll have to prepare if we're going to go there to look for her," Katie said. "And we'll need to make sure we have the things we need to—if things get really bad—survive there."

"All right then," Cassie said, grabbing her backpack and emptying its scant contents of paper strips, dried-out pens, and empty mechanical pencils onto her bed.

Katie retrieved the largest backpack she had and placed it on the floor of Cassie's room, beginning to pack items into her bag as they checked things over with each other.

For a few minutes, they looked over the things they'd packed, evaluating what should and shouldn't be brought considering what would fit into their bags.

By the time they had completed their packing, they were aware their bags could weigh them down so they scrutinized everything, discarding items.

Fortunately, in the end, everything they needed could fit somewhat well into one bag.

"Is there anything else we should add?" Cassie said to Katie, her bag still unzipped.

"I thought I heard Avery say, 'What if it's just like the books?' So, maybe we should pack some of the books from her series? Just in case something in them is important where we're going, considering the way she looked at it."

"Yeah, it's probably important if she said something specific about it; it's all she's been thinking about, after all."

"I'll go get the book that she dropped, then."

When Katie returned with the books, Cassie slipped all six volumes of Across the Universe into her bag, slinging it onto her back and switching off all the lights upstairs.

Cassie waited for her sister to make and pack a few egg-salad, turkey, and BLT sandwiches in her bag, before she joined her at the portal with the food.

As they began to put on their jackets, Katie couldn't help but feel worried about whether they'd be able to make it back. Because, even if she was just overthinking, what if they never made it back home? What if she never saw her home again? Her friends? Her parents?

"We'll make it back home," Cassie said, as if she'd been able to read her thoughts. "And we'll see Avery again." She gazed back down at her as she adjusted the straps of her backpack. "I'm sure of it."

Katie nodded as she took her sister's hand, prepping herself to jump into the green light.

Even if she was scared, at least Cassie was here.

At least Cassie would always be here for her… right?

"We jump on three," Cassie said, trying to ease her sister's fear, so it seemed from Katie's perspective.

"We'll make it back home…"

"One…" Cassie started.

"And we'll see Avery again."

"Two…"

"I'm sure of it."

"Three!"

As they leaped together into the green light, it swirled rapidly around them, shifting into a bright marigold orange.

The color began to fade away as they observed the red light beneath them growing in vibrancy below, shining brighter and brighter until its vibrant tint consumed the space surrounding them. Almost instantaneously, the pull of gravity no longer affected them; it was as if they were weightless, as if traveling on the surface of the moon.

Katie enjoyed the feeling, the liberating sensation of freedom from the shackles of her looming dread. Even so, her eyes bulged with apprehension as she looked around frantically for a solution. But all she saw was Cassie trying to do the same.

Despite the sense of security of previously, they were now plummeting toward the light much faster and more obviously than before, screaming at the top of their lungs even though the sound of rushing wind drowned out their voices.

Through all of this though, Katie never let go of her sister's hand, because even if it was fire, just as she feared, as least she'd have Cassie here with her.

Even if it was roaring, dancing, and waiting to devour them, they both knew one thing for certain. They would always be at each other's side.

"No matter what awful things happens to us," Cassie whispered to herself with the background of the rushing wind in her ears, "I'll take care of her. Whatever happens in these next few seconds, I know I have to take care of Katie."

She stopped for a moment.

"I promise to take care of both of them."

And with a deep breath, she uttered the last part, something that Katie managed to hear despite all that was happening. "No matter what happens to me. I promise."

Chapter 2
Escaping

THEIR JUMP TOWARD THE LIGHT SEEMED TO have knocked out both girls, their heads now fuzzy, painful and distant. As they regained consciousness, they could hear a beeping sound, similar to that of an electrocardiogram tracking a heartrate.

It was somewhere in the backs of their minds but even so, both could hear it.

"What's that noise?" inquired Cassie, massaging her forehead as her eyes raised to look up. "And where…"

She stopped short at the sight of a luscious, emerald-green forest with glowing flowers of different colors and towering sequoia-like trees. They turned to admire the violet mountains in the distance, summits barely visible in the clouds that were hovering above them.

When they turned back to see the garden-like forest they had witnessed before, they only saw a horrifying, shocking sight. In place of the beautiful forest, a seven-foot, twin-headed tiger was looming over them, rancid-smelling drool dripping from its razor-sharp fangs.

In that moment, their hearts dropped so low they could feel them in their feet.

Grabbing her sister's arm in her hand, Cassie pulled Katie through the forest, sprinting so fast that the foliage of the forest blurred past them.

They kept running despite the increasingly heavy breaths escaping their lips, their legs tiring, and their backs cursing them for putting them into this painful situation.

They continued running, slowing with each step.

Cassie caught sight of a cliff up ahead.

She threw herself and Katie behind a large bush, breathing as quietly as possible despite her lack of oxygen. They couldn't stay here the whole time; they'd probably be smelt out.

It was common knowledge that big cats had a terrific sense of smell; this cat could sniff them out in a heartbeat—and if they just kept waiting, that twin-headed tiger would surely find a way to catch up to them. The tiger's soft paw pads were audible, coming ever closer.

Damn it, thought Cassie, trembling and wide-eyed.

They were running out of time.

What am I supposed to do?

She was deeply afraid, more for Katie than for herself. *I'm supposed to keep her safe!*

Her thoughts trailed off, catching sight of the cliff only a few feet away.

She crawled a bit closer to the edge and found a river there. Before she even gave her sister another moment to think, she gripped her arm again and leaped with her over the edge.

"What the heck are you doing?" Katie spat out. "You're gonna kill us both!"

They skidded down the hill into the creek, a cloud of dust coming up from behind their feet, blanketing the roots with even more dust as they descended.

Katie fell, then faced her as they reached the bottom of the cliff, the shore of the creek dry with dust; Cassie pulled her toward the wall of the cliffside that hung over their heads.

"What…were…you…thinking?" Katie breathed.

"Shhhh!" her older sister hissed, pointing upwards as the ground shook with each of the tiger's heavy steps.

The two tiger heads looked over the edge for a moment, observing the skid marks left by the girls' shoes and the small crater of dirt that Katie had left behind near the river's shore.

"What d'you think did that?" said the tiger's right head in a raspy voice. "Must've been something unnaturally large considering the size of those prints. Those are not pawprints."

The creature's paw, gestured toward the marks in the dust.

"Some human, I'm assuming," the left tiger head responded, its voice much smoother than that of the other.

The steps of the abnormal creature began to fade, allowing the two sisters to rise from the spot beneath the overhang, where they hid. Both sisters sighed a deep breath of relief.

"So where are we going then?" Katie questioned.

They began walking downstream of the babbling brook.

"Not sure right now," Cassie answered, kicking at the dust of the shore. "But this whole adventure thing is starting off pretty crappy. Although, it's what I signed up for after all."

"Of course, you know it is." Katie said this without thinking, not expecting her sister to provide any sort of rebuttal despite her, in retrospect, poor choice of words. *"Everything* about this is bad. Even if I've only been here a few minutes, I already know this journey's gonna be laborious. But like you said, you promise to take care of your younger siblings."

She looked up into the twinkle of her older sister's eyes as she started off at the calm creek. "Meaning me and Avery. And it'll be worth it in the end once we finally find her."

Cassie was surprised when Katie said this, and it took a while for her to truly take in the words. But when the realization came to her that Katie was right, she nodded.

She continued walking forward.

Cassie knew what she'd signed herself up for—and what she's signed Katie up for, too. But she also knew it'd be worth it in the end when Avery finally came home safely.

But as she raised her head, she caught sight of something horrifyingly perplexing.

A vine, it seemed, was whipping toward them, its smooth green internode wrapping tightly around them both as its wide leaves obscured their view; it was as if the vivid plant was doing it on purpose! Before they knew it, they were atop the cliff from which they had worked so hard to escape, writhing in the grasp of the vine.

But both girls were achieving nothing but making the nasty vine's grip tighter than it already was. Until now, neither of them had realized how the end of the vine was a sunrise orange tiger lily, one of Cassie's favorite flowers from back home.

Yet despite how much she loved it, it couldn't help but bring an array of questions.

Was it alive? Well, of course, it was. It was a plant, wasn't it?

But was it properly alive though, like a person? Could it move? It seemed as if it could.

It looked as though it even had the ability to make conscious decisions.

Do plants like this even exist? she thought. *The only thing I can think of is anemones, but I know for certain this isn't one. But it's also not a tiger lily despite the flower. Bizarre!*

The plant began to pull them toward the two-headed tigers they had seen before, the animal crouching, eyeing them both, observing the sisters' gradual approach.

One head came much closer to Katie, so close she could smell its rancid breath. She would've loved to tell it that its breath smelled like rotting garbage, yet she knew that doing so would be a death wish. Instead, she backed her head away so she couldn't feel the heat of the two heads' breath anymore, keeping her face as straight and emotionless as possible.

It snarled menacingly, ferocious eyes boring into Katie's.

Rearing to snatch her by the neck, the other head moved the shared body away, giving Cassie and Katie a threatening look as it ambled to the far corner of the clearing.

"Calm down," the head on the right said in its signature raspy voice. "The Crystilifier will know what to do with them."

Katie's expression seemed to say, *The Crystilifier? Who or what's that?*

As the creature's two muscular arms grabbed Cassie and Katie, it dragged them through the forest, caking the waist of Cassie's dark jeans and the hems of her lavender blouse with dirt. Katie, meanwhile, was dealing with the same problem, scratching at the skin beneath her black hoodie, the grass somehow finding a way to make her uncomfortable even through her clothes.

"Where are we going?" Katie asked, arm aching in the tiger's grip.

No answer came from either head, still dragging the pair of sisters across soft grass and patches of dirt until they reached a white marble castle. Katie hadn't expected an answer, yet it shocked her to witness the fairytale-like castle looming over her.

They were forced to plop down on the ground, inches away from the polished tile entrance as they looked around in awe.

Four acute turrets stood high above the surrounding forest, while several of the windows on the building flooded sunlight into its halls and chambers.

Crystal blue flags danced in the wind at the turrets' summits, shadows visible through the high windows and intricately stained glass.

As the girls sat, the tigers walked through the castle doors, giving Cassie all the time she needed to rummage through her bag and find the first book of Across the Universe.

She began to flip through the pages, because if there was anywhere they should start searching for more information about this crazy new place, it would be these books.

"Okay, I can't find a more in-depth explanation, but I was able to find that these creature things are called Tigrisia." Cassie used her finger to track where she was on the page. "Says here, they're usually used as guards for royal citizens, like kings and queens and stuff." She glanced up at the castle before them. "Explains the reason why we were brought here then."

Katie's eyes glimmered with excitement.

"Royal? So, we're going to meet royalty then?"

But before her sister could provide an answer, Katie caught sight of a woman in a burlap potato sack, her brown hair disheveled and dirty as she was unwillingly dragged into the castle. Katie looked back to Cassie. "Where's she going?""

"Not sure," Cassie answered. "But that's probably where we'll be going too."

After sitting on the grass for almost an hour in anxious anticipation, the castle's entrance door burst open again, a regal rhinoceros emerging.

Its fluffy silk robe was a shade of dark red, bejeweled with red and green crystals that shimmered in the sun, concealing most of the navy-blue suit it modeled underneath.

It wore a golden crown with blue jewels that flashed your eyes with light when you caught sight of them, its crystal blue wand tip lit up with blue.

The rhinoceros also wore an infuriated frown, making it appear as if it was a disappointed ruler looking down on its subjects, which, in this specific case, it was.

"WHO ARE THESE PEASANTS THAT STAND BEFORE ME?" it shouted in anguish in a royal yet ear-splitting voice, standing over them in dark brown boots.

They both stared up at it momentarily, taking in the darkness in its brown eyes. But seeing the burning rage reflected in them too, they looked away immediately.

"What is this?" said the rhino in a softer voice as it picked up Katie's arm by the sleeve and looked it up and down, as if it was a piece of utterly disgusting garbage. "I've never seen such before."

She gulped and said reluctantly, "If you wouldn't mind me asking, who are you?"

Its eyes widened and it dropped Katie's sleeve immediately.

"You don't know me? Preposterous! Absolutely ridiculous!"

It waved its gigantic foot dismissively, like a hand.

"You must think I'm a numbskull or something," the beast insisted, apparently mortified and embarrassed not to be recognized and revered. *"Of course,* you know who I am…"

It stared at her again intently for affirmation but Katie still seemed confused, gasping in shock as it walked a few steps away from them.

"You really don't know me, do you?" the rhino inquired as it set its hands on its indiscernible hips. "Why, I am the royal Crystilifier, member of the Council of the Realm and sorcerer responsible for the crystallization of the evil sorceress, Lilliana Orbin."

To its dismay, this raised no questions or thoughts in Cassie, nor seemingly in Katie.

The Crystilifier rolled its eyes.

"Guards! Come pick up these... *specimens.* They need to be removed from the premises immediately." As it walked away with thundering steps that shook the earth, the Crystilifier murmured under its breath, "Doesn't know me? How can you not know me? I'm one of the most popular beings in this entire universe... It's preposterous, I say! Ludicrous!"

"Yes, Your Majesty," the twin heads said in unison, prowling toward them.

Right before the Tigrisia could lay its hands on them, the ground beneath Katie and Cassie's feet collapsed, and they plummeted.

Down…

Down…

Into the earth.

***

With a thud, they landed in an underground room split cleanly in two, one bright green side beautifully decorated with green banners, potted plants, and faux vines along the walls, whereas the other side had been painted dark blue and had been littered with various pieces of trash that looked to have been there for days on end. Besides these, the room held one pristine electric guitar, and a navy loveseat bearing a huge pile of laundry.

Not long after their impromptu arrival, however, two foxes, one dark green, the other navy, appeared out of a nearby room as the girls dove behind the little couch they'd previously witnessed. They watched intently as the dark green fox walked close to their hiding place first, their heartrates beginning to speed up as it approached.

Foxes? Why were there foxes in this underground house? Why was there even an underground house to begin with? Foxes didn't have opposable thumbs so how would they even put the space together? How could they move furniture and…

"So many questions…" Katie whispered. "Yet no way of answering them all."

"My ears are twitching," said the dark green animal in a rather feminine voice.

"Why?" the blue one asked, masculine tone heavy in contrast. "Did you hear something?"

Perhaps the foxes knew each other, the two sisters suspected.

"Don't know."

"Is it coming from over there?" said the blue one, pointing its furry paw at the couch behind which the girls were currently hiding. "'Cause I'm picking up on something too."

They walked over to the navy loveseat, inspecting it for a few moments and sniffing around for any change in odor.

"Don't think anything's there, sis," the blue one said, backing its snout away.

"C'mon, Conner, there's gotta be."

"They really do know each other then," Katie and Cassie whispered almost simultaneously.

Katie peeked over the couch, only the cowlick of her dark ginger hair visible to the foxes over the back.

"Did you see that!" the green fox shouted as Conner turned to leave. Cassie tugged her sister back down. "I just saw something!" the green female fox yelled.

"Aria, you're going crazy," Conner sighed. "Just admit you're wrong and move on."

He turned away from her and began walking toward the hall entrance.

On his way out, he picked up a small keychain.

Grumpily, the fox by the name of Aria followed the other fox, Conner, out of the room, only to see Katie's small face peek up over the couch far more noticeably.

"Oh, are you torturing me?" Aria trudged toward the couch again.

She froze to see Katie and Cassie's backs against the walls in fear, hiding their heads between their knees, coat hoods covering their heads to stay somewhat safer.

"What are you doing?" the green fox chuckled, reaching out a paw to help them out. "And why are you two sitting like that?"

Cassie was hesitant to provide a response, breathing heavily while the fox continued to flick her eyes from Cassie to Katie.

"Like I said, what are you doing?" Aria repeated.

Katie peeked up from her hood at the fox for a split second, Aria catching her eye and Katie shrinking back into her coat again.

"I won't hurt you guys, I promise."

Aria waited for a few seconds, then walked away, leaving Katie and Cassie to stay behind the couch until the two sisters finally seemed comfortable greeting the two foxes.

"What the heck was that?" Katie whispered to her sister. "How'd these foxes get here? And why can they talk?" She looked up at the couch. "But I mean if they *can* talk, doing human things like moving stuff seems not to far off."

Cassie glanced at her. "Well, maybe they're safe then, right? We should try and talk to them, shouldn't we, Katie?"

"You're right. Maybe they could help us get out of this weird place." Katie looked up at the hole far above the main room then back at Cassie. "We must've fallen from up there."

She pointed up at it. "Although it must be concealed in something for us to not have noticed it immediately. But even then, we'll have to find some way to get up there."

Katie checked above the couch to observe whether their surroundings were safe, then nodded at Cassie to confirm.

When they had emerged from behind the chair, Katie looked up at the hole again, checking how high they would have to pull themselves up. "We'll need a rope with a hook tied at the end or a ladder or something to get up there." She looked back at the room they were in. "But where would we even find one?"

"We could look around here for one," her older sister suggested. "Or maybe ask those weird talking foxes for one."

"Weird talking foxes?" said a familiar voice. "That's a bit rude, don't ya think?"

They jumped at the new addition to their conversation, looking in the direction from which it had come. It appeared to be the fox from earlier, specifically the green one that had attempted to speak with them beforehand.

"Oh-um-sorry," Cassie quickly apologized. "We were just looking for a way out of here. And we don't wanna bother you—"

"You wanna leave that bad?" the fox chuckled, sitting down on the dirt floor. "Didn't know we were that intolerable."

"Oh jeez. Sorry if that came off as rude." Cassie pulled her backpack straps tighter around her body to distract herself from the fox's gaze, even if just for a few moments. She couldn't help but feel ashamed. "We'll try to get going now."

"Oh, don't worry about it." The green fox beamed a toothy, sly grin. "We can help you."

"We?" Katie asked. "Do you mean the other fox? The blue one, right?"

"Huh, actual human guests," the masculine voice they had heard from earlier chipped in. "Haven't gotten any of those in a while, now have we?"

The blue fox had emerged from their cavernous hallway, strolling in nonchalantly with a steak quesadilla in his mouth. "I'm Conner," he said through his chewing. He gestured toward the green fox and said, "That's Aria. My sister."

"Older sister," Aria corrected.

"Will you shut up about that?" Conner argued. "And it's not like that even matters anyways. I *am* the favorite, after all. Am I right?"

"I won't dignify your immature lie with a response, so respectfully, I'll ask you to shut up, okay?"

Conner smiled at Aria artificially, allowing Cassie to continue with her part of the introduction as he shot his sister death glances.

"I'm Cassie," she introduced after a few seconds. "Fifteen, with barely any experience in, well, anything. Not gardening. Definitely not notetaking." She chuckled at herself. "I should just stop talking, in fact." Her eyebrows jumped as she looked down at the ground. "That was really bad. I did *really* bad."

"Yeah, it was," Katie agreed, "And yeah, you did bad."

Cassie shot her a glare similar to that of Conner to his sister.

Katie resumed their introductions.

"Anyways, I'm Katie. And we have another sister, but she's lost somewhere in—um—whatever this place is. With all these talking animals and two-headed tigers."

"Lost in the Magic Realm?" Aria piped up, seemingly perturbed at the mere implication of such harrowing news. "How did that happen?"

"And I know it sounds crazy, but a magic portal opened in our pantry, and then she—our sister—fell into it," Katie explained. "And I know that story seems stupid, but she's lost somewhere in this dimension. And we have no idea how to find her on top of that."

"The chances of something bad happening to her, especially here, are relatively high," Conner said, rather emotionless considering the words that he spoke. "There are deadly plants unlike anything you've ever seen, evil sorcerers, and perilous animals that can tear you limb from limb in this place." He saw their worried faces and smiled hopefully. "But we'll find some way to locate her, won't we?"

Aria nodded at her brother and looked back to them. "Yeah. We promise we'll find here." She glared at her brother. "Right, Conner?"

Although the two were attempting to assure the sisters that everything would be all right, Cassie and Katie still exchanged nervous glances with one another.

They had never expected this world to be as dangerous as Conner had described it to be. But so far, all they had ever known—the only planet that existed in this universe—was Earth.

And this place certainly did not seem to be anywhere on Earth.

All they wanted was to rescue their sister.

Was this the universe expressing that wanting to have their entire family together was too much to ask? That they didn't deserve to ever see Avery again?

And even if they didn't find her, would they even be able to return home? Would they continue their lives stuck here forever? Or what if they ran into an evil sorcerer?

What if someone had taken Avery?

What if—by now—she was already dead?

No, Cassie thought. *Don't think like that. It isn't true. She's okay. She'll be okay. You promised yourself, didn't you?*

Even if she was trying to stay positive, she still harbored one thought in her mind, a thought of which she was desperate to let go, despite how awful she felt about it.

What had Avery been doing when she'd fallen into that portal?

Chapter 3
Learning the Spells

BEFORE THEIR EYES, THE TWO DIFFERENT colored foxes became a bright flurry of flipping and twisting sparkles, Aria now a ball of bright green and Conner a magical sphere of cyan.

When the ball of green faded away, Aria, a young woman of average height, now stood before them in a light green blouse and a ripped light blue pair of jeans.

Her dirty blonde hair was tied into a short choppy ponytail.

Conner, on the other hand, had transformed into a tall young man with his sister's curly dirty blonde hair. He was wearing a dark gray sweatshirt with the words *MADRIC ACADEMY* spelled out in upper-case orange lettering lined with white.

He appeared to have eyebags, a sign of regular lack of sleep that, considering the state of his room, didn't exactly come as a surprise.

Cassie's eyes flicked from his face to his sweatshirt, then back again. "What's the sweatshirt for? What's Madric Academy?"

"She forces me to wear it so scouts nearby will know she's interested in Madric Academy. It's this fancy-shmancy school," Conner replied, frowning at his sister, who smiled widely back. It was obvious she found joy in using her twin brother as free advertising.

"I personally think her deciding to go there is kinda dumb, but…" He scoffed. "What'd I know? I'm just the stupid twin."

"Yeah, you are." Aria turned back to the sisters.

Cassie looked around the room, searching for some sort of parent or guardian, eyes stopping back at the twins as Conner spoke up.

"There's no point in looking," Conner stated, as if reading her thoughts seamlessly. "They live back in the Earth Realm. But we prefer life here; it's simpler and less demanding.

"We did use to live with our grandma, Ruler Marjorie for a few weeks though…" Conner said. His frown disappeared. "But she…" He took a sigh to release tension. "… she died."

"Could you tell us what happened to her?" Katie hesitated, quickly adding, "If it's fine with you, I mean."

"She was killed protecting a friend," Aria responded, tears coming to her eyes. "She was a selfless person, truly. And an amazing grandmother."

Cassie understood that any further questions would hurt Aria in the tense moment, so instead she gave her a moment to feel her emotions, staying silent and withholding her questions as they stood in silence.

"What are those wands you're holding?" Cassie questioned, trying to change the subject after several silent and tense seconds.

"Oh! These…"

He held up the crystal stick, its two pieces twirling together toward a glistening tip. "They were given to us by our grandmother." He pointed to his sister's wand, appearing to be an almost exact copy of his own. "We use them for spells and magic and stuff."

"Spells?" Katie's eyes lit with excitement in a wondrous way. "If they can do magic stuff like that, then how were they made?" She smiled and gestured toward Aria's wand.

"They're made in the Caves of Crystalia, a bunch of underground caverns where magic gems are found and powered with magic to be made into magical devices," Aria elaborated further. "And since all gems in the Magic Realm possess magical properties, things like charms for bracelets, necklaces, rings, hairpieces, earrings, crowns, and all that other stuff can be used for magical purposes."

"Well then, if that's true, does that mean you guys used your magic to become those foxes? All those colors and lights and stuff have to mean something, right?"

"Yes, exactly," acknowledged Aria in a sisterly manner. "Our wands can perform all sorts of spells like Conner said. And all you've gotta do is say the spell incantation and point at the object you want the magic inflicted upon."

Conner observed how intently Cassie and Katie were listening, and he proceeded with, "Like, when we did the spell that turned us into those foxes, we used a transformation spell, *Dorsiti calcuntactu*. It's a family spell, invented and only known by the Smith bloodline, our bloodline. All except for those who had been directly taught the spell.

"It only lasts for six hours, but you can undo the spell when you need to. Wanna try?"

Conner twirled his wand around his fingers.

"Of course, we do!" Katie chirped, looking to her sister, not for confirmation or agreement but purely because she didn't want her to debate.

"You sure it's safe?" she whispered to Katie skeptically. "I mean what if they're lying?" She paused. "They could be, but if they did, wouldn't—"

"Cassie, it'll be fine. You've seen them use magic before and they're completely okay, aren't they? And what reason do they have to lie to us anyways? They seem nice enough."

"Well, fine." She glared down at Katie again. "As long as we don't use any spells that'll cause us some sort of lasting effect or pain, it's fine."

"Awesome, awesome," Katie murmured quickly, snatching a crystal blue wand out of Conner's hands.

The wands they held in their grasps appeared to be crystal, tinted with blue.

It reflected into their eyes as the two pieces wrapped together in a spiral, just like the crystal stick of the twins.

"And you'll need this book of spells too. Not to keep, just for reference."

Aria handed them a mahogany brown book with tattered covers, a large, shining dark purple jewel in the center. Then, between the covers were ripped pieces of parchment with various notes scribbled on them, and these were also in between the old, crumpled pages.

"That book is one of the most important artifacts—if not *the* most important artifact—in the Smith Dynasty of Sorcerers,"

Conner said rather haughtily. "Our grandmother wrote a lot of it herself. She tried every one of those spells and wrote them out, even invented some too."

Cassie peered over her sister's shoulder at the book in astonishment.

A magic spell book. A real magic spell book! There in her little sister's hands was the recipe to magical powers. The thing she'd never thought existed.

Yearning to perform the spell immediately, Katie frantically opened the spell book to a page near the middle before her sister could continue examining it, in a desperate search for the spell previously performed.

"Dorsiti calcuntactu!" Katie cast shakily, pointing the wand at herself, this causing a rush of hot pink sparkles to release from the tip of the wand.

She found herself engulfed in the magical matter encapsulating the twins, sparkles wrapping around her in a swirl of fuzzy light that obscured and blinded her vision.

Cassie cast the same spell, a lavender light releasing from the end of her wand, swallowing her in a slowly turning ball of light.

It rose high into the air, falling to the ground with a thud.

Her head throbbed ferociously, and the room felt as though it was spinning at a thousand miles an hour, but she still managed to raise her head despite a faint ringing in her ears.

"God, my head hurts."

"Yeah, that usually happens," Conner added. "It's just your brain and body reacting to the magic. It's nothing to worry about so don't dwell on it. If it doesn't happen again, I mean."

"Okay…But what's on my hands?"

She ran her left hand over her right, noticing the thick black hair that grew over them. From her feet to her chest, she noticed she was still wearing the clothes she was previously wearing, but her body seemed to have transformed itself into some kind of gorilla.

Katie, on the other hand, noticed the way the orange fur on her arms was blowing in the gentle breeze left behind by the sparkling magic.

She was wearing the same outfit she'd been sporting before, just like her sister. She smiled at the feeling of her fluffy orange paws, noticing a single stripe in the middle.

"Out of all the animals you could've chosen, why'd you choose a gorilla, Cassie?" commented Conner bluntly. "A bit boring, don't you think?"

"I thought it would be better considering the species is closely related to humans. Seems a safer bet than something like..." She gestured toward Katie. "…what Katie chose."

Katie dismissed Cassie's remark by saying, "God, Cass, you're so boring."

After a few moments of taking in their animal appearances, Cassie's headache started to subside, replaced by an immediate sense of urgency. "We should get back to looking for Avery." She glanced at her younger sister for a moment. "Should we?"

"Well, if you we need to get going that bad, then all right." She paused as she held her wand to her chest. "What's the reversal spell? Or some way to turn back, maybe?"

"Just say the spell backwards. That's how it is for all spells after all," Aria directed. "You should turn back into a human after that."

"Calcuntactu dorsiti!" Katie and Cassie said in unison, consumed by the sparkling magic that had swallowed them once before.

They fell to the ground reverted to their familiar human forms, and Cassie couldn't help but feel a wave of relief rush over her. The magic had truly worked!

She glanced up at her wand that she still gripped tightly in her hand.

Magic was real.

***

After a small meal of quesadillas that Conner had made, Cassie and Katie began to pack their things away while the twins cleaned up the kitchen, the sound of running water faint as the two hoisted their bags upon their backs.

"Thanks for the hospitality!" Cassie said farewell to the twins as they walked in. "And thanks for the wands and the spell book too; they'll help us out a—"

"Hey, backtrack a second, did you really think you were gonna leave without us? With our family spell book?" Aria questioned, rather perturbed by the idea of the sisters leaving after she hadn't talked to anyone besides her brother for so long.

"Oh, I can just give it back then." Cassie slipped the thick book out of her bag and handed it over to Conner. "Here. And thanks again for the food as well." She gestured toward Katie and whispered, "Didn't really know what we were gonna eat for a while."

"That's not what I meant at all," Conner replied, pushing the book back into her hands.

"What he meant to say was that we want to…" Aria paused for a moment as if pondering over the request, then she continued hesitantly, "…to come with you."

The sister's eyes widened at this request. "Come with us?"

"Why would you want to anyways? You don't even know us," Katie said bluntly.

She could've phrased it better, but it was the truth. Why would these two strangers want to tag along on a journey to rescue someone they didn't even know or care about?

"But we could watch out for you guys while you travel, couldn't we, Aria?"

Conner looked warily at his twin then back to Katie and Cassie. "And—and we could teach you spells that'll help you guys find your way around this place."

From the way he spoke, it was clear he was growing desperate.

Cassie put the spell book back into her backpack and slung it over her shoulder once more. "But we wouldn't want to intrude on you."

"But you wouldn't," Aria interrupted immediately, just as desperate to tag along as her brother. "And in case you ever run into any extreme problems, we could help you with advanced spells." She paused and added embarrassedly, "And—to be honest—we're really just bored here at home."

"Seems convincing enough," Katie mumbled to herself, loosely thinking it over in an attempt to convince Cassie that her opinion, after such thorough thought, was a good one. "Why don't you guys come?" She glanced back at Cassie. "Right, Cass?"

She weighed up the options in their current situation, talking to herself as she pondered aloud. "I mean they could help us with spells and keep us safer than we'd be without them, but what about their life here? We'd be disrupting it, wouldn't we?"

"Does she always do this?" Aria said quietly as she watched Cassie think aloud.

"Yeah," Katie admitted. "This is her thought process most of the time when it comes to making both simple and complex decisions. She can be indecisive sometimes, and when it comes to things like this, she likes to debate it with herself."

"All right then," Cassie concluded. "If you guys really want to…" She smiled and finished, "You can come. As long as it's not putting you—"

"Yes! Yes! Yes!" Conner and Aria cheered jubilantly together, the latter pulling her brother down the hallway as she cheered. "Let's go pack!"

"It's nice how excited she is, y'know?" Katie observed. "It must've been boring here in this home. No matter how much they could've loved it. Maybe we helped them out."

"Helped them? What'd you mean helped them? If anything, I feel we've just made things a lot harder."

"Oh, Cass, you're worrying about them too much." Katie sat down on the couch as her older sister followed. "Would they have been so excited if you, this random person who'd just appeared in their home, showed up and made their life a lot harder?"

She shook her head no.

"Exactly. Now stop looking at yourself as this gigantic burden," said Katie. "Not only did we manage to get two wands, but we also have a whole book of magical spells that can help us." She looked at the emptiness of her sister's eyes, despite her hopeful reassurance. "Cassie…" She looked down at her. "Is something else bothering you?"

I don't wanna burden her with my problems right now. At the very least, not here. She deserves to be free from the sort of feelings I've been experiencing lately.

I don't wanna do that to her…

…but she did ask.

"Yes, something else is bothering me." She sat down on the couch beside her sister and cupped her face in her hands. "And it's about Avery."

Katie watched intently.

"I know I worry about her a lot, but she's just gone. And I feel so responsible. I wasn't being as attentive as I'm supposed to be. I wasn't taking good care of her. I was ignoring her.

"And I—"

"Cassie, you weren't ignoring her. And her getting lost here isn't your fault," Katie responded, her blunt manner of speaking having faded, now replaced by a much softer tone of voice. "What happened to Avery was an accident. An accident that wasn't anyone's fault. Not Avery's. Not mine. And especially not yours. Blaming anyone in this situation won't get us anywhere. Just finding her is what's important."

Cassie nodded, opening her mouth to add something just as the twins walked in with matching black bags strapped across their backs.

"You guys ready to hit the road?" Conner finally said, appearing from around the corner.

He smiled as the sisters joined him beneath the entrance hole of the cavern as instructed. He was pointing his wand upwards toward the cavern exit. "That's how we'll be leaving."

"But how? You can't just—"

"Before you say anything," Aria said, similar to the way a tour guide would speak to their customers, "this is gonna be a bit…damp. Sorry."

And with that, Conner pointed his wand at the ground and said, "Aqua exponentia!"

His wand tip illuminated at his words.

He drew a wide circle around their feet, directing them away to allow him to draw a ginormous water droplet in the middle of the light circle.

"I'm gonna need you guys to hold onto each other as tightly as possible." As soon as he tapped the center of the circle with his wand, with the three others huddling around it, a strong blast of cool water began streaming from the tip of his wand.

The pressure of the water was so strong they were barely able to make it to the ceiling of the tall dirt cavern, gripping tightly to the dirt and the thin grass rim around the hole.

Finally, they hoisted each other onto level land.

Aria covered the hole over with large leaves and grass, concealing the hole so well it was as if it had never existed in the first place.

"This feels so much better. I can't remember the last time we were above ground," Aria told her brother as she inhaled the scent of the forest, at the same time ignoring the castle that stood right beside them. "Don't you think, Conner?" She received no response, observing how empty-eyed her brother looked. "Conner, is something wrong?"

Her brother was gazing out at the space before them, his eyes making it seem as if he were somewhere else, despite his body being present.

"How'd she do it? How'd she defeat her? How'd she muster the courage to give her own life to save this place? She sacrificed her own self, all for this. All for this—this ruined world.

"Well then what'll we do now? Conner said to himself loud enough for Cassie, Aria, and Katie to be able to hear. He appeared teary-eyed about this *she*.

"What is he talking about?" Cassie whispered to Aria. "Who's this she?"

"Well, before you hear this, you can't tell anyone, okay?"

Both Cassie and Katie nodded, pulling their backpacks even tighter around themselves as they braced for what they were yearning to hear.

"Tell them about what happened with Grandma," Aria said, nudging Conner from his trance. "How she died."

Moments later, Conner snapped out of his daze and sighed as he told Aria, "Yeah, okay."

Chapter 4
The Story of Ruler Marjorie

CONNER LOOKED AT THE REST OF THEM, all seated in the emerald grass.

"As you may know, there are many realms or dimensions in this multiverse we live in, including our realm, which is the Magic Realm, and yours, known as the Earth Realm, if I'm correct? Well, some people also refer to your place in the universe as the Without Magic Destination since it's the only dimension where your system of physics doesn't allow the principles of magic to work."

Aria continued for him.

"After the kingdoms in the Magic Realm were established hundreds of years ago, the Council of the Realm, a collection of important figures in magic history, decided to choose two members to have a chance to become rulers of each kingdom when one of the rulers passed away. Although, it doesn't work like this anymore.

"It's usually their children who succeed their reign nowadays."

She took a parchment map out of her bag, spreading it out on the lush grass before the four of them.

The paper had been divided into five parts, each consisting of various sketches.

Both cities and forest had equal representation. She described the five kingdoms.

"The kingdoms were the Animal Kingdom…" She pointed to the top right corner of the map, and added, "the Kingdom of Magic…" This time, she indicated the middle.

"The Land of Elves…" Her hand moved to the bottom right corner.

Then she said, "And the Kingdom of Sorcerers."

After this, she placed her finger on the bottom left section. "And finally, Crystalia."

She stopped with her finger on the top left corner of the map.

Conner took over the explanation. "And each kingdom had a choice of two possible candidates to be decided by two members of the Council of the Realm.

"The Ruler of the Realm, Ruler Marjorie, was the one who chose which of the ten members of the Council of the Realm would be deciding—"

"If your grandmother is…" Cassie stopped as she reconsidered her words. "I mean if she *was* the ruler of the realm, doesn't that mean one of your parents is the Ruler now?"

"Well, not exactly," corrected Aria. "After she died, the Council decided that if they did have a ruler of the entire realm, this would be too much power for just one person.

"Paired with the fact that that person would probably be hunted for their position, it seemed obvious to eliminate the role altogether rather than try and salvage it. Not to mention that our parents live in the Earth Realm, so it's not as if they know about this place anyways."

"So, you're saying you guys have been living here all alone?"

"We moved here without them knowing because they thought we would be living with our grandma who lived in-state," Conner elaborated. "So yeah, we have been living here without them."

"So, you still don't feel like moving in with your parents? Aren't they at least a little worried about you two? And what'll happen when they realize that you've just been living on your own for the past… who knows how long? Why don't you just go live with them again?"

"We've already taken the lie too far at this point. It's been such a long time since Grandma died and if we go back to Earth, we'll have to tell them about all this stuff that's happened. It's why we lied to them. They were both so close to her and it'd be so hard to hear that Grandma died, so we just didn't even bother saying anything," Conner responded.

"Well, haven't they ever called you guys to say anything? They should've found out at this point," Katie pointed out. It did seem rather illogical that after all this time, neither parent had made an effort to contact their kids.

"They can't call us when we're here." Aria's breath hitched and she continued, "If we just stay here the whole time, we'll never have to tell them anything. We'll never have to tell them about what happened. We'll never have to hurt them if something bad does happen."

Conner peered down at the ground as he said under his breath, "We don't wanna hurt them more than we have. We might as well exit ourselves out of their lives." He looked back up at them. "To them, I'm guessing we're as good as dead."

"Hey," Cassie said immediately. "Don't say that about yourselves." She looked between the twins. "You'll still always be their kids. And they'll still always love you. I promise that they'll always love you. You just need to give them the chance to tell you that again." Her eyes lingered on Aria's for several moments. "You can do that, can't you?"

Aria looked down, and, unsure of what to really do, Cassie wrapped her arms around her.

"I can't really say that I understand what's going in your head. But I do know that, at the very least, I could try to help," she softly whispered.

She pulled away as Aria said softly to her, "Mom and Dad would always talk about how boring visits to her house were, with all the tea and fine China and news-watching and piles of knitted scarves." She let out a chuckle. A soft, sad, melancholy chuckle. "Dad always said Mom loved her like her own mother. But, even so, Dad never saw his mom that often because he'd always be at his cousin's house so much."

"Sometimes, I wonder if he missed her. If he missed having a mom always there with him," Conner added in.

Cassie had almost forgotten he was there, but she still listened carefully to his words.

They were two different people.

But in the end, the way they experienced grief was so similar.

It was good that they had each other.

"Sometimes…" Aria began to choke on the tears that built in her eyes. "…I wonder if she can see us…See us from that faraway universe she'd tell us about before we slept."

She slipped from the rock face as she buried her head in her hands.

"I miss her. I miss her so much. And now all I have is memories. Memories of her being her with me. But she's gone. She's—"

Cassie embraced her again. She didn't want to say anything to her, didn't think anything would be comforting enough in this situation. She deserved an honest consolation, but that wasn't something Cassie thought she had the ability to offer.

As Aria cried, there was always the occasional mumble, but all Cassie wanted to do was hold her tighter. She wanted to help her somehow, and this wouldn't do it.

She'd never be able to understand the sort of pain Aria was going through, but she wanted to be a shoulder for her to cry on. She wanted to be there for her.

Eventually, Conner began crying too, not as heavy or intense, but the slipping of tears that occurred when someone just couldn't hold in their sadness anymore.

And inevitably, Katie started too, Cassie wrapping her arms around her younger sister.

She was the only one not crying.

She wanted to help everyone, but she wasn't inherently sad. All she wanted to do was give them the comfort they needed. Not with words. But with what her mother would use.

Hugs.

Hugs always make things better, Cass.

And a single tear fell.

***

As the melancholy heaviness of their tears began to subside, Conner started his story this time, eyes and tone a lot brighter than before. It seemed as if the crying rejuvenated him, giving him a moment to breathe, respite from his usual happy self.

"Anyways, on with the story," Conner said, his voice much softer and less punchy than it had been before his conversation with Aria. "After the members made their decisions, the rulers were chosen. Ella would rule the Kingdom of Magic; she was a princess possessing powers of telepathy. The members chose Clara to run the Kingdom of Sorcerers; she was a princess skilled in healing and communicating with animals.

"For Crystalia, it was a girl named Lona Lohan who was excellent at teleportation, a skill that few sorcerers have, in fact. Then, the ruler of the Land of Elves was Lady Marilyn, once a teacher at Abilinium, a school in Crystalia that taught its students how to use the powers they had to benefit the wellbeing of the people around them and to get further in life.

"And the Animal Kingdom was ruled by Vitina Orbin, a sorceress who studied under some of the greatest sorcerers in the land."

"And once they were all chosen, they went off to care for their respective kingdoms. Everything was running smoothly for a while until after the Choosing Ceremony when Vitina started telling people that her abilities and upbringing would make her an exceptional Ruler of the Realm. Ruler Marjorie, our grandmother who was the current ruler at the time, was kind enough to give her a chance in the selection process.

"In order for one to become the Ruler of the Realm, you would have to be tested by the current ruler depending on the conducts they saw fit. And so, the ruler tested her, and she ultimately failed, even though she had exceedingly great potential considering her excellent magical abilities. She wanted the position all to herself, and the fact that the ruler she saw as inferior wouldn't give it to her was what threw her off the rails.

"A few days afterwards, she entered the Council of the Realm's building in the Kingdom of Magic, demanding the position.

"She used empty threats that inevitably didn't work, resulting in her attacking Ruler Marjorie and casting a fatal spell on her, landing her in the hospital."

Aria took over.

"The spell, one you can only perform with murderous rage on your mind, caused our grandmother to collapse right in front of Vitina," Aria said. "Before she could leave, the Royal Guards found her and turned her in to the authorities.

"Some of the members rushed Ruler Marjorie to the hospital just in time. Unfortunately, the doctors were unable to heal her because she was too far gone, and Ruler Marjorie ended up dying. Vitina had committed a serious offense in the Magic Realm, and she lost her position as the ruler of the Animal Kingdom. Then, after her hearing, they convicted her as guilty and sentenced her to exile," Aria added. "Unfortunately, she escaped before her removal from the Magic Realm, so…" She sighed. "…no one knows where she is now."

"So, our sister is lost with a killer psycho on the loose?" Cassie reiterated. "Well then, what *do* I do? I didn't think this journey could get any harder, but apparently, I was wrong!"

She was looking down at the ground, her vision blinded with rage and with overwhelming stress and fury. She was so frustrated she wanted to throw something. Curse something out. Stuff that she used to do back at home. It was some sort of way to cope with the stress.

But with what Cassie had said, Aria wasn't sure how to deliver a response.

She needed to thank Cassie somehow, for the way she'd consoled Aria before.

"Well, even so," Conner said in his signature Conner way of changing the subject. "That may not be one of the only problems on our plate. What about that portal? That portal that opened in your house? What about that?"

"I don't have any idea what happened with that thing. I have no idea how those things even open. Especially not specifically in our house," answered Cassie.

"They're attracted to places or objects with strong magical energy," said Conner as he scrolled through his phone. "There must've been some sort of magical presence in your house that caused it to open there. Some magical energy beckoning it."

"Well, I'm assuming we would've known about something like that, right?" Cassie debated. "Our parents don't know magic even exists, let alone have any magical objects."

"Looks like that's a dead end for now. I really thought it'd be able to give us some answers for how to send you two home once we find your sister," Aria said regretfully.

"But back on the topic of Vitina. What happened after she escaped?" Katie questioned.

Aria nodded.

"According to some news reports and articles, some people started by finding a person who's associated with Vitina, known as Andromeda Colburn," said Aria. "She escaped prison at a young age. Right now, they seem to be working together to plan their domination, but the authorities haven't thought to arrest them yet." Aria paused before continuing with, "I don't think they really know what they'll be in for. So, it's best they just don't try for now."

Cassie couldn't help but chew the tips of her dark ginger hair at this chilling news.

Vitina and Andromeda must have been planning what they were going to do to Avery right now if they had her. What if they had her and a whole army of people right now?

They could kill us on the spot, even if we do become at least pretty advanced in magic. How do we do this? How'll we survive? How'll we find her?

How'll we save her?

I thought I promised to keep them safe. This isn't keeping them safe at all.

I just put her in danger with my carelessness so I'll try to find her later tonight. I should try to find her later tonight. This is my responsibility. Not Conner's, not Aria's, not Katie's. It's my fault we're even in this situation. And I'm gonna be the one to find a way out.

I have to.

Chapter 5
The First Night

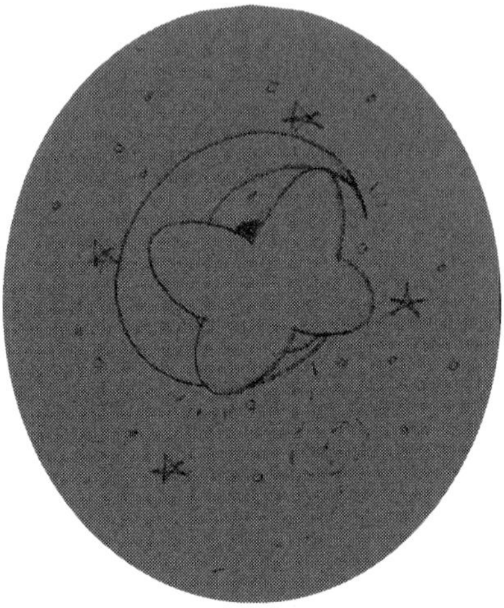

AS THEY WALKED, CASSIE OBSERVED THEY were back in the same forest she and Katie had seen when they'd first arrived here, before they'd been apprehended by those Tigrisia, of course.

"Where are we?"

"Let me see." Aria pulled her phone out of her bag and clicked on an app. "Looks like the Animal Kingdom at the moment."

"Ooh! The Animal Kingdom!" Katie piped up, eyes alight with a twinkle of excitement. She must've been quite bored and weighed down by all this heavy fun. It was nice to see her so genuinely happy. "Do they have any cats around here? I've always wanted to have one!"

"Not really, it's more wild animals and anthropomorphic ones than domesticated creatures," Aria answered, turning fast enough so she didn't have to watch Katie's bright smile dissipate because of her words.

It was the truth of the matter. There just weren't a lot of happy things in this world, only blankets that obscured the misery and fear beneath it all.

"Oh, and don't forget the Squadrons!" Conner added, receiving an elbow nudge. Wait, no—it was more like a jab, from his sister.

She scowled.

"Why'd you say that? Now they're gonna—Squadrons? What are those?" she inquired as Aria and Conner's eyes flicked to her. "They sound like sparrow-robot crossovers."

"Squadrons are drones that patrol the forests of the Magic Realm. And if they see anyone using magic, they'll take them in," informed Aria. She could tell that at least one of the sisters was about to pipe up with a "why?", and so she went on, "They're looking to find new members for Vitina's army. You see, they were never meant to roam the woods of this world, picking on unsuspected magic users, but during a spike in soldier intake during Vitina's alliance with Andromeda, they were able to get their soldiers to put them together."

"Well now that they are, we have to be really careful to make sure we aren't caught," Conner reminded them. "Or else our journey'll be thrown horribly off track."

No one noticed that as they spoke, the sky went from a light cyan to an elegant ombre of bright orange, light pink, and dark blue that shone down on the trees and colored the grass.

Eventually, they finally became aware of the sudden chill breeze of wind that blew over them and took a glance at the setting sun.

"We should find a place to stay for the night," Cassie suggested as they all stood. "It's best we're not out here late at night."

They continued their trek through the unsettling quick-dimming forest, watching in the dark for any sign of movement around them.

It was a sense of apprehension that made Cassie wish the day could just be over already. She had never liked feeling this vulnerable, especially when out at night.

Minutes later, they caught sight of a clearing canopied by leaves, elms and pines, the short grass that covered the space sprinkled with small lilac candytuft flowers, their tiny little blossoms circling around the clusters of mauve seeds in the center.

"I think here's a pretty good place to set up camp," Conner said, setting his bag down beside a nearby a pine tree trunk. "We should be able to stay here tonight."

Katie watched the twins for a few moments then asked, "Why aren't you guys using your wands? You can do that, right?"

"Our magic doesn't work like that," said Aria. "Most of the magic in our wands comes from magic cell towers, which help to regulate the flow of magic in the Magic Realm.

"If you aren't close to one of the towers, the magic your wand can produce will be limited. For instance, we can't conjure items, but we can use our Family Spell and use spells for attack and defensive purposes."

Aria pulled her wand out of her pocket and examined it with wistful eyes.

"That means we can't just conjure a place to stay for the night, so we'll just have to build one for ourselves."

Katie groaned tiredly as she stood, stretching her arms over her head, listening to Aria.

"So," Conner began. "We'll split into buddy groups to get the materials we need. We're gonna need some leaves for the floor and ceiling, strong sticks for support, vines to tie supports and leaves together, and a couple more sticks to use as weapons just in case our wands aren't able to do the job well enough."

Aria glanced from Katie to her twin. "Katie and I will be on leaves and vines and you and Cassie..."

"...will be on sticks," Conner finished.

The two groups dispersed into the dimly lit forest under the setting sun, heading in opposing directions in silence.

"So, do you know any places to find some big sticks?" Cassie asked awkwardly, staring down at her feet as she kicked a rock through the grass.

"No. Why would I?"

She looked up at him. "I mean, you know everything about this place, don't you? You know the landscape, the animals, the history. You must be really good at observations and retaining information in class… or must've been."

"No, not really. The only class in the Earth Realm where I got a higher grade than C minus was math; it was the only thing that actually made sense to me then. But here in this realm, Aria and I decided to stay back, y'know? We're not really going to school or planning to. At least, I'm not. She's planning to go to Madric Academy when she turns eighteen."

He pointed to the logo on his sweatshirt. "That's why she's forcing me to wear this thing all the time. It's really growing on me though, so I don't really mind."

"Well, maybe you'll find an advanced magic school to go to, too."

Conner frowned. "Not really, I'm not interested in all this magic stuff, I'd much rather work one of the normal jobs here rather than become a potions master or work on the Council of the Realm like Aria is planning to do when she gets older."

"Oh, well, don't give up just yet, Conner," Cassie assured. "I haven't seen you use your magic that much yet, so you could surprise me..."

She gestured back into the direction they'd come from. "…and Katie."

Just as Conner began to let a small grin slip across his face, Cassie noticed a pine tree, roughly five hundred feet from them, covered from head to toe with branches.

"Those are perfect!" she announced, hurrying over to where the tree stood.

Conner, sprinting after her, could feel his breath dwindling slightly as she continued running at a quick pace.

When he had eventually caught up with her, he had to bend over in a frenzy of shallow breaths, taking in as much oxygen as possible since he wasn't used to running so fast for so long. "How..." he panted. "...are...we… Oh, God, I can't breathe… Are we supposed... to... break 'em?"

"Didn't think about that…"

She was staring at the tree in thought, her breathing just fine in comparison to his.

When Conner finally looked up, she had already hoisted herself near the base of the branch, putting all her weight on it, causing it to shake with each subtle jump.

It was a foolish plan, Conner realized almost immediately, but almost seconds later, the branch snapped as she fell into a pile of pine leaves, cushioning her otherwise painful fall.

"There," she said, handing him the branch she had just broken off. "You just do that while I go get some sharp sticks, all right? Just like I did."

Conner took a glance at her as she walked away, then turned to the tree. "Guess I should get started." He looked back at the sticks and froze for a moment.

The sounds of nature drifted all around him, his vision still locked on the branches. Despite the time continuing to pass, he carried on standing there for a few more minutes, his vision blurring as he stared into nothingness.

Back to reality, he shook his head to try and focus more.

Cassie and Katie had to come first.

***

"Got it!" Katie exclaimed in triumph as she pulled a long vine covered with large leaves from a stubby tree, almost the height of a regular bush.

In a mere ten minutes, Katie had collected roughly twenty-five vines, all approximately the same length.

Aria, meanwhile, was holding several large banana leaves from nearby trees in her arms.

"Okay, Katie, that should be enough for the two forts," Aria declared, leading her back toward the campsite. "We should start heading back to the clearing now or else we'll be stuck in this dark forest and have trouble getting ourselves out."

The suffocating silence resounded through the space almost to an insufferable degree as Katie and Aria walked through the dim foliage, the only noticeable sound the crunching of leaves beneath their feet. Unlike when they had first encountered the camp—when that silence was unsettling and eerie—this was just simply boring.

And both Katie and Aria already knew that.

"So, how has this adventure been so far, Katie?" Aria asked as she looked at her, working to break the ice a bit and get her mind off the weird ringing in the back of her mind.

"I've been doing fine for the most part, but I do kinda miss my mom and dad. Although I do love Avery, she can be a bit...troublesome at times, which causes her to make some really dumb decisions, y'know? But as soon as we save her, we'll get out of here and see Mom and Dad again. I just know it."

"If you didn't know already, when my brother and I first came to the Magic Realm, we started to miss our parents, too. And y'know, sometimes, we still do. I mean, living with them was really calm and…"

She clearly didn't feel like finishing; after all, it seemed as if she had a knack for taking the attention from other people when she didn't need to.

She should just stop talking for the time being.

"What happened?" Katie asked, their steps in sync now.

Her words were soft, as if she genuinely cared.

"Our dad married someone else, and, I feel so selfish for saying this, but it was like she took him from us," Aria admitted. "They moved across the country, so for a while, all we could do was call him. I miss seeing Dad on the weekends and him taking us to the arcade during the summer. I remember that he had a pretty good relationship with Mom then too, just two pairs of friends taking their kids out bowling. It wasn't a family everyone would immediately envision, but it was *my* family and I loved it.

"The two of them always looked so happy after they weren't married. And although they were never good romantic partners, it was awesome that they were great friends with each other. The problem is Brittany, my dad's new wife, hates it when he and my Mom are around each other. Hates me. Hates Conner. Hates us as a family.

"It's like she's jealous of us, but jealous of what exactly…" She paused for a second as she allowed Katie to think about the words more. "…I'm not really sure."

Katie frowned, but ultimately said, "I don't know what you're going through personally, Aria, but I do know that even if your parents aren't married anymore, you guys are still a family, right? And if Brittany is tearing rifts in the family you have, then she isn't a part of it. She doesn't want you to be happy.

"So, it's all right if you don't accept her as part of your family either. Because until she tries to make your happiness important, she doesn't truly care about you."

Aria let out a quiet chuckle, the type she made when she was contemplating words with a sense of melancholy to the way she sounded. "Thanks, Katie. Truly."

Despite her words though, Aria's genuine smile was enough of a thank you.

They continued on quietly for a few more moments until Katie spoke up to say, "But I do have a problem myself. Or more specifically, Cassie does. Something I feel is better to talk about when she isn't with us."

Aria didn't say anything, allowing Katie to continue on with what she was saying. "Cassie's dedicated. Super dedicated. She's an amazing big sister and is super devoted to taking care of me and Avery, but it's just that sometimes, she can take it too far.

"She's super protective of us and would even put herself in harm's way just to keep us safe. I love her so much, but she needs to realize she still has to take care of herself sometimes. I'm worried that at this rate, she's gonna try to do something stupid she *can't* do and get herself killed. All because she wants me and Avery safe."

Katie looked down. Then she continued with a big breath.

"If you could do anything for me, even though I barely know you, could you watch my older sister for me? Make sure she doesn't try to sneak away tonight and see that she stays here with us? I want her safe as much as she wants that for me, and I feel like I can trust you enough to ensure that."

"Of course, I will," Aria said. "I want all of us to stay safe, even my brother, although I don't show it that much."

"Thanks," Katie said quickly, grinning as she looked up at Aria like a big sister.

"No problem."

***

Conner sat alone, muttering to himself quietly.

"If only I could tell her. If only I could talk to her, but she won't even notice me. I'm not the scholarly type. Forget it, I'm not even the regular type. She's the brightest princess anyone's ever seen. Not to mention she's nice to everyone she meets. Sweet and beautiful… She's amazing…" Conner's face looked longing as he sat on a large rock.

"Conner!" Cassie shouted, pulling—more like throwing—Conner out of his daze. "You slacker! You've only broken four branches we need at least twenty! Hurry up!"

Together, Cassie and Conner climbed to the lowest branches on nearby trees, snapping them quickly. With Cassie helping, in a little over five minutes, they snapped all of the branches required, Conner still left confused as to why she was acting so odd.

"Did you collect all your sticks?" Conner asked softly, trying to avoid Cassie's overwhelmingly prominent irritation by methods of deflection.

"I finished my work. All twelve needed." She didn't have a fuming sort of anger to her, more one of disappointment and overall frustration.

And it pained him even more.

He wanted to get straight to the problem. There wasn't time for this beating around the bush method he always played when someone was mad at him, so in his softest voice, he asked, "Why are you mad?"

Cassie didn't even pay mind to his words and stormed ahead toward the campsite. Conner hurried in her trail, cradling the sticks in his arms.

"Well, I did phrase that terribly. Of course, she's angry now," he mumbled.

"Is it about your sister again?" he said, rather insensitively before he could stop his words. "She'll be fine, Cass, we'll save—"

"Stop dismissing the problem like that," she groaned. She moved even faster in the direction of the clearing.

Despite only making it worse, he continued with his questions. He wanted to know why, but he wasn't as good with words as his sister was. Not to mention how awful his tone was.

Almost at the clearing, he found himself nearing where she had stopped walking and looked at her.

"One, don't call me Cass," she hissed beneath her breath. "And two, if you're really that sure, why don't you figure it out for yourself?"

You sound petty, Cassie thought. She knew she did. But some part of her wanted to.

She was angry and if it wasn't yelling or throwing stuff, it was petty words that helped relieve some of that frustration.

Conner stood and thought for a moment, contemplating her demand. "Uh, no idea. Could you give me a hint, maybe?"

She walked farther ahead.

"C'mon, Cass. I mean, Cassie. You know I'm an idiot. I'm bad at taking hints," Conner claimed in an effort to help with her attitude, at least a little bit, right?

Discreetly, Cassie smiled and continued to walk. "I'm mad cause, well…" She stopped. "I'm just mad, y'know?"

Conner stopped as she did so.

"I'm frustrated 'cause I'm so useless. I'm frustrated 'cause I'm supposed to be the responsible one. I'm supposed to be the one keeping everyone safe."

Conner didn't say anything as she continued talking.

"And I can't come to terms with the fact that I failed them." She looked down at the ground, vision blurring as she continued.

"That I failed Avery. That I failed Katie. They have to go through all of this because I was too stupid. I wasn't careful enough. I wasn't paying enough attention and now look what happened. Avery's somewhere in this magical death trap and I have no idea where she even is. If only I had just been better. I keep beating myself up over this when I know whining about how crappy I handled everything won't make things any better. I wasn't even downstairs when she fell into that portal.

"I wouldn't have even heard her screams. All because I—"

"Stop."

Conner looked at her with a gaze of affinity. He evidently knew this feeling.

"I understand where you're coming from. If you love someone, you want them to be so safe to the point where you become irrational. You feel responsible for every bad thing that happens to them even though you barely have any control over it.

"But stop beating yourself up over it. You're not whining. You're trying to be better, which you should be proud of. You really do want to keep your sisters safe, and this one mistake doesn't make you a bad sister. You're only a bad sister if you don't do anything to try and fix it. Or at least that's what I tell myself."

She gazed up at him. "Yeah. I guess I am trying to be better. I'm trying to find her and to fix the situation."

"Yeah, you are, and if it makes you feel any better, I'll tell you why I was slacking off."

"Why then?" An expression of curiosity had replaced her frown.

"I, um, I have a little crush on someone and..." He saw Cassie smile at him, and he blushed incessantly. "I'm not telling you who it is!"

He looked away again, but in his peripheral vision, he could see her smile.

He carried on, "But you do get to know that that's why I was being stupid. There you go." He couldn't stop blushing and speed-walked toward the campsite, knowing very well that Cassie would be questioning him later.

Behind him, she could feel laughter building in her throat and let it out.

***

"Finally, we're done!" Cassie shouted, full of pride as she smiled at the two forts they had built, their frames supported by thick sticks tied together by vines, holding up the banana-leaf roof Katie had woven together.

By that time, the sky was already dark and Cassie, with her bit of knowledge of living outdoors, lit a small fire between the left and right forts they would be staying in.

"You guys hungry?" Katie asked, digging in her bag for some sandwiches as they sat around the fire. "I have turkey, egg salad, BLT—"

"I'm starved!" Conner interrupted, watching hungrily as she set them out on napkins for them to have.

Everyone took their own egg salad sandwich, and began eating them viciously, extremely hungry after all that had happened that day in comparison to calm lives previously. It would probably have to be like this for a long time afterwards.

"You know, eventually, we'll run out of these delicious sandwiches," Conner said, pointing at his half-finished dinner. "We'll have to start learning to hunt and do things without magic." He looked at his sister and quipped, "That'll be hard for you, sis."

"Well, it's not like it's any easier for you, dumba—" She saw Cassie and Katie staring at her. "Yeah, sure...We can learn sometime."

She shot Conner a nasty look and continued eating.

"I used to go to campsites with my mom and dad," Cassie said, taking another bite of her food as she ignored the air of hostility between the twins. "Maybe I could teach you guys some camping tricks later on."

"That'd be great!" Aria piped up as she looked away from her brother. "We could start tomorrow."

"Of course, I can, but it's kinda fuzzy," Cassie added in, on second thoughts. "But I guess fuzzy is better than nothing, right?"

While they silently ate for a moment, taking another one of Katie's sandwiches, Aria watched Cassie's behavior. She had looked around the clearing almost five times tonight, eyes flicking back and forth, looking for fast exits and entrances, it seemed.

She also took mental note of how Cassie would tap her fingers against the ground, indicating some sort of impatience to suggest she was waiting for everyone to get to bed so she could leave. Aria would definitely have to keep watch of her later tonight.

"Ahhhhhh," Conner yawned, retreating to the left fort. "I'm gonna go to sleep. 'Night guys."

"'Night," Katie said back, heading to the right fort.

Only Aria and Cassie still sat there in the quiet of night, Cassie studying her sandwich intently and Aria scrolling around on her phone, quiet enough to still manage to hear Cassie.

It was getting so late that Cassie began yawning, retreating to the fort where her sister was staying with a quick 'goodnight' after putting out the fire.

Aria's eyes still looked that way, seemingly intent on watching everything Cassie did tonight.

***

It was getting to be around midnight when Aria heard the rustling of a large leaf, perhaps one of the banana leaf blankets Katie had put together for them.

Cassie.

Aria pulled out her earbuds as quietly as possible and listened as the rustling turned to the sound of crunching grass.

At this point, if she didn't hurry, Cassie was going to disappear into the night. She couldn't let that happen.

When Aria emerged from the fort, she found a confused Cassie looking back at her; it appeared she was writing some sort of note.

Maybe one to say goodbye before she left her sister.

Aria sat down beside her. "Don't."

"Don't what?" she chuckled nervously. "What'd you think I'm doing?"

"You're gonna leave, aren't you?"

Cassie looked taken aback. There was no way she could convince her otherwise. "H—how'd you know?"

"Katie warned me about this. She told me you'd do anything to save Avery. Even sacrifice your own life by doing something as stupid as this."

"It's *not* stupid," Cassie grumbled as she plopped on the ground beside her. "I'm doing this because I love Avery. She needs to be safe, and this is the only way to ensure Katie stays safe too. I just need you guys to take care of Katie for the time being, then we'll just—"

"No." Aria gripped Cassie's hand, stopping her from slipping the note to Katie. "You're not going anywhere. We promised that we'd come with you. We promised to keep you safe, didn't we? Me and Conner? We can't keep you safe if you're going off on dangerous missions all on your own in the dead of night. Just trust that we know what we're doing."

"But I've gotta…save her!"

Cassie pulled her arm back, releasing Aria's grip on it and throwing the note into Katie's fort. She stood up as she stated, "I'm gonna save Avery and you can't stop me from doing it."

Just as Cassie began running off, Aria chased after her, trying to keep up with Cassie's quick pace as she ducked behind trees and stones, caves and bushes.

Aria was trying to stay as emotionless as possible when she was with Cassie in the clearing, but that façade faded away so fast it had gone without notice.

She didn't know what she'd do without her. She couldn't let her do such an insanely dangerous thing, unsure if she'd ever come back alive.

When she had caught up to Cassie, she locked her in a hug, just before she was able to duck behind another rock and manage to get away.

"Don't go, please," she sniffled. "We need you here, Cassie. Please don't do this. We want you safe, do you get that? We want you to stay with us! Please, Cassie, stay!"

"Hey Aria. But…"

"No 'buts'. We want you safe. If you're gonna do this, don't do it alone. Please."

She looked her straight in the eyes, seeming to be on the brink of tears. "I don't want anything bad happening to you, Cassie. Please stay. Stay for me and Conner and Katie. Stay."

Even the silence of the night, the stillness of the birds and the beasts, the quietness of the usually crackling leaves, and the big moon seemed to say, *Stay. Stay.*

She had to stay.

That was what they kept having to repeat to her. What was so hard to understand about that? She would be dead for certain if she tried going. She had to stay. More than that, she *wanted* to stay. For Conner. For Aria.

For Katie.

She nodded as she could hear Aria's sniffles. "Oh, stop crying, will ya?"

"Hard pass," Aria laughed through her tears.

And with that, even Cassie cried a little.

"I'm sorry I put you through all this, Aria."

She didn't say anything, just lost in a swirl of emotions as she cried. Why was she even crying? Was the thought of losing Cassie that heavy on her? Was it really that scary to her?

"Is losing me really that scary?" Cassie breathed. "I wouldn't think it would be to you."

"Don't ever say that," Aria said, sternly staring into her eyes. "I can't think of ever losing you. And I'm sorry if you ever feel that way."

Cassie couldn't help but think about what her mom had said about hugs. How they made everything better. Was that what was happening now? Was this how Aria wanted to console Cassie in her time of need?

Well, it's working, she thought. *Mom, you were right.*

***

"Conner, do you hear that?" Aria whispered, shaking her brother; he was on the opposite side of the fort. It was a few hours after her conversation with Cassie and she was hoping Cassie was feeling a bit better now.

"There aren't any breadsticks here, Vanessa. Let's just leave," Conner groaned, eyes still shut.

"What? Conner, I said wake up!"

"Huh?" His eyes slowly began to open. "What'd you want?"

"I think I heard something."

"Oh." He shut his eyes again, getting into a more comfortable sleeping position. "Thinking isn't knowing. Goodnight."

"Conner, c'mon!" There was a rustling in the distance, which she knew for sure wasn't Cassie, who she was sure would have gone to sleep already. "Conner, get up!"

Conner reluctantly grabbed a sharp stick that lay next to him and quietly crawled out of the fort on hands and knees, holding his wand in his free hand. It was pitch black outside, signifying the middle of the night. Aria stepped out too, holding both her wand and Conner's.

Conner looked around, feeling a presence near him.

He turned to his sister, who he could barely see in the dark forest, the only light providing the faint moon above their heads. "Where's that noise coming from?"

He looked both left and right, trying to find a sign of what was lurking in the darkness and obscuring their sense of sight.

"No idea," Aria replied, heart pounding in her ears. What was it? A bear? A deer?

As if they had appeared on her call, three bright green pairs of eyes appeared from a bush to the right side of them, stopping as it watched Conner and Aria intently from afar.

As she whipped her head around, holding her wand in her hand, she pointed it at the faces of the creatures emerging from the brush, trying to keep herself together despite the scream forcing its way up in her throat and the incessant pounding of her heart.

"L-lux ex-p-p-ponentia."

The light from the tip of her wand illuminated the space around them even brighter than the moonlight could, allowing them to see the horrible sight prowling before them.

Now, they were fully aware of what was waiting there for them, the snout of the animals covered in short light gray hair, baring deadly sharp teeth.

And in this very moment, Aria wondered whether ignorance and death were better than the obstacle she was certain to face at this very moment.

Wolves. They were wolves.

As Conner cast spells at a wolf, attaining scratches and bites, Aria alerted Cassie of the threat, but only after several bouts of screaming at the growls from outside.

They stepped out of their fort with their crystal wands held high, Aria and Conner pointing theirs at the largest of the three. Using the only spell they knew, Katie and Cassie shouted simultaneously, "Dorsiti calcuntactu!" at the two dark gray wolves on opposing sides of the clearing, hoping the magic would work for them despite their limited experience.

As soon as the golden, shimmering sparkles shot from her wand, Cassie was already thinking about what plant or animal she would turn the wolf into, contemplating on the least threatening option to knock a wolf off their list.

"Rocks...Flowers...Leaves... a Leaf! Yeah, a leaf!"

The sparkles transformed the creature into a large leaf, its green color on display under the luminescent moonlight as it descended to the ground like a feather in the breeze. And with that, Cassie leaped in the air in triumph, thrusting her fist in the air.

She turned to see that Conner and Aria had already turned the largest wolf into a blueberry bush, taking up a large amount of the clearing.

But it seemed that now, Katie was missing.

"Oh God," she murmured to Aria and Conner. "Where'd Katie disappear to?"

She received no response and continued calling for her, her words ever growing in volume, although none came back to her.

"KA—"

"Cassie," Conner began from behind her, cutting her off. "There's still one wolf missing."

Cassie looked back at him blank-eyed. "One wolf missing? What'd you mean 'one wolf missing'? Does that mean it got to her?" She took off into the space around the clearing, running in circles as the three of them called Katie's name over and over.

As she ran, Cassie disappeared farther and farther into the forest, the trees darkening her path as she trekked. Each second, her thoughts got more and more irrational.

Not now. Not today. She couldn't lose Katie now, not when she was finally back on the right track to finding Avery.

"I can't lose her," she whispered to herself, clenching up her fists. "I can't lose both of them. I can't. I can't. I won't be able to face Dad. I won't be able to face Mom."

She looked at the bush before her for any sort of sign of her sister's presence.

"I won't even be able to face myself."

After yelling Katie's name a few more times, it seemed hopeless. Katie was gone and she had done nothing. Nothing to help her. Nothing at all.

"Katie," she called more quietly this time. "If you can hear me, please come back. I won't be able to go on without you. Katie, you're the reason I was able to know to come here to find Avery. You're the reason that we might have a chance to find our other sister. I know that we have our fights sometimes, but please."

No response.

"I know you were the person who told Aria to keep me from leaving. I know you were the person who did. Who else would've? You know what I'm like. And I wish I knew more about what you were like. I can be a pretty bad sister sometimes, can't I? But this time, could you let me be a good one. Please?"

"You're already a good one, Cassie," said a voice from behind her.

There, standing before her, was Katie. Scuffed up with a few scratches on her arms and face but happy as ever. There she was.

"Katie!" cried Cassie, throwing herself into a hug. "I thought a wolf had gotten you."

"Well, one almost did," she said. "That's why I have all these scratches on me. But in the end, I was able to turn it into this really large lavender butterfly and here's the crazy part: it talked to me!"

Cassie pulled away from the hug and chuckled a bit. *"Talked* to you? That's crazy. Butterflies can't talk; you know that."

"But it did! I'm serious!" There was a fluttering of some sort behind her, and she caught sight of the lavender butterfly she had just told Cassie about. She checked its right wing, marked with a dark purple bruise. "I think this is the one."

"Seriously?" Cassie said. "You transformed a wolf into a butterfly all by yourself?"

"Yeah, in fact. But before you say anything else, stay here and watch them; I've gotta go get the spell book."

"But why were…" Katie had already disappeared before Cassie could finish her question.

For a few minutes, Cassie sat in the grass, waiting for Katie's return. She stared at the butterfly's massive bruise. *Did Katie do that?*

Perhaps she did to weaken it before it killed her. That seemed to make sense.

But then how did she inflict that pain? She doesn't know any of those spells. So, does that mean she threw it, maybe? Katie, no way. She was able to do that?

Eventually, Katie came back, carrying the tattered spell book the twins had given them and Conner and Aria following in her steps.

The twins sat down near Cassie and watched as Katie began skimming through the spell book for an incantation used for fast healing.

"What're you doing?" Conner asked.

He wasn't questioning the large lavender butterfly, Cassie had noticed, so it seemed like this wasn't a very out-of-the-ordinary experience for him.

"Looking for a spell for fast healing," she said with eyes looking fast from page to page, so quick it looked as though they were vibrating. "Maybe it'll heal this butterfly's wing."

Aria questioned, "But didn't you say that thing was a wolf? And didn't it try to kill you?"

"Well yeah." She had finally found the spell she was looking for and raised her wand to the butterfly's bruise. "But just because it did doesn't mean it deserves to live life with this terrible bruise. I already put the thing through too much when I threw it at that tree trunk to stop it from getting to me."

There was a hint of regret in her words, that in fact she did, truly, feel bad.

"Medicas adhibere aquam exponentia," she cast as light streamed slowly out of her wand to the butterfly's bruise.

Aria, Conner, and Cassie watched intently as she did this, all perplexed about how she'd manage to pull this off.

The light spiraled around the creature as a water-like liquid, its translucent fluid shining in the moonlight. It wrapped the butterfly in a sphere of water, steam emanating from the tops as the water swirled inside, the butterfly still as if it had never been alive in the first place.

"Wait." Katie checked the spell book again, worried that it would cause the butterfly to drown. "Is this the right—"

Her sentence was cut short by the rush of water flowing to the ground, hitting the grass in a puddle as the drops made their signature *plop* sound.

The creature looked at Katie through its large, solid black bug eyes. Even though it disturbed her a bit, she continued to look into its pupil-less eyes that blinked back at her.

Its gaze seemed to say, *thank you for healing me.*

"My pleasure," said Katie.

"Well, it was a big problem for me," came the tiny almost inaudible voice of the butterfly. "It was very painful." Although the tiny voice was very faint, it was deep, and that of a male. Its voice was reverberating in her cranium.

"Could you explain to me how I'm doing this, again?" Katie asked, as if speaking into thin air. "I'm still really confused about the mechanics and all."

"Well, you see, you're an animal telepath; you can speak to animals using your thoughts, as long as you've locked eyes with the creature, I must add. You will hear it as a voice. Just as you hear me now."

"But why didn't I have powers like this where I'm from?"

"Magical powers must not be able to exist from your home, but they're very real here. If magic exists here, the prospect of powers isn't all that far-fetched. The first time you perform magic, your brain discovers its ability to perform magical feats. This allows you to have an individual power. And yours just happens to be animal telepathy."

"This is all still so crazy and cool to me. I can't believe how amazing all this is. It's like I'm living in this magical dream, huh?" Katie said back.

"I guess you could say that young Katie. And quite the strong power you have as well."

The butterfly began to fly higher into the sky…

"Where're you going?" Katie asked, eyes locked with the large creature once again.

"To my home, of course."

"But you're a butterfly. The wolves in your pack won't recognize you."

"Oh, that's not a problem. I needed some time to myself anyways."

The butterfly began to flap its wings again.

"Are you sure you're gonna be okay? I don't want this state to cause any trouble for you because of me."

"I appreciate the worry, Katie. But really, I'll be okay."

The butterfly nodded its head and flew up and over the trees.

Chapter 6
Out of the Woods

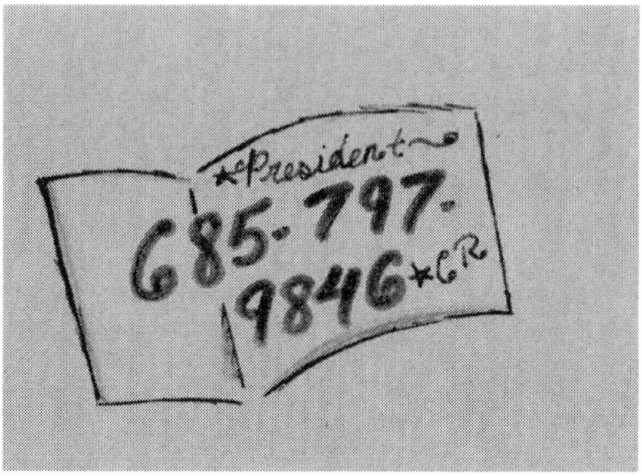

"**LISTEN, I'M REALLY SORRY FOR GETTING LOST** last night."

Cassie hugged Katie tight for the third time that morning. "Oh, don't apologize. You defeated that wolf all by yourself, learned a new spell, and saved me from making the stupidest decisions ever all in one night. You're the best baby sister ever!"

Katie smiled so bright she couldn't even feel an ounce of negative emotion.

"Thanks, Cass."

Cassie hugged Katie for a few more seconds, then held out her pinky to her sister.

Katie looked from her sister's face to her hand in confusion, inquiring, "What's this for?"

"Promise me something."

"Promise you what?"

"Promise me that you'll always look out for me."

"I'll only promise you that if you promise that you'll always look out for me," Katie said back immediately.

"Of course. Pinky promise?"

Katie interlocked her pinky with her older sister's. "Pinky promise."

"This includes not telling Mom about this, too," added Cassie.

"Oh of course, I know that. Mom would ground me for my whole life—plus future reincarnations."

The sky was a faded blue, as it was about eight o'clock in the morning and there were barely any clouds in the morning sky.

The sun was piercing through the leaves of the pine trees above.

Moments later, they heard Conner yawning, followed by him crawling out of his fort in the clothes he had worn the day before. "G' morning, you two."

"Morning," Katie replied.

"Morning," Cassie responded. She breathed into her cupped hands, scrunching up her nose at the scent. "I've gotta brush my teeth fast. Not sure my nose will be able to take the smell again."

"We'll find a river to brush our teeth in," Conner suggested. "It shouldn't be too hard to find one."

"Then let's get our stuff and get going," Aria said from beside him. She had appeared so fast without anyone noticing. It seemed as if she had just teleported to his side.

As everyone packed their belongings, Aria took out a map from her backpack.

"Looks like we're in the middle of the Animal Kingdom. And we need to get to where our magic is the strongest or find someone to help us locate Avery's location. Maybe somewhere in the Animal Kingdom City or the Kingdom of Magic."

"Is there any way to do the spell ourselves, without the hassle of asking someone in a more populated area?" Cassie inquired.

Conner answered, "No. We'll need a Seeing Portal Spell, which none of us, not even my sister or I, know how to perform. It's an advanced spell and takes a lot of magical practice and ability."

"Can't we just teleport to the city?" Katie inquired. "There's gotta be a spell for that, right?"

"There is, but that's also an advanced spell. And it's a pretty risky one, too. When they're performed incorrectly, you can become trapped in the place between your teleportation starting point and your destination. Or you can get your atoms spliced in half and just end up dying altogether. The safest and best thing to do overall to just get there would be to walk."

"So, if we walk, how long will it take us to get to the city?"

"A few hours. We won't be able to conjure any vehicle due to the limited magical cell towers around, so looks like we'll just have to use our legs."

They all groaned at the thought, all except Katie, who was happy to lend them each another egg salad sandwich to silence their rumbling stomachs.

They started packing up again, checking the campsite for any belongings left behind.

"Let's get going then, guys," Aria said, leading them away from the clearing as Katie picked up a handful of candytuft flowers and played with their petals.

She threw the flowers aside after a minute of doing so, walking in silence behind the group until they reached a thin stream, the water so clear and translucent they would've mistaken it for glass if it wasn't moving.

They kneeled over the water with face soap, toothbrushes, and toothpaste in their hands, dipping their toothbrushes in the water and applying toothpaste before brushing their teeth.

When they had finished, feeling cleaner and refreshed, they continued on their journey, Cassie rustling through her backpack for her smartwatch or phone so she could tell the time.

"Here it is…" She stopped on the path as her friends continued walking ahead of her.

She pulled out a small, lavender phone from the front compartment in her bag and turned it on, showing a picture of her and her best friend dressed as twin Grim Reapers for Halloween as her lock screen.

She typed in a numbered code so fast you could barely see it and unlocked to the home screen, tapping on an icon with a small, white clock against a violet background.

The screen popped up to appear various times in different time zones, and she searched for that of her home, Los Angeles, California, where it was late at night, it seemed.

"What time zone would we be in here?" she inquired, searching through the available list.

"The time is based on which kingdom we're in. That's because every one of them faces a different amount of sun at a different moment since the Magic Realm is a flat-faced rock spinning in a way similar to that of Earth," Conner explained. "Just look up the

Animal Kingdom in the time zone search bar above and you should find the time."

Cassie typed "Magic Realm" into the search bar and her phone quickly rose into the air, convulsing back and forth as it rose higher and higher.

"What's going on?" Her phone was almost near the top of a nearby pine, its branches high in the sky. "What's it doing?"

From five separate points in the sky, aquamarine beacons of light shot at her, levitating phone, stopping it from ascending any higher. With the phone still in the light's grasp, it got hotter and hotter, to the point where electric blue flames covered it completely.

Is it going to destroy my phone? I can't pay for that!

As fast as it had appeared, the light disappeared in a flash.

It caused her phone to fall to the ground.

She looked up, narrowly avoiding the falling phone knocking her out, only to see Conner catching it effortlessly at her feet.

"Here you go," he said, handing her the unusually warm smartphone.

"Thanks." Her worry was beginning to subside with relief, and she gratefully accepted the device from him. Everything in her phone was the same.

Same apps, same home screen, same passcode.

The only thing that had changed was that her phone had adapted to the new dimension.

If she looked up the Magic Realm in her search engine, it gave her thousands of tabs and websites that held lots of information about the new world she was in. And when she looked up 'Magic Realm' in her clock app, the world was no longer full of countries, but it now had a modern map of the different kingdoms. She zoomed in on the Animal Kingdom, the time popping up before her.

"Says here it's only 8:30, so we seem to have plenty of time to get there in good time," Cassie declared.

As they traveled, their shoes crunching on dead and dried leaves, they talked, played rounds of games on their devices and watched movies.

They took a walking breather every hour or so.

After a little less than five hours of walking, the lush forest scenery had transformed into a bustling metropolis full of towering glass skyscrapers and hovering motor vehicles.

"This place is incredible!" Katie praised, eyes lighting up at the mesmerizing beauty of the city. She turned back to them. "This is the Kingdom's capitol, right?"

"'Here in the Kingdom's capitol, you can find statues of their founders, incredible structures, and all modern contraptions this place has to offer'," Conner read off his phone.

"We can stay here for the night, right, guys?" Katie asked, eyes still twinkling. "It'll be so awesome!"

"Sure, but just make sure you keep your guard up. Squadrons like to take citizens when others aren't looking around places near the woods."

Their feet quickly adapted to the smooth concrete sidewalks instead of the uneven grasses. On their right, the hovering motorcycles, cars, trucks, and eighteen-wheelers used magnets to suspend themselves over entirely metal roads. At the wheel, were anthropomorphic animals in human clothing, whereas on the sidewalks, a variety of animals walked at different paces, some running and narrowly avoiding collisions with other citizens while others were walking leisurely.

The city, though, wasn't only filled with anthropomorphic animals, as there were fairies with brightly colored wings as well.

Aside from the difference in their appearances, they all gave Cassie, Katie, Conner, and Aria a burning glower from afar, staying as far away from them as possible.

"Where are the people?" Katie inquired.

Aria quieted her instinctively, receiving a confused glance from Katie and Cassie. "Don't say the 'P' word."

"Why?" Katie asked. "It's not like that's a bad word, right?"

"We need to go somewhere more private," instructed Aria, leading them to a darkened alley beside a casual restaurant, the lights overhead hung by thin pieces of string.

"Why can't I say that?" Katie asked again. "The 'P-word', I mean."

"Well," Aria started, eyes flicking back and forth for any sign of a passerby. "Years ago, after the kingdoms were already separated, the Animal Kingdom felt that they were being ignored by the Council of the Realm. This was because their ruler at the time, Vitina, wasn't working to help them. In the time when the Council was struggling to find a new ruler with the old one now a criminal and roaming free, the people of the Animal Kingdom were able to create their own system of government.

"One with democracy, and a court system, and all that other important government stuff."

"So, like their own America?" Cassie suggested.

"Pretty much. But anyways, everything was going well until a person from the Kingdom of Magic came to tell them to fall back under the rule of Ruler Marjorie—despite her still being in the hospital at the time and having trouble doing her work—and the Council.

"As a kingdom, they refused and protested as Ruler Marjorie's condition worsened over the next few days.

They then decided to elect a president every two years and a law was put into motion that their court system would work to enforce the law on the kingdom's citizens.

"Those who failed to follow them were prosecuted. To create equality between the animals and fairies, the presidential and vice-presidential seats would each be represented by a member of one of the species. Of course, though, this depended on who won the election."

"That's a really well-developed system,' Cassie commented. "And they did this all without the help from a ruler?"

"Yep," Conner answered. "And that's why the Animal Kingdom hates humans so much. 'Cause they ignored them and their problems for weeks on end, so they ended up having to solve those problems on their own, completely throwing away their need for humans."

"So, is saying the word…" Katie lowered her voice to a whisper. "… 'people'…" She raised her voice to normal volume. "…is it outlawed or something?"

"People aren't illegal, per se, but everyone here hates them.

"Not to mention hate crimes against them are legal, at least in some cases." Conner pulled his wand out of his bag, everyone else doing the same. "If we wanna stay safe here for the time being, we'll need to make sure we aren't people."

"Dorsiti calcuntactu," Aria whispered quietly, her wand pointed to her chest.

A wave of emerald-green light surrounded her in a ball of sparkling light, illuminating the dark space around them and filling it with the light's bright hue. The movement ceased as the ball of sparkles stopped turning, the light fading to reveal Aria had now transformed into a fairy with olive skin and large, jade green wings that shimmered in the light of the sun.

The fairy's hair was long and brown, mint stripes at the front.

Despite the media depiction of fairies as the size of pencils, Aria stayed the exact same height. She adjusted her seafoam green blouse dress and smiled at how well her transformation turned out, watching as her wings flapped behind her.

"Dorsiti calcuntactu," her brother said next.

The spell caused a wave of cyan light to wrap around him, flipping and spinning him in a sphere of sparkles, moving faster and faster with each passing second.

From the fading orb appeared a fairy with the same skin tone as the fairy-Aria peacock blue-winged fairy. His cyan tunic swayed gently in the breeze along with his now light-brown hair tipped with blue.

Aria and Conner engaged in conversation as Cassie cast the spell upon herself, causing her to become a lavender cluster of magical matter. She emerged from the magical ball with ivory skin, lilac wings, and a boysenberry dress with flowing sleeves that ended just below her elbows. Her hair was the color of the twins, so light someone could easily mistake it for being blonde hair with violet tips.

Her hair blew back as her wings flapped against the chatter.

Aria flicked her eyes to her and smiled, immediately turning away.

"Katie," Cassie directed to her younger sister. "It's your turn."

Katie nodded at her and pointed the wand at herself. "Dorsiti calcuntactu."

Her feet lifted from the concrete as she spun effortlessly in the air, so quick that she had become a pink blur building up wind at an alarming rate.

It seemed odd how extreme the transformation was, considering the fact that those who'd proceeded were rather calm in comparison.

This observation frightened Katie, leading her to believe that she had done something wrong. She could feel her pace of breathing quicken and her heart increase in pace.

The pink sparkles that had surrounded her and caused such a remarkable amount of distress disappeared in a split-second and a relieved Katie took a deep sigh.

She returned to the ground once more, a fairy with wavy brunette hair striped with pink and a fuchsia dress with a dark pink belt.

The dress billowed in the gentle breeze flowing through the intricate modern metropolis.

She began flapping her wings as soon as she noticed them, quickly shooting into the air, wind blowing her short hair back. She sailed the skyscraper, the glass windowpanes beneath her creating a blur of blue similar to that of the sea passing beneath a fast-moving boat.

"Katie," Cassie yelled over the powerful wind. "What're you doing?"

Yet Katie never answered her question, soaring ever higher into the sky, so high that she had reached the clouds circling the top of the building.

"Katie," Cassie breathed, observing the sea of fluffy clouds at her feet.

She arrived just as her sister had.

"Just leave me here," Katie interrupted absentmindedly, staring off into the clouds beneath the sun that shone above. "I'll be fine. You three can go and come back when you've found someone to help us. And just come back to this tower to tell me."

"That'll take us too long, Katie," Cassie chided, pulling her bag tighter around herself.

Then, the twins arrived.

"Then just text me. And then I'll come to you guys," said Katie. She still wasn't looking at her sister.

"Shouldn't we be looking for someone to help us in the city? Y'know, on the ground?" Conner quipped.

"You're not funny, Conner," Aria snapped.

"Well, Mom said my jokes were lovely, in fact."

"Mom has a horrible sense of humor; you knew that."

"Yeah, we should." Cassie glared from Conner to her sister. "Right, Katie?"

Katie had already gotten the message and stood from her seat at the edge of the building, clutching her backpack straps tight as they began their descent. The wind was in their hair and the rays of sun warming them as the city came into view again.

The buzzing of their wings soon ceased, and they lay their feet gently on the gray concrete overlooking the stone steps into the main city. There was an array of wide meadows and clearings outside of the city's boundary. Roads around the buildings led vehicles out of the city and far into the sun-kissed, grassy countryside to the east.

Yet none of the city compared to the regal beauty of the Capitol.

They turned to see a pristine white building with a golden dome roof soaring over them, reflecting sunlight back over the city with a lustered appearance. And with a background of the clear afternoon sky, the picturesque sight looked straight out of a storybook.

As the group walked through the wide entrance lined with golden roaring lions, they entered an enormous silver room with steps going on forever toward its ceilings.

"Someone here should be able to help us. Maybe the President if she isn't busy at the moment," Aria suggested. "And if not…I'm not really sure what we'll do."

She said her words calmly, but something in her eyes told Cassie she must be panicking; this would have to work.

On the first floor, animals and fairies in formal wear walked in and out of the marble-floored space carrying papers and forms in leather briefcases and portfolios.

The building had several levels, way too many to even count, and taking a few more steps inside, they noticed how every floor overlooked where they stood in the cylinder-shaped location known as the Main Hall.

Katie enjoyed the main hall most out of the four, staring at the never-ending staircase as if her eyes were glued to it. "Is that where the executive office is?"

Aria was only able to start nodding when Katie's wings began to buzz, and, soon after, the wings of the other three of them too.

They flew quickly, reaching a halfway point in the staircase in hope that they had saved at least a little bit of strength in their wings in case they needed to get out of there fast.

They had already traveled thirteen floors up, not including their flight to the halfway point, yet they still had to pass several floors.

Yet as the stairs continued to twist forever, now was when Aria eyed the floors of the building, apparently realizing they had made it to where the Presidential Garden was.

"We must be close," gasped Aria.

She wiped sweat from her forehead.

"Looks like we're almost there," Conner breathed, checking his phone for a map of the building and putting it back in his pocket again.

His legs ached as he adjusted his grip on his backpack. Cassie would hear the fatigue in his words. His heavy breaths, his deep inhalations. She noticed the sweat that glistened on his forehead. From her backpack, she pulled out a water bottle, handing it to him.

"Here," she said. "Take it. You seem kinda tired."

"Thanks, Cass." He snatched the water from her hands and downed most of it in mere seconds, putting the bottle away to save at least a bit more for later.

Cassie was rather astonished at how quickly he had finished most of the bottle, but thinking back over it, he wasn't surprised considering how far they had climbed at this point.

After about three more floors, they had finally arrived at the long-awaited golden doors that must've led them to the executive's office on the top floor.

As Cassie observed the letters of the entrance, Katie stared down over the railing, her hands gripping the metal. She looked over the lethal drop to the first floor, so far below them the citizens below looked like ants.

Above, a silver board read in large black letters: EXECUTIVE OFFICE.

They walked through the doors cautiously, realizing they were in a hardwood-floored room where three sturdy men stood in solid black clothes and sunglasses.

They stood in the same stance before a door on the opposite side; it must've been the President's office. Resting on the walls were small torches that flickered, illuminating their emotionless faces in the faint light.

Aria's face showed worry was overtaking her. Perhaps this wasn't the best idea…

The guard on the very left had a caramel brown scalp bouncing light into their eyes. He wiped a bead of sweat from his face, his quick and subtle movement wrinkling the top of his tight suit. A silver pin on his lapel read DERRICK.

It was rather comforting to Cassie that you couldn't see his eyes through his sunglasses, or that of the other two.

If she did, she was afraid his mere gaze would cause her to abort the mission immediately.

In the middle was a guard with black hair frayed at the tips, favored more toward the left side of his head as light reflected off his ivory skin.

His silver name tag read FLYNN in the same bold letters.

Unlike the other two though, the one on the right emanated an unmistakably pleasant energy. His deep brown hair reached his lower neck, flowing in a way, adding distinction to his otherwise normal hair. He had a strong jawline, no trace of facial hair anywhere and his lips, whilst similar to his peers, were upturned just enough to tell that he was a rather calm individual in comparison to the others.

Apparently, his name must've been Charles.

Hoping for the best with what she was able to pick up, Aria walked up to Charles and timidly asked, "Excuse me. Charles, is it? Could we enter the President's office please?'

Charles lowered his tinted sunglasses to reveal glaring deep brown eyes, causing Aria to pull back a bit from him. "Not at the moment. The President is on a call with close relatives and mustn't be interrupted."

He spoke in a low voice, eyes moving from Aria to her friends, then back again.

"I'm sorry," Aria started. "But we really need to see the President."

She didn't want to seem short-tempered the way she usually was, especially not right now, but she couldn't help but feel a flicker of frustration as Charles did nothing but blink in response. "We have a problem we're certain she can help us with. We just need her to perform a spell for us and then we'll be out of here. It'll only take up to five minutes."

"You should've scheduled an appointment then. And I don't think it would be that hard to find someone else to perform the spell for you. Or maybe, say, perform it yourselves?"

There was a hint of a smug smile on his lips with his emphasis on his last words. It was clear he was attempting to get under their skin, specifically Aria's.

Aria breathed deeply to relieve some tension. "Can't we just see her for five minutes?"

"Why do you need to see her so bad, anyways, huh?" Charles returned to his prior stance and kept his emotionless expression. He looked back at the entrance door to the room. "She doesn't have time for some kids with a superiority complex at the moment."

Obviously, Aria couldn't tell him why they needed to see the President so badly. It was illegal according to Dimensional Law to use the Seeing Portal spell without the supervision of an official authoritarian figure. And of course, these guards, who were humans and probably not considered such, couldn't verify that they wouldn't be using it for criminal purposes. Only the President could do that right now.

The new law had been developed a few months after Ruler Marjorie died, to keep Vitina from having access to watching and picking up on the locations of her victims. Of course, though, it did end up affecting citizens who merely needed the spell for things like this.

But it seemed this was just a problem they would have to deal with for now.

And yeah, they could just go down to the police station to ask for this, but the police barely ever had any magical experience.

They were always devoting their time to police work. Meaning no magic or wands.

Just guns, tasers, and a variety of other non-magical weapons. And no shop in town would just be giving out things like this, especially not for free on their budget.

The President was the only convenient choice they had that wouldn't get them marked as fugitives.

"We don't know anyone else who'll be able to help us," Conner said as he neared the guard. "And just because we think that someone like the President might have time to help the citizens she's required to serve doesn't mean we're entitled."

There was a hint of smugness to his words.

At that point, Aria could already tell her brother had screwed up.

A vein popped on Charles head, and he said quickly, "But that doesn't seem to be my problem, does it?"

Aria let out an internal scream of frustration and pulled her friends to the exit door, all confused as to why she would give up so easily.

But just as Conner was pushing the door open, Aria set her wand on an angle pointing to the light switch near the entrance, her body covering it from the guards' view.

Conner stopped midway as he saw this from the corner of his eye, quick to pick up the plan, and he walked over to the guards. "Are you sure she isn't available at the moment?"

The exchange between the two gave Aria enough time to say, 'Aqua exponentia', draw a water droplet inside of a small circle with her shining wand tip, and position her wand in a way the guards still couldn't see it. Just then, she tapped the center of the circle, and it shot a thin, almost unseeable, stream of water at the light switch, causing it to turn off the lights in an explosion of embers she narrowly avoided.

She wasn't expecting it to work as well as it had, considering the fact that these lights they had were fire, right? But it seemed, by some magical stroke of luck, that something had finally worked out in her favor today.

"What just happened?" Derrick boomed. "Turn the lights on now!"

"And why would we do that?" Conner said as he avoided the guards' flailing hands. "It's not like you can see us anyways."

"But we'll find you," Flynn grunted, running uselessly as he searched for them

As the group made their way around the guards, hoping they wouldn't accidentally run into something, they desperately searched for the entrance door.

And to their dismay, it was much harder to find than anticipated.

Conner's spirit lifted as his hands ran over something smooth with engraved wording on it. And in triumph, he shouted, "I've found it!"

"Yeah," another voice disclosed, "I found something, too."

The bright lights switched on, everyone surprised to find themselves in their new locations. Conner was standing near the doors to the executive's office. Cassie and her sister were searching a plain wall, Aria was searching the one opposite, and Flynn and Charles were staying somewhat in their original spots.

"We're gonna have to take you in for trespassing and public property damage," Derrick said nonchalantly as he walked away from the light switch, somehow fixed again as the fires of the lights roared back to life. "And for this little stunt you pulled, all of you'll have to come down to the police station with us. They'll probably fine you…" He grinned. "…Maybe even stay a night or two in the city's jail."

Derrick grabbed Aria's forearms, causing them to grow pale, starving them of blood circulation by the tightness of his grip. Flynn grabbed Conner by his as well, but Conner tried to punch at him as he attempted to free himself from his grasp. Taken by Charles, Cassie too writhed as she tried to break free from his pull while Katie fought to do the same.

"Hey!" Aria shouted, trying to punch Derrick with her free arm, "I swear to God!"

"Oh, shut it," Derrick said as he dragged her. "We've heard that story hundreds of times. 'I swear to God I'll punch you when you let me go', 'You'll be sorry'. It's all just a bunch of empty threats you don't have the strength to fulfill.

"So quit your tantrum and let us take you down to the police station."

Derrick was cut off by Aria's grunts as she tried to weasel herself out of his grip, pulling at her shoulder to at least slip herself out a little bit.

After moments of trying though, she stopped when they had reached the exit door that led to the staircase to take them to the main hall.

"We can't have you escaping, so we'll have to take you to the station ourselves," Flynn said as they set off walking down the long flight of stairs leading them to the Main Hall.

Aria probably shouldn't have provoked them, and now she was searching for a solution but not finding one.

And now, they were going to be taken down to the police station for who knew how long.

She looked at Flynn and noticed something she should've seen earlier.

He had no wings.

Neither did Derrick or Charles.

"Damn it, Aria!" she said to herself quietly. "Of course, they don't. They're humans, duh! I just need to get a running start on 'em, then just fly back up to the office. I just need to get free somehow…"

She kept running over the plan in her head several times, looking at possible reasons why it would and wouldn't work, perfecting it over and over based on unknown variables, such as people passing by and how fast the guards were.

It was the only thing that would work. She had to try at least.

With her right arm, she felt around in her pocket, finding her wand and hiding it behind her thigh and right wing for the time being.

She angled it at Flynn's arm, which was gripping Conner's arm painfully.

In a voice so quiet she had trouble hearing it, she whispered, "Stupefaciunt exponentia" and shot a fine line of light at Flynn's lower leg.

According to her plan, Charles and Derrick would either rush to help Flynn or interrogate them, so she quickly put her wand in her pocket and watched as Derrick inched so close to her face she could feel the heat emanating from his bald scalp.

"Did you do this?" he spat.

"No. Of course not." She tried to sound as sincere and surprised as possible as she lied.

Charles and Derrick went to help Flynn, asking questions and inspecting where it hurt the most, sort of the way a friend would.

It all seemed to be going according to plan.

Conner, Katie, and Cassie looked at her.

It took barely any thought to understand what they needed to do now and with a powerful leap, the four took off flying back to the top floor.

It was a long and tiring flight to the office as they had already traveled more than halfway down, the three guards supervising them only seconds ago.

Below them, Charles and Derrick were carrying Flynn by the armpits.

He'd uselessly tried to climb the stairs himself, despite the numbness overtaking him.

By the time they were in the room, they took a breath of relief, but knowing the guards were only mere steps away at this pace, they pushed their bodies' weight against the doors to keep them from entering.

Yet, they burst open not even a minute later to a fuming Derrick and frustrated Charles carrying Flynn's limp body.

"The hell is *wrong* with you kids?" Derrick yelled as they began darting for the door. "Do you really think you can get away with something like this? Do you really think what you did was okay?"

"And for what!" Charles added in.

Aria was tuning out Derrick's lecture as she was thinking about how they would make it to the door without the President hearing her guards from outside.

Maybe the room was soundproof? Maybe she'd just gotten used to hearing a lot of noise? No. The President would probably be suspicious if her guards kept saying there was a group of criminal kids in her office, and he'd come out to investigate the issue as soon as possible.

"Hey, you!" Derrick bellowed, snapping Aria from her daze. She looked at him with an empty and straight face, her usual thinking face most of the time. "Not only did you destroy property, but you also stunned a guard, didn't you?"

She continued staring at him with empty blue eyes, no remorse in them.

"I know you did it! You're just trying to keep yourself from getting locked up, aren't you?" He took a deep breath and set Flynn to the side where Charles held him up, standing still as he observed what was about to occur.

Derrick was bounding toward her with his wand raised and Aria, still for some reason taking in the situation, observed him holding it like a sword or dagger.

It was also very long.

Derrick thrust the wand on her right side like a sword.

Maybe it didn't have any magical uses?

She avoided the wand again and Derrick drew it back, about to cast a spell at her, proving her previous thought incorrect.

Conner, desperate to save his twin, pulled his crystal blue wand out of his pocket and shouted a spell unfamiliar to Cassie or Katie. "Invisibilia vis agri exponentia!"

The electric blue light hit Aria's arm, yet she continued on with her thinking undisturbed.

Derrick shot a stun spell at her head, yet it deflected back toward him, and he narrowly avoided the same fate as Flynn by leaping out of the way.

Derrick ran up against the force field, leaving no mark or infliction on the magic and smiling cryptically as he panted, "Fine then. I'll just have to make you leave."

He was now pointing his wand at Conner, Cassie, and Katie, the latter two pulling out their own wands and acting as if they knew at least one spell to defend themselves in an attempt to provide some stability to the situation.

"It's gonna be your own fault when your friends go to jail, kid! You wanna be responsible for that? Are you sure, now?"

Aria looked up at Derrick and smiled. He didn't know how much of a disadvantage he was at. She looked at her brother for confirmation and he nodded then, leaving a confused and disoriented Derrick wondering what it was they were plotting.

When Derrick had finished his victory speech and looked at the three, he smiled as he charged toward them.

But Aria, too fast even for Derrick, knocked him out of the way with her forcefield like a ball in a pinball machine.

Derrick hit the exit door with a bloodcurdling cry of pain.

Charles, the only guard left standing, began shooting spells at Conner, Cassie, and Katie, the three still unprotected by a spell.

"Stupefaciunt exponentia!" Charles cast, a ray of golden light making its way toward the three of them.

Before they could even cast a spell, Aria jumped in front of them.

Her force field was around her, deflecting the spell back at Charles, who chuckled as he watched Conner lower the force field around Aria.

It was likely Aria was hoping to create an enormous sleeping spell to keep the guards quiet for up to an hour, and that way, they could finally speak to the President in peace and get the spell they needed. After all that had happened, in the back of her mind, she was no doubt wondering whether all of this was truly worth it.

But it was for Cassie, of course.

She blushed for a moment, flustered at the embarrassment from that acknowledgement. This was supposed to be about Avery, not Cassie!

Yet the only way she could put a sleeping spell on the guards was by lowering *her* guard, which would give someone the opportunity to sneak up behind her.

"Shouldn't have let your guard down," Derrick laughed. "Was an amateur move for kids your age." He took his wand out and backed away from the four, tension building and hearts pounding as they watched him in fear.

"STUPEFACIUNT EXPONENTIA!" Derrick yelled in triumph.

In the air, he created a circle even taller than his own six-foot stature, one that would surely end the four's plan for good.

Aria looked around desperately for some answer, but the circle he had cast was much too wide for them to avoid without at least one of them being hit. And there also wasn't any time to cast a force-field spell before Derrick shot his magic at them.

That was it. They were stuck.

The plan had failed.

Derrick chuckled menacingly at his success.

Aria looked at Cassie. She hadn't talked in a while and seemed to be clenching her fists.

A burst of energy flowed throughout her, and she looked up at Derrick, so angered and infuriated that she might as well have lit him on fire with her gaze.

She needed to know where her sister was.

She needed to find her and wouldn't let someone get in the way of that.

With her bag still on her back, Cassie sprinted around the circle of the spell faster than anyone could notice.

She had moved so fast, Derrick had just turned around when she took her wand out.

Cassie looked from the ground, staring at him with a burning fire in her eyes, wand pointed at his chest. "Don't do it or I—" She was hesitant for a split second but went on. "I'LL STUN YOU!"

He laughed at her pathetic attempt to be the heroine and said, "Don't provoke me. You haven't seen the worst of my training just yet."

He knows I'm no good at this.

When Derrick turned back to the three standing before his spell, he noticed they were all gone and standing behind him. Involuntary distraction.

Guess I should've kept a better…

Conner cast a sleeping spell on him before he could even finish his internal sentence, causing the spell Derrick had just created to dissipate as he collapsed before Cassie.

Charles was bounding for them while Flynn, on the other hand, moved pitifully using only his arms to worm his way to them, a bit of feeling returning in his upper body.

"Dormiens exponentia!" the two twins cast at the guards, watching them fall asleep right at their feet.

They walked into the executive's office with no words to each other, just a deep sigh of relief and hope that the guards wouldn't wake up before they left the President's office.

They entered a gorgeous room with grayish-white painted walls. On the walls either side of them were looming bookshelves stocked with several political books, and others with records of past events in the kingdom before and after the so-called "Vitina Crisis".

On the wall opposite them was an eight-paneled window overlooking the city, gray curtains swept to the side to allow the warm sunlight in. In the middle of the room was a large desk with a small silver sign in the corner that read, PRESIDENT.

Strewn across the deep brown desk were sky high stacks of as yet unsigned forms beside a two-screen computer monitor, each separated by a few inches.

They took in the beautiful room for a few more moments until a fairy walked in and sat in a leather desk chair, curly black locks of hair either side of her head bouncing with each subtle movement.

At the same time, they noticed the white blouse she was wearing beneath her navy-blue pantsuit, and she had subtle makeup done on her chestnut brown skin, enough so it wasn't too noticeable but at the same time, didn't make her look unready for work.

"Why hello!" she announced, a light shining into her deep brown eyes. "Welcome to the Executive Official's office, or President's Office, if you will. My name is Christina Robel. What about you four?"

"Aria Thomas."

"Conner Thomas."

"Cassie Smith."

"Katie Smith."

"Well, nice to meet you all." She shook each of their hands, exposing her purple nails to each of them. "What is it that you require?"

"Well, we have some friends here." Aria pointed her thumb to Cassie and Katie. "And it seems that their sister became lost somewhere in this dimension, and they're really worried about her safety. Do you have any ideas on how we could find her?"

"Not at the moment, but I do know you need a teleportation spell, yet I'm afraid I can't help you with that. There are too many liabilities around risky spells like that for me to perform that for you, y'know?"

"Yes, we're aware of that," Conner said as he walked up to her. "But if you could create a seeing portal for us to use, that would be really helpful."

"Of course, I can." She paused and smiled warmly. "For a small fee, of course."

"What fee?" Cassie questioned skeptically.

"Well, you see, our kingdom is hoping to use taxpayer money to pay for the construction of a few more magic cell towers. We can't do that by giving people free goods and services, right? So, if you want the help, I'll need you to pay me."

She smiled as if what she said hadn't just completely changed the course of their conversation, sticking her hand out for payment.

"You want money? Our sister could possibly be in danger, and you want us to pay you?" Cassie spat, a condescending look in her hazel eyes that were usually so calm and composed. Conner hadn't seen her this angry since that night at the camp.

"Oh no, no, no, no." She punctuated each 'no' with a wave of her hands. "It's only a small fee of one hundred films. You can easily pay that, can't you?"

Cassie and Katie exchanged confused glances.

What were films?

"How much is one hundred films exactly?" whispered Cassie into Aria's ear.

"About two hundred U.S. dollars," Aria breathed back. "But they don't take that type of currency in a completely different dimension."

The thought had just occurred to Cassie then. They were all humans, and no one probably had any films, let alone one hundred of them to pay her.

No one would give this type of money to some random, broke strangers. How would they pay her, one of the few people on their journey who was actually being quite nice to them?

At that moment, an idea hit Cassie that she should've picked up on early.

It looks like we'll have to break her trust.

They would have to take her wand.

"Um, is your magic strongest here?" It seemed as though Aria had picked up on the idea at the same time and was now working to get the information they would need.

"Of course. The Capitol building had been purpose built near several magic cell towers; that way, all of the officials here can use all of the magic they need to maintain order within the building and city. Mine works especially well."

She held up her translucent lavender wand, the sunlight reflecting into their eyes as they caught sight of the magical object.

It was so clear that they could see a refracted image of Christina's face in it.

So clear that they could see spotless reflections of themselves and the room behind them if they looked hard enough.

The group exchanged glances, all having a relatively easy time understanding what they needed to do. If they were able to get the President out of the room, they could use her wand without paying the fee. The plan was perfect.

"So do you have a meeting with the vice-president to attend or something?" Conner inquired, hoping she would say yes.

"Well, no. But now that you mention it, I do have a meeting to attend with the High Court tomorrow on their system of prosecution. So, I guess it would be a good idea to get to crackin' on that. I just need a couple of papers."

She looked at them and smiled. "I'll be right back."

With that, the President sashayed out of the room and into the hall. The clacks of her wedges on tile faded as she walked farther down the hall to the copy room.

"All right," Aria whispered, "she'll only be gone for two minutes tops. We have to take her wand, stuff it in someone's backpack so she can't see it and do the Seeing Portal spell behind the building. We'll leave the wand back there when we're done. No one'll know it was us and we won't have to try and pay her. It's perfect."

Everyone nodded in understanding of the plan. It was simple with a low risk; as long as the President didn't try and question them, it seemed difficult to fail.

As quickly as possible, Cassie snatched the lavender wand off the executive desk. She had barely finished zipping up her backpack when she heard the familiar sound of the President's shoes coming down the hall toward them.

The President walked into the room and groaned as a tower of paper landed on her desk, covering her from their sight. "I've got so much work to do." She blinked and opened her eyes to force a smile at them. "If it's okay with you three, maybe I can speak with you tomorrow." She stopped and inspected her desk. "Cassie, Katie, Conner, Aria, where did my wand go? I placed it on my desk only a few minutes ago if I'm not mistaken."

They glanced between each other.

Was she going to find out? Was stealing someone's wand against the law? But they were going to give it back, yet neither Cassie nor Katie knew about the rules in this place.

Wouldn't Conner or Aria say something about it?

What if she found out, and fined them? Threw them in jail?

Executed them?

"Oh," Cassie said, struggling to keep herself from breaking down in a nervous fit. She had never been a good liar, especially in a circumstance as important as this. But on the other hand, if she just didn't say anything, that wouldn't be an actual lie, right?

"Truly is a shame."

"Are you sure? Because it's very important I have my wand. By Dimensional Law, it's actually a crime to steal someone's wand for magical purposes, as it gives the criminal access to the spells the wand owner already knows how to perform.

"This can give bad-intentioned people who aren't at the prowess level access to powerful spells with which they can do horrible things." Christina eyed them suspiciously for a few seconds, suspecting they might be up to something.

"Are you four really sure you don't know where my wand is?"

"Of course, we're sure. We just hope you find it eventually," Aria lied seamlessly, making Cassie extremely jealous and, somewhat impressed.

Cassie gasped internally at how easy that was for Aria compared to how much she had struggled to do the same only a few moments ago.

"I guess I should just wait for it to turn up then. Could've just knocked it off my desk or something. If you need to contact me for more questions, here's my card." She stepped out from behind her desk to hand them an index card that read:

685-797-9846

"Thank you," Cassie responded, smiling a fake grin as she kept the truth from blurting out of her mouth. "We'll be on our way." She stopped at the door and faced Christina. "Oh, and by the way, those guards of yours—Charles, Derrick, and Flynn—we saw them sneak into your office while you left and search the place for a minute."

She stood immediately. "Seriously?" She began walking toward the door as she murmured, "I knew I shouldn't have hired those humans."

"Oh no." Cassie stopped her. "They won't own up to what they did just yet. You have to wait until they're ready to spill the truth. Once the guilt gets to their heads."

"You're right." Christina nodded as she returned to her seat. "By the time they wake up, I'll take them in for questioning down at the police station. Maybe then they'll own up."

Christina stopped for a moment before continuing her work when they left, thinking over the words Cassie had just told her. Were her guards really thieves?

She had hired them because they were good people, some of the only humans in this kingdom with clearance to go into the Capitol building. Were they taking advantage of the privilege she had given them? The privilege they didn't even deserve?

Maybe they were…

***

Outside of the President's office, they found the guards grumbling on the floor and rubbing at their eyes as they began to wake from their slumber. Without even a moment's delay, they sprinted across the space as fast and quietly as they could.

Flynn was the first to wake. Looking from his working leg to the lavender wand, he could just barely make out the zipper of Cassie's backpack.

He'd seen that wand before.

He gasped and smiled. The President's wand. Those damned kids must have stolen it. He smiled even wider. Now he would have even more of a reason to throw them in jail.

He stayed silent as he rushed down the stairs to catch up with them, hoping to catch them in the act by the time they used the President's wand or if they started flying off with it. And with that, a new vengeance toward them formed.

He would catch them in the act.

He was sure of it.

He would get revenge in the name of his kingdom.

In the name of Flynn Albecon.

Chapter 7
The Seeing Portal

FINALLY, OUTSIDE OF THE CAPITOL building, Aria, Cassie, Conner, and Katie landed on the ground at the back where trash bags piled into dumpsters. They lay beside them in the slowly cooling heat of the sun. It wasn't exactly hot per se, but hot enough for the heat to add onto not only Cassie's, but also Aria's anxiety about the situation at hand.

Cassie rapidly searched through the spell book she had pulled out of her bag to find the Seeing Portal spell. After intense searching, she had finally found the spell she needed.

It was near the middle of the book.

It was a page with detailed descriptions and pictures of how to perform the spell.

She placed the tip of the lavender wand on an empty spot on the building's wall and cast, "Visum portal exponentia!"

The spot where the wand had touched the building turned a blend of black and blackish purple, the colors swirling faster and faster to form a deep purple oval that swirled hypnotically before them.

"How do I make it look for Avery?" Cassie asked, eyes flicking around to check for signs of people.

"Just say it into the portal," answered Aria. "And hurry!

"Find Avery Smith." She stared at the screen, hoping it would work. Just a second of information would be enough. *Please. Please.*

The screen swirled for a few seconds then turned into a visual of a girl with peach white skin, dark ginger hair, and brown eyes. She wore scuffed jeans and a white blouse that flew in the breeze, her eyes making her look especially dead.

Under them were large bags, indicating sleep deprivation, and her hands were tied behind her back with a thin rope. Behind her was a hooded figure in a navy-blue cloak, watching her intently to make sure she didn't pull any tricks as they trekked through the forest together.

"What's going on? Who's following her?" Katie worried. She hadn't seen her sister in so long, but what was happening? Where was she going? "Where're they taking her?"

"Oh God," Conner slipped from his mouth, feeling the blood drain from his cheeks. "Those blue-cloaked people work for Rubidium, a school for kids to become soldiers for Andromeda and Vitina. They 'founded' the school themselves when they stole the building from Kingdom of Sorcerer's officials, hoping they could earn more workers in the process. She can't go there." He looked at the despair in Cassie and Katie's eyes. "If she arrives, she'll never be able to escape. And if she tries…" He looked back at the screen again. "…they'll do whatever they can to find her and hunt her down."

"You're kidding right? Right?" Cassie looked in his eyes for some sort of joke.

It would have been a cruel and disgusting joke to make but at least it would mean this wasn't her sister's reality. "You have to be joking, right, Conner!"

There was desperation in her eyes as she looked to him.

"Why would I joke about this?" Conner looked at her with serious eyes she rarely got to see. "We've gotta get her out of there before they do anything really bad."

She dropped the President's wand to the floor, the portal disappearing as gravity tolled on the object. "Do you know where Rubidium is?"

"It's in the Kingdom of Sorcerers, the best place for becoming magic users, to be able to use as much magic as possible."

The growing worry was clear in her eyes and he seemed to be trying to make his expression more relaxed despite the harrowing circumstances.

"The school is a horrible place even if I haven't been there myself, but I know for certain that they'll feed her and give her somewhere to sleep. They can't let their students die and if she stays in line for the time being…"

"They will?" She looked at Aria for verification.

"Yeah," Aria responded solemnly, setting her hand on Cassie's shoulder. "They won't take the best care of her, but they'll at least keep her safe for the moments she's there until we save her. And you look like you deserve to relax a bit more before the real journey begins; we have been traveling all day, after all." Her hand quickly retreated as she gazed into Cassie's eyes. "You should go somewhere to relax."

Cassie nodded, breathing deeply.

"Yeah, yeah…" She shook the worry from her head. "You're right."

"Let's stay here for the night, all right? Then we'll head to the Kingdom of Magic in the morning then the Kingdom of Sorcerers the next day," Conner proclaimed. "We can conjure a trailer later today for us to stay in on the trip."

"Won't it disappear when we're in the forest?"

"As long as we're in a ten-mile radius of at least one magic cell tower, the trailer will stay intact," he assured.

Cassie checked her watch. "It's about 4:30. We can still take a look around the city. Our transformation spells last about six hours, so we have some time left until we transform back.

She set the President's wand behind a pile of garbage bags; they'd be able to leave this place behind without consequences. And not only that…

Shouts of a gruff voice coming from her right cut off her happy moment.

When she turned her head, there she saw him.

Flynn.

He was sweating profusely and had a look of craziness in his eyes as he bound toward them at breakneck speed.

But by the time he had reached them, they had already flown off, watching them from his spot on the ground.

He smiled like a maniac, talking to the police station on a walkie-talkie.

"Yeah," he said, trying to sound emotionless. "My squad in vector Alpha have found four fugitives. They've stolen President Christina Robel's wand and assaulted three guards of hers. If you spot them, send me extra information. They're flying at the moment."

"Do you know what they look like?" the voice said on the other side. The man slurped his coffee quite loudly at Flynn's news. "Their names? Addresses?"

"I don't know where they live," Flynn began as we started walking back inside, "but I might know where to get some answers."

Cassie watched as the guard disappeared behind a wall and her worst nightmare had come true. *Oh God. He knows. And now, the President is probably gonna find out too. Cassie, why'd you have to screw up so bad? What've I done?*

Conner, next to her, noticed she was looking as if she was on the brink of another meltdown and smiled at her in a way she'd notice.

She smiled back at him. Even though he hadn't said anything, just the notion that he understood and cared made her smile.

As they flew toward a more secluded part of the city, they found themselves far from the Capitol building in a lush grassland full of RVs, trailers, and vans.

They landed on damp grass and Conner pulled his wand out of his backpack and held it to the late afternoon sun. "Creo exponentia!"

Before them, the air transformed into a long cylinder of beige sparkles, Conner tightly shutting his eyes, apparently thinking long and hard about what he was conjuring.

The cylinder began to gain more definition, transforming into a large trailer with two vibrant red stripes, six colossal tires, and a model name *E450* imprinted in silver on its side.

Conner received shouts of praise from his sister and friends as they walked inside the newly created vehicle. It had a sleek hardwood floor and beige seats facing the black leather dashboard at the front of the vehicle. There was also a seating booth with crimson red seats to their left and a rosewood dining table separating the two sides.

On their left, they observed a small twin bed with two lavender pillows and boysenberry purple sheets, a four-foot separation wall keeping the headboard of this bed from touching the footboard of a full-sized bed of the same color.

As they continued taking in the sight of the van, they noticed a door leading to a polished bathroom with a Jack and Jill sink and a shower also counting as a bath.

The trailer, quite thoughtfully, had also accounted for face soap and toothbrushes, even though they wouldn't need them since they had their own.

Across from the bathroom was a small kitchen equipped with a conventional oven underneath the black counter, and a microwave. On the far right of the kitchen, they could find a buffed sink and to the left of it a gas stove with two black burners.

Exploring further, they found themselves in a large sitting room with two full beds on the right side with a four-foot emerald separation wall between the footboard of one and the headrest of the next, much like the beds they had just seen minutes ago. The two full-size beds were covered in green from top to bottom, mint green pillows, seafoam green sheets, even a dark green frame. Sunlight warmed the beds through a window on the wall beside them, so when Conner claimed one of them, he could feel the warmth as he sat down.

"This van really does have everything," Cassie commented as she sat herself down on the brown couch on the right side of the sitting room. Her feet sank into the black carpet as she played with the TV remote she had just found on one of the side tables.

Cassie and Katie eventually sat their bags down near the two purple beds at the front of the trailer as the twins put their things on the beds in the sitting room.

As Cassie waited for everyone to get out the door, she looked at her phone for a moment, thinking she could call Avery. But she couldn't, could she?

She doesn't even have her phone with her.

And it's not like you could call Rubidium either.

Everyone was out the door by the time Cassie had gotten her things together, locking up the van with her keys as she placed her wand in her pocket.

She put her phone away solemnly.

I just wanna see her again.

When she was level with them in the sky—though still several feet behind—they had already begun their gradual descent, avoiding buildings, cars, and citizens with their sights already set on a place to visit.

The had arrived at a light gray building with a neon green sign that read *Bowling Alley.*

As they stepped inside, they heard the loud clacking of shoes and crashing of heavy bowling balls. They walked toward a granite counter to the right of the door, where an anthropomorphic female skunk stood near a labyrinth of bowling shoes.

"Which one would ya like?" the skunk asked in an accent similar to that of someone from New Jersey, sliding a sheet of laminated paper toward them.

Sounds just like one of our relatives, Cassie thought. *Can't place my finger on which one.*

The laminated information sheet included all the deals the bowling alley offered, some that Cassie considered rather cheap relative to the number of customers it covered.

"We'll take the four for the price of two deal, please," Conner answered as he handed the skunk one piece of mint green paper that read IN ANIMALS WE TRUST in obnoxiously big letters, a picture of the city's capitol underneath the words.

The skunk examined the two sides of the bill, which looked exactly the same. Then she shoved it into the metal cash register.

She pulled a stick of gum out of her beige employee's uniform breast pocket and chewed with her mouth open, blowing a minty bubble in front of them.

She handed them bowling shoes matching their sizes and they walked toward an empty lane when Cassie remarked to Aria, "I thought you didn't have any films."

She wasn't exactly angry, just sort of feeling betrayed. Why would she hide that from her? Especially now? "Why didn't you give that to—"

"Listen, Cassie. All Conner and I have is thirty-five; we don't—"

But Cassie didn't really seem to be listening.

Cassie looked away from Aria. She wasn't really sure how to feel. Why hadn't she been telling this stuff to the President? How could she…

"Why didn't you tell the President? Why didn't you tell the rest of us this before? Why didn't we get to be involved in this?"

"Well, because…" Aria hung her head and faltered because clearly, she'd upset Cassie. But perhaps it wasn't the wrong thing she'd done, yet Cassie still had obvious reason to feel mad. "I should've. You're right, Cassie." She sighed. "I'm sorry."

Cassie didn't know whether she should accept this apology, but the way Aria looked to her was making her feel all weird in her stomach.

"Look, Aria. Would you stop looking at me like that?"

Aria smiled and persisted playfully, "Like what, Cassie? Like this?" Aria stared at her in the same way and Cassie let out a chuckle.

"Yeah, stop that!" she said, playing along effortlessly.

After a while of this banter, though, Aria finally said, "I really am sorry if what I did upset you, Cassie. I should've talked to you first."

She breathed deeply as she walked away from her.

Once they had arrived at an empty bowling alley, they typed their names into a small screen connected to a large monitor overhead. Their names each popped up as white letters against the dark blue background and they went up in order of their names, Cassie casting occasional glances at Aria.

Her stomach started doing that weird thing.

Crap! she thought. *Quit that, will you?*

She thought that as if it would do anything to obey, when all it did was make it worse.

They laughed and told silly stories and jokes over the course of almost three hours, the time inching ever closer to when they would transform back.

They had played a total of three long rounds, with Aria winning the first, telling all of them every ten seconds about how she had been the first victor.

Conner was the next to win a round and he let out a bellowing cry of victory when he'd beat them all by a single point, causing a few animals in the bowling alley to look at him with confused and condescending looks.

This caused the rest of them to fall over with laughter.

And finally, to Cassie's surprise, she was defeated by her little sister in the last round as they were starting to cut it close to 7:30.

They walked out the door happy and chatting, walking through the streets looking for a place to get dinner. The dim lamplight lit the streets, preventing evening darkness from consuming the roads. They stopped at an organic tea shop called Blue Rose and strolled into a small room packed with several customers, some sitting in seats near the kitchen counter, others at tables, and some simply standing and talking to their friends.

In the back were at most ten employees in marigold orange employee shirts and beige khakis. They sliced and diced numerous vegetables and steamed them over clean stoves in pots that glistened in the lamplight.

On the right side of the kitchen, employees worked on refreshing drinks, warm teas, and iced coffees, while on the left, staff worked diligently to cook the foods the café served.

"Why hello!" a cheerful gray tabby cat employee with a name tag reading *Rosa* greeted. "What would you like?" She took out a small pen and a tiny blue lined notepad.

As the group discussed their orders, they decided on two small cucumber, egg, and pistachio sandwiches on rye bread with a cup of papaya drink for Aria.

For Conner, he would be taking two small BLTs on Italian herb bread with a cup of iced tea. Cassie would be taking on lamb and parsley soup with a side of white bread and a cup of pomegranate acai and watermelon refresher drink.

And for her little sister, she would have a cheddar grilled cheese and a small lemonade.

Rosa was able to get the entire order down and checked with them for confirmation that she had gotten all of their things. "Will that be all?" She looked up at them.

"Yes. That will be all," Aria verified.

Rosa rushed to the kitchen and gave the drink makers one sheet of paper she had just scribbled on and the cooks another, shuffling back toward them as she entered their order into the cash register. "That'll be twenty-four films, including the tax of one film."

Aria handed her five mint green bills, which Rosa inspected.

Then she slipped them into the cash register.

"Oh, do you have *to-go* boxes? We were planning to eat at home," Aria said as Rosa was just about to take another customer's order.

"Yes, we do actually," Rosa smiled. "Would you like plastic or Styrofoam?"

"Plastic, please."

"All right then." She turned to the workers in the kitchen and shouted in a less chirpy but still happy voice, "Make sure it's packaged in plastic, okay?"

They sat down at a table near the door as they checked the time, the hour at which they should be transforming back approaching much faster than anticipated.

"It's already 7:24," Cassie whispered urgently. "We're running out of time, you guys."

They got up from their seats when the cat called them up to the counter to collect their meals, quickly thanking Rosa and barreling out the door as they shot into the sky faster than they ever had previously.

With the time crunch and the amount of time it would take for them to reach their trailer, it seemed as though they would barely make it.

But even so, Katie still observed the city as they flew; the lights, even the blaring honking noises all seemed so beautiful against the darkness of the night that surrounded them.

"Katie!" Cassie grunted as she caught her sister's food and drink just before it fell.

"Huh?" Katie noticed her things were now in her sister's hands and chuckled nervously. "Sorry…"

After more stressful precious minutes had passed, they finally arrived at the trailer park, Cassie using her key to the van to unlock the trailer and let them in.

She quickly set their food down on the table.

"Just in time," Cassie breathed, seeing it was already 7:30.

With a flash of light, Conner returned to his original appearance, a lanky teenager with curly dirty blond hair, jeans, and a gray Madric Academy sweatshirt.

By this time, Aria had already returned to her normal appearance, now appearing as a teenage girl of average height with dirty blonde hair like her brother's, flowing at her side. She also wore an airy light green blouse and ripped light blue jeans.

The two had already taken seats at the dining table, indulging in their meals as Cassie appeared before them with her peach white skin, dark ginger hair, lavender blouse and jeans now returned. "Finally don't have to worry about sitting on those stupid wings."

"I thought they were kinda cool, honestly," Katie remarked back. "And pretty helpful too, especially during the time crunch."

"I never noticed how you two really are spitting images of each other," Conner said over a mouthful of his sandwich as he looked back at the two sisters.

They both scoffed and started to eat their food.

Katie pulled her black hood over her head in anguish.

"Well, we have this RV as long as there's at least one magic cell tower ten miles from us, so we can manage to take a path through the forest." Aria pulled up a map of the dimension on her phone and showed it to them. "Right now, we're here." She zoomed in on the bottom left of the Animal Kingdom located in the right corner. "If we take a path through the forest, we don't have to worry about transforming into fairies in the morning."

"Yeah," Conner muttered, his voice muffled, gobbling down the last of his first sandwich and washing it down with his iced tea. He then turned to Cassie.

"You're still going to teach us how to hunt, right?"

Cassie nodded her head quickly as she slurped her lamb and parsley soup.

"We'll need weapons for that, though. And I doubt we'll find any in the city. We'll probably end up making them ourselves."

"Now what's the plan for breakfast tomorrow morning?" Katie piped up.

Aria looked down at her. "We'll still be in the city tomorrow, so we can just conjure something to eat."

"Conjure food? Won't it just disappear when we eat it?"

"No actually. Magical matter makes up all conjured things, the light, sparkles, and diamonds you see when a spell is performed. This matter can take all shapes and can create solids, liquids, gases, plasma, and everything in between."

"Resicus is the scientific term for magical matter," Conner continued for his sister. "And when there aren't any magical cell towers around it disappears because there isn't enough coming from the towers to be used. Although, you can still use attack and defense spells when there's at least one cell tower in a ten-mile radius.

"This is because every time you perform a spell, there's a little bit of Resicus left in your wand and that, plus the magical matter from the cell tower, can allow you to perform those types of spells."

"This magic stuff is really complicated, huh?" Katie commented. "How do you guys manage to remember all this, anyways?"

"Yeah, it is complicated," Conner said. "But when you fully understand you'll really get to appreciate how great it is. But anyways, if you need me, I'll be in the living room."

Conner threw his plastic container into the trash and walked to the sitting room, closed the door, and began changing out of his clothes. By the time he had opened the door, he was already walking toward his bed in nightwear.

About two hours or so later, Conner continued to scroll through his phone, falling further into the covers providing him warmth and comfort.

His eyes flicked to the windows, a looming figure hiding behind the curtains.

He blinked to see if he was just hallucinating.

And the figure was gone.

He was searching for some way to rationalize this.

Maybe he was just seeing things. Maybe it was just a fern or a tree or something.

He nodded his head to himself as if to say, *yeah, just seeing things. Having hallucinations. Or a waking dream kinda thing.*

He turned back to his phone once more.

Katie was first to fall asleep, despite her promising herself she'd at least try to finish two chapters of her book, while Aria fell asleep next. By the time they were entering the early morning of the next day, Cassie's eyes were becoming heavy despite the light emitting from her phone. She set it aside to finally get some rest.

Conner, on the other hand, stayed awake through almost the whole night, wondering if the figure he had seen was a hallucination or was really there until roughly 4:00 a.m.

But he hadn't been tired then. So, it must've been real, right?

He would investigate this more, try and see if there really was someone waiting for them outside their van. But the weightlessness and comfort of sleep were pulling him in deeper and deeper until he couldn't hold onto consciousness anymore.

Even though everyone was fast asleep now, outside, the figure Conner had seen was watching them slumber, a cryptic smile spreading on their lips.

The figure realized they'd finally found their victims.

Wrath flowed through their veins, words ringing thorough their head.

Words that most likely said, *Finally, I've found you.*

I've finally found you.

Chapter 8
Conner's Crush

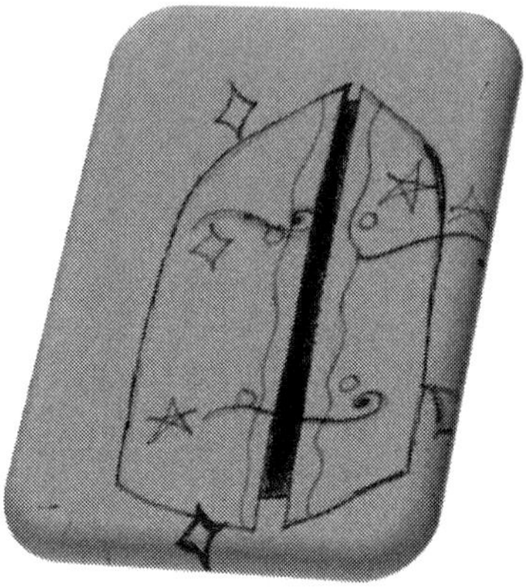

"HEY, GUYS," CONNER BEGAN. "Did you see something outside the window last night?"

"What do you mean, Conner? There wasn't anything outside," dismissed Aria. "At least not that I know of."

"I mean before I fell asleep, there was this thing. I saw it outside and it was staring at me. But when I blinked, it just disappeared. I stayed up most of the night wondering if it would come back, but it never did. It was someone wearing a black cloak, but I couldn't see their face. You guys didn't see anything like that?"

Everyone shook their heads no and Conner appeared to brush off the thought again.

It was already late morning and everyone had showered and changed into a new pair of clothes, Conner being the only one left smelling and feeling unclean.

As he took his shower, Katie, Cassie, and Aria leaned over the map of the Magic Realm, planning out their driving path for the day.

Aria held her pen over the map and drew a line from the corner of the Animal Kingdom to the middle kingdom. "I'm thinking we should move through the Kingdom of Magic."

"Kingdom of Magic?" Conner blurted. His hair was still dripping with water, but he had already changed into a black sweatshirt and baggy jeans.

Aria looked at him with confusion in her eyes and replied, "Yeah… Is that gonna be a problem?"

"No, it's gonna be great!" He walked back to the bathroom with an unusually cheery smile and the three of them continued to look over the map after his absurd interruption.

Before they could even get back into their discussion, Conner threw open the bathroom door and sat down at the dining table with them, speaking with a joy in his voice.

He hadn't possessed this level of enthusiasm before.

"Are you okay?" Katie asked him as she handed him an egg salad sandwich she'd stored in their tiny fridge. "You've been acting kinda…weird."

"Of course," he said and the rest of them dismissed him.

"So, will we stay human when we're driving? Will we transform before we get going?" Cassie questioned.

"If we stay low and keep any eye out for people passing by, I guess we'd be fine. The cops around here are particularly hard on humans so make sure to drive safely so you aren't pulled over." She glared venomously at her brother to make sure he was listening.

"Well, I'm not at all ready to drive. That's gonna be really boring," Conner groaned. An idea popped into his head. He looked at his twin. "Aria, my favorite sister…"

"You mean your *only* sister," she grumbled back.

He brushed off her comment and continued with, "Anyways, I know you *love* to drive…"

"Um—drive magical artifacts and steer mystical creatures. Not stupid trailers." She crossed her arms over her chest and puffed, "I'm not going to."

"But you are the oldest sibling, so…"

"Yeah, by mere seconds!"

"But *favorite* older sibling..."

"Still your only sibling."

"Why don't you drive? Great idea, don't ya think?"

He pushed his sister toward the driver's seat and received a fiery glower from her, which caused him to back away. "Fine, fine… I'll drive."

"All right then," Cassie said, taking another bite of her sandwich. "Well, since whatever just happened has been resolved now, I think it's important to know that it's almost noon." She put her phone in her pocket. "It's about time we got going."

Conner's previous excitement had returned; he was smiling widely once more, chirping in with, "When'll we get there?"

Aria looked down at her phone and back at him.

"About five hours or so and we'll have arrived."

His face betrayed all his feelings. In his glowing, happy eyes, he seemed to say, *I'll see her soon! Maybe even get to talk to her!*

Conner pondered even more, as if thinking about a million things. "Are we stopping in the Kingdom of Magic for a day or two? Hopefully, a day perhaps?"

"We'll stay there the night," Aria stated, staring down at the parchment map and circling places they would stop on their journey.

Conner's face noticeably lit up and his sister, sitting beside him, took immediate notice of how dazed he was looking. And before she could say a thing, he skipped off to the living room and plopped down on his bed, earbuds set firmly in his ears.

He lightly tapped his foot and peered out the window.

"What's wrong with him?" Katie questioned, taking a glimpse at Conner.

He appeared on the brink of insanity!

Cassie shrugged while Aria motioned for her brother to start driving, clearly dismissing Katie's question due to its ultimate insignificance.

He was still as he watched her hands move toward the driver's seat. "Maybe we could—"

Aria's pen dropped to the table with a clatter. "Can't you just *listen* for once!"

The excitement drained from his features as he walked to the driver's seat, hands in his pockets and locks of hair covering the top of his head. He strode across like a berated child.

"Are you always like that to him?" Cassie said between held-in laughs. She couldn't help but feel bad for him, but the situation was a bit hilarious. "Isn't that a bit harsh?"

Conner nodded and said with arms crossed, "She's right, y'know!"

"Oh, shut up and drive!" Aria barked back.

"'Shut up and drive'," Conner mocked as the trailer began to lift off the ground.

It then shook slightly from side to side as they rose in the air.

Cassie was struggling to grasp something to keep herself steady, and she held on tight to her little sister as she wavered and shifted about.

Beneath their vehicle, grass swayed ferociously as balmy air spewed out of the bottom of the van. Its six ginormous wheels adjusted themselves inside the vehicle, soon replaced by six massive magnet plates, sleek and black in the lustrous sunlight reflected by the magnets below. In an instant, they sped forward with blasts of blue fire coming from the back of the vehicle. The two sisters almost immediately took notice of the wobbling of the RV becoming smooth sailing, as if it were flying.

Yes, it was flying now, flying over metallic roads lining the streets of the city.

They headed toward the outskirts of town.

During the next five hours, Aria, Katie, and Cassie entertained themselves in a variety of ways. They began with a bout of gaming with the beloved Animal Kingdom game known as Microbial Quest, in which you fought to survive as a bacterium in the Kingdom of Sorcerers.

Afterwards, they watched a two-hour comedy film on the TV in the sitting room, laughing for the majority of it as Katie struggled, doing her best to understand the jokes.

They were definitely not catering for her age demographic.

In the final hour of their trip, they played a lengthy game of hide and seek, which served to show up how little space there was within the van, and how few spots for them to hide in.

Then, after several hours of wait, they finally arrived at the beautiful scenery in the Kingdom of Magic. As the trailer parked in a nearby clearing of grasses swaying gently in the breeze, the six magnet plates retracted back into the van, replaced by the original wheels, the tire grooves now hitting the ground with a thud.

"We're here! Yes! Yes! Yes!" He was jumping up and down jubilantly. He settled down as he asked, "How far are we from Ivory Princeton High right now?"

"Twenty, or maybe fifteen minutes," Aria said as she checked her phone. She glanced at Conner's obnoxiously wide smile. "Why would you even want to go there, anyways? Sure, the school's nice, but we have no reason to stop there, 'specially not now."

Something's going on here… Cassie thought as she stared at him.

The beautiful city towering above them revealed luminous baby blue glass skyscrapers reaching above the pristine white clouds. Beside them stood tall golden hotels, etched with the names of their founders in luminescent gold.

Vehicles flew above the metal roads at swift speeds.

Lining the roads were gray sidewalks where regular humans walked.

They were openly carrying their wands, some making their way toward the back end of the city where a white marble had been cast upwards in the shape of an elegant, glossy castle.

This was roughly twice the height of the nearby hotels, its four turrets acutely sharp, each propping up a white flag lined with gold.

The etched word SPELLS was on one, in shimmering, golden writing, another with BALANCE, the third with POTIONS. The last bore the word WANDS.

"Why is that castle there?" Katie asked, eyes twinkling with admiration as she stared at the regal structure. "What's inside? A school or something?"

"That's where the ruler of the Kingdom of Magic and the Council of the Realm reside. That's why it's so large; has to fit all those people," Conner explained. "The school, Ivory Princeton High, is a bit farther from it—over there." He pointed to the east of the castle, to a lush clearing in the near distance, a palatial school standing high. He continued speaking.

"Ivory Princeton High is the school where kids from the Kingdom of Magic go to learn about things like potions, spells, and all that other magic stuff from ages twelve to eighteen."

"Well, it's really pretty," Katie began, admiring the four sky-high pine green turrets with that signature, childlike twinkle in her eyes. "I wish I could go there."

"Me too..." Conner stared longingly at the tower, a bit odd considering he had no reason to. Everyone sent quick glances his way; he was acting rather giddy at the moment, especially considering how boring their day had been so far.

What is going on with him? He's turning into some weirdo! I swear, he is!

Cassie glared at him once more, his gaze still unchanging.

Is the boy sick or something? Drowsy?

She snickered at another thought her brain came up with. *No, not that.*

"Conner," Aria said to her brother. "You've been driving for a while and you look like you need a break, so we'll be staying here overnight. You, Cassie, and Katie can go somewhere, but I need you guys back by sunset since it seems like you really wanna go someplace. We have to head to the Kingdom of Sorcerers after this."

She noticed how her brother still wasn't listening and snapped her fingers in his face. "Earth to Conner." His eyes were still unfazed at the sound and motion. "Conner!"

"Yeah, what did ya say?" He snapped his eyes back to her.

"I was just telling you that you, Cassie, and Katie can walk around the city until sunset, but when the time is up, I need you guys back here, all right?" With that, she followed his gaze to see what he was eyeing. With a sigh of disappointment, she went on to say. "Conner, it's been a year, and she doesn't even know you exist. Either get over this crush or actually talk to her…"

He smiled even more than he had before.

"That's not what I meant! I meant after we save Avery and get her and her sisters back to Earth! You can't ask her out after all that's happened."

"Sure," he agreed. "Promise I won't."

"You'd better not do it!" she yelled back at him as Cassie, Katie, and Conner walked off. It was obvious that he wasn't listening.

At some point, she'd have to come back in to save his butt.

Despite his outer demeanor, he was rather terrified of what his sister would tell him after he'd done what she had specifically told him *not* to do.

"You better not visit Ivory Princeton High, no matter how much you like her. We don't have time for you to get stuck there," Aria said quietly to herself, still glaring at him as he walked off. She had to trust him to some degree though.

He couldn't be that stupid…

…could he?

But even though the better option was clear for Conner to see, he still had his sights set on the place he wanted to visit. At least, one day.

And just maybe, hopefully, that day was today?

"We're here!" Conner cried out, a fake grin spreading on his face as he looked back from the building to Cassie and Katie standing behind him.

He didn't want to get in trouble with his sister, so for the first few minutes of their visit, he planned to actually keep his word. If Katie or Cassie said they wanted to visit Ivory Princeton High, then they would. That way, he wouldn't get in trouble with his twin since he wasn't the one who made the decision.

That made sense, didn't it? It seemed like it did. At least right now.

"You guys can go look at the Kingdom of Magic History Museum. Then we can explore the city for the time left until sunset."

"Conner, you don't really want to come here, do you?" Cassie questioned, voice rather cynical contradictory to her words. "Where do you wanna go? If it's that Ivan Princeton High or whatever, that's okay with us."

"For one, it's Ivory Princeton High. And two, Aria doesn't want us to go there," Conner grumbled. He looked angrily at the gray concrete patio outside of the museum.

He scuffed his shoes, intent on kicking away a loose chip of cement.

The building's pristine white pillars supported a white sunroof protecting the wicker armchairs and stone-white side tables from the sun's rays.

Above the main building was a navy-blue dome roof, reflecting the sun's rays into their eyes, propping up a golden flag that waved in the cool breeze.

Cassie was staring at him again. "Oh! Ivory Princeton High. Yeah. We don't have to go. Why would I even want to go to Ivory Princeton High, a school for prestigious students, when I can't even make a potion correctly? I wouldn't be interested in the school. No, no, not at all," he blabbered, punctuating his words with a fake, wide grin.

She was still looking at him with confusion, trying to persuade him to explain a little further than these vague and nonsensical sentences he was spitting out. "We'll just visit some other place instead. We could do a museum tour or something."

"Yeah, great idea, Cassie," he sighed, blue eyes full of regret and his expression downcast.

Silence followed seconds after, no one moving or uttering a word.

"Conner, it's okay if you wanna say something," Cassie said as she focused her brown eyes on his. "If there's something wrong, you can always tell me. I am your friend, y'know."

"Well..." He looked at the ground, blushing against his own will. "There is Vanessa."

"Who's Vanessa, Conner?" He was looking away, seeming to be rather flustered and she went on, "C'mon, don't be embarrassed."

Cassie held her gaze, looking as non-judgmental as she possibly could.

"Vanessa is the Ruler Josephine Caswell's daughter, who's ruler of the Kingdom of Magic. I've only ever seen her once in person, but I know for sure that she's breathtakingly beautiful. She has gleaming golden skin, beautiful brown eyes, and wavy brown hair.

"But not only that, she wears the nicest clothes and outfits and looks amazing in anything." He sighed, lovestruck it seemed to Cassie, and stared into the partially cloudy sky.

"But I don't just like her for her looks. I mean, that'd be really superficial, and I am not superficial. But she *is* stunning." He looked lost in a dreamland. "Even though I've only met her once, I know from friends who live there that she scores top marks in every one of her classes. She's incredibly talented at magic and just everything, y'know?"

He was making himself sound like Vanessa's stalker now! It appeared he must have put in a lot of high-end research to find out everything about the girl. But he wasn't even done yet.

"Even in advanced classes, she maintains good grades, as in Human History and Magic Realm History courses. I've seen her on the news a couple of times, and she just loves doing kind work. She volunteers to help out kids at the local orphanage... kids who want to learn magic. She tutors students, even advocating for social justice for citizens of the Animal Kingdom. I swear she's just the perfect girl, isn't she?"

He looked to her for a sense of confirmation, and Cassie nodded.

But this was usually a rhetorical question.

It clearly would not matter what Cassie thought because the boy was plainly smitten!

Cassie gaped at him, eyes bulging wide, and her mouth dropping to her chin.

Just then, the realization that Conner had just shared all his feelings about a girl he had barely met to someone else he barely knew, and it hit him like a freight train.

He shoved his head in his hands and ruffled at his curly blond hair, looking mortified.

"That's wonderful, Conner. Truly!"

Cassie closed her gaping mouth, eyes now full of reassurance and warm, the same way they had been before. "I wasn't being judgmental. I love that you feel you can share your deep feelings with me."

She opened her arms wide, looking to him like a friend she'd known all her life.

He was rather perplexed, yes, but hugged her anyways, Katie eager to join in as well despite her confusion in the situation.

"Isn't that what friends are for?" Katie chirped, looking to them happily. "Helping and looking after one another? Caring for each other at your worst?"

Conner looked down at her and nodded in agreement. She was right.

That was what friends were for. And he turned to Cassie once more, seeing how she truly was a friend to him. It hadn't even been that long yet and they'd both proven themselves to want to look out for one another.

He hadn't had a friend like her in a long time and now that he did…it was nice.

"So, are we going to Ivory now?" Katie questioned.

Sure, I mean if Conner wants to." She looked at him, still looking into the clouds. "You're going to meet her, right? Aren't you excited? You guys will go on a date, and it'll be so romantic and…"

But he could only grimace, most likely going over what his sister had said to him.

Conner, it's been a year, and she doesn't even know you exist.

Either get over this crush or actually talk to her.

It must have made him cringe to think of Vanessa now.

But did Aria not want him to see Vanessa?

Maybe she was saying he should do both, but wasn't that impossible?

Maybe he was being stubborn but what would be so bad about visiting Ivory Princeton High? It was a school after all; what bad things could happen to them there? He knew already that the security there was top-notch, and they would be able to get back by sunset.

He balanced the pros and cons mentally, coming up with the conclusion that going there wouldn't be that bad anyways, even if only for a few minutes.

His sister couldn't be that angry if she didn't end up finding out.

As they walked along toward the pine green castle looming before them, Conner stared out into the bright blue sky. His year-long dream was finally coming true.

He was finally going to see her.

He acted giddy and excited like a little kid waiting for their present on Christmas morning. He couldn't help but smile as he answered the question Cassie had posed.

"So, where'd you guys meet?"

"Well," he began, deep in thought as the memory resurfaced. "It was a Monday, I think, and I was stopping by the school to take one of the summer potions classes that Aria had forced me to do. I probably argued with her about it now that I think on it.

"There, I remember being extremely nervous, so scared that I was gonna walk out miserable. And then once class began…"

Cassie took immediate notice of how he had paused for a few seconds.

She was staring at him intently, silently encouraging him, willing him to continue on.

Her eyes burned into him and he went on with, "I noticed her staring at me…and smiling. I didn't know why, but I smiled back, and she giggled and waved.

"During the class, we learned about making invisible potions with simple ingredients like sunflower seeds and roots of clovers and stuff, and she aced it with ease. After she'd made hers, there was still some time left and she made her way over to my desk.

"She could see how I was struggling and offered to help me out. My heart was beating really fast in my ears as I managed to get out a 'yes', and she helped me mix the right ingredients together. She was so sweet, so kind, and I really wanted to talk to her again."

Cassie, deeply invested in this story, was now waiting for a conclusion.

She received one as soon as the thought came to her mind.

But it was not exactly to her liking.

"That day, I left the class, and waved her goodbye; she returned my wave with a bright smile and a wave like she had done at the start of the class. But that was the last I saw of her."

Cassie's eyes glossed over.

How sad it must be to meet someone in such a way and never get the chance to see them again. She shook away the emotions threatening to bubble up and took a quick glance at her phone. "Well, lucky for you, Conner. It seems we're only ten minutes from the school."

Cassie and Conner talked back and forth amongst each other, the occasional comment from Katie either adding a hint of confusion or farce to their back-and-forth banter.

Eventually, they arrived at a towering pine-green stone wall, a large, arched stone entrance blocked by a wooden door obscuring their path. It was rustic in a way similar to something from medieval times, something Katie was quick to take notice of.

She got a hold of the latch that would allow the trio to enter school grounds.

The stone arch they walked beneath scanned them in a red wave of sparkling Resicus, flowing around them in a glorious and alluring sparkle of sorts, too spectacular to miss.

"What was that for?" Katie inquired as she shut the wooden door behind them.

"The school uses this as a system of scanning your thoughts; they wouldn't want people with evil intentions on school grounds. It's able to detect your intentions by probing your brain and collecting data. Then when it does eventually find someone who's here for a bad reason, it summons the Royal Team to remove them from the premises for further investigation," Conner nonchalantly explained.

He tended to sound like his sister when he explained things, further reminding him of the mistake he'd made and weighing down his mood.

"Meaning neither Vitina nor Andromeda can get in here," Katie concluded. She stared out across the grounds in longing. "If only she had ended up here…"

"Or any psychopath for that matter." Conner had noticed the last thing she said; it wouldn't take a genius to figure out who this 'she' truly was.

With its towering acute turrets, billowing white flags etched with eloquent golden lettering dancing in the gentle wind, and gleaming, translucent glass windows that arched high over them, Ivory Princeton High was the absolute picture of elegant beauty.

To attend such a school, one that, according to the white flags above them, cherished Spells, Balance, Training, and Potions more than anything else, appeared an extreme honor in the eyes of all the three. And Katie, first to move from the surprise and awe, was quick to dash off toward the castle, disappearing into the grassy area of Higan cherry trees.

Their leaves hung down in alluring drapes of petite light pink flowers, flowing in the gentle wind as they canopied the area in a dim light.

Unlike what one would expect, it was far from ominous, but calming and tranquil.

"Katie!" Cassie called as she darted into the curtain of trees. "Come back!"

Conner was quick to follow, chasing in after her as she ran at an alarming pace, similar to the way she had run back at the campsite.

Gradually, the Higan cherry trees were becoming a grove of cherry blossom trees, littering the short grass below with small pink flowers over which they quickly trampled to catch up to Cassie's shockingly wiry sister.

Through the school garden they ran, the environment around them rather resistant to change, making them unsure if it would ever end.

Perhaps they were running in circles, Katie luring them along to allow herself a moment of calm. That seemed like something she'd do.

Eventually though, they found themselves standing before a massive, towering structure, the picture of grandeur and elegance that, even if anticipated, still left them standing in awe.

"We're here," announced Conner, taking heaving breaths as he stared up at the castle.

The emerald door standing tall before them was nearly five times Conner's height, so tall that they could barely make out the gleaming silver board suspended over the arched crystal entry. It read, *The Ivory Princeton High School for Elite Magical Teachings.*

Two thick pillars stood either side of the doors, each propping up a twisted wooden wand on a flag pedestal. The wand hovered above the stone, bound by some sort of magical force most likely, the occasional wave of gold Resicus swirling around it.

Together, they managed to crack open the door, allowing the three to successfully get inside and integrate themselves into a crowd of unbothered students.

They walked around for a bit, not wanting to disrupt the flow of the students, especially at a time such as this. The marbled floors on which they walked, polished to absolute perfection, clacked beneath the students' shoes in a symphony of subtle sounds.

Katie couldn't help but grin as she looked around at the elegant halls, illuminated in the light of torches propped along the ceilings and walls, each one bearing flickering fire.

Conner though, was much more preoccupied with other things, such as where Vanessa was. Sometimes, students would take other passes during transition between classes, but couldn't at least some good luck work in his favor right now?

But just as he was about to tap Cassie on the shoulder for them to bail, he locked eyes with someone talking in a group in the crowd. The gentleness of their brown eyes shimmered against the weak light of the torches above, and the girl with beautiful golden-brown skin had her silky hair tied up into a bun.

Was it her?

Conner approached her silently, creeping about the crowded halls and watching as the group to whom Vanessa spoke all flicked their eyes his way.

Unsettling, yes, but he had to know for sure.

"Hey, would you happen to be Vanessa Casswell, by any chance?" he asked, trying to make this entire situation as non-awkward as possible.

He was surely miserably failing though, and now, Cassie was approaching too.

"Yeah. But you…" She stared at him for a few moments. "You look really familiar. I must've seen you somewhere, but I'm struggling to remember."

"Last year!" Cassie spoke from behind him. "You met him last year at the summer class on potions."

"Yeah!" she piped up, not even seeming confused at this outburst and going along with things rather well. She glanced back at Conner. "Conner, right?"

"Yeah, Conner." He smiled, a blush coming on as he quickly glanced away. "I was kinda hoping you'd be here."

"Well, I mean, she *does* attend school here after all," said a rather lanky boy from behind her. He had red dreads that draped over his eyes and eyelids that were unmistakable, but he still smiled brightly. "It'd be weird if she wasn't here 24/7."

Conner let out a light chuckle at what the boy had said.

Vanessa spoke up again. "Don't worry about Seth, he's just…" She glared back at him. "…a lot sometimes."

"Um, yeah. I guess," Conner hesitantly agreed.

He wouldn't want to get on this kid's bad side, but he was not here for anyone but Vanessa. But it wasn't as if Seth seemed to mind what Vanessa had said anyways.

He could have stepped closer to her, given her a handshake or a hug, anything.

But he danced from foot to foot, a strange kind of hop as if he wasn't exactly sure what to do. They were in a pause in their conversation; it seemed neither knew how to continue it.

She started talking to her friends once more and Conner looked mildly embarrassed.

Sweat was building on his forehead and his demeanor spoke of the heady, confusing mix of doubt and missed opportunity.

As the five friends slunk away, though, Conner muttered to Cassie under his breath, sounding both frustrated and disappointed, "Damn it!"

They made their way back into the main crowd again, hoping to get out of the school without appearing too suspicious to any of the passing students.

Conner's head was looking down, as though he liked to examine his shoes as he moved. More likely, he was ruminating, thinking over everything he had just done wrong.

He was probably thinking, *Conner, you idiot! Why'd you do that?*

It's clear that she likes you. Or I think she likes you, doesn't she?

She looked like she liked you. She seemed like she liked you. So, just ask her out on the stupid date, idiot! You should've done it! Should've done it, man! Idiot!

Before Conner could attempt to push open the door, he found himself running into a man wearing all black from head to toe, the only other color exposing the wrinkled white of his button-down. "You're not going anywhere."

Conner gazed up to see a man of around fifty with ivory skin and flared black hair, his librarian's spectacles shining under the light from the ceiling. "You and your friends will go to your dorms and study for lesson reviews tomorrow. Come along now."

Conner, Cassie, and Katie followed the man through the corridors lined with gleaming navy-blue lockers under the flickering torchlight. By the time they'd reached the stone flight of stairs they were meant to scale, Conner looked even guiltier than before.

His plan was going south just like his sister had anticipated. Just like she had warned.

She must have known he was going to act impulsively and get himself into a situation like this, so she'd told him to explicitly not do it.

But he did do it.

And now he had to find a way to fix it.

Chapter 9
A New Friend

"**HE BETTER NOT BE TAKING THEM** to Ivory Princeton High right now," Aria muttered to herself under her breath, plopping down on the couch in the trailer, grabbing the remote, and turning on the television. She took a deep breath. "Calm down, Aria. It's been a while since you really relaxed. Today is all about you. It's Aria Day. Yeah, Aria Day. Anyways, he wouldn't do something so plain stupid, would he? No, he wouldn't. Not Conner…

"Happy Aria Day…" she whispered again, slouching into the couch as she began to get comfortable. "Watching TV, eating snacks… Oh! I do need snacks don't I?"

Swiftly, Aria shuffled to her bed, seized her crystal blue wand, and leaped back to the couch. "Creo exponentia!"

In a flurry of orange diamonds, a lump of solid orange appeared in the white bowl in her hands. As it gained detail and jagged edges, then separated, the pieces became triangular seasoned chips, some of which she happily stuffed into her mouth.

"Aria Day has just begun," she whispered to herself, chomping on another handful of chips and falling further back into the sofa.

Hour upon hour passed, allowing Aria to finish episode after episode of her show and two whole bowls of chips. In her relaxed state, she took the opportunity to catch up on some spell studying, since she was planning to attend an elite magical school when she turned eighteen. And so, she set down her chips to start getting to work.

From her backpack, she pulled out a pamphlet, the cover showing a lush, green campus with looming trees over the vintage brown buildings. Inside the crimson clay-tiled roofed buildings were thousands of dorm rooms, libraries, and classrooms, from what Aria already knew. Above the picture, it read *Madric Academy: The School for Elite Magical Prodigies.*

"Okay, if I want to get in, I have to study. Study like I've never studied before," Aria reminded herself, the way she did every study session. She stopped for a second. "Conner would totally think I sound like a nerd for that."

Conner. Her brother. It had been a while since she'd seen him.

But she was giving him space right now.

After all, this was one of the first times he'd been away from her in a whole year.

She furiously scribbled notes of spells, their origins, how to make potions, and the history of magic in preparation, calm music playing faintly in the background as she worked.

The school had given her a thick book with hundreds of pages to help her study for the exam, allowing her to take notes and make points wherever she pleased.

For the entrance exam, a student would have to perform a few actions in every one of the main nine magical subjects: Nature, Spells, Magic Training, Potions, Elemental Magic, History, Real World Magic Application, Magical Biology, and Counter Magic.

Classes and acceptance depended on how well someone did out of five in each of the subjects, one being barely acceptable and five being exceptional.

On reaching at least a three in each of the nine categories, the student would be given the chance of acceptance into the school.

Those who did relatively well with scores of mostly fives were guaranteed a spot in Madric Academy, while those scoring more threes than fours or fives would be placed on the waiting list. Anything lower than a three in any of the categories, even if it was just one score under three, and that meant complete rejection.

The school had three levels for each of the classes: beginner; intermediate; and advanced. This all depended on the attained scores in the entrance exam.

Mostly fives put a student into the advanced class.

Mostly fours would mean going into intermediate, and mostly threes in beginner courses.

When first taking the entrance exam, the candidate would perform their magical skills before a group of five to ten judges who were observing, depending upon what category it concerned. Those not accepted immediately had to take a written and a performance exam, testing all of their abilities in a more normalized testing fashion.

She was doing well in most of them, all except for some of the questions in the Potions sections. It would be unbearable to fail, especially having never been given a way to know what the testers would throw at her. But for now, she wanted to get to work on something she was familiar with: the Spells section.

'If you're looking to use an invisibility spell, what would the incantation be and what object would you cast the spell upon?' the practice question asked, a few thin lines below it left blank for the candidate to write in the answer.

She drummed her pencil against the rosewood side table on her left.

Her glass of sweet orange juice also rested there.

"If I'm going to use an invisibility spell, what incantation would I use and what object would I cast the spell on?" she asked herself.

"Hmm, what would I think of? What would I think of? Well, I know all spells come from Latin words, so the spell will most likely end in the words 'exponentia' or 'cantamen', in fancy cases of course. But that doesn't include the transformation spell Grandma taught us since that's in the Smith bloodline, and they wouldn't let me use it at the school.

"I'd get denied right away according to their Code of Conduct. What is the Latin translation for *invisible* again? *I—in—invisi—invisibilis!* Invisibilis, yeah!"

She quickly wrote down the spell on the line, peering at the next question.

Airily, her eyes lifted to the ceiling, lost in her own reasoning. She carried on muttering, barely audible, more or less just mouthing her thoughts. "But wouldn't an invisibility cloak work best? The whole point of invisibility is to be unseen and unnoticed.

"And even though it's quick, you could be seen by the light emitted from your wand. Just putting on a cloak dipped in the anti-glare coating of the glasswing butterfly with ground ranunculus flower will do the trick just fine. That way, you'll be in a cloak both soft and unseen. I would love to make one of those potions someday."

Aria turned her attention back to the book, reaching for her mechanical pencil, about to write down the potion for invisible cloaks.

That was sure to get her more points in the entrance exam.

But as soon as Aria felt the plastic in between her fingers, she stopped.

A look of realization passed across her face.

Invisibility cloaks had to be created with the petals of the ranunculus flower and the anti-glare coating found in the glasswing butterfly, an insect occupying warm and humid areas of the world, such as places like the Summerlands in the Land of Elves.

As for the ranunculus flowers though, they grew in places with long, cool winters, just like the Snowlands of that kingdom, too.

For this new plan to work, they couldn't deplete themselves of precious time when picking up the potion ingredients. Perhaps if she found someone to teleport them there, then perchance this plan would actually work out in their favor.

And finally, with their ingredients collected and put together in the required potion, they could simply dip their clothes in the mixture, granting them undetected access to the deadliest school in the world.

With a foolproof plan set into motion, Aria seized her phone and went to call her twin, the phone ringing for more than a minute before it gave up and diverted to voicemail.

"Seriously, Conner, you really can't pick up?"

She set her books aside, snatched her wand, scribbled down the things she needed to find, and clutched at the smooth leather of her purse, stuffing the note and RV keys inside.

Before the sole of her shoe could even graze the tips of the short blades of grass, she was off, locking the trailer with a swift click of a button.

Exploring the streets, she was able to find a small hickory brown store, a neon-green sign hanging from the shop window, reading in flowing calligraphy writing, *Karrie's Magic Store.*

A number of neon figures surrounded the sign, much like the ones Aria would've loved to have in her own room.

A room she'd never get to see because of her lack of a home.

But as for the building itself, it had a domed roof, gleaming sunlight into her blue eyes that momentarily blinded her at a specific angle.

Maybe she could find someone to sell her a teleportation spell there.

There was a familiar smell in the place, one of cinnamon and nutmeg, as if someone were eating a muffin or pastry consisting of these sweetened spices.

A small bell rang above her head, one she could not see.

Across the room from her were tall stone pedestals displaying wands of every color, size, shape, and material imaginable in the mystical and magic wand industry.

During one of her spontaneous night internet searches, she had educated herself about them, learning how to harvest them from the Caves of Crystalia, an underground cavern in which gems for Magical Charms were also harvested.

Unlike the charms though, the type of material making up the wand didn't determine its strength; all of these materials had the same amount of Resicus and magical energy in the beginning of their wand life.

Aside each wand shelf were short rosewood nightstands, and small pocket spell books placed intricately at the tables' center.

Tissue paper honeycomb balls decorated the ivory tile ceiling of the building; they were all colored periwinkle blue, small light bulbs beside them illuminating the store. The light was so feeble that its effect was barely noticeable against the harsh light of the sun.

Behind a granite counter sat a young woman with beige white skin, a shoulder-length black bob with red highlights, and a wrinkled black employee's uniform.

She licked her paper-thin lips as she flipped a page of her mystery novel titled *Render Her Guilty* written by Mallory Quincy.

"Excuse me?" Aria glanced at the silver name tag on her shirt, which read *Jade.* "Are you selling any spells here?"

"Yes. But I don't know about those," Jade answered, a hint of rasp in her monotone voice as she cast a brisk glance at Aria, then her eyes wandered back to the pages of her book. "But talk to my manager and you'll find someone to help you."

Her arm wafted in the direction of a hickory brown door on the left side of the store, bearing a silver board that said *Manager's Office.*

The door was open for some reason, and she cracked it wider a few more inches.

The beige office had a windswept look. The papers on the brown desk lay strewn across the table and floor, and a single empty white coffee mug was dripping coffee onto the carpet.

Where was the manager and, more importantly, who had done this?

"Jade," she began, closing the door to the manager's office as she could hear the faint drip of coffee hit the carpet, "I can't seem to find them. Any other ideas where they might be?"

She sighed. "Look, whoever you are," Jade announced, raising her voice, plopping her book face down on the counter, and standing up from her chair. "I'm trying to read my book! I know I work here, but this is my break. I would appreciate a little peace and quiet after working a shift, so either leave or solve your own problems, all right?"

Aria stared at her, taken aback and clenching her fists. "Okay, look." She took a step toward Jade's counter, her eyes widening at her action, "I'm sorry if you've got no one here to help you, but you're responsible for the store right now. And I'm a customer, right? Doesn't that mean it's your job, as an employee, to help me? At least a little?"

"Fine then," Jade sighed reluctantly. "What spell do you need me to perform for you?"

"Teleportation, please," said Aria, noticing emptiness in the pools of Jade's amber eyes.

Even if she was talking, she seemed lifeless and empty. It was something about her.

The way she talked, the way she moved, all dead.

"Hey? Are you even listening?" Jade had risen her monotone voice, adding a bit more character to her dead expression.

"Y-yeah. What did you ask me again?"

"Do you want an advanced type of teleportation spell?"

"Um, yeah, one that can teleport across kingdom borders."

"All right then. Pretty sure I can do that for you."

"Could you also transfer the spell to my wand?" She held her crystal blue wand at Jade's wooden one, their tips aligned in an oddly straight line.

"Yes, for only two gold pieces and two copper ones, which does include the cost of the spell being performed and its transfer."

"Here then." Aria gave her two rectangular pieces of gold.

They bore markings etched front and back. She gave her the copper pieces as well, each appearing to have different markings than the gold pieces.

"Thank you." She accepted and put the pieces into a cash register, then she held out her carved wooden wand with both hands on it, casting, "L—l—Oh God." She looked at Aria with a weary face. "I've forgotten the spell."

"You have?" Aria cried. "Won't your manager let you check a spell book or something? Or can you use one from the store?"

"We're not allowed to touch store merchandise and he usually takes the only spell book we have with him when he leaves!"

"Maybe there's some way you could. Maybe you could just look on your phone, I guess?" Aria started typing on her own, looking in the search engine for a teleportation spell.

The internet would provide. It always did. In her times of need, at her most hopeless, it was always there for her. It gave her answers and help and…

Nothing.

For at this moment, it had eclipsed on her. The great internet could not do the things it usually did for Aria, for this poor girl.

The sadness in her eyes couldn't be cured with the simple click of a button. Her emotions, her pain, were far too complicated for such a straightforward object to aid.

"I'm gonna get fired!" she blurted. "No! I can't! Not until I have all the money!"

"It seems like this is stressing you out. I can just go if I need—"

Poor beleaguered Jade stuck her hand out desperately and cried, "No, you can't! My manager left me in charge, me, because I'm supposed to know what to do. Always! He left for the day because he trusts me. But if he learns I couldn't perform a spell for a customer…"

She looked away.

"Jade, I promise, it isn't—"

"He'll fire me and I won't be able to get a job anywhere else! I can't go back to living with my parents. This is exactly what I didn't want to happen!"

"JADE!" Jade looked at Aria and froze. "It's okay. You can keep the money. I can just go without the spell—"

"But my boss…"

"Doesn't need to know."

"What if he asks about business today?"

"Just tell him you performed the spell and nothing else, okay?" She started walking toward the door to the shop but Jade speaking up stopped her short.

"Lie to him? I can't do it. And even if I did, he'd find out anyway…wouldn't he?"

"Listen," Aria uttered, her back to the store counter, "You've already gone through enough with my stupid irritability relating to me and my time crunch, but do yourself a favor and lie for me, all right? Consider that to be what you did for your customer, okay?"

Jade took a deep breath and promised, "I will."

"Oh, and here." Aria pulled five gold pieces from her purse, all looking similar to those she had given Jade only a few moments ago. "The internet was always able to help me when I went through stuff. And I feel bad because it wasn't able to help you."

Jade took the gold pieces in her hands, looking at Aria, a twinge of hope in her formerly empty eyes.

"Your problems, it seems, even if I don't know them, are so much deeper than mine. I can't relate to what you're going through because it's never happened to me.

"But I know you need something, so take this money as a gift from me. To help, I mean."

Before Jade got the opportunity to even thank her, Aria began walking toward the door.

"Wait!" Jade stopped her, Aria turning at her call.

She met her at the door, the gold pieces set upon the counter. "You understand what I'm going through so much better than anyone I've ever met. Especially my parents."

"What d'you mean?"

"They never believed in me. They never believed in who I wanted to be. That's why I moved out of their house a few months ago." She paused for a few moments, then continued on, "I would love to grow up and become an actress in theater or an animator or something that makes lots of people happy. I want people to be happy, unlike how I wasn't able to—"

Aria scribbling something down on a notecard cut Jade off; then, she quickly handed it to Jade. "Here. Another 'tip' you could say."

Jade took the paper into her hand, a single sentence, it appeared. But it held so much strength, so much resonance with her.

You are so incredible, so amazing, so marvelous, and I hope your parents see that, too.

And as fast as she appeared, this random stranger, with so much to offer with just her words, who had end up impacting her life in ways she'd never dreamed, disappeared from sight. Disappeared forever.

***

Darting through the streets, Aria searched for any sign of Conner, Cassie, or Katie, the heat of the sun turning tepid as the ombre of sunset began its nightly conquest of the sky.

Where could they be? She had told him to bring them back by sunset.

As she delved farther into the evening darkness, her search through the various-colored buildings, skyscrapers, and stores was coming up empty.

Where could they be? She had searched every crevice and alcove of the city, yet somehow, they were still nowhere to be seen.

Oh no.

Did they leave to visit Ivory Princeton High?

"I knew I shouldn't have trusted Conner! I knew I shouldn't have. I told him not to visit that place! He knows he can't do this stupid stuff. It's already sunset! Conner!"

She was pacing back and forth near the bench, slipping her hand into her skort pocket, a shade of yellow as warm and strong as the rays of the sun upon her skin.

Delving even further into ever-growing worry, she fiddled with the hem of her blouse, thinking perhaps that would ease the worry.

Wait! She stopped and pulled out her phone from her purse, scrolling through notifications to see if her irresponsible train wreck of a twin brother had called at any point.

Nothing.

It was hopeless.

"This is awful. God, Conner, you couldn't have just listened to me! You do this all the time. Doing *whatever* you want without thinking of the repercussions or how it'll affect the people around you. You're so *selfish*, Conner!

"I'm so sick and tired of this! Now that you've got them trapped inside that school for sure, there's no way now they'll be able to get out.

"Mr. Clemont will surely go to extra measures to keep them there."

She took a glance at the device in her hand. Already past eight. There was only a little time until the sun finally set for her to get there and get them out of school.

She darted across seas of gravel and grass, stone and wood verandas of nearby shops, all so she could finally arrive at the pine-green castle in the distance.

If she made it, she would be home free. Back to what everything once was.

Yet, as she ran, heaving with each step, she uttered a small thought.

"What if Conner did this on purpose? What if he actually wanted to avoid me? To get away from his nagging sister for a few hours? Maybe he's tired of me. And maybe, since neither Cassie nor Katie stopped him, they are tired of me too."

She slowed her pace, approaching the gates of the school.

The plan in her mind was now devoid of attention.

"What if everyone I've met wants to avoid me?"

This emotion that bubbled up every few months or so, Aria didn't know what to call it.

She had never tried to put a name on such a thing. At points, she appeared as if she believed her world was crumbling and the things around her were all going downhill, even if they had nothing to do with her at all.

It seemed she often felt responsible. Responsible for all the wrong things going on.

Like now, *was* she responsible?

The only reason Conner had left…had it just been to get away from her?

Had he been so desperate to leave her behind that he had let their entire strategy get thrown out of the window of *who cares?* and *so what?*

No. No one was responsible but her. She was the cause of this disorder, this disruption.

She hid her head in her hands for a minute, as if even when she tried to fight this invisible voice, this invisible feeling, it only grew stronger.

A few moments later, she found herself back in her own body, that out-of-body feeling dissipating like steam from a pot of boiling water.

The stone—marble to be exact—of the school wall was a quality of rock she had never seen before. Smooth and intricately carved, not a single defect anywhere.

With the push of a door, she charged through the stone wall into glorious school gardens.

Through the gorgeous pink Higan cherry trees, their vines draping down over her head like a natural canopy before her, the space around was ever so slowly transforming into a grove of slim cherry blossom trees.

A wave of nostalgia came, of her world before all of this. Before her parents divorced. Before her grandma died. Before she'd known magic existed.

Before her life turned upside down.

When she'd been a small kid, her family would go to Washington, DC and walk through the gorgeous gardens of cherry blossom trees. Some were taller than a mountain, it seemed at the time, others looking almost as short as her.

She cherished those annual escapades, finding joy in the intricate yet simple parts of nature, ones she didn't get to experience that often. Back then, everything was new and glorious, another gift of life.

She still thought like this, yes, but not as much now.

Nothing seemed old, yet nothing seemed new either. She would experience new things, just like this adventure, but wouldn't go through it with the same type of wonder and twinkle in her eyes as she had as a kid.

And sometimes, she wished she still did.

"Stop flashbacking," she said to herself. "You need to focus on what's ahead. You need to be there." She wiped off a number of sweat beads from her forehead.

Eventually, after minutes of heavy breathing and slowed running, Aria had finally reached the stone castle doors, towering far over her head like the barricade of a fairytale castle.

"I'm finally here!"

Without even a moment's haste, she pushed open the entrance doors, landing her in quite an odd predicament.

Students groaned as the door pushed them out of their paths, knocking books onto the ground and dropping belongings. During all of it, Aria winced and blushed.

"Sorry!" she said to the boy whose thick Animal Kingdom History book had landed on the ground in a thud.

Another person, a girl this time, with wonderfully bouncy and curly brown hair settling at her shoulders, had dropped her things due to Aria's clumsiness.

"Oh, let me get that for you!"

"Oh no, it's all right; don't worry." The girl had picked up the thin notebook so quickly Aria didn't even have enough time to watch as she walked away.

She didn't even get to apologize to her.

She continued walking through the halls again, hoping no one would notice her from the mistake she had made the very first time she'd set foot in this school.

Well at least it wouldn't last long.

"Conner! Cassie! Katie! Where are you guys?" she called, cupping her hands around her mouth to amplify her sound.

"Hey!" a burly voice called out.

She looked to the source of the noise, a tall young man with curly, black hair and smooth honey brown skin.

He was wearing an Oxford blue jersey with two stripes of white on each side and had deep brown eyes, but despite his 'jock' appearance, he seemed rather timid, twiddling his thumbs and pulling at the hems and edges of his jacket nervously.

His denim jeans were baggy and seemed a bit too large for him, the fabric fading out at the ends of the pants where the white strings stuck out at the laces of his black high tops.

Aria didn't pay much mind to him, only proceeding to continue through the crowded corridor unfazed.

"Wait! Come back!" His voice was wary despite its baritone, and as he walked—bumping into multiple people—he found himself apologizing over and over again.

As she walked through the halls, the hundreds of people sloughed away the farther she went. Down the hall, a wood door stood tall over her, its polished silver sign reading, SECRETARY'S OFFICE.

"Oh, c'mon! I need to get the Dean's office!" she grumbled under her breath, looking around to see if she would be given any sort of clues.

She began jogging through the halls now and, without looking where she was going, ran into someone.

Another student.

Yes, indeed it was a student, but definitely not the one she was expecting.

It was that boy she'd seen in the hallway.

"You were the boy in the hall, weren't you?" she asked.

"Yeah," his familiar voice responded. "I'm sorry for yelling at you. It's almost time for dinner and I was wondering if you needed any help finding the dining hall. Or if you just needed someone to show you to our dorm building. But anyway, I want to introduce myself.

"Darius Johnson of the line of Johnson potion makers."

He held out his gigantic hand, exposing his dark blue fingerless glove and flashing a shy smile. "Nice to meet you."

"Oh," she realized, glancing from his hand to his face. "Same, Darius. I'm Aria Thomas." She firmly grasped his hand and shook it once, formal in the way one would to a client in a business meeting. "Um, could you direct me to the Dean's office? I'm looking for some of my friends."

"Of course, if we're quick. Follow me," he said, leading her through the empty corridor to a pine-green stone staircase.

As they climbed, Aria gazed at the burly young man in front of her. "Why are you helping me? It's not like I'm a friend of yours or anything."

"No reason, just being nice I guess." He glanced over his shoulder at her. "You don't want to miss dinner, right?"

For a moment, Aria's mind went blank.

Dinner? Why would she miss dinner…?

By the time she realized, Darius had lost his smile and turned away from her. "Wait, but I don't need to go to the dining hall."

He stopped and looked at her. "Really? Are you not a student then?"

She shook her head no and Darius looked at her for a few seconds then back to the stairs.

"That's why you're heading to the Dean's then. How silly of me to assume you were a student," he chuckled, leaving Aria in a state of shock and wonder about whether he'd read her mind. "We'll arrive at the Dean's office soon and then I can drop you off, Aria."

"Thanks for helping me. I don't go to school here, and wasn't expecting to get any help from anyone."

"So why do you need to find friends? It seems like they go to school here. Were you guys just planning to go somewhere together?"

"Actually, my friends don't either. It's just that my brother took them here to meet one of the students and he can't seem to find a way out." She pointed to her phone. "Not picking up any calls either."

"Why didn't he just ask Mr. Clemont? Just tell him the truth?"

It seemed that, up until that specific moment, Aria hadn't really thought about it that much. As a dean, Mr. Clemont surely would've let out someone who he couldn't prove was a student. And—even if he didn't—wouldn't that person try to leave as the school wasn't theirs to attend? She thought about how nonsensical the situation really was.

But besides all that, Conner really didn't want to see her.

So did it truly matter, then?

Surely, that was the answer? That her brother, so desperate to get away from her nagging and yelling, had actually left.

After Aria hadn't answered his question for a while, Darius continued to stay silent, walking up the winding staircase as the chatter and footsteps of the sea of students below fell back like the retreating sea.

Although, after a while, they finally reached the Dean's office.

Before her a tall, wood door with a silver doorknob, light sparkling back into their gaze under the tinted yellow light.

Aria walked into the Dean's office without another word to Darius, not even a *thank you,* leaving him alone, confused, and rather intrigued about her situation as he looked down from the railing overlooking the main hallway.

But nonetheless, even if she'd left him feeling worse than before, he stayed right there.

Right there, waiting for her to return.

Chapter 10
What He'd Been Waiting For

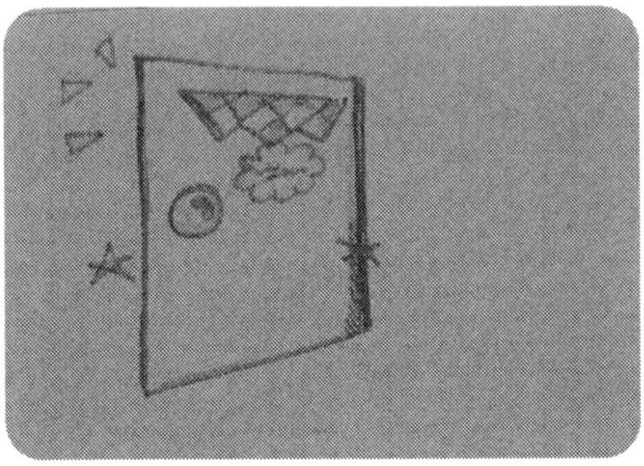

"**YOU WILL STAY IN THIS ROOM** and study, young man," Mr. Clemont said, adjusting his librarian's spectacles. "And I expect you to study well, Mr. Thomas."

He slammed the oak door with a deafening boom, his shoes clacking along the smooth tile outside of his door as the man retreated to his office.

"Oh God," he sighed, looking out at the dorm in front of him. "Aria's gonna kill me when she finds out what a mess I'm in!"

He had always known Aria to be an overbearing and controlling person as, with the lack of a parent, she felt herself responsible for filling in the position.

Ever since the first month they had been in this new place, she'd been acting as a sort of caretaker to Conner, despite them being the same age and him being well capable of doing so himself. At least, that was what he told himself.

And because of this, there had been moments where he asked himself, "Then why don't I just find a new place?"

In fact, he had thought of this multiple times, mostly after she'd berated or chided him like a mother would tell off her child. He could find an apartment in the city, get a job, take care of himself since he was already sixteen, on the verge of the age of seventeen already. Why did he need his sister when he could just depend on himself?

No Aria meant no yelling, no breaking into his room at night asking if he'd done the dishes, no arguments, no fights. Just him and his thoughts.

Yet, even with all this, he'd still never moved away.

Maybe it was because he knew he'd miss her or because he knew that she was the one who made all the dinners.

Or maybe even it was because, deep in his heart, he knew he needed and loved his sister.

When their parents divorced, the only thing they were certain of having was each other. They knew that, even with all the bickering and objects hurled across the room during arguments, they would have the other's backs in the end.

Their bond was the only thing that had brought them normalcy back when the wounds of their parents' divorce were still fresh.

Through everything, they'd always had each other, and Conner, at least in the back of his mind, wasn't ready to accept that they didn't need to rely on each other like they had as kids.

And because of this relentless subconscious mindset, he stayed with Aria, even when he appeared to detest her. It seemed he could never bring himself to move away from his twin.

This thought was always there whenever he considered how his sister might react to his futile attempts at defending his decisions, and whenever she grew irate at him.

But the problem was, he needed her so much more than she did him. But if he really did care about his sister, then perhaps moving away would free her of the burden of him.

Yet he could never bring himself to do it.

***

It had been nearly an hour since the Dean had deposited him in this empty dormitory, and with each moment, Conner simply sat upon the cool, hardwood ground, taking in the room as he waited anxiously for this elusive roommate of his to arrive.

Yes, he very much could have made himself comfortable on the spare loft, hanging a few feet over the workspace below, yet it wasn't his to begin with.

None of it was.

He didn't belong here. He didn't belong in a place full of well-brought-up magical students destined to be great in their adult years.

There was one and only one reason why he came to this school and that reason hadn't even arrived. At least, not for long.

Without someone, he would be alien, alone, outcast from the other students.

He wanted to get out of here and tell the Dean what was happening, but didn't feel like being castigated about how stupid he was. God knew, he'd heard that enough from Aria.

He was much too old for this, too old to be such a hassle. Such an annoyance.

Such a burden.

"Stop that!" he told himself aloud. He had no reason to feel so awful, so broken down.

Not at any point in his life, even with how harsh his sister seemed, even with how abrasive her comments, it all meant nothing.

Not once had she ever meant those things that she said.

It was always clear she really did care about her brother, despite how foolish he seemed.

Everything they said back and forth to one another was all simply their dynamic, not a true representation of how they felt about one another.

It was simply something they found funny. They didn't mean it, they each said, though at times, it could appear quite vicious or mean—especially to onlookers who assumed a sibing feud was underway and that it could even drive them apart.

Aria had always said whenever explaining it to their mother, "It's just the way we act, y'know? We're just being stupid together."

When she'd said this as a young child, she didn't think of how much this single statement would affect Conner. She never imagined he'd remember it.

She'd especially never guessed how it'd stick with him nearly five years after she'd proclaimed this wonderful statement.

It told him that whatever mean thing she said never really mattered, because she never meant it. She never took it too far and it was never an accurate representation.

He tried to think the way she would.

I don't really mean this.

I don't actually think this about myself.

But sadly, even with the love and support of those around him, he did.

He did mean those horrible things he said to himself, those awful thoughts that appeared in his mind when he was at his worst.

He had never found a way to confront this way of thinking, only to stop it temporarily until it inevitably came back, hitting him even harder the next time.

"And now that I actually have time to think about my thoughts, rather than to distract myself like I always do…well, sis, I guess I realize I need you. I need you to help me."

Especially, he needed her to help him with those awful, destructive inner thoughts.

There was a knock at the door.

When Conner gripped the silver doorknob, pulling it back, it revealed to him the person he'd been thinking about just this moment.

Vanessa! She was finally here.

"Hey, Conner," she greeted. "Just came by to say sorry about what happened earlier. I felt bad that I wasn't able to properly talk to you after such a long time." She looked around the hallway for a minute, obviously uncomfortable with the situation.

"Oh, well, don't feel too bad about it. It's really no one's fault that happened."

He tried to laugh off the stiff atmosphere of their exchange, worried that this would be how all of their conversations would end up being.

But, even with his nervous and rather funny laughs, Vanessa's face stayed sober. "Conner," she whispered. "I saw you weren't in class today. If the teachers find out, you'll get major detention!"

"Oh yeah, class…" He looked back at her with a nervous smile. "I don't go to school here."

Vanessa had picked up on his enunciation of a few of the vowels he had spoken, along with the way his speaking pace had sped up toward the end.

He obviously hadn't told anyone, and was now trying to play it off somehow.

"Then why do you have a dorm?" She peered over his shoulder at the right loft and workspace. Although empty, presumably, another student occupied it.

"And how are you already living with someone else?"

He looked back at the room, the right oak loft personalized with a variety of posters and lights, while his was simply white bedsheets, a single pillow, and an empty desk.

"I *don't* actually live here," he said to her. "The Dean just put me in here 'cause he assumed I was a student."

"Then why didn't you say something?"

Conner mulled over her question. Indeed, why didn't he say anything?

Was he worried about what his sister might say?

Was he tired of helping Cassie and Katie, or was it that he did want to get away from her? That he did prefer being here?

No! Of course not! Aria was one of the only people in this world who actually cared about him. Why would he want to leave her? There was only one real explanation.

"It's because I wanted to see Vanessa," he thought aloud. "That explains why I haven't left yet."

Vanessa blushed cherry red, flattered and flabbergasted.

"Me? What d'you mean?"

"Yeah." He took a hesitant step toward her. "I wanted to see you. Corny, I know."

She couldn't help but laugh at what he'd said, her smile difficult to miss.

The two of them were silent for a long while, although it seemed awkward to start up some kind of conversation after such a thing had been said.

She then moved into the dorm room, seating herself on the floor near the occupied loft.

The floor was covered in pens, suggesting Conner's roommate may have left the room in a hurry. And so, with silence as an opportunity, she picked each of the utensils up one by one.

Such an action seemed so kind, helping out a person she had never even met with such a simple task. The person wasn't even in the room, yet she still felt obligated to help them.

He appeared embarrassed and a bit ashamed that he hadn't noticed this in his pensive stupor, bending down to help her out with the gathering as if in an afterthought.

"Oh, don't worry about it," she dismissed, picking up the last pen with the words *Ivory Princeton* inscribed in gold lettering. She stood from her crouch, setting all of those pens and pencils into a blue pencil holder on the loft desk. "I was able to get all of them anyway."

She lingered at the desk for a moment, taking in the assortment of notebooks, sticky notes, and dry erase markers atop the table, and the large laptop sitting in the corner. Conner's roommate obviously wasn't doing anything important at the moment.

The black desk chair sat right next to the table, warming under the light of the tall lamp.

She clicked it off quickly, giving the baby blue jersey covering the entirety of the chair's back a break from the inexorable heat.

The dresser was much shorter than her, allowing her to view the hairbrushes, variety of different hair gels, charging cords, and a number of other unorganized objects set—well, more like thrown—onto the drawers.

Although, when Vanessa looked from the right loft to the left, the one in which Conner was supposed to be staying, it looked so barren.

Its white sheets had been folded to perfection, the desk left untouched, and the dresser sat deserted with no sign of any sort of recent interaction.

"You didn't even try to move in yet? For someone who wanted to see me, you sure didn't make it seem like it," she joked, hoping that maybe it would lighten the atmosphere.

It did not, in fact.

Conner laughed awkwardly at her almost laughable attempt, but it was reassuring to know that the next heiress to the throne of the Magic Kingdom was as horrible at small talk as he.

They could share something in common. Even if it was that.

Finally, after such a tense and awkward halt to their conversation, Conner spoke up,

"Hey, could I ask you a question?"

She looked at him, looking surprised he had said something after such a long time, but she was likely grateful they'd be talking again. "Yeah, sure."

"Would you be interested in helping me out with something?" he started, watching her eyes intently. "You see, my friends, Katie and Cassie, and my sister need to find someone.

"Katie and Cassie's sister is lost somewhere in the Magic Realm, and we need someone as good as you at magic to help us out."

She stayed quiet, so Conner continued.

"We've been doing fine already, but extra help wouldn't hurt. It's just been us four for the past few days and maybe another party member would help make the trip a lot more fun."

Her face stayed the same, and Conner looked twitchy and ill at ease.

"We'd really like someone who's as good as magic as you are to help us out. Or I would."

Vanessa smiled with the same warm grin as before, and Conner beamed too.

Apparently, he had said the right thing for a change!

"Conner, I'm flattered that you would want me to come along with you four…"

His face lost its cheerful blush, and, taking immediate notice, Vanessa went on to reassure, "Which is why I'd love to go! Even though the first time we ever met was that potions class a year back, I never forgot you. I was pretty sad that we weren't able to become closer friends, so an opportunity like this seems incredible."

She stopped smiling, looking from the tiled floor to him.

He had noticed the change in her face, her expression having drastically changed.

Had something happened?

Was asking her to come along too grand of an idea?

Maybe he should've planned it better, but as ever, impulsivity got the best of him.

"But how am I supposed to leave school, though? An adventure with new friends seems awesome and refreshing after the end of this stressful school year. It's just that…" She took a deep sigh. "With Queen Prep classes in the castle and summer homework and all the other stuff I have planned, I don't think I'll be able to have such a good time."

Of course, she had a booked summer vacation full of important work and classes and a bunch of other honor student stuff. She couldn't possibly have time for a boy like Conner.

And doubt and loss, hurt and abandonment showed on his face. It was as if he wished he had never asked. It was obvious she could not fit him in.

He should've bitten his tongue and said nothing, just staying quiet so as not to make an idiot of himself again with the girl he liked.

Vanessa stared at the emptiness of his eyes. Her gaze might have been pitying or compassionate; it was anyone's guess what she thought and felt.

His shattered hopes and broken optimism were things he tried desperately to hide.

It didn't work, and they came flooding from every pore. His eyes looked watery.

And, in that moment, whether it *was* pity or maybe something else, she looked at him and said, "Maybe I could work something out. At least, I guess. I really do want to go, but my parents are always signing me up for stuff and my schedule's always jampacked."

There was a potential chance here, a light on the dark path he was now trekking through. "So, what do you have scheduled?"

"For the two weeks of summer break…" She scrolled through her phone for a few moments. "There's magical practice for the Monday through Friday, which are classes set up by private tutors on subjects from school pretty much. Then on the weekend, I'll be booked for Queen Prep in poise, appearance, and presentation. That's the boring part, although I do kinda like the shopping for clothes bit. Then the week after, I'll be doing more magical tutoring practice, with the same instructors probably."

"Magical practice?" he said. From his face, it was obvious a storm of thought was brewing in his mind. "That's what our adventure will be like. Or that's what it's been so far."

"Really?" Her mouth turned up in a smile now.

Conner's face flushed anew, seemingly overcome yet again by that same overwhelming joy he had felt the first time he'd seen her eyes light up. Now, he smiled that *she* smiled.

Whether it was because she would get to hang out with friends or to get away from her tutoring lessons, Conner didn't care, just that her smile insinuated she was genuinely excited at the idea of getting a time to venture around the Magic Realm alongside him.

Sure, there'd be three other people, but that didn't really matter, did it?

She had deprived him of an answer for so long that maybe she had lost her enthusiasm.

But he needn't have worried. She was just considering it all, lost in thought.

He tried again, taking a different angle to fish for a reply at last.

"During the trip, we'll be training with spells for things we run into along the way, working on potions, and that kind of thing, and not to mention the application of all the stuff you've learned in class. It'll sorta be like your summer classes, right?"

"That's perfect!" she chirped, obviously too eager to be leaving her tutors and extra classes behind. "I'll just have to call my parents to cancel the tutoring for this week…"

She looked back at him from her phone, a gleam in her eyes.

"We'll be coming back, right?"

Conner had never asked himself this question before, the question of whether this adventure he and his sister had impulsively embarked upon was truly safe.

With the recent discovery that Avery was at Rubidium, perhaps it wasn't.

Or at least, not as safe as he'd once imagined.

Was taking Vanessa really a good idea?

Would she perhaps get hurt, even worse, killed if she were taken along?

It stung that this was a possibility, that he might end up hurting someone he cherished.

And all because of stupid pity.

And so he answered with all of his honesty. "I-I don't know, Vanessa. I don't know if we'll be able to come back."

She didn't say a word after, just shoved her phone in her pocket and made her way to the dormitory door.

"I think I need some time to decide," she said, her voice cold and dim, so different from the way she'd spoken previously.

Conner only nodded his head, showing a look of understanding. After leaving her with such a heavy decision to make, she would likely say no.

Of course, someone as important as Vanessa couldn't go risking her own safety for someone else. Especially not for someone she barely knew.

And Conner needed to find a way to accept that.

Chapter 11
A Dormitory Expedition

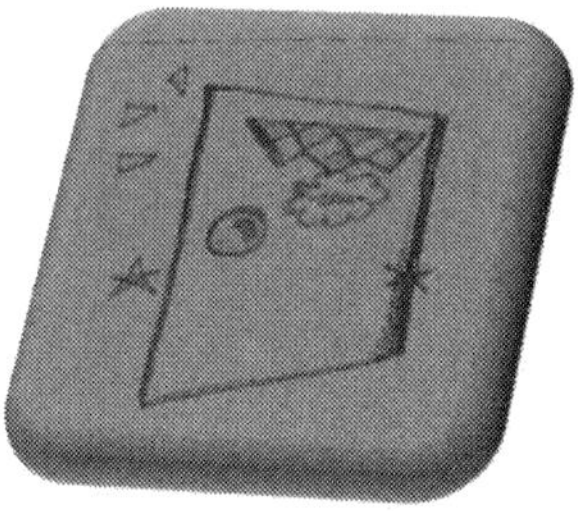

"SIR, YOU HAVE TO TELL ME where Conner is!" entreated Aria. "I need to see my brother!"

"Indeed, I am quite apologetic about such a mishap, Ms. Thomas, but I cannot allow registered students off school grounds at such a late hour! The sun's almost set!"

He slammed his hand against his desk and the drawers rattled with his fist's contact. "You must either get to your dorm room or leave this school immediately!"

"But my brother isn't a registered student here! He just came here to see someone!"

"Then why didn't he tell me such a thing?" Mr. Clemont remarked smugly. "If he weren't a student at this institute, I would expect he would inform me of this.

"I wouldn't just let in any random person."

"But you did. That's what I'm saying. Conner's bad with this kind of thing and relies on me to do it for him. Either that or he hasn't done what he came here for."

"If you really are telling the truth, Ms. Thomas, then I presume you also know of his goal? Hmm?"

She paused for a moment, desperately grasping for some sort of way out without embarrassing her brother. Slowly, the assured tone lost in her voice, she said, "I don't know why he wanted to come here." She took a deep sigh, then her voice became strong once more. "I just need to get him out of this place. You'll be able to forget I was ever here."

Mr. Clemont chuckled a bit, focusing in on a single quill sitting in a miniature mahogany pot of ink, then to her. It was odd that he had such an old-fashioned writing utensil.

He had a number of pens right there before him, but she didn't question such a thing.

"You could just have told me, y'know?"

He was writing on a small piece of parchment, intermittently dipping the light gray feathered quill tip into the inkwell. "I just wanted to know that you wouldn't end up doing something to destroy the school I've put so much love into. That's all, you see.

"And it appears to me that you really do have good intentions. So here."

He handed her a piece of paper, Aria nearly crumpling it as she gripped it in her hands.

Dear Receiver,

Do not worry about the individuals in the hall who are walking around during the time most are in their dormitories.

If this young lady is walking around alongside others, do not question them either. I have given all of them, however many there may be, an excuse from punishment.

Sincerely,
Dean Augustine Clemont

Aria stared at the sheet of paper in shock and ecstatic disbelief.

"Thank you so much!"

She folded the sheet into a small piece and shoved it in her pocket, throwing open the door as the Dean called, "You may find Conner in one of the boys' dorms! Good luck!"

"Thanks for your help, Darius!" Aria shouted, running down the winding staircase as Darius ran in her wake.

There was not even a moment to stare as she ran unwittingly down the stone steps.

She leaped from the stone, fingers breezing past the railing, her shoes landing with a clatter on the white linoleum floors.

Darius watched her run unwittingly along the hallways, knowing she would lose herself in the place he had found to become his second home.

"Any idea where the dorms are?" she finally asked, having given up on self-reliance.

"The dorm buildings are where you'll find the students. Past the courtyard and auditorium. Now, there are seven dorm buildings with common rooms, and a bathroom on every floor. Each school year has its own dorm building for both the girls and boys of the year, and since there are one hundred twenty students in each year, that's how many there are in every building. The bottom three floors of each building hold the boys' dormitories.

"This is where you'll probably find your brother. But since each year depends on age…" He stopped for a moment, considering how he hadn't asked such a crucial question yet.

"How old is your brother by the way?"

"Sixteen."

"That means we'll either find him in the fifth-year building or sixth-year building."

"I'll search the sixth-year building and you search the fifth. On the three bottom—"

"No," Darius cut her off. "We should go to each building together to save time if we end up finding him sooner than we thought."

***

"So, the system is to knock on each door and ask if any Conner is there," said Aria. "That should be simple, right? It's not like anyone'll see me? And no one will try to ask more questions… at least I hope…"

Climbing up the steps of the fifth-year dorm building together, Aria showed confidence. She also showed something she had not exhibited for quite a time, and not with anyone else.

It was trust that everything was going to end up all right in the end.

Trust that she would find her friends and fix everything.

Only, as she glanced at the burly boy in front of her, so kind yet huge, she still looked unsure. How come it was this boy, the boy she had only known for mere minutes, around whom she was apparently so comfortable? She had no problem talking to people, having always considered herself pretty social. Yet, Darius made her visibly relax, unlike some of the people she talked to. She was opening up to him without hesitation.

Perhaps he could truly become a friend.

Maybe he wouldn't end up leaving her at the end of their time together, like her former best friend Heather, or Sienna, or even Cassie and Katie.

They all seemed destined to end up leaving her, too.

Then there was Conner. Her brother. Her twin. Her friend for life.

She loved him, quite a lot actually, but the moment she and her brother went on to live separate lives, when they didn't have the same group of friends, when they went to different schools, lived in different places… She was going to be all alone.

"Aria, we're here."

She snapped from her pensive trance at the announcement of their arrival, realizing they had reached a hall atop two dorm hall stories, stepping from the winding steps to the floor.

"How do you know it's this hall?" Aria queried as they walked the length of the deserted room.

At the other end of the collection of doors was another staircase, Darius' eyes leaving the collection of carved stones to look back at her.

"It wouldn't hurt to try."

In front of them, a door rattled.

"What was that?"

"I don't know."

She took a glimpse of his taken aback features, and queried, "You okay?"

"I usually feel uncomfortable around people from my school. Well, I mean, don't get me wrong, they're sweet and all, but they're all so friendly that it feels like they're forcing me to make conversation with them.

"It feels—if I'm being honest—that they don't really wanna be around me."

She looked ahead, the words Darius had spoken resonating in a way she couldn't seem to comprehend. The words were both foreign and familiar at the same time, the fine line between the two descriptions blurring with each second that passed.

But, even with this deep thinking, she still couldn't resurface a memory in which she could relate to the emotions Darius must've been feeling.

And this realization…made her feel ashamed a bit.

She couldn't help him.

"Well then," she attempted to continue, trying to present herself as recollected, "we shouldn't have to worry about that. It's not as if anyone is going to be trying to talk to us anyways."

He didn't say anything, so she suspected that he was feeling a bit better than before, hopefully because of what help she had provided—or in her opinion, attempted to.

A door farther down the tiled hallway opened, and an olive-skinned boy in baggy pants and a large blue shirt, wrinkled and much too large for his petite frame, emerged.

He turned to the door from which he'd appeared from and called, "Hey, Tobias, what d'you want from the dining hall again?"

"Maybe a bag of chips or something? I don't really care that much though," the disembodied voice of Tobias rasped. "And maybe something to drink."

"All right," the golden-haired boy replied, making his way down the hall toward Aria and Darius.

He strolled down the hall, eyes empty and tired as he mumbled, "Can't believe that they didn't even think to invite me to that hang-out last night. I had to spend all of last night…"

He caught sight of Aria and Darius when taken from his jealous gaze, noticing how quickly the pair of them were attempting to walk past his view.

Despite Darius' previous fears, the boy walked past with nothing but a held-back grin.

They had just started climbing up the stone steps, when Darius could hear a faint knocking from the floor they had just left.

A jumble of words, followed by his name.

His name.

Darius couldn't help but curse in his head.

This was exactly what he didn't want to happen. He didn't care *what* they were talking about, but the fact that they were talking about him at all might as well have been the thing that caused him to finally drop out of this school.

He was one of the topics of their conversation; whether bad or good he didn't care, but he had to get out of there.

Without even an explanation to Aria, Darius clambered up the steps, hands precipitating at the thought of people talking about him behind his back. He couldn't be dealing with this, not now, not with the summer break so close at this point.

He couldn't wait for it, isolating himself in his dorm room and finally getting a chance to hang out with his siblings, his parents, and with Marc.

It would be wonderful, people he already knew, and most importantly, people he already knew he could depend upon. They were the light at the end of this hellish tunnel of bad thoughts, of feeling out of place…

"Look! It's Conner!" Aria shouted, far below him on the staircase.

He must've been so deep in his own thoughts that the world around him had faded away. Oh, how he wished that would stop.

Before he got the chance to take in the current events, she was already far ahead of him, having caught sight of Conner in a dorm room, a dirty blond-haired boy with his arms wrapped around his knees and head lying flat on the wrinkled fabric of his jeans.

His hood, sprinkled with leaves from the garden, it seemed, lay roughly over his head, concealing the most part of his forehead's curly locks.

She approached him quietly, tapping on his shoulder with a gentle look in her eyes.

He jumped at the sight of his twin and stood up quickly.

No one said a thing for a few moments.

She put all anger into her tight grip on his arm as they set off running again.

"Where're we going?" Conner finally said when they had made it to the common room on the bottom of the dorm building.

"I have to get you guys out of here before the school closes," Aria said, a hint of frustration in her voice.

It was clear that Conner wasn't feeling the best about himself, and she would have to be a horrible person to have to add on to that.

She wouldn't want to be the reason he chose to leave her.

She wouldn't know if he would be okay after that.

Darius on the other hand, had an entirely different dilemma on his hands.

The rumor of Aria being his girlfriend had spread faster than his mind could grasp, and it was his top priority to get out of here before people started bombarding him with questions to which he wouldn't have the answers.

As soon as they were out of the door, Darius led them toward the wall on the back side of the fifth-year dorm building, allowing them a moment to catch their breath before running once more.

"My…God…I'm…so…tired," wheezed Conner, glancing at the two others, eyes stalling upon Darius. "Who…is…he?"

Aria, too tired to answer, continued to take in much-needed breaths, Conner taking advantage of such an excellent opportunity and taunting, "Is he your new… Your new… God, I'm even too tired to pick on you."

Aria propped herself up and took a deep breath. "This is Darius. He's a friend I met looking for the Dean."

As soon as Conner and Aria started running, Conner stopped them.

"Mr. Clemont took Cassie and Katie to dorms, too. From what I know, they're either in the fourth or fifth-year building."

"Well, how old are they?" Darius inquired. "I need to know that if we want figure out the dorm they'll be in."

"Cassie said she's fifteen and I think Katie said she was around ten," Aria said in place of Conner, who had no answer at the moment and was still thinking.

"They should be in the fourth-year building then," he concluded, starting to make his way to the fourth-year building.

"But why isn't it fifth?" Aria asked as she pulled her brother along. "Isn't that still a possibility?"

"Right now is around the time when the current school year ends, and we go on our two-week-long summer break. After that, we start a new school year, and those in fourth year are required to be fifteen years old by year end."

And with this clarification, the trio dashed toward the door to the fourth-year building, Darius so quick that he was already nearing the third floor by the time they had cracked open the glass door.

When they arrived at the sixth story, the hall was completely empty, all except a pair of dark ginger-haired sisters, one tall, one short, standing in front of an open door and looking around the hall.

"Katie, Cassie!" Aria gestured for them to come by her side. "Come on guys! We've gotta hurry!"

Cassie and Katie followed her without question, catching up with her as they had started their descent down the east staircase.

They had just started racing toward the main school building when Conner stopped before them, locks of his hair blowing in the faint breeze appearing with their halted movements.

His eyes were alight with euphoria, and his lips turned in a childlike smile. Something, it seemed to his twin, was on his mind, and oh, how elated it seemed to make him.

"We have to wait for Vanessa! She's coming too!" Conner smiled hopefully, making Aria suspect that with his wavering grin, there must've been some doubt in his mind at that statement.

Just as Darius opened his mouth to question him, he had already started running toward the fifth-year building, in the opposite direction of their previous destination.

He dashed through the common room, the stone marble walls decorated with posters the students had hung themselves, as well as with bulletin boards and a variety of other things they had put together to make the building their own for the year.

He left the gray carpet trampled with every step of his feet.

"Vanessa!" he called from the steps as he walked up the staircase. "Are you ready to go? You're coming too, right?"

Minutes later, she appeared, a black backpack strapped on. "I'm here!" She draped her medium-sized purse across her chest and took a deep breath. "I was barely able to finish calling my parents, but luckily, I was able to pack my stuff in time."

She really did.

She came along!

Conner couldn't help but smile, chirping, "We'd better get going then."

They calmly sauntered down to the bottom of the stairs, Conner refraining from telling her about their crunch of time in order to cherish these few blissful seconds.

Unfortunately, they had reached the door to the common room much too quickly, and Aria was staring him down as he arrived, obviously exasperated at his carelessness with time.

Vanessa smiled and waved at them, taking notice of Cassie's stare at Conner, in which she briskly looked away. Maybe the glaring girl was his girlfriend.

Not that she was bothered, anyways, of course, since she donned her *see, I don't care* face to the best of her abilities.

"So, where's Darius?" inquired Conner.

"He went to go back his stuff," Aria said quickly, tapping her foot impatiently. "Told him that we'd meet him at the back door of the main building, so we should get going now."

As they commenced their walk through the grounds, the dorm buildings passed slowly in their peripheral vision. Katie weaved happily through the wide buildings, Cassie chasing after her, steps becoming ever more sluggish with each passing second.

Aria gazed out at the scenery before her, taking in the way the puffy clouds made their way across the blue sky, the colors of a beautiful sunset becoming more prominent as time passed. The garden surrounding the school was lush with a variety of foliage. Katie seemed totally enraptured by its beauty, stopping here and there to exclaim.

And so, the ten-year-old girl made her way across the grass to a fly agaric mushroom, gasping as she piped, "Oh look! It's a red toadstool!" She looked back at her sister as she bounded toward her. "I'm not gonna touch it, obviously," she dismissed. "I've already learned so much about these mushrooms from the book Mom got me for Christmas."

Cassie smiled as her sister stared intently at the mushroom, pulling out her phone to take a few pictures of it.

Katie looked up at her in confusion.

"So that I can print them out. Why don't I put them up in your room?"

Katie smiled and quickly hugged her. "Thanks, Cassie!"

Back to the intended path, Cassie kept looking at Conner, thinking about how he must have been feeling now that he had found a way to not only have an actual conversation with Vanessa, but also to ask her to join them on their adventure.

On the other hand, Vanessa was taking notice of the way Cassie would make sure to stare at them, and she, slowly and subtly, moved away from Conner.

And, as a form of respect for this girl who must've been important to Conner in a way she couldn't be, Vanessa let their conversation fizzle out.

She didn't seem mad, sad, or jealous—just a bit surprised.

After all this, she had probably hoped he would have feelings for her, but maybe he was just being nice. Maybe he just wanted to befriend her.

And that was okay.

Conner's face had been radiating jubilation moments ago, but that faded from his expression after Vanessa's one-word answers and overall disinterest in their conversation.

"Hey, wait up!" Darius shouted, running from behind them with a bulky backpack and duffle bag.

They stopped before being cast into the shadow of the auditorium building, the sun blinding their eyes as he ran to make it to the main class building near the Admissions Office.

"Sorry I took so long," apologized Darius. "Wasn't sure where I put my phone."

Without even a moment for directions, they hurried inside the building through the back door, searching for the entrance that must have been locked.

They passed through the halls silently, creeping under staircases and steps for fear of someone spotting them on the security cameras.

Of course, students had permission to be in the halls at times before curfew, but a group of teenagers and a ten-year-old with a collection of bags seemed more than a bit suspicious.

Too suspicious to allow them to get out of here seamlessly.

Finally, they had found the entrance door to the school, ramming it open without even a moment's notice of the sound reverberating through the halls due to this contact.

"Here!" cheered Aria, far ahead of them as she pulled open the school's entrance door.

They had made it through the doors, elated to have done it quickly enough, just as they heard the shrill sound of a P.A. system overhead.

"All students must report to their dormitories," the voice of Mr. Clemont said over the speaker, rotund and stern.

At his words, there was a loud click from the entrance door.

"So, they lock the doors at a specific time?" Conner asked Darius.

"Yeah, for the safety of the students and the staff, the dorm buildings and main building are closed from nine p.m. to six the next morning."

Aria was still holding the Dean's note in her pocket, sure she would use it if a teacher or anyone of the sort wanted to ask them why they weren't in school while they made their way across the lush grounds.

By the time they had made it across the wide school lawn, disappearing from view of the main building, they found themselves within the garden once more, the area surrounding them decorated with cherry blossoms.

"Oh, look at this, Conner!" beamed Vanessa, the flowers in her open palms, her brown eyes sparkling in the setting sun like a polished smoky quartz gemstone. "Aren't they beautiful?"

Conner watched in delight as she pulled a few blossoms from her hair.

"Conner?"

When she turned to look at him, his face was alight with joy again as though she was straight out of a romantic movie. He gazed at her as if they were the only two people there and everything else in the world had simply slipped away at the sight of her.

"Are you all right?"

Lost in the sparkling of her eyes, he looked rather bewildered for a moment. Taken aback, flummoxed… too slow to respond. Then he came back to his senses as if he'd slapped himself across the face.

"Oh, um… Yeah, I'm fine. And you're right; these blossoms *are* really beautiful. But not as beautiful as… as…"

He couldn't finish, his cheeks flushing a deep red.

***

"Did he forget that we're still here?" Cassie asked Aria as they sat on a large, smooth stone together.

"Probably." Aria took a swig of the bottle of water Darius had offered to her. "This happens a lot whenever he's around some girl he likes. But Vanessa *is* his first love after all. What I mean is, he really has a thing for her. More than I've seen before."

"Really? I would have thought he'd at least had a middle-school girlfriend or something."

"Oh no. He was way too scared to ask any girl out then, too scared they would reject him. Then embarrass him in front of everyone and become an outcast in school. It's always been his insecurities that've never allowed him to find that special someone.

"I've always felt kinda bad for him for it. But I think things with this girl will be different. I know things between them might not seem that good now, but I think she'll be able to help him with the things he's been going through for a while, and it's clear that he likes her…"

"We just need to know if *she* likes him," Cassie finished.

"Exactly."

"But how though?"

"We could ask her later tonight. But we can't let him find out. We can't have him knowing she doesn't like him. At least not having him find out while she's still in the room."

"If I'm being honest, I think she does. Just look at the way she looks at him. There must be at least some chance there."

"That's true, the signs are there, but we should still ask so no embarrassing assumptions are made."

"Agreed."

"But besides that," said Aria, "what's been happening with you and Katie?"

"Well," Cassie began, remembering what had happened in the dorm. "When we were separated from Conner by the Dean, he took Conner away and lead us to another dorm building. The rooms were nice, but they gave us a dorm room for two students, one of the lofts inhabited by someone named Stephanie.

"We talked to her for a while, then she left, saying she wanted to go study with some friends in their dorm. We were left in the dorm for a time, then looked around in the halls of the dorm building for someone, but returned when we didn't find anyone. One thing was different when we came back though. There was this note on Stephanie's loft desk.

"I didn't really know what it was for, but it appeared so fast, like it was magic or something. So, then I stuffed it in my pocket just in case it was a bad omen toward Stephanie or something." She stopped for a moment, looking at the crumpled piece of paper in her hand. "But now that I think about it, that was probably a stupid thing of me to do."

Without another thought, Katie took it from her hands.

"Katie! That's not your letter to read!"

"Neither is it yours, Cass," she retorted quickly. "But you still took it anyways."

Cassie's eyes bulged in shock and surprise at her clever response but didn't say anything for fear of getting embarrassed in front of Aria again, whose snickers were so loud they attracted the attention of her twin sitting across the wide clearing.

"Well then, what does it say, Katie?" Aria asked, leaning over as her snickers subsided.

Katie's pleasant features were gone like the light from a weak flame, and she looked to Aria solemnly. It seemed that she had already read the note, and if she was this stricken, even with it not being about her, it must've carried quite a distressing message.

Hesitantly, she scanned her eyes again over the top of the note:

You must not go to the Land of Elves.

There will be a group of people apprehending your arrival.

They can track you down from there. Please, if you want to stay safe, do not go to the Land of Elves. I only want you to be safe.

Stay safe and love you,

Mom, (or formally, Mrs. Fulton)

Chapter 12
The Intruder

"WHO'S MRS. FULTON?" Conner queried immediately.

He turned to Vanessa, then to Darius, searching for some sort of understanding in their muddled eyes, as deeply confused as they appeared.

No one spoke for a moment until Vanessa piped up, "It may be a note from Stephanie's mother though. One conjured into her room to avoid the journey here."

"That makes sense," Darius replied, the crumpled note now sitting in his open hand.

But only then did Aria notice something written hastily on the palm of his glove, a glistening silver marker, it seemed. The inside of his hand had been open for such meager moments that she didn't have time to read it, but such a thing was hard not to notice.

She looked away as if not wanting to be nosy, not wanting people to think she was someone all up in everyone's business, but she kept glancing back whenever Darius exposed his opened glove for all to see.

"But I wonder why she has to have a note of warning? Who's even looking for her?" Darius replied after Cassie had said something.

Aria's pensive state was abruptly disrupted, looking to Darius to somewhat be able to understand what the girl beside her had said.

"No idea, but for now, it seems she should be fine. The note said it was the Land of Elves, wasn't it?" Conner added.

"Hoping she won't go there," Katie chimed in. "But Stephanie—"

A girl appeared from behind a tree, by means of magic it seemed to the six of them.

And this girl, with short, coiled twists in her kinky black hair and luminescent brown skin, lit by the warm light of the setting sun, stepped from behind one of the bushes.

"Stephanie, isn't it?" Cassie said, brushing a loose leaf from her shoulder.

It was apparent that she hadn't expected to be the topic of anyone's conversation, not to mention a group of six school-aged children outside of school during such late hours.

She chuckled, standing up properly.

"I was just out here looking for one of my friends. They hadn't come back since earlier today, and I was thinking, since they're so obsessed with our school garden and all, that they'd be here." She observed each of them for a moment, taking in the confusion in each of their expressions. "Although, I wasn't really expecting to see people other than them."

She stopped speaking for a moment as it seemed her odd circumstance did not entertain them as much as it did her, and so she turned to Cassie.

"But Cassie, what're you doing out here? Why aren't you unpacking your stuff?"

"Don't worry about that," Cassie dismissed, clutching the note Darius had in his hands. She slipped it into Stephanie's; Stephanie's face appeared surprised for a moment as she watched Cassie recede to her original spot in the clearing.

"Sorry I took that. It's from your mom, I think. Saying something about not going to the Land of Elves for the time being. I'm sure she must've texted you about it, right?"

Stephanie's smile faded as she looked at the piece of yellow piece of paper in her hands, looking up to Cassie. "No, she didn't, but…" She read the note again, muscles tensing, and it looked as if her mind must have been racing as she tried to take in the information.

"It's not like you're in any sort of danger or anything though…" When this comment didn't help to soothe her uneasiness, Cassie went on, "…right, Stephanie?"

"Mom told me about this before," Stephanie said in a solemn voice, all traces of joy removed from her soft features. "She told me that they—"

She clutched at her throat and rubbed her nose as though they burned, her eyes moving over the ground. Tears came flooding free.

There was no one else in this situation now; at this moment and this moment only, Stephanie's Mom was the only one who mattered.

"It's already happened once. The things they would do to try and find Mom. Try to kill her like they did Ruler Marjorie."

Cassie stopped, not knowing what to do.

Give her a hug? No. I have to let her keep talking. Let her get all her feelings out before I try soothing her with words.

Stephanie, without any sort of interruption, went on, "I need to go see her, but I can't. Not with school in the way. I wish there was a way I could, but not with her being hundreds of miles away." She crumpled into her hands, rubbing tears away with her palms' heels, evidently wishing she wasn't tearing up in front of a group of strangers. "I wish that—"

Cassie instinctively wrapped her hands around her, Katie quick to follow as they allowed her to cry for a few moments.

Cassie knew Stephanie was feeling embarrassed, ashamed of her emotions, but now, that didn't matter either. All she needed was a friend. Someone to lend a shoulder to cry on.

And so, as a friend would, Cassie did.

***

They sat in silence the few minutes after Stephanie had left, taking in her words, her actions, her emotions.

It felt good to Cassie to know she was someone Stephanie could confide in, yet it was painful knowing Stephanie wouldn't have her around whenever such an event occurred again.

"Guess we know Vitina's motives now, don't we?" Conner remarked, trying to add some light to the bleak occasion. "We—"

"Shut up," Cassie said from under her breath, eyes penetrating through his.

Even with the warm tones of her brown eyes, he couldn't help but flinch at her gaze.

"WHY CAN'T YOU UNDERSTAND THAT THIS ISN'T THE TIME!" She stood up, anger and sadness mixing in her eyes. "IT'S NOTHING BUT A NUISANCE! WERE YOU EVEN PAYING ATTENTION TO WHAT HAPPENED!"

He winced away from her, obviously not used to seeing Cassie as infuriated as this.

He looked away from her, clearly flinching. "I'm sorry. Guess I shouldn't—"

"NO, YOU'RE NOT SORRY! YOU NEVER ARE! YOU JUST JOKE ABOUT EVERYTHING WITHOUT THINKING! STEPHANIE WAS RIDDLED IN GRIEF AND DESPAIR AND YOU THINK JOKING ABOUT THIS IS FUNNY?"

"Cassie," Vanessa interrupted before she could speak again. "Please stop. Just look at him."

Her enraged stupor subsided as she looked at the fear in Conner's eyes.

No longer did they carry that joyful glow, just an empty sea of blue.

She sighed and slumped away to her original seat. "Look, I'm sorry. I was just… I just got caught up in my emotions and stuff. I'm sorry, Conner."

He nodded, obviously not accepting her apology after she had chastised him so harshly.

But he nodded, maybe realizing he did deserve it. He was quiet, morose, introspective.

He certainly had been acting like a nuisance these past few days.

But why was it Cassie was the only one who could reveal such an epiphany to him?

He looked ashamed and angry…most likely, at himself.

He was older than her and should've known so much better. But for her to have to explained such a thing to him at such a crucial point in his life? Maybe this was why people hadn't liked him in middle school.

He *was* a nuisance.

And, thanks to Cassie, he had finally come to terms with it.

The six of them stayed silent several moments on end, the atmosphere no longer bleak and hopeless, but undeniably awkward to the point where all were hesitant to speak.

Aria, usually the first one to speak up in this sort of situation, announced, "Um—so, I have this idea for how to get into Rubidium that I've been thinking about for the whole day."

They all looked to her, obvious boredom and discomfort in their sunken eyes.

The five of them were gazing up at her, but their earlier smiles were gone, all receded.

Cassie's chuckle had died away. Katie's youthful grin, dead. The bright twinkle in Vanessa's eyes… All of that, all those smiles, those grins, those genuinely happy moments, gone. Nobody was happy anymore. Everyone lost themselves in their own sullen thoughts.

It appeared she couldn't take it any longer.

"Look," she sighed. "I know that everything is feeling off right now. We used to be so happy together, me, Cassie, Katie, and Conner. Smiling and giggling and just having a great time on this adventure." She stopped and looked to them from her reminiscent daze. "To distract ourselves from the real reason we all came together."

"To find my sister," Katie finally said after what seemed to be days of not speaking a word. But this ten-year-old, who very rarely felt as if she contributed anything, started tearing up, nose tingling and throat closing up as she looked down at the ground.

"I-I miss her a lot. And I just wish we could all be happy all the time. Happy and smiling. Because when I'm sad…" She sniffed as her head fell in her hands. "…I don't like it. I feel like we'll never find her. That horrible voice in my head tells me we'll never find her again. That she's lost to this crazy-weird world that I wish sometimes never existed."

At this point, tears were already streaming down her cheeks.

Grief and despair were plainly overtaking her thoughts.

"Because if it didn't, she would've never disappeared."

Cassie knew she should've chastised her, said something about how important this place was to people like Darius or Vanessa, but even she knew that Katie didn't need it.

She knew what she'd said, and she would come to regret it, but right now…

It was the only thing she wanted to say.

"You're right," Vanessa sniffed.

"Yeah," Darius said, rubbing at his eyes.

Were they crying too?

So, she really did matter to them. Katie looked at them in turn, taking in their sadness too. Through all the tears and sadness, they all cared for each other.

Even her.

Cassie wrapped her arms around her younger sister, wiping her tears and keeping her close. "I'm sorry."

"Sorry for what?" Katie mumbled. "You didn't do anything?"

"I'm sorry that you have to feel that way. Like the things you say don't matter to us. Like *you* don't matter." She looked into Katie's eyes, both compassion and sternness mixing in her eyes. "Because you're just as important as everyone else here. Me, Aria, Darius, Vanessa, everyone."

And with another warm sisterly hug, Katie couldn't help but smile.

Cassie had just shown that her fears had been disproven.

Cassie had shown that she had worth here. She mattered.

***

"Since we'll have to sneak into Rubidium to find Avery, I came up with a plan while you guys were away," Aria stated, the atmosphere from before having finally subsided. "I was studying for an entrance exam to Madric Academy when the idea hit me."

They leaned in closer to listen and she continued.

"We can make ourselves invisible with a potion of the ranunculus flower petals and the anti-glare coating of the glasswing butterfly. Then, once we dip our cloaks in it, we'll become invisible to the human eye, allowing us to slip into Rubidium undetected.

"We'll need to collect the ingredients for the potion too. Glasswing butterflies live in warm places with lots of trees, just like the Snowlands in the Land of Elves. And when we have that—

Darius—" He looked up at the mention of his name. "You can whip up the potion."

"But can't you just perform an invisibility spell?" Cassie questioned. "That would be the easiest way around having to go on another one of these laborious quests."

"Invisibility spells don't last as long as potions do, and it would break if we were touched, defeating the entire purpose of the spell anyways."

"Then that seems like a pretty good plan, Aria. I think I've learned something about that potion in one of my classes. I have the brief memory of making it," reminisced Darius. "But how'll we even get to the Land of Elves? And why are we talking about Vitina's school?"

"Cause that's where Cassie and Katie's sister is." She pointed at the two light-haired sisters and Cassie looked up from her phone with shock in her eyes.

"Did someone say my name?" she interjected.

Aria ignored her and continued to Darius, "That sister Katie was talking about is named Avery, and from what we've learned, she was taken to Rubidium."

"Rubidium?" He stood from his stump swiftly, clenching his fists as if the word had done something to his composure. "She could die! We've gotta find a way!"

"We know that," Conner disrupted flatly. "But going in without a plan would end up with us dead. What's the point then?"

"But there's gotta be some way to get to her faster, hasn't there? Teleport there? Anything?"

"Teleporting is too risky," Vanessa debated. "We don't need ourselves getting stuck in the space between our entrance and destination for all eternity. We need to go about this methodically, and teleporting there is not the way."

"Also, if you didn't know already," Cassie said after pulling up an article on her smartphone, "Rubidium tends to not kill their students as soon as they enter the school. At least now, we know that she's still alive. And no matter how far-fetched it may sound…" She glanced up at them briskly, then back at the screen as if in timidity "…we'll find a way to save her."

Even though Avery wasn't his sister, Darius' nerves appeared to have been settled, at least a bit, by Cassie's optimistic statement.

He sat back down on the tree stump of a seat once more, breathing deeply as he began another important topic in their conversation, "So, how'd she end up in Rubidium?"

"There was a portal that appeared in our house," Katie started, beginning to get sick of having to retell this story over and over to people. "She had fallen into it, transporting her to somewhere in the Magic Realm. Based on what we know, she's probably at the Rubidium School in the Kingdom of Sorcerers, so we need to bring her back home before anything really bad happens to her."

"And having this potion is the only way we can ensure that this plan works perfectly. Cause if we don't…" She paused as they took in the gravity of the situation. "… We might not have another chance like this again."

"Rubidium is run by the sorceresses Vitina and Andromeda, right?" Vanessa queried. "I'd heard that Vitina was the one who killed Ruler Marjorie a few years ago, one of the most powerful, if not *the* most powerful sorcerer in history. And not to mention Andromeda being even worse than that. What'll we do if they end up catching us?"

"But they won't," Aria said, seeming rather presumptuous. "Which is why I'm saying we've gotta get that invisibility potion."

After a moment, Darius was the first to speak up out of the hesitant crowd.

"Well, if that's the plan, then I'm in," Darius finally answered.

With his words, the others found the courage to eventually comply, and Aria announced, "Sun's setting pretty fast, so we'd better head back to the trailer."

"Trailer!" Vanessa piped up. "We'll really be staying in a trailer!"

"Well, yeah, that's where we've been staying since we got here," Katie explained.

As they headed toward the surrounding wall of the campus, strolling through the expansive garden, Conner was walking much farther ahead of the chatting, rather jubilant group of adolescents. He was off on his own, alone in his own thoughts it seemed, and Cassie, quick to take notice, hurried to catch up to him.

His eyes stayed on the sunlit grass swaying beneath his shoes.

"How was it, Conner?" she asked him, quiet enough that Vanessa, only a few paces behind them, couldn't hear her.

"How was what?" he mumbled. "Me missing the chance to ask her out or the absolute embarrassment I was when I met her for the first time in a year?"

"Oh, don't be so hard on yourself. It's always hard to talk to your crush."

"Not just that, but, after a day of hanging out with her, I was reminded of why I liked her in the first place. I didn't really tell her I liked her, but she seemed excited that I had come all this way just to see her. There's a chance I think. And that conversation we had…"

He sighed happily. "…it made me realize that I should continue having the feelings I have. Try not to bottle them up so long they shrivel up and die."

Cassie squealed quietly in triumph. "That's incredible, Conner! Me and Aria are rooting for you two, y'know?"

"Aria? Why would she care about this anyway? She didn't even want me to come here knowing Vanessa would be the only reason. I can still remember what she said.

"To either give up or finally confess to her. I know I sound stupid, but I just can't do that. At least not now. Not when I'm not really sure what she'll say. What if…"

There was genuine worry in his eyes.

"What if everything goes wrong?" he said plaintively.

His eyes lost their shimmer and he stared back at the ground again. "What if she just wants to be friends? What if she'll be so weirded out by me, she just wants to leave all together?"

"Conner."

"What if she likes someone else? What if it's Darius? What if they start dating and I have to watch her fall in love with someone else? I know I'm not entitled to any feelings from her but—"

Cassie started to raise her voice more. "Conner."

"What if she just leaves when I tell her this? What if she has a boyfriend and will be so hurt by me asking her out without even asking her about that first, that she hates me?"

"CONNER!" Her scream was loud enough for everyone to hear, and they stopped.

The Higan cherry trees rustled in the utter silence, everyone standing still in confusion and disarray at the abrupt stop to everyone's composure.

"Conner," Vanessa said, resting her hand on his shoulder as she broke the silence. "Is something wrong?"

"What? No! Nothing at all! Nothing is—"

"Stop lying to yourself!" Cassie echoed, voice reverberating around them once more. "Stop saying everything is okay! Everything isn't. You're clearly upset, and you need to at least ask her. Ask Vanessa what you couldn't before."

Vanessa looked from Cassie to him, worry and bewilderment swimming in her eyes.

"Ask me what, Conner?"

"Go ahead," Cassie directed. "Ask her what you need her to hear."

"Vanessa," Conner sighed, attempting to look into her eyes, but ultimately failing, "I've been wanting to ask you this for a while..." His body started tensing up despite his mind begging it not to. "...Would you... I mean only if you'd like to. Only if you *really* want to. I mean you don't have to if you don't want."

Vanessa stopped his blabbering with a smile, removing her hand from his shoulder as he kept going on incessantly. "*What* did you want to ask me?"

"A date?" he finally professed with a heavy breath. "Maybe tomorrow."

"Of course, we can. A friend date sounds nice."

Conner looked up, surprised and assured, happy yet disappointed.

A date, but a *friend date.* That didn't sound too bad. It wasn't what he expected but the fact she had accepted this at all was more than he thought he even deserved.

"Yeah. A friend date."

"If that's what you wanted to ask me, then great! I'll see you tomorrow. Maybe the date can be during a search for some of those glasswing butterflies Aria was talking about."

"We could do that, yeah."

Cassie silently slipped away from Conner's side, leaving Conner and Vanessa to talk amongst themselves when she stepped next to Aria.

Conner glanced at her, sunlight bouncing off his sweatshirt. His eyes looked happier, much more cheerful than before, and he mouthed to Cassie, "Thanks".

"No problem," she responded, yet no sound escaped from her lips.

Cassie sighed with triumph.

"What was that all about?" Aria asked as if she had instantly appeared. "Was it Vanessa again?"

"Yeah," she said, "but luckily, I, the best friend ever, got him to ask her out. I'm a pro at these sorts of things, y'know?"

"What are you guys talking about?" Darius asked, leaning his head in as they approached the wall surrounding the campus.

"Conner's got a little crush on someone and needed help asking her out. Luckily, I was able to get him to do it," Cassie said, pride still radiating off her as she was the last to close the latch on the door. "I'm the person you need to look to for dating advice."

"Yet you've never had a boyfriend," Katie joked from her side.

"Well…no, I haven't." She looked down in impromptu embarrassment

Aria and Darius shared a small chuckle at her, and she shot daggers at them, prompting even more chuckles from them.

"But guys. Oh, c'mon!" she said, trying to stop them from laughing at her even more.

Eventually, even Katie started laughing a bit, and Cassie smiled, embarrassed but amused at the outcome of her prideful statement.

Vanessa, standing at Conner's side, looked back at them all laughing uncontrollably. "What do you think they're talking about?"

He waited for a moment, thinking over her query. "Cassie or Aria probably said something stupid again."

"HEY!" the two yelped furiously at him, Conner ending up cracking a laugh as well.

"It was definitely them," he whispered in Vanessa's ear.

And with those four words, even Vanessa laughed along a little too.

***

"This trailer looks really nice," Vanessa complimented as she walked in and out of each room, steps slow as she took in the place around her.

"For something that's been conjured," Darius said from around the corner, "I must say this place was really well done."

"You can go ahead and conjure your bed if you need to," Aria said, sitting on the couch as she watched Darius raise his wooden wand to the illuminated ceiling.

"Creo exponentia!" he cast, the tip of the wand immediately turning shades of blue so light that they appeared almost white.

In a wave of sparkles, they witnessed a round-edged rectangular blob appear before them on the farthest wall of the room, placed directly left of the couch's nightstand.

And as the object gained detail, they watched as the bed appeared before them, the colors not even fully established before Darius sank down on it to rest his weary legs.

"God," he said as he looked to the ceiling coated in soft yellow lighting from the surrounding lamps. "That was a lot of walking."

The others though, it seemed at the time, were much more concerned with other matters, or more specifically Conner was, and everyone else was simply watching him growing flustered as he spoke with Vanessa.

"So, I'll just sleep on the couch maybe. Then I just put away the blankets in the mornings," she suggested.

Conner spoke up quickly, unnecessary worry filling his words. "Is that okay?"

"Yeah, it is," she swiftly said to him, reassuring his worries that he must have been a bad person for doing this. "I just need you to give me some blankets though."

At this point, everyone else had already left the living room, and Conner had gotten lost in the depths of her brown eyes, so rich and luminescent in the lamplight, he knew he would have trouble regaining composure once more.

"Where are the blankets again, Conner?"

Vanessa was almost immediately cut off by Aria, waving a hand incessantly in front of Conner's empty eyes. He then shoved a few of their thicker blankets in her direction. "He's just—" She looked at him briefly and turned promptly, his eyes nothing but a pool of blue, appearing lost in zero thought but the statement he would tell her every day.

'Vanessa's so pretty, y'know?'

"He's just being an idiot," she finally said, walking away just as Conner had begun to seem his typical self again, at least the same Conner he always was around Vanessa.

"Oh, um, do you need me to get you some blankets?" he asked Vanessa.

Vanessa shook her head and smiled, putting her bag to the side as she proclaimed, "No, your sister brought me some already. But thanks for asking."

"Oh," Conner breathed, shaking in a fit of panic and surprise.

Darius and Vanessa began unpacking their bags, Cassie and Katie gathering beside the twins at their dining table for dinner, the older Smith sister emerging from her seat to sweep beige curtains over the windows in the van.

"Oh, wait," Vanessa stopped her, taking the silky cloth in her own hands, luminous in the light around them.

Conner was indeed right, Cassie had realized immediately. Vanessa was radiant like a summer afternoon sun, one Cassie would've wished to have the opportunity to just lie and bask in after all that had happened.

The girl, even though all she had done was offer to help her, reminded her of a simpler time in her life. Watching the summer sun as it bathed the vibrant grass in its light, the symphony of the cicadas, the feeling of cool water down her throat after a long day of lounging with her friends at the park, all came back to as an unprecedented wave of nostalgia.

She missed those times.

She wanted to go back to them.

But she couldn't.

No one could, not her, not Katie, not Avery. Not unless she managed to save Avery, anyways. Then everything would be able to go back to normal.

At least that was what she hoped for.

But maybe, just maybe, despite all that she had told herself, the nostalgia exceeded the real thing, because at the same time she realized she had nothing to really go back to.

All except for maybe her parents, it seemed, and the ways she tried to distract herself from…

From what?

What am I even saying? What am I even talking about? What am I distracting myself from?

At that moment, Cassie realized that was a question she could not answer, for she had never wanted to ask herself such a thing.

Because asking the question meant an answer was bound to appear.

And she was dreading that answer.

"Cassie?" a small voice called from behind her. "Are you okay?"

She flipped her head to Katie in a delirious, deranged way she hadn't wanted, causing Katie to take a step back. "I-I'll just leave you alone. Dinner's ready anyway."

She met with them at the dining table, squashing in beside Vanessa and Conner awkwardly as she looked at the plate before her.

Lamb shanks seasoned with lemon pepper and rosemary and several other spices made her nostrils feel alive and jubilant. Whisks of steam escaped from the meat set beside the vegetable medley, all of which she seemed to be quite enjoying.

It was one of her favorite meals, but even so, she was clearly still struggling to feel her typical self again. Anyone could see she didn't feel okay, but she also didn't say anything.

Everyone was so happy and she likely didn't want to spoil things.

Anyways, no one would want to listen to her ramble on about her dumb problems.

At least that was what her old friends had always told her before.

So, everyone chattered around her, laughing and complimenting Katie about her amazing selection.

But Katie *hated* vegetable medley! And there it was, languishing on her plate!

Katie looked to her sister across the table, smiling and pointing at her food as she held up her thumb, as if to say she was loving the food.

She was obviously lying behind those eyes, obviously aware that Cassie knew it too.

And, with what little she could do, Katie seemed to be trying to find a way to make her sister feel a bit better again.

Cassie listened to them discuss their plans, smiling at the way the food tasted in her mouth. It was a comfort meal for her, tasted of home, tasted of good memories and good people and good friends and…

…of feeling happy.

"How are we planning to get to the Land of Elves?" Vanessa questioned, taking a bite of one of her lamb shanks.

Aria looked up at her, mouth full. "I was thinking we could teleport there."

"Teleport!" Darius blurted, his fork falling with a clink on his plate. "Didn't you hear what Vanessa said? Do you know how dangerous that is?"

I should've been a better sister, the voice in the back of her head said.

"I know, but I didn't even get the teleportation spell anyways. I can't perform one myself, so I went to a store in town to find someone to transfer one to my wand. In the end, the employee couldn't even perform the spell, so I just left to go look for Conner." She looked at Darius, surprisingly no hint of frustration or negativity in her expression. "I appreciate you worrying about me, but I promise, I know the risks of a teleportation spell."

"That's a relief," Darius sighed, "but how are we actually going to get there then?"

I should've been taking better care, the voice proclaimed.

"We can drive to the Land of Elves for the potion ingredients than move west to the Kingdom of Sorcerers," Conner elaborated.

"So, when'll we leave?" Vanessa had just finished off the last of her broccoli.

"We can leave tomorrow morning, but who'll be driving?" Conner looked around at them. "Any takers?"

This is all your fault, the voice accused.

"I'd rather not," Vanessa admitted. "With me being a princess and all, I usually have a chauffeur, so I don't have a lot of driving."

"Excuse me!" Cassie shouted over the conversation at the table, rushing off to the bathroom before anyone could stop her.

Her mind was racing with bad thoughts and wistful memories and people and blurred faces. She couldn't take it. It was becoming too much.

This adventure, this world, everything, everyone.

I don't think I can do this anymore.

She had experienced something like this before, years ago when she was around thirteen.

But she didn't want to remember that time.

But now it seemed that was all that could fill her mind.

All those tears, all those horrible promises, all those lies that she was all right. It hurt. Hurt more than she could even imagine.

And so, sitting on the cool, white tile of their shower, she cried, covered by the dim light as she stared at the ground and convulsed with overwhelming despair or anguish or…

"Don't question it," she said to herself, lying back as she allowed her nose to tingle, tears falling from her eyes once more. She sank into the dim light of the curtain.

She cried.

She thought.

And she spoke, to herself, to the voice in her head.

She wanted to reach some sort of compromise with it, treating it like some kind of person who could be reasoned and negotiated with, and not a sign of something that needed desperate attention.

It refused her compromise, seeming to insist on coming back at a later time.

But, with its weakening effect, she allowed herself to cry freely.

And it made her feel…

…better.

At least, so she thought.

***

Darius was the last out of the four to get to bed.

He was sleeping in a large dark blue shirt and black pants that Conner had lent to him, a kind deed he hadn't expected from someone he'd met less than a day ago.

In the still quiet of the night, Conner and Vanessa spoke beneath the faint light from the lamp in the living room, laughing and gossiping and showing each other videos.

"Could I have your number?" Vanessa yawned. "I wanna be able to talk to you more, well, without waking everyone else up."

Conner blushed and froze. Was she flirting with him? But she said their date would be a friend date, not a romantic one. Or did she just want to talk to him more as a friend?

Well, maybe that didn't matter? She had just asked for his number!

"Sure," he smiled, saying his own number so she could type it into her phone.

She gave him her own and made her way toward the living room, Conner hurrying after her as he inquired, "Where're you going? It's only midnight."

"I just wanted to watch a movie; of course, I'm not tired. Don't you want to watch one?"

"A movie?" His face radiated, as if fireworks had gone off in his head, and it took all of his strength to keep himself from combusting with pure joy.

"Well yeah, that's what friends do at sleepovers, right? I would at least consider this to be a sleepover."

He smiled and followed her, finally able to pipe up, "Yeah, sure."

He sat on one end of the couch, wrapped in a blanket of his own while Vanessa sat on the other end. He didn't want to avoid her, and wasn't making it seem as if he was doing.

He was behaving in a way that she couldn't misunderstand. Doing that seemed unfair toward her, especially since this was the first day he'd actually spent with her.

He was barely paying attention to the movie, just gazing at Vanessa from the side as she cracked smiles and laughed.

He matched her actions, because if this was one of her favorite movies, he would have to make an effort to make it one of his favorites as well.

She was radiant like the sun, as he'd told Cassie, yet as cool and refreshing as the light of the luminous moon. She was gorgeous and she was funny, and she was lighthearted…

She's just wonderful… conveyed his dreamy face, smiling stupidly, lost too deep in his lovesick thoughts to even comprehend the things happening before him.

And so, he fell asleep, as well as her, long before the movie had even ended. And Conner's thoughts, no doubt, were filled with her.

***

"Where's Cassie?" Katie murmured, stirring from her light sleep as she picked up on the sounds from the living room.

She peered her head in, seeing the television still on, quickly turning off the obnoxious background noise.

She turned to Cassie's empty bed for a few moments, looking from there to the bathroom door, the last place she had seen her older sister.

But no one could be in the bathroom for that long. It had been hours.

There were no lights beneath the bathroom door, leading her to believe Cassie had probably left at some point. But if so, why wasn't she already in her bed?

She set her fingertips on the smooth silver of the doorknob, pulling open the door and flipping on the bright lights.

She heaved a sigh of relief; her sister wasn't anywhere near the sink or toilet.

The shower wasn't running, so she pulled back the smooth white curtains. A girl was sitting there, her back up against the opposite side of the showerhead.

Her face fell, shocked and horrified. *Oh no,* her expression displayed.

Something like this had happened before, back when she was around the young age of seven. She had wanted to clean her sister's bathroom since she had been feeling down for the past few days, and so she'd made her way down the hall to get to work.

But her bathroom was filthy and littered with paper towels and used tissues, and so, confused and terrified, she ran back to her room.

She never told her mother, never told her father, and especially never Cassie.

She had been worried and scared and…

…the only thing she knew to do then was give her a hug and tell her that she loved her.

Because that *was* all she could do.

She shook Cassie's shoulder a few times, causing her to stir.

She moved from her rest, shifting slightly with watery red eyes.

"You need to go to sleep," Katie managed to say, helping Cassie out of the shower. "In a real bed."

Cassie locked eyes with her younger sister for a moment; her eyes were solemn and serious in a way they weren't most of the time.

Somehow, someway, her sister understood her, at least more than most did.

Cassie had never told her anything about the way she was feeling after that day when she was thirteen; she also didn't understand what was happening, but Katie, even as an inquisitive, loud-mouthed seven-year-old, never said anything.

Cassie was afraid she was making her grow up too fast, forcing her to face things that some kids beyond her age could not even comprehend, but Katie never cared.

All Katie cared about was that her elder sister was all right.

Cassie was first to leave the bathroom, and Katie followed her out soon.

As Cassie drifted off to sleep, Katie was the only thing on her mind.

Does she really know?

***

In the dead of the night, a figure cloaked in black slunk up to the van's windows, obscured by the safety of what seemed to be thick, opaque curtains.

The figure was watching the shadows' soft breaths of those inside.

They gripped a crooked golden wand in their nimble fingers, raising its point to the glass of the window, keeping it steady as the light swiftly expanded.

Intense vibrations reverberated throughout the vehicle, causing Conner's unexpected and unfortunate awakening from such a blissful sleep. As he rubbed the sleep from his eyes, they cleared to see a lanky shadow through the curtains.

Maybe a gnarled wand held against the window.

He lightly shook Vanessa awake, and she rose her head so swiftly it seemed as if she had been conscious the whole time, watching intently as the shadow's lips faintly contorted to recite some sort of chant.

"Get your wand," she breathed, so quickly and sternly that Conner seemed to be pondering for a moment, wondering if she was irritated.

He ignored the notion and did as told, no doubt quietly hearing her doing the same, staying as still as possible, despite the pure darkness inside the van.

They slowly crawled toward the vehicle door, sure to keep out of sight of the numerous windows in case they should be spotted out of the corner of the shadow's eyes.

They both crouched before the van door, wands held at the cloudy, black-tinted glass, hidden in the shadow of the opaque metal surrounding it.

"On three," Vanessa whispered, eyes boring through the darkness of the glass, keenly watching the grass swaying outside the window.

Conner's eyes darted to the ominous stillness of the outside, grass swishing this way and that in the gentle night breeze as he worked hard. The task must have been distracting him from a looming anxiety over the situation.

It had all happened so fast. He surely wasn't ready for this to happen.

He couldn't allow Vanessa to know he was afraid. Not after he had managed to finally establish some sort of friendship with the girl he had been pining after for a year.

He had to lock up his emotions. For her sake. Just the same way he had his entire life.

She had to think he was brave, right? A shoulder she could cry on when she was down and a source of comfort in times of hardship.

That was who he had to be.

Even if that was not how he felt about himself.

"Three!" Vanessa said, Conner quite confused, snapping back from his pensive trance.

Despite the build-up, Vanessa had slowly opened up the van door for fear of attracting unwanted attention, the moonlight illuminating her golden-brown skin in an angelic way, a way at which Conner couldn't help but smile.

In spite of Vanessa's efforts, the masked figure pulled their wand from the window, a magnetic tug causing the job to become quite difficult.

"Impetum exponentia!" she cast, watching as the baby blue light of Resicus blasted from the tip of her wand.

"Claudicatio exponentia!" the anonymous figure cast in opposition, a wave of red magic firing from the wand with a deafening crackle.

Vanessa narrowly avoided her own spell deflected in defense, jumping out of the way as the figure cast an invisibility spell over its bodily frame rather swiftly.

Conner looked about the grassy field frantically for some sign of movement or, really, anything that would help him to pick up on the intruder's presence.

It seemed that without a moment's hesitation, Vanessa had already cast a force field around the two of them, something similar to a large bubble or hamster-wheel.

She led the way as Conner frantically ran in her wake, watching as she effortlessly deflected magical shots from their opponent as if she could clearly see them, the invisibility spell they had cast not working well to their advantage.

The flurry of shot spells seemed to consist of obliteration ones as well, causing the immediate destruction of a patch of grass where the spell had landed as soon as the invisible individual had stepped on it.

They fired another spell, this time from a new angle, almost hitting one of the van's colossal tires. But as they stopped to take a breath, Vanessa pointed out the embers of a flame beginning to spark in the nearly empty grounds.

The small fire was only a few feet from where they were standing.

She audibly cursed herself for letting the opponent get the better of her, dragging Conner along in the circular force field as she watched a ring of dancing flames build around the trailer.

And now, she was trapped. Cornered.

There didn't seem to be enough time for her to drop the force field and put out the fire simultaneously.

Undoubtedly, she hadn't expected for this to happen.

And she was supposed to know what to do.

She was supposed to know how to behave and how to control the situation.

She couldn't let Conner down.

She let out a faint sigh, adrenaline pumping through her bloodstream as she brought down the force field.

"What are you doing!" Conner cried out, feeling a sting of guilt at his bitter tone, but he pressed on. "That was our only source of protection!"

With all that was happening, Conner's words seemed to be the least of her worries as she struggled to deflect spells with her wand at the same time as trying to decipher a solution.

"I've got it!" she chirped. "Get me up there!" She quickly gestured to the roof of the trailer, the metal illuminated subtly in the dim light of the moon.

He had just made his way to the top as she cried, "Aqua exponentia!", drawing a symbol of a water droplet in the air surrounded by a circle of light, her swift yet subtle movements similar to that of an experienced artist.

She swiped her open hand across the symbols, sending a wave of water over the flames as she held her hand high, chin raised in the air as she looked over the quiet meadow.

The only sound for miles, it seemed at the moment, things slowing down in Vanessa's mind as the intense blast extinguished the flames. In her peripheral vision though, she watched as the water moved in a rather peculiar fashion, along with the faint sound of a cough on the wind.

"Volans exponentia!" Vanessa and Conner cast together, shooting off into the sky as soon as the last syllable left their lips.

They shot a series of spells at the invisible figure, hoping to somehow scare them off if any of them even happened to hit them. And with the thud of a body in the soft grass, they returned to the ground where they joyfully delivered the last spell.

"Nulla gravitatis exponentia!" they shouted together, wands side by side as the blasts of light went shooting toward the collapsed figure, struggling to move their appendages to leave.

And then they disappeared, far into the starry night of the atmosphere.

Conner let out a sigh of relief as Vanessa embraced him in an unexpected yet very welcome hug. He smiled as her head rested on his shoulder, the faint smell of vanilla in her silky dark brown hair wafting through his nostrils as she nestled her arms around him.

Regardless of how short the embrace was, Conner wanted to prolong this moment for however long he could. It wouldn't last long, but just this moment alone…just this warm feeling of embrace from her would be enough.

As they silently made their way back into the van, the stinging scent of ash from the fires and burnt grass reminiscent on their clothing, the warmth glowed from their wands as the Resicus that had been pulsing through them only seconds ago made the objects work a lot more than they were accustomed to.

“That was crazy, Vanessa! Like, I thought I was gonna die, but to walk out unscathed…” He sighed quietly, a happy twinkle in his blue eyes as he smoothed his hair back, gazing at her. “…just goes to show how amazing you are.”

As the words left his lips, Vanessa could feel an overcoming blush begin to form, looking at him and simply smiling. Something about his words, paired with the look in his luminous blue eyes, made it seem as if she couldn’t help but smile.

Her heart was beating fast now, but from what?

It wasn’t adrenaline, and her fast pulse from the fight had already faded.

It was…something else.

Something new.

But anyways, he continued, “I noticed that figure’s wand was stuck to the trailer for a few seconds, like a magnet.” She sat herself down on the couch where Conner was sitting, a frown on her face despite the inevitable quick beating of her heart. “I’m scared they might’ve wanted to do something to it. Like set it on fire or something. Or make it combust!”

She paused for a moment at Conner’s lack of a reaction.

“Or you know, maybe I’m just overreacting. I guess I tend to do that some—”

“No!” he jumped in, tensing as she froze. “You’re right, Vanessa. They were using a fire spell, which means they had the skill level of one who uses Elemental Spells, some of the hardest known in magic history.

“They take so much wand practice and spell knowledge that they had to be taught that.”

“But taught by whom? Because if there are educators in—well—whatever’s going on here, that means there can’t just be one person who’s up to this.”

“Okay, so we know that this group of people, whoever they are, have advanced magical capabilities.” He counted ‘one’ with his index finger. “And they are concealing their identities with black cloaks.” He counted ‘two’ by adding his middle finger. “And have a crooked golden wand.”

Vanessa gasped, quickly putting an idea of hers into motion. “What if they’re tied to Rubidium?”

"Rubidium? No way." He stared at the kitchen table for a moment, obviously contemplating something. "The different colored cloaks."

"To disguise themselves," Vanessa finished. "You remember the story of Vitina's exile, right?"

Conner nodded but didn't speak.

"And how she vowed to create an army to take over the Magic Realm once and for all?"

Vanessa's deep brown eyes widened with realization.

"And those cloaks must be for her growing army."

She paused for a moment, frowning as she let out a halted sigh. "But what if we're jumping the gun here, Conner? We can't just suspect this kind of stuff without any proof. What if it was just some pyromaniac or whatever, who saw us as an easy victim?"

"But what about all that strategy though?" Conner replied in defense of his claim, his tone unusually defensive. "They were looking for us. Us specifically. A regular pyromaniac would've attacked multiple people in the RV park. But they attacked us, just us, and wouldn't move onto anyone else. We were targeted, Vanessa."

The blood drained from her face, Conner noticed, as she spoke so softly it was as if there was no sound at all as she looked to the ground.

"You're right. It's her army. It has to be."

"Vitina's army," murmured Conner, just as softly as Vanessa would speak.

"But why would Vitina want to get rid of us? They shouldn't have anything against us. We've done nothing to them, right?"

"I don't know why she would want to do something like this," Conner responded, rather influenced by the gravity of the situation as he attempted to emanate some sense of calm.

"But Rubidium and those black cloaks. We know Rubidium is a school for people to become soldiers under Vitina and Andromeda, right? Whoever attacked us could've been a part of that growing army of soldiers."

"Those two colors are used so no one knows it's them. Like I said before, to disguise themselves from authoritarian and civilian watch."

Vanessa watched as Conner's eyes widened with terror and apprehension.

"They were trying to kill us."

He quickly took her hands in his, noticing how soft and warm they were in his grasp.

Vanessa laid her right hand across her heart as if worried by how fast it was beating. She had done the same at the start of their conversation.

"I'm so sorry, Vanessa," Conner apologized, sorrow and regret mixing in the pools of his blue eyes. "I shouldn't ever have told you to come on this quest with me. It was selfish. And I should've known better before putting you in such danger. I'm so sorry I did this to you, Vanessa. You don't deserve to have to—"

"Conner, it's fine," she said, covering his hands with her own. "It's a wonderful gesture, y'know, but it's not your fault if something bad happens to me. I'm still my own person, making all my own decisions."

"Yeah, yeah," Conner murmured, looking sheepish and embarrassed at his unneeded outburst and her calm reaction in opposition. "I don't have to be blamed for everything."

"No, you don't." She smiled, hand still atop his.

She didn't bother moving, enjoying his warmth and his comforting words. The way he cared for her. The way he wasn't afraid to take fault.

She laid her hand on her heart again. "It's beating so fast," she voiced as if she hadn't even planned to state it aloud. But Conner seemed to have missed it, lost in his own thoughts.

"So, you know how much Vitina hated Ruler Marjorie, my grandmother. She's the reason Grandmother's dead. She must've found out I'm her grandson."

"So is she trying to kill you because you're related to her?" Vanessa let out a faint gasp of awareness. "What if she's planning to kill everyone related to important figures in power? Everyone who stands in her way?"

Without even realizing it, Vanessa was tensing up. Conner could die? All because of Vitina's stupid lust for power? All because she wanted the Magic Realm for herself?

"I wish I knew a way to stop her somehow, though," Conner said after a few moments. "Some way to stop the destruction that's inevitable at this point. The cities that'll be destroyed. The families broken apart. The lives lost." He looked down with a glint of shame in his eyes. "If only there was something I could do."

For the second time tonight, Vanessa wrapped her arms around him, this time a lot closer than before.

"You're such a wonderful person," she said, "and the things you say and the things you do…just go to show how amazing you are. Just like you said to me before. You're so kind and good-hearted. But the things you want to do, you simply *can't* do them…"

He looked her dead in the eyes, his gaze boring into her instead of the softness she usually saw in those hypnotic pools of blue.

"…alone," she continued.

Then she smiled and took his hands in her own. "That's what friends do, right?"

Her eyes were gazing into his and he couldn't help but smile at the sight, his hands enveloped in the warmth of hers.

She had called him a friend again though! Just a friend!

He looked contemplative, maybe mulling over her *friend* statement.

But even so, even with these romantic feelings bubbling within him, just being here, being here with her, just knowing she cared so much about him…he looked to be on cloud nine.

His eyes said that he wanted to enjoy these moments with her.

Enjoy them for as long as he possibly could.

She bid him goodnight. He made his way to his own bed and changed into his nightclothes, having spent such a long time with Vanessa.

"She's so beautiful and kind and always knows what to say. She's amazing," he whispered to himself as he nestled into bed.

"Maybe," Vanessa was saying to herself at that moment too. "Maybe I might see Conner as…a bit more than a friend."

Chapter 13
A Failed First Date

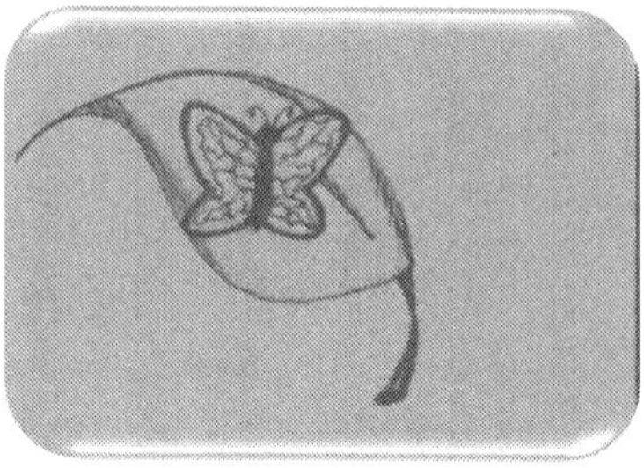

"**WHY ARE YOU BELIEVING** his crazy story?" yawned Aria, rubbing sleep from her eyes. "He was probably just describing some stupid dream."

"But Aria, I actually saw them. With my own two eyes," Vanessa puffed. "And if I heard something like that from Conner, I probably wouldn't have believed it either. Based on how crazy and ridiculous the whole thing was."

In the darkness of the 4:00 a.m. moon, Aria and Vanessa talked, in fact the first time they had ever spoken to each other one on one.

They sat at the dining table, taking bites of the turkey sandwiches Aria had conjured up and placed in an a more ornate manner than the situation warranted.

"Okay then," Aria harrumphed. "If I believe what you're saying about this 'mysterious figure', will you at least tell the rest of us when things like this happen?

"I don't want two of our friends getting hurt or worse because they thought they could handle some murderous psycho all on their own."

"Yeah, yeah," she sighed, obviously not lacking in the lecture department. "I get it."

After growing up in a castle where officials didn't take her seriously as the non-blood-related heiress to the Magic Kingdom throne, she had heard one too many lectures about safety. Especially when it came to those who found themselves far more befitting of the throne wanting to take her place.

"Despite how nice it is here in this castle, with all these guards and stuff," her brother would remind her, "there are some real crazies, you got that? Hold your place against them, but if they get really bad, get out of there immediately. They disguise themselves behind their brilliant work ethic and skills, but some have few to no morals whatsoever, sis."

She would take those words to heart as a child, acting jumpy every time somebody from the castle outside of most of the Council and her family called her name.

Luckily though, she had never had to deal with such a thing happening to her, but lectures were still never out of the question—and usually on the agenda—during familial meetings.

"But can I trust you to convince everyone else about what happened? 'Cause Conner and I were able to come up with an idea that we think might be beneficial to us later on."

Aria leaned in, ready to listen to this newfound beneficial information.

"Oh no," said Vanessa now. "I'll tell everyone in the morning. I'm feeling a bit foggy right now actually."

"Well then…" Aria sighed, and an idea went off in her head. "Oh! Could I ask you a question?"

"Yeah, shoot."

"All right, don't tell Conner I asked you this, but—"

"Are you gonna say something bad about him? 'Cause if that's the path this conversation is taking, I'll gladly go back to—"

"No, I wouldn't do that. Well, not around you." Vanessa's frown became noticeably prominent. "But do you happen to like anyone? Like right now?"

"Like anyone?" Vanessa screeched, voice cracking as her cheeks blushed scarlet despite her brain fighting that they wouldn't. "We don't have time for this type of crap, Aria. We've got a potion to make and a girl to save."

"Yeah, of course. I know that, but I'm simply asking because they wanna know if you reciprocate their feelings?"

With the peculiarity of this conversation and the questions being asked, Vanessa was inclined to somewhat believe whoever this mysterious 'person' was, had a likelihood of being her, but she wouldn't ask those types of questions before getting all the details.

"Well, do you happen to know who this 'person' is?" It seemed she was hoping Aria would pick up on the message she was trying to convey.

"Yes, but I won't tell you who it is for fear of embarrassing them."

"Can I at least get a hint then?"

"Okay, I'll give you one, but then you have to answer my question."

Vanessa nodded quickly, leaning forward as she said, "Okay, I get it. The hint?"

"This person, name and gender unknown, has liked you for quite some time. They've seen you only around one location and they care about you quite a lot. They're a tad bit insecure about this crush and how you feel about them, but they do enjoy the little things you do for them. Of course, this doesn't count as a hint 'cause that could be really anyone.

"The true hint is…"

She observed as Vanessa's soft features contorted into an expression of inquisitiveness. "…this person is here right now."

"Here right now? Like in this van?"

Aria gave her a single nod, a look of pure superiority on her features, happy to act as the big sister in this situation.

"So, is it Darius or Conner?"

"I can only give you one hint."

"But it's a boy?"

"I told you, the gender is unknown."

"So, they're not a boy then?"

"I cannot disclose any more information."

"Well fine," Vanessa harrumphed, seeming rather proud with herself rather than upset, rising from her side of the table. "I'm pretty sure I figured out who it is anyways. It is pretty obvious, after all."

Aria looked a little confused. And bewildered, likely thinking that Vanessa no way could've figured it out on so few clues.

Not unless she'd grossly underestimated her. Maybe she dealt with this type of stuff all the time? "Wait!" Aria whispered, stopping her at the entrance to the sitting room. "You never answered my question, even though I answered yours."

"Oh, that."

She turned to Aria, the hint of an impish grin on her face as she said, "I do happen to 'like' someone as you call it. Not an extreme amount, but enough that I would consider it to be a crush. Now, about who it is—"

"I already know who it is," Aria interrupted, an arrogant expression on her face as she walked off.

The color drained from Vanessa's face, her secret she thought to be well-kept exposed. "But I didn't even—"

"No need. I mean, it's so obvious!"

Frustrated, Vanessa made her way back to the couch as Aria settled into bed. She examined the window for a few seconds before closing her eyes, some residual apprehension left in her racing mind after the earlier incident.

As her eyes closed, the worry subsided, allowing her some much-deserved rest.

Yet it was evident her mind continued to race through *Rubidium... Black cloaks.. Golden wands... Elemental Spells…*

But, as she was unnoticeably whisked off to the void of darkness that was sleep, her body stayed restless and fitful, over-active thoughts inevitably invading her dreams.

Her flailing, restless body that tossed and turned in bed betrayed how these thoughts were only adding onto the earlier worries far more than she could have consciously imagined.

Throughout the brisk early morning, Conner too struggled to rest.

He too was tossing and turning in his mint green sheets, and eventually giving in to watching the moonlight fade away bit by bit as the sun slowly cut through the dark.

He desperately needed to sleep as he watched the sun rising in the sky, but sleep just showed no interest in him in return. The clock ticked on, the night's cloudy sky giving way to birdsong, and the darkness making space for the inevitable dawn.

At some point, however, faint snores gave away the fact that he too was finally being whisked off to a land of dreams, similar to Vanessa.

He too slept restlessly, however, his dreams no doubt filled with the events causing so much anxiety in Conner before, events that intruded into his dreams against his will.

It would appear he had no gateway out of the hellish reality his mind had created for him.

***

"Oh God, oh God, oh God," Vanessa whispered to herself, pacing the sitting room.

"Vanessa?" Conner stretched as he rose from bed, eyebrows turned down as he watched her pace back and forth. "Are you all right?"

"Oh," she acknowledged blankly, left abashed at her failure to recognize him as she folded her blanket. "Nothing—nothing. I'm fine. Really."

Conner looked from her to the window, the sunlight peeking through the fabrics of the curtains as its warmth bathed the carpet that lay before the couch.

And as Conner was paying attention to the way dust particles danced while Vanessa was opening the curtains, she quickly strode off to the bathroom, a ball of clothes in her hand. Poor Conner was left perplexed by her sudden disappearance.

"Aria, do you happen to know why Vanessa's acting so weird?" Conner interrogated her, his tone rather accusing from Aria's perspective, as Conner made his way to the dining table.

She was filling a pot with water from the sink, her nightwear indicating she had probably just woken too, although quite contradictory to the things she had already done in the kitchen.

"I might have an idea, a teensy, small, really meaningless i—"

"What did you do!" Conner grumbled. "Did you tell her? I thought I told you that I wouldn't be—"

She could sense the exasperation in his words as he spoke, and went on to declare, "Don't worry about it, okay? It isn't anything crazy and no, I didn't tell her."

"That barely answers my question," Conner sighed deeply. "Anyways, why are you filling that pot with water?"

"I was planning to hunt for dinner this time around. Or me and Darius specifically."

"But I never said I knew how to hunt though," Darius admitted defensively from the driver's seat.

"But it's pretty simple, Darius. Just stab stuff with pointy objects. And try to aim for the neck so it dies instantly."

Darius looked warily from the overhead mirror to the road once more, the hovering cars passing by at speed, Conner's eyes wide at the unexpected sight of them all hurtling past.

They must've been on the roads between kingdoms, as the interllor citizens would refer to it, although neither twin had ever been on these roads in their years living in this dimension.

"Guess it can't be that bad then," Darius said, admitting defeat after his short and rather one-sided argument for his part.

"So where are we?" Conner questioned, hands pressed against the window, awkwardly struggling to balance his weight on the footboard between Cassie and Katie's beds.

"The interllor connecting the Magic Kingdom and the Land of Elves," Darius said after a quick glance at the navigation map on his phone. "We've been on the road while you've been sleeping, so now we're headed toward the Summerlands in the Land of Elves."

Rather peculiarly, Aria set a map of the Magic Realm down on the dining table.

Conner, for a second, looked stunned; how had she retrieved the object so fast?

But he never said a word.

"We're in the northwest corner of the Land of Elves, the Autumnlands.

"And, since every sector of the Land of Elves endures different seasons year-round, it's pure autumn where we are."

She turned back to the map, using a pen as a pointer to indicate the kingdom about which she was talking. "In the northeast corner is the winter portion of the Land of Elves, the Snowlands, the place we'll be heading tomorrow. And in the southwest corner is the Springlands, and finally, the summer of the kingdom is in the southeast corner, the Summerlands, where, like Darius said, we're heading right now."

The grasses of the countryside became gradually more faded as they made their way down sleek metallic roads with towering red, orange, and yellow oak and maple trees, liberated from the weight of their multi-colored leaves.

Yet as the road encroached on the autumn wood, very few magic cell towers stood, and even those that did barely hit one hundred feet, barely considered adequate.

"Those cell towers," Conner pointed out. "They don't seem too tall." He turned to his sister, who was intently scanning the map at the dining table. "Sure they'll be able to do the job for us out here?"

"Oh, likely not," Darius answered for Aria. "That's the thing about places like this deep in the forest. The magic cell towers aren't top priority around these parts, so we'll just have to rely on attack and defense spells for the time being. That and Elemental ones of course."

"So, for dinner," Aria spoke up, "I was thinking rabbit and then maybe something else, like fish or something." She quickly folded up the map and shoved it in her pocket.

"If you actually manage to kill it," Conner said as he mounted off of the footboard. "You couldn't even hold Grandma's staff without dropping it in the next twenty seconds."

"Yeah, that," she sighed. It appeared that as the time passed, Grandma's death was getting harder on her, even though it was steadily becoming easier for her twin.

She was supposed to be the older, more mature twin.

The one who knew how to handle situations. How to handle grief.

She couldn't let Conner take her place as the one for whom her parents held high expectations. As the one they used as an example.

Grandma seemed to be the only person who understood how much these expectations weighed on her.

The only person she could truly talk to about this without feeling judged or pitied.

She didn't have the energy to come up with a remark aimed at Conner as she usually did, and with a worried look, he went back to gazing out the window

After several moments of eerie silence, the sound of sloshing water and the flow of the tap reverberated in the kitchen, and Conner walked up behind Aria quietly.

"You okay?" His words were calm, soft, unlike the way he usually spoke to her, or really anyone for that matter.

"Yeah, of course," she breathed, smiling at him as she set another pot of water on the counter. "Thanks for asking."

She couldn't make him worry. She wasn't allowed to make him worried.

"But um—" she said, clearly floundering for a topic she could use to change the subject. "Last night, after you and Vanessa fought off that shadowy figure…"

"How'd you know that!" Conner piped up, his tone back to the way it usually was.

"Well, Vanessa told me last night," she answered dismissively as Conner's voice rose.

"WHAT DID SHE SAY!" he chirped, so loud that he could hear Katie and Cassie stirring from their lengthy rest, indicating he had been far too noisy.

"Calm down, okay?" She turned to face him. "I made a deal with her that if she told me whether or not *she* liked anyone, I'd give her a hint about who liked her."

"Does—"

"And," she said, indicating to Conner that it was high time he shut up and simply listened, "I'm not sure."

She stood still, head tilted to one side, obviously pondering the conversation they'd had for a few seconds, replaying certain events in her head.

Probably, Aria's mind would be replaying the way Vanessa looked at her, the way she'd looked at Vanessa herself, tones of voice.

She would be picking apart and analyzing every part of their discussion.

She gasped and an extreme blush built on her face with the realization.

"I—perhaps, though probably not, but maybe I did, but maybe I didn't."

"What the hell did you do, sis!"

"I…" She lowered her voice as she felt herself simmering in the embarrassment, boiling in it. "…might have made it seem like *I* like her."

Conner slumped against the wall, a dead and cloudy look in his eyes as he fell to the floor.

He looked to her as a door rattled in the background; no one paid it any attention though it was probably the same girl he was worrying about right now! "And does she like you?"

Aria lifted Conner up by the armpits without opposition, something that seemed very unusual based on past experiences of him fighting back whenever she laid a hand on him.

"Probably not. In all honesty, I think I like someone else anyways. And…"

She breathed deeply and backed away in preparation for his inevitable outburst. "…she probably likes you."

Conner let out a smile, a sincere, heartfelt smile that made Aria visibly reel.

"Thank you, Aria. Genuinely, thanks…for saying that, I mean."

"Oh and…" Conner looked back at her smugly as he was about to leave, a sly grin on his face that Aria couldn't help but be happy was back. "…I think I know who you like."

Aria's smile dissipated.

"Remember the night we fought those wolves, right? And when Cassie almost left?"

She would have asked him how he knew, but to ask Conner such a question when Katie was already stirring into consciousness was out of the question. Of course, Katie had been the one who'd informed her about the possibility of something like that happening.

She wouldn't be telling Katie that her worst fear had come true without her own notice.

And so, after a moment, Aria responded, "Yeah, I do."

"I know you left to make her come back. To stop her from leaving us to go save Avery." He sighed as he started walking away, allowing his words to just fall from his lips so slightly and softly, it was difficult for Aria to hear.

"I know how much you care for her, Aria."

And with that, he left, a discombobulated and embarrassed Aria standing in his wake, just as Cassie rubbed the sleep from her eyes to see her.

Cassie gazed at the blank stare on Aria's face. "What's wrong Aria; you okay?"

Aria stopped at the sight of her, hair in disarray and streaks of discolored skin on her cheeks. Anyone who had been asleep would've assumed she'd been crying when she left dinner last night. Aria looked crestfallen that she had not noticed, not consoled her.

"Aria?"

Without a word, Aria ran from the kitchen to the living room. "Aria!" she hissed. A heavy blush of embarrassment colored her peach-white cheeks. "How could you let him get to you like that? Stupid girl! Of course, you don't…"

She looked at Cassie who was staring at her bewildered.

She felt the corners of her mouth upturn in a smile.

Oh no.

***

"The date," Conner gasped, as the realization appeared to hit him. "The date. My date. With Vanessa. Oh God, how'd I forget? That's why she was pacing around this morning."

"It's fine. It's fine!" he said under his breath, pacing. "It's your first ever date, but she'll enjoy you as just you. You won't ruin your chance with her. It'll be fine. Just calm down, Conner. And it *is* just a friend date, isn't it? That's what she said, right?

Yet as Conner struggled to organize his thoughts, Aria began examining the cabinets, coming across a pack of gleaming knives, oven mitts, and a variety of other staple items all lovingly conjured in the creation of the van.

As Conner stood awkwardly in the middle center of the living room, he eyed Darius from the driving seat, his deep brown eyes boring into Conner's as they twinkled with worry.

And so, Conner, uncertain of this stranger with whom he had become stuck, sat in the passenger seat, buckling in his seatbelt as he watched the gravel of the road pass.

It was calming, relaxing, and his worry melted away as his eyes stayed on the blurs of the road and the sway of the grass as they passed.

"I can see you're pretty nervous, huh?" Darius acknowledged, keeping his eyes straight on the path.

Conner took notice of his tone of voice; it was not deep or stern in the way one would possibly expect from such a burly looking man. But in fact, there was a certain worry, even anxiousness one would say, to his words. And his voice was much higher than expected.

Conner looked to him, then wiped the sweat building up on his forehead and slumped into the cool leather of the seat. "How'd ya guess?"

"You've been sweating like crazy all morning. And you barely talked to Vanessa."

"So, do you know her?" he questioned. "Are you in any classes with her?"

"No, I don't think so. But I do see her sometimes on the routes to some of my classes." He stopped speaking for a moment.

"I do remember that there was this one time when I dropped some of my things in the hallway, and she helped me pick them up. She talked to me afterwards, saying something about how she was always lonely at lunch and was hoping to make some new friends during our first year at the school."

"Did you go to lunch with her that day?"

"Yeah, and she was fun to talk to, in fact," he answered, smiling as he reminisced. "We bonded over having trouble making friends and later, found out that we had the last classes of the day after lunch together in our first year."

"So, what I'm collecting from this story is that you've met her before, but now you guys are friends on occasion?"

"Well, not really, but kinda, I guess." Darius glanced at Conner, then back to the road. "She's always surrounded by people asking if she wants to meet up on the weekends to hang out anyways."

"So, she's popular around school? Y'know, I'm not surprised at all, truly."

"Not really sure she enjoys all the attention she gets though. Whenever I see her, it's like she's uncomfortable and her smile… her smile is nothing like it used to be when she was younger. It looks fake. Fabricated. Like it's a new one she created to make other people feel better even when *she* isn't feeling too good."

He sighed, changing the topic quickly before Conner could ask any more questions.

"So, why were you so afraid to talk to your sibling about this? After all, she seems like she would understand, right?"

"Yeah, Aria's nice and all about this stuff. But I don't think the problem is her. I think it's…" He let out a heavy breath. "…me."

Darius' expression showed familiarity with the situation, with being made to feel as if *he* was the one doing wrong. Feeling he was the one who had messed up somehow was familiar to him. And it was a feeling of familiarity which he didn't like.

"I just don't like to talk about this type of stuff with people. It makes me feel like I'm susceptible to heartbreak. And I know how bad it is. I've seen it in my sister with platonic relationships, but I have zero experience myself of how awful romantic heartbreak can be. And the thing is, I'm afraid I won't be able to handle it that well."

"Well, Conner. Here's what one of my siblings taught me to do."

He fixed his mirror so that it was facing Conner, his crystal-like eyes shimmering in the sunlight as he gazed at the reflection of himself.

"Look yourself in the mirror, and ask, 'This thing I'm worrying about, this thing that I'm doing right now—would I have been able to do this before? Would I have been able to do this, say, a month ago?'"

He chuckled, and went on, "When I was a kid, I always thought doing this was kinda stupid. 'Cause, I mean, I thought it made me look like a crazy person. But as I grew up, and my anxiety continued to get worse, I started listening to my siblings' advice. Because, maybe they were right, and maybe, somehow, doing this would help me."

"And so," he took a glimpse of Conner, who peered back at him and nodded, "since this was able to help me, maybe it'll help you."

Conner shrugged as if questioning the efficacy of this method, but he didn't question it; Darius had already managed to surprise him before.

So, why not now?

He repeated the questions Darius had posed. But now, as he replayed them in his mind, he projected the questions as a new voice. "Conner," the voice said as if aloud.

The voice was softer, foreign, and sounded nothing like himself. It was like someone else was speaking to him. Someone pervading his thoughts.

It was a strange voice, yet one with which he appeared familiar.

"Conner," the voice said again. "Do you think you would've been able to do this? Asking this girl out on a date a month ago? Do you think you would've given yourself the chance to, let alone asked?"

Conner looked pensive, pondering on all of it, studying the question for a few moments as if someone had asked it of him aloud.

Eventually, he answered, "No. I don't think I would've been able to."

"And so? Don't you think that you deserve to feel at least a bit proud of yourself for this? At least a bit accomplished?"

"I do," Conner responded to the voice now brought forth from inside his own head.

"Conner?" Darius inquired, interrupting Conner's internal conversation with the peculiar voice. "Did it work?"

"Oh, yeah. Your advice." His lips upturned into a smile as soon as the words left his lips, and he unbuckled his seatbelt as he rose from the passenger's seat. "It did."

He set his hand on the shoulder of the passenger seat as he leaned over and thanked Darius for his sage words, spoken at just the right moment.

"Thanks for the advice, Darius. It really helped, and I see why my sister was able to become fast friends with you."

Darius beamed at Conner's words as he ambled off, for he was always the one saying 'thank you' for things. Yet, being the one who provided the thing worth saying 'thank you' for, being the one who could finally say 'you're welcome', was so amazing that his smile was broad and beaming and steeped in joy. Clearly, it felt incredible.

For now, he seemed to be coming to the realization that it was Conner who was changing *his* perspective on things.

The one giving him the opportunity to look at things from the view of the giver.

And he was rather enjoying it.

***

"You were in the shower for a while, weren't you, huh?" Aria asked Vanessa, glancing from her own reflection to Vanessa's as she set about tying her silky brown hair back into a small ponytail, most of her hair falling toward her lower back.

"Most of it was just me pacing around in the bathroom, or really just simmering in my own embarrassment in the shower if I'm truly being honest."

"You worried?"

"A lot actually," Vanessa said, obviously perturbed, lips turned down in a grimace as she spoke. "Because I'm worried that…" She sighed and looked away, pulling out her hair tie to do her hair for the third time in a row. "…oh, never mind."

"Worried about what?" there was a certain sincerity in Aria's voice that didn't leave Vanessa completely shocked, but she looked a bit surprised. She rarely ever spoke to—well—anyone this way. It was a new way of seeing her that Aria hadn't thought about until now. And, getting to know her better was, if not completely, at least a bit gratifying.

"Well, you see, I'm worried about if I'm gonna mess this up.

"Like I've done before with some of my other friends. Every time I see them, that must be what's on their mind—at least, that's what I think."

As soon as she spoke, Aria took Vanessa's hair tie into her own hands, taking a brush from the counter and beginning to do the task Vanessa seemed to have been struggling with.

"Go on."

As the steam from the shower started to subside, Vanessa talked, volume wavering as she spoke, and emotions fluctuated. And Aria simply went on styling her hair as she listened, letting her speak without interruption.

After Vanessa had finished, Aria, after several minutes of staying silent, reassured her.

"Well, here's something I learned when I used to go to school."

She set down the brush she was using and used her fingers to comb through Vanessa's locks, making sure to remove all possible knots from her hair as she continued.

"When I first started hanging out with people—without the company of my brother, might I add—I was always nervous. Nervous they were judging me, somehow, in some way, and that, secretly, even if they never showed it, a part of them didn't like me.

"It made me feel anxious about myself most of the time, and self-conscious about everything I said and did about them. It would keep me up late at night, replaying the events of the day, running through what I felt I not only could've done better, but had done badly."

She switched out the comb for another brush.

"But one day, after I had first started living here with my brother, I came to a realization. All this worry that I was doing, it revolved around them, the people who made me question myself extremely. Even if I thought they were good people at the time, as I reminisced on memories with them, I realized that they weren't as good a set of friends as I thought."

She set the brush down, examining what she'd done with Vanessa's hair as she said in conclusion, "And that they were the reason I kept feeling so self-conscious about myself.

"'Cause once I separated myself from them, I was much happier. Much happier with myself and around the people who I knew for a fact cared about me. Like my brother and Cassie, and Katie and…" She made her way to Vanessa's right side. "…you."

She smiled, a beam so bright that Vanessa couldn't help but smile back at Aria as she was setting her hand on the doorknob to the bathroom.

"Although I can't be exactly sure if this advice would help you in this situation. But, if you need to talk to someone about this, remember I'm always here, okay?"

And she left.

***

"And we've arrived," Darius said calmly, unbuckling his seat belt as he stretched and rose from his seat.

He stood with his hands in the pockets of his white breeches, which—apparently—were to his liking, baggier than in the description. He had felt tempted, he said, to put on a sweatshirt over his black polo, but eventually, after some internal debate, agreed with himself that outside it was much too hot to do that.

Despite that, he did tie one of his summer sweaters around his waist just to make sure.

As he walked toward the living room, he caught sight of Conner nervously fiddling with his dirty blonde hair in the mirror to no avail; his eyebrows downturned as he frowned at each new style he produced.

Darius knocked on the door to the bathroom but was met with silence.

Well, anyways, Conner had shown him he needed to solve his problem on his own, meaning Darius could only rely on the efficiency of his own advice, despite how miniscule it may previously have seemed—and still seemed in his eyes.

Eventually, Darius was speaking nonchalantly to Aria and Cassie, taking notice of the way Aria would mind her words in a way she never had before.

Especially when she would speak to her brother.

She would brush her own hair out of her face in a peculiar way and found it oddly easy to laugh at the jokes that Cassie would tell, even when Darius didn't find them all that funny.

Conner knocked on the door frame of the entrance to the sitting room and grinned, rather awkwardly, but charming nonetheless.

"Hey, Vanessa. You ready for our date?"

"Our friend date?" Vanessa stood happily, a grass-woven basket in her grasp as she walked toward Conner.

She briefly looked back at Aria, then to Conner, and gulped briefly. "Definitely."

Conner's face was red, a flush that had come over him as soon as Vanessa reiterated the dreaded words: *friend date.*

No, not just date. *Friend* date.

His face crumpled each time someone said that term now, unable to hide his displeasure.

They made their way to the trailer door beside one another, Conner still appearing in a bad mood—or at least downcast and not very chatty.

Vanessa beamed at him as they strolled as if nothing had changed between them at all. Or if she had noticed the change in his mood, she was good at covering up.

She cast him a warm, genuine smile, and he visibly relaxed, his shoulders losing their tension. How could he not be grateful for how amazing these circumstances were? Even if it wasn't a romantic date, it was still a moment with her, even if just between friends.

Katie watched as Cassie bid Aria goodbye. Aria walked off with Darius and, watching the clearing intently, they searched for any sign of movement.

"Cassie?" Katie said, pulling her own wand from her bag, shoving it in her sister's face to indicate her objective. "What d'ya say?"

"Well, I don't know…" Cassie looked from the clearing to the jubilant twinkle in her younger sister's eyes, to the glint of her wand in the bright sun. "Okay, sure. Let's do it."

And as soon as those words left her lips, her sister had already gathered everything they'd need, shoving her out the trailer door in a not-so-elegant way.

"All right then," Katie announced, cradling the open spell book in her hand as she raised her wand to the sky. "Let's start with something easy."

She glanced back at the pages, then to her sister.

"How about a light spell?"

"Lux exponentia!" she cast, watching as the light from her wand built above her, expanding to a size suitable enough to use as a sort of magical flashlight.

"Lux exponentia," Cassie repeated, yet instead of raising her wand like Katie had done, she drew a circle as soon as she had cast the spell.

She was probably hoping this unconventional action would result in an unfamiliar result.

"Oh my God!" Katie exclaimed, astonished as she observed the light her sister had created, extending her arm to—

"Wait!" Cassie stopped, backing away just as Katie was grazing the particles of light from the spell. "What if I do this?" She tapped the center of the circle with the tip of her wand, noticing it would stay in place, watching as light began to bleed into the center.

It was filling the circle with golden light. "What does the book say about the circular movement of wands to perform spells?"

"Give me a sec…" said Katie.

Katie began flipping through the pages, so swiftly that it seemed as though she hadn't even had the opportunity to see their content. "It says here that creating a circle with the light from the spell can increase the circles' strength, which is why the light from your wand managed to shine brighter than that from mine."

"Weird…" Cassie moved her to the other side of her, watching as the circle of light stayed in its place the same as before. "What if I just—" She chopped her arm through the center of the circle, watching as it disappeared as fast as it had shown up.

"Well, why don't you try another, Cass? Maybe an attacking spell this time."

"Incantation?"

"It says here it's Impetum," Katie said, squinting as she read the text.

"Impetum exponentia!" she said, moving her wand in a circular motion as she watched the light begin to build at the tip. With a circle of light created, she tapped the center of it with her wand, watching as it filled with golden light.

Particles of Resicus from the spell were seemingly evaporating into thin air.

She aimed her wand at a nearby pine tree, ushering her sister out of the way by nudging her head at her, thrusting her arm forward and sending the golden disc of light at the tree.

It left a gaping hole in the trunk as steam whisked into the air from either side.

Cassie shrugged. "Seems the same to—"

Interrupting her external thought, the disc of light returned to the tip of her wand, the way a boomerang would return to the hands of the one who threw it.

She watched as it levitated in the air in front of her, eventually whirlpooling back into her wand like the flow of water down a drain.

"What'd it do to my wand?" She inspected the nib of the crystal, noticing nothing strange or odd about it, and pointed it at the same tree once more.

Without an incantation, the disc of light had magically reappeared, and frisbeed across the clearing as it sliced off a side of the already inflicted-upon tree trunk.

"Well then," Katie said, rather obviously if Cassie were to take notice of anything. "I guess it did do something, huh?"

"So, the spell can be performed with just a whisk of my wand?"

"Well, that's what it seems like." She gazed back at the thick spell book, eyes glinting with delight as she scoured the pages once more. "Seems that circular spells really do make the original spell more powerful."

She raised her wand to another tree surrounding the clearing, the bark peeling from the trunk, as if wilting away at the thought of her spell casting.

"Now it's my turn!" she beamed.

***

"Glasswings, glasswings, glasswings…" Vanessa mumbled to herself. "Oh, where are those infernal things?"

"Here, found one!" Conner cheered from afar, setting an unmoving butterfly into their basket. The creature, black and white striped on its thorax and split black and white down the middle of its abdomen, had primarily clear wings.

The wings' borders were painted with streaks of orange, black, and white, colors so bold and vibrant that Vanessa couldn't help but gaze at them.

"So that's one," she said, getting back to her tree examinations. "Just forty-nine to go."

After a few more moments of useless sifting through the wood, Vanessa concluded, "Y'know, Conner, it's only been twenty minutes. So, why don't we split up, okay? And I'll meet you back here in an hour."

Her words stung as he comprehended them, especially based on the fact this was a date of sorts. But he obliged and reluctantly nodded. "See you in an hour."

As she searched, Vanessa was plainly struggling to take her mind off of what had happened. How she'd ended up ruining her own date for both herself and Conner.

"There's no way it can be that much of a problem, right?" she asked herself. "I mean, it seemed like he didn't mind that much. But maybe he did? I did this to myself, didn't I? But maybe it's his fault. No, Vanessa, are you crazy! Of course, it's not Conner's fault. All he wanted to do was to ask me out, which is completely normal and completely fine!

"And, well, sorta inconvenient to be honest."

She stopped herself. "But that doesn't mean that he caused this. Or maybe he doesn't even care. The only person I can really blame, if I'm going to be honest, is me. And I caused more of a problem for Conner than I truly did for myself…"

"Anyways though," she said, shaking the current worries from her mind. "I need to find these things faster. Maybe I could use a spell or something…" She glanced at the wand in her pocket, taking a glimpse of the twinkle of a gemstone on her wrist.

She raised her right arm to her face, smiling as she realized. "Yeah, my Nature professor gave me this charm."

On her wrist was a single piece of black string melded to a lapis lazuli, the blue gem twinkling as she moved beneath the patches of sunlight in the towering trees.

He said a person could only activate these nature charms when the wearer uttered a phrase special to them. Using that phrase, you could activate any magical charm to your own use.

"So, what's mine again? It had something to do with one of my pets as a kid. And it began with an 'A', I think. An 'A', then it was an 'L', then a 'B'? At least, I'm sure that's it. Albi—albio—albino—Albion! Albion! My castle bird that I had as a kid! I remember him!"

She carried on mumbling to herself like some crazy woman.

"Albion," she cast, tapping her wand to the gemstone on her arm.

As the words left her lips, the lapis lazuli glowed brilliantly. 'After it glows, you must say what you want the charm to do,' spoke her professor's voice.

"Track glasswing butterflies," she said, keeping her words as clear as possible as she spoke into the gem.

From the gem, Vanessa watched as a circular screen of light blue arose. Then dots of gold and a single black dot appeared on the screen.

"So, if I'm the black dot in the center, that means that those dots of gold must be the butterflies. Huh, there are a lot more than I'd expected."

She followed a path to the gold one nearest her, finding a single butterfly hidden beneath a patch of grass once the black dot was close enough to one of the gold ones.

"If I keep following this," she smiled, following another path to a gold dot, "then I should be able to find twenty in no time!"

And so, as she discovered glasswing butterflies hidden in the grass, in the bushes, on the crevices of tree branches, she showed excitement and gratitude for the charm, something for which she hadn't expected to thank her professor as much as she did now.

And by the time the hour was up, she returned to the clearing where she'd last seen Conner, seating herself on the grass as she waited for him to show up.

As the time passed though, there was a temptation to use her gemstone to track him. It had already been more than twenty minutes, so where could he be?

"Where were you?" she questioned as soon as she saw him.

Her voice sounded impatient and frustrated, even if she was trying not to allow it to.

"It was just—I got lost looking for the clearing. I was thinking I could take this one path and ended up taking another and—well—yeah." He looked away from her, clearly avoiding the way her deep eyes were boring into him as they began walking toward the trailer.

Without a word, he placed the ten glasswings he'd found into the basket, finding them barely able to fit in comparison to the number that she had managed to collect.

He couldn't help but feel ashamed, not because of how well she had performed, but how he had managed to upset her. He felt guilty, even if he hadn't intended for this to happen.

But as he looked at her, the emotionless stare on her face—compared to the smile she usually had when she was around him—it stung.

Stung a lot more than he would've liked it to.

Vanessa tried to ask him a question to somehow lighten the mood, but everything felt too uncomfortable, so extremely stiff that even small talk wouldn't work.

And so, she didn't bother.

And with this, they kept their eyes permanently focused on the path before them, without even a single glance in the other's direction as they traveled, the birds of the forest chirping in the background as the cicadas sang their symphony.

"Just get back to the trailer with no problems. Everything is completely fine, okay?" Vanessa murmured, struggling to convince herself of something she knew wasn't true.

"Once we get back, you'll be fine. It wasn't that bad, y'know?"

Conner also was quiet but seemed positive enough.

Despite that, their miserable faces showed this date had been a complete and utter failure.

Chapter 14
The Magic River

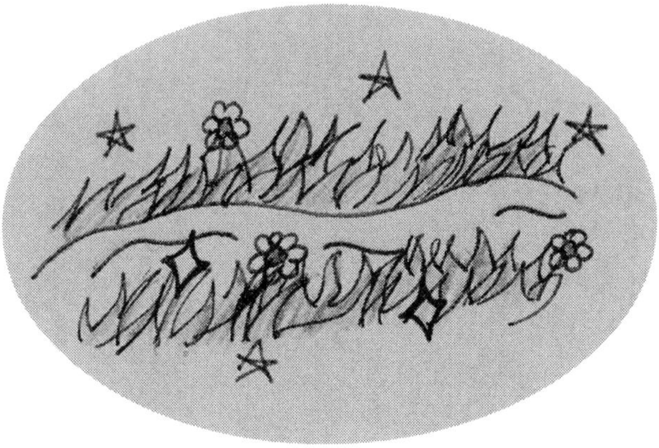

"**HOW DO YOU PLAN** we start hunting? 'Cause, I met up with Vanessa in the afternoon and found out that she'd used a bracelet charm to find the things she was looking for. One from her class apparently. Do you have one? We could probably use it."

"Well, yes, but do you have a minute."

She stopped for a moment, seeming rather perplexed, but overall agreed. "Yeah—sure."

He led her toward a path of short, vibrant green grass.

Guarding the path up ahead, two banyan trees on the left and right side of the footway towered over them, their branches intertwining to create something similar to a colossal tree with a double-rooted foundation The path on which they walked stretched on for miles, to a point where both were struggling to see the end.

"So, why'd you want to bring me here?" Aria questioned. "It's not like there'll be anything to hunt over here."

"Aria, just listen," he interrupted, eyes glaring at her as she quickly silenced at his stare. "Listen, Aria. I understand where you're coming from with this. I understand why you feel so responsible for everything. But today, for at least a little bit, I want you to take a moment to relax. So, you don't have to stress over your responsibilities for at least a little while, okay? 'Cause, I mean, don't you think you at least deserve that?"

She paused, and, with a slight smile, nodded. "Yeah, I do."

"And with relaxing, you see, comes conversation. So, to start off, who's your best friend?"

"My best friend?"

She glanced at the banyan tree to her right side, her brain starting to collect memories as she started to reminisce. "I have a best friend—or at least, I think I do. Well, if I'm being honest, I think I should be saying that I used to have a best friend. Heather."

"Heather?" Darius inquired.

"Yes. We'd do everything together. I'd go on vacations with her family, and she would come on vacations with mine. We'd take the train with each other every day when we were going to school, and even used to have a band—well, I should call it a duo."

She sighed despondently.

"Although, despite how much fun we'd have together, when we left middle school, and turned fourteen, our friendship started to sort of wilt away. Shriveling up and dying like a dead flower, I like to say. We would talk less with each passing day, and it felt like she lived on a completely different side of the world, even though we went to the same high school."

'Then what happened?" Darius felt inclined to ask, yet he didn't. He let her continue.

"And toward the end of freshman year, I never saw her in the hall, never saw her at lunch, and even in our matching classes, she never even took a glance at me. And, even if I didn't know it at the time, it was the end of our friendship."

Darius stayed silent, witnessing Aria's wistful recollection of bittersweet memories.

"Then there was Sienna. She was a kind girl I'd met in my freshman year after Heather and I officially stopped being friends. She was always there for me, always stuck up for me.

We'd bond over our similarities and would always pair up whenever we had a project in our Home Economics cooking class."

"We were friends in freshman year, but when I was introduced to this dimension, it seemed so interesting, so exciting, like so much fun. As if it could open my eyes to a whole new world of possibilities and learning and…" She sighed. "…anyways. Sienna hated how I'd never tell her anything about where it was that I would disappear to for hours or even days on end. And because I knew it would be dangerous for her if she knew, I just told her that all friends kept secrets from each other."

"But once I said that, she left. Left me in the corridor, without even a 'goodbye'.

"And so, without a friend, I'd try to tell my mom, but she'd never believe me about this place. I would try to tell my dad who lived across the country, and he said I was crazy.

"So, because no one believed me, and I didn't think I had anything to stay on Earth for, I packed my bags, told them I was going to live with Grandma in San Francisco.

"I got on a bus with my brother. Yet, unbeknownst to them, Grandma, Ruler Marjorie, lived in the Magic Realm, a whole other dimension. When we got here, she said that we could stay at her place until we felt the need to go back home or just wanted to live somewhere else, as long as me and Conner stuck together."

"And so," Aria spoke, the words softly falling off her lips as she went on, her story coming to a close. "That was the end of my non-magical friends. My normal friends, my non-magical home." She gazed back at Darius; after she had been speaking for so long, she had expected him to become disinterested in her story, yet he was as intrigued as when she'd started. "And now I have one. Although it may not be a permanent one at this rate, I enjoy living here. A lot, in fact."

Darius looked forward solemnly and said, so soft it could qualify as a whisper, "Do you ever… Ever think you were the one responsible for your friendship ending? The one between you and Sienna, I mean?"

What type of answer was he expecting from her?

Was he hoping for just something to somewhat soothe his own guilt about his failed friendships, the ones he seemed to think he'd ruined?

It appeared he was passing on his twang of guilt to her and this was selfish and unfair to her, using her own emotions to feel better about himself.

"Most of the time, yeah," Aria admitted, although with the liberating of the truth about her own feelings, surely she should have had a delighted look in her eyes.

Yet, her blue eyes conveyed only melancholy, in a bittersweet expression.

"Well, how come?" Darius inquired. "Why do you feel responsible?"

"I didn't trust Sienna enough, and me simply saying that 'all friends hold secrets from each other' just felt like a shallow attempt at making myself feel better."

She took a deep sigh and continued, "True friends trust each other. They may not tell each other all their secrets, but at least the important ones. Because at the very least, I think I could've told her about this place instead of just dismissing her questions over and over again like she was bothering me.

"I should've expected our friendship to start ending the moment I began doing that."

"Do you really believe that?"

She glanced at him, then quickly back to the path. "Believe what?"

"That it's your fault? Because in that case, I think that the reason most of my friends left me once I started going to that fancy border school was because of me and my own actions."

"Wait," Aria interrupted. "The things that *I* did… The things that were a product of my own wrongdoings, those have nothing to do with you, okay? Because every case is different, y'know? I've already come to terms with what I did wrong, but you…"

She gazed at him, the light of the sun framing her face in an angelic sort of way. "…you following your own dreams doesn't mean you deserved for your bonds to break."

"Remember, Darius, I know the things I did were wrong, but my feelings about the event don't dictate yours. All right?" She lightly chuckled, turning back to the path again as they strolled along under the warmth of the afternoon sun. "Or maybe I'm just rambling."

"No. Thank you, Aria," Darius replied, and he spoke solemnly, contrasting with the way his lips upturned into a grin. "Genuinely."

Without another word, Aria walked off, examining the thick trunk of the banyan tree of which they had caught a glimpse back at the start of the path.

Setting her arm on a branch, she began to climb in a rather agile fashion considering she didn't usually do this sort of thing.

"How'd you know how to do that?" Darius asked, looking up from the base of the plant.

"When it was just me and Conner staying in the Animal Kingdom, before Cassie and Katie came along, then sometimes when I was bored, I'd climb trees to take in the view of the land. Especially the Crystilifier's castle since we lived so close to it."

She set her hand on another branch, raising her higher.

"I'd stay on the branches and sketch out drawings of the castle from my higher view. It was calm, and serene. I loved it."

"Well, if you're that good at climbing, could you help me out then?" he asked, legs flailing as he struggled to place his feet somewhere.

They worked together side by side, Aria teaching him her own way of scaling the branches. Yet even though the way she taught him seemed rather complicated for a beginner, Darius stuck it out, and so, at the very top, he was finally able to sit and relax.

So far above the ground, the forest below looked simply like a sea of green beneath them, Aria's long skirt blowing in the faint breeze as she set their empty basket on the branch.

They were silent for several minutes, relishing taking in the way the sun reflected on the lakes in the distance, illuminating the wood below.

"Amazing, isn't it?" she said, voice faint as she tried to speak over the wind's whistling.

"Yeah, it is," he agreed. "Oh, and I know this sounds stupid but, in a place called 'the Land of Elves'…" He chuckled awkwardly. "…where are the elves?"

"If I'm being honest, I'm not really sure. But I guess that they don't really inhabit the forests like they did years ago; they probably just live in the cities now. But do you have any idea where the ruler's castle is? I haven't seen the princess of the Land of Elves on the news in a long time."

"Evelyn Remona?"

Aria nodded. "Yeah, I haven't seen her in a while."

"Pretty sure she isn't a princess anymore. I think she turned twenty-one a few months back. But the thing is, even though her parents were killed in an attack over a decade ago, she still hasn't gotten over it. Which honestly, I wouldn't be surprised about."

"Y'know I still feel bad for her though, because as the ruler of an entire kingdom, she's got all this stuff to do all these citizens to take care of, but on top of that, she has no one to take solace in—or really just talk to."

"Well, at least her brother has monthly visits with her, so they get the opportunity to catch up with each other."

"I know, but monthly? You're saying she has to wait an entire four weeks before she can actually talk to someone?"

"You're right," Aria admitted. "That is a long time to wait for an opportunity to talk to someone. Especially considering that sometimes—more like oftentimes—her brother's schedule is too tight to visit her."

"Well, on another note," Darius said in an attempt to change the mood of the conversation. "What about Vanessa? How has she been doing as a princess?

"From what I know about her already from the times I've spoken to her, she doesn't talk about her royal status that much, so I don't have much to tell you."

She solemnly sighed. The silence between them would give her a moment to ponder about whether her going on would end up souring the atmosphere of the conversation once more. "But it really is a shame what happened to her brother Francis Caswell," she said at last.

"Y'know, I can still remember the news headline broadcasting during lunch that day. 'Prince Francis Caswell of the Kingdom of Magic, son to King Alistair and Queen Josephine Caswell, has mysteriously gone missing.'"

"'Mysteriously.' Pfft! Yeah, right! How am I supposed to believe that bullcrap? He was clearly kidnapped by one of Rubidium's guards and taken to their school, but no one wants to admit it. Everyone already knows about Vitina's inevitable return to power.

"But they're all too scared to actually do anything about it," Aria said.

"Yeah, I understand that," Darius argued back. "But how'd they manage to get past castle security? It's one of the strongest security systems in the entire world—if not *the* strongest."

"Well, I wouldn't know," Aria admitted. "But I do know that what happened must've been really hard. For both Evelyn and Vanessa. Losing the people who are important to you and having to pretend that everything's fine for the sake of everyone else. They're always worrying about other people but are never given the opportunity to worry about themselves.

"And because of that, I'm really happy that Vanessa was able to find Conner."

"Your brother? Why?" asked Darius. "It honestly seems like them being together just results in a lot of stress for them both."

"Perhaps it looks that way to you, but I feel like, with that, there's also the solace that they're able to find in one another. And not only that, but Vanessa found and met all of us."

"Yeah, you're right, Aria. I don't think Vanessa had the opportunity to have many true friends at home. With all her honors classes and extra studies, I'm assuming that she needed a well-deserved rest to finally get a moment to breathe." He smiled, his brown eyes captured in the light of the sun as he grinned. "I'm glad that we found her."

"You mean that we found each other?" Aria questioned, her lighthearted tone cutting through the stillness of the woodland.

"Yeah. That too."

***

"All right, let's get going," Aria directed, a sharpened stick held in her right hand as she gripped the basket with her left.

"Well, I'm hoping you sharpened me a spear."

"Yeah, here." She lent him a three-foot stick, its tip razor sharp. "Oh but be careful. Pretty sure that thing can pierce skin."

"You know—why do I even need a spear when I have my wand? I—I'll just use that," he chuckled apprehensively.

"No way. Using our wands will draw attention from whatever it is that lurks in this forest. The spears are our best bet. And you don't get the real hunting experience when you use a magical wand."

She walked off into the forest when Darius came rushing up behind her. "Hunting experience? And what would you know about that?"

"Lots of things." She seemed to rack her brain for a quick answer. "Like how there's…hunting. And it's an experience."

He burst out laughing for a few seconds, Aria now walking ahead of him even quicker.

"Can't you give me a better answer than that?"

"But the answer was correct, wasn't it?"

"Well."

"Exactly."

He rolled his eyes, rather contradictory when paired with his rather prominent smile.

"So, what d'you think we'll find?" Aria asked, their shoes crunching through the footway of short grass, the faded shade of green faintly upsetting seen against the vibrant colors of the rest of the forest.

"Maybe a rabbit or something," he answered. "But it would be much better if we could find something like fish."

CRUNCH!

"What was that?" Darius whispered, flipping his head back and forth.

There came another crunch, followed by the rustle of leaves from a bush, a fluffy white rabbit emerging from the brambles, warmed beneath spread-out spots of sunlight.

"It was just a rabbit," Aria said in Darius' direction, quiet as possible as she stood completely still. "Don't make a sound."

The rabbit, feasting on thick grasses, sat oblivious to the towering creatures that were Aria and Darius, intently watching for subtle movements. Its ears twitched for a half-second, not looking up from its meal as they neared.

Only two feet away from the rabbit at this point, it looked up at them with fear in its eyes—and bounded off in the opposite direction.

"Damn it," Aria complained, sharp words sliding across the wind, her voice echoing on the breeze as she gave chase.

"How're we supposed to catch up at this rate?" Darius breathed, the rabbit already twenty feet from their grasp.

"It'll slow down eventually, right? We just have to wait," she sighed, breathing heavily from her mouth as she gained speed.

Although, after five minutes of intense sprinting, the animal had gained speed to the point where they began to fall back. Eventually, the rabbit, tiring as well, slowed to mild leaps, to a slow hop, to a normal plod.

They crept up on the rabbit, its back turned to a neighboring raspberry bush; it was feasting on the pinkish red berries that lay in the grass, shielded by the lowest leaves.

Darius towered over the creature, extremely aware of the way the rabbit's ears twitched with a sense of wariness, and he raised the tip of his stick over the neck.

I'm so, so sorry, his expression gave away. But they needed food.

Without a moment's hesitation, he speared the stick through its neck, the rabbit turning too slowly to realize it had just been stabbed.

Yellow liquid the color and consistency of mustard seeped from the wound, drenching the tip of his stick as Darius turned away from the lifeless creature.

"Caught it!" He shook his head of the guilt of the killing as he beckoned Aria over.

"Nice!" she said, a triumph washing over her demeanor. That seemed odd, considering it was Darius who had been the one to catch the rabbit. He lifted the limp body at the end of his weapon, placing the rabbit into their basket as he removed the stick, the yellow blood continuing to drench the rabbit's pristine fur. "Will this be enough to eat?"

"The rabbit's relatively small, and probably enough for, at most, two people. We're gonna need two or more." He picked up on the faint trickle of water in the distance. "Oh! But how about a different type of protein instead?"

"Yeah, that should probably finish the job."

She gripped the basket in her hands again, now following him east toward the sound of the dripping water, growing louder with each couple of steps.

Reaching the river, Aria hurried toward the water's edge, seating herself down on the grassy bank where the grass was warm beneath her from the light of the sun.

"What're you doing?" He peered over her shoulder as she took the spear from his grasp, the sharp tip facing the water.

"Obviously, trying to catch some fish." She turned back to him. "What else would I be doing?"

"Oh really?" He chuckled. "Well to me, it looks like you're just stabbing the water as if it owes you something."

"Oh, shut up," she groaned, turning back to what she was doing. "If you think it's so easy, why don't you try it, huh?"

"Oh no, I never said I was any better," he teased. "Just that most experts say the technique you're using can result in you getting hurt."

He pointed out the way she was sitting, her legs in the water and the spear between them.

"Well, you said, *most,*" she grinned smugly. "Not all."

"Keep telling yourself that."

He sat beside her at the bank, the river rather small in comparison to those that Darius had seen before. Occasionally, the rushing water would wash over the stones that visible over the water's surface, Darius watching as the orange trout swam beneath, reaching depths so low that they disappeared from sight.

He peered over the edge of the bank. "This thing's pretty deep."

Without a response, Aria pulled her feet from the water and set them on the grass, lying down on the warm green blanket as her hair splayed out around her.

"So, you're tired?" he taunted.

"Not at all, in fact," she bluffed, sitting up immediately. "Just taking a breather." She began stabbing at the water once more, then setting her stick down on the bank. "Actually, why don't we make a bit of a bet, hmm?"

"All right. What's the bet?"

"The person who catches the most fish gets bragging rights. How does—

"No, let's raise the stakes," Aria interrupted herself immediately. "And can shut the other person up as much as they want for an entire day."

He thought over the rules for a moment, eventually holding his hand out so that she could shake it. "Okay. Deal?"

"Deal." She firmly shook his hand once, then fell away from his tough grip.

Darius sat on his knees, watching the trout moving through the water, hearing the splashing as Aria stabbed at the liquid in the distance.

He stretched his head even closer into the river.

"Um, Darius," she said, her voice wavering with worry. "My stick is stuck."

"Stuck? What'd you mean stuck?" He gazed back at her as she let go of the spear for a moment, watching as it stood in place. "It won't move."

She rose as she tried to pull it out from every angle.

"Just leave it be," Darius dismissed. "It'll probably—"

In that instant, the fast-moving water of the river pulled her in, the only thing keeping her from drowning being the stick in her grasp. She hugged it as it breezed down the river, praying it would snap and break on her.

"Oh God," Darius whimpered, bounding down the grassy bank.

As he raced, he noticed a glimpse of the waterfall downstream through his anxious and apprehensive cloudy vision.

He'd never catch up to her on land at this rate, and he made a drastic decision.

He plunged into the river.

The ice-cold water stung at his legs, but he had to brush the sensation away, gripping his own spear in his hands the way Aria had done.

He began kicking his legs ferociously behind him as he swerved around the rocks peeking above the surface.

Persistence ran in his bloodstream, the freezing liquid feeling as if it was evaporating; he could feel his body temperature increasing as the sweat ran down his head.

He was going to save Aria. He was so close.

She was much closer, but not nearly close enough to save. And in this moment of pure desperation, he let his stick collide with a giant rock, shooting him several feet into the sky and roughly onto the branches of a banyan tree.

He landed with a painful thud, the wind knocked out of him, yet he persisted, hoisting himself onto the top of the branch as he jumped.

He was watching his feet as he hesitated over the deathly drop.

He had no time to be hesitant. No time for excessive worry as he neared Aria, there far below him.

He dropped into the water in an explosion of freezing water, now only a foot away from Aria's stick at this point. He kicked his leg with vigor, his vision blinded momentarily by the drips of water falling from his flattened hair.

By the time he had caught up with her, he clutched the back of her stick, the dull end, heaving her and the stick toward the bank with the last bit of energy he could manage.

"What do we do!" she exclaimed, struggling to steer the stick.

"As soon as you find the biggest rock, I want you to run the stick into it!" he exclaimed over the rush of the water.

She gazed back at him with a worried look in her eyes, truly wondering if she would be able to survive this. "You sure?"

"Just trust me on this! Please, Aria!"

She leaned forward, a flare of uncertainty combating with determination in her eyes the color of the river water; a ginormous rock lay up ahead, not too far from the cliff of the waterfall.

If she failed, they would certainly both die.

She centered the stick as well as she could with the rock face, watching as the stick collided with the smooth edge, wood splintering as Aria held tight to the grip Darius had around her as they both were flung high into the air.

The angle at which they flew was risky, yes, but high above the water, they were able to grab onto a deep brown, twisted vine, its tip hanging over the edge of a rapidly flowing waterfall.

Darius took hold of it as soon as he saw it, holding onto Aria too as she looked down at the harrowing grip. Aria took hold of a neighboring vine, climbing it precariously.

They were over a lethal drop in the lake that appeared to be rather shallow, considering how the sun reflected the light of the sand below the body of water.

Not to mention the way the water flowed down hills in smaller streams that went branching off.

They balanced on the tree branch, walking with caution.

They neared the tree's trunk, shimmying down.

At the base of the tree, they started sprinting away from the cliffside until they had reached the place where the basket sat.

Both were glad that the rabbit they'd found hadn't been stolen by a lurking creature.

Aria gazed back at Darius, gawking happily as her chest rose subtly from the extensive running. "Darius, oh my God! You saved my life! How did you know that'd work?"

"Well, I tried it myself…and it worked. So, I just trusted my gut, I guess." He gazed back at her. "If it worked for me, it should work for two people, right?"

"Darius, you risked your life for me! I owe you one—like a big one!"

"Like what?" He grinned at the realization as she locked him in a hug.

"Well, firstly, I can't not hug the person who saved my life." She examined his face for a moment, narrowing her eyes. "Why are you smiling like that?"

"Let me win the bet."

"But—"

He looked at her again, and she sighed, grumpily accepting the deal to which she'd agreed. "I hate you, y'know that? But you—you did save me, I guess."

"And what do I get in return?"

"You win the bet."

She watched as he strode off into the forest with their basket in his hands and hurried after him with his long strides. "But remember that if I didn't run into that rock that—"

"Who told you to do that?" he dismissed, examining the trees that surrounded them.

"You," she groaned. "But still, I'm just saying maybe I could help you with—"

"You almost died like five minutes ago."

She followed him in silence, a look of bitterness on her face.

Although, not completely known to her at the time, it still felt nice. Bickering playfully with someone who wasn't her brother. It felt like…

…like she finally had a friend again.

And so, she couldn't help but grin.

Chapter 15
A Quest in the Land of Elves

SET INSIDE THE SINK was a skinned rabbit, four small orange trout, and two cream-colored quail eggs inside of a grass-weaved basket. The sky overhead was gradually losing its blue shades, replaced with reds and oranges as the sun sank into the horizon.

Aria turned around while the basket was filling with tap water. "Hey, Ca—"

"Hi, Aria," said Katie at her feet.

"Oh! Hey, Katie. What'd you need?" She was taken aback at her sudden appearance; she'd never really noticed how tall Katie was for a ten-year-old.

"Just wanna know what's for dinner."

"Rabbit, fish, and quail eggs since that's all Darius and I were able to find before we had to start heading back. Will that be okay?"

"Oh definitely," Katie smiled, bright and childlike in the way Aria remembered looking back at people. Yet, before she could ponder on it any longer, Katie disappeared as fast as she appeared.

Just how did she did do that?

Seated on the couch with her older sister, Katie watched as Cassie focused on a game of Solitaire. "Would you want to come hunting with me tomorrow?" asked Katie.

"A) you know you're gonna hate it," Cassie pointed out nonchalantly. "B) you don't know how to hunt. And C) it's worse than you'd think."

"But I want to—" Katie remonstrated.

"No, you don't." Cassie looked from her phone to the melancholy look in Katie's eyes, then looked back at the screen in guilt. "Anyways we just studied spells today."

"Well, if we can't do that," Katie said, switching up rather fast, "How about studying circular spells?"

"You know what, yeah. That sounds cool."

"Ooooh! Did I hear someone mentioning circular spells?" Vanessa said, plopping down on the couch beside them.

"Yeah, and they were really cool," answered Katie. "Cassie and I used them today and they made the spells even more powerful than before."

"Guess my Spells teacher was right," realized Vanessa, quietly. "But anyways, that seems incredible. I've only ever used one for a levitation spell, but I'd love to see some more.

"Maybe tomorrow before I leave, I could look at some of the spells with you guys."

"That would be great!" chirped Katie and looked back at her older sister. "Can we show her the Disc Attack?"

"You gave it a name?" Cassie chortled.

"Of course! It deserves a name. But can we? It's just so cool!"

"Yeah, we can." Cassie grinned genuinely at Katie's excitement, a sincere expression of joy that she hadn't experienced or shown in a while.

***

Behind Aria, Darius approached, his black socks assisting him as he stupidly glided across the floor. "Need any help?"

"Uh..." She turned to him, away from the boiling pot of water on the stove, decreasing the heat. "Yeah, I could." She led him toward the sink and pointed at the basketful of meat. "I'll need you to clean these. And then, if you want, you can start on the rice."

After her brief instruction, she ambled to the bathroom, setting her apron on the booth seat.

"Anything else?"

She didn't answer, so he started scrubbing the meat with his washed hands.

For the minutes that Aria was gone, Darius cleaned the food carefully with hot water as instructed, burning his hands slightly rather frequently.

He checked the cabinets for the rice Aria had mentioned as she emerged from the restroom, and he took out a five-pound pack of dry grain, one knife, and a variety of spices after reading the labels.

He took no mind to her arrival, setting the ingredients down on the counter near the boiling pot as he cracked his knuckles.

"You seem to be a pro at this, huh?" Aria commented, watching as he cooked the meat in a large sauté pan with oil.

"Yeah, it's just like making potions back in class," he said happily. "I can make the rest of dinner if you need to relax." He watched as she just stood and observed. "Well, I mean if you don't, I'll need you to make sure the meat is cooked correctly. Then turn off the heat and take the meat out of the pan and add it to the rice that I'm making."

Darius added four handfuls of hard grain to another pot of water.

"You sure that's enough?" Aria pointed out as she examined the grain.

"Don't worry about it. I've been making potions since I was in diapers and cooking can't be any different," he boasted.

She rolled her eyes as she waited for the meat to cook through while the quail eggs boiled in another smaller pot of water.

She examined the meat a few times through to see if it was cooking thoroughly before she added in a few spices, turning down the heat but not decreasing it completely.

By the time the eggs had finished, she drained the water and took note of the way they looked for a moment, peeling the shell away as the golden-yellow yolk revealed itself to her with a bright egg-white. "Are these things really safe to eat?"

"Definitely, or at least if you cook them the right way. Even though they look like regular eggs, they taste like creamy chicken, like the chicken in a pot pie alongside the gravy. I used to eat them all the time." He took a white serving plate from the cabinets.

"They taste best with broccoli harvested from the Kingdom of Sorcerers," Darius continued. "The broccoli is filled with an abnormal amount of salt and pepper naturally; they just magically grow like that. My family used to eat them all the time when they were just getting off the ground. Living off Pop's money made working at a magic charging station, and part-time at local fast-food places was always pretty hard.

"I felt so bad. And I was never able to do anything because I was just this useless twelve-year-old with barely any money, no skills, and no friends.

"But that's when I learned my family's secret ability."

"What was it?" Aria asked, draining the water from her pot into the sink.

She had never asked Darius about his life before everything about Vitina happened, or even before she and her brother showed up.

She wanted to know more about him, but she'd never gotten the courtesy to ask.

"Making potions. My family, the Johnsons, had been creating potions for people for over two hundred years. We invented the potion that helped you grow vegetables, the one that could incinerate the material it was poured on, but the last spell..." He sighed deeply. "…the last spell ended all of that."

He looked back at his rice, placing the soft grain on the large serving plate.

"This potion allowed the performer a way to see the future. With the simple incantation *videte futurum* and a drinking of the potion, you could see the future in your mind.

"Yet, the potion, as people said, seemed to be a false prophet, and gave people predictions of unfathomable things that could never happen to them. So, my family stopped making the potions, only to realize everyone else had already invented others, meaning we couldn't sell them potions anymore. We couldn't keep up in the growing market."

"Darius," Aria turned to him, eyes glossing over at the prospect of something so melancholy. "That's so sad. I didn't know that's what happened to your family."

"Don't feel bad," he said. "I'm fine and my family's fine. Ivory Princeton is providing them financial aid for my admission." He looked at her. "And they're happy at home with the money they used to purchase their own apartment."

He set the rice on the white serving plate, laying the meat on top of it as Aria intently decorated the plate with quail eggs and trout.

As he brought the complete serving plate to the table, Aria held utensils in her hand along with a larger steak knife, trailing after him to set them down on the table.

***

"Hey," Aria breathed, shaking her brother's shoulder at his bedside. "Dinner's ready. C'mon, wake up."

He flew awake from his nap as he saw her standing over him, vision clearing as he said, "What did you say?"

"Dinner's ready," she said again, starting to walk off.

Conner, last to the table, looked across at Cassie, Katie, and Vanessa, who looked at him for a moment and smiled awkwardly. It was rather obvious to him that she still had trouble with looking at him after what had happened earlier that day.

Was she embarrassed? She had no reason to be.

He was the one who should be embarrassed. Not her.

Aria sat beside him after she had set the plates out in front of her, and without a single word, she sliced off a leg of rabbit and set it on her own plate. She scooped a ladle-full of rice, fish, and quail egg onto her own plate.

Everyone indulged in conversation, all besides Conner and Vanessa, who looked up every now and then to catch a glimpse at the other.

"So, Vanessa, is everything okay with him?" Conner overheard Cassie whisper over the chatter of mainly Aria and Katie.

"Yeah, it's just everything is kinda awkward now."

"Well, are you gonna at least talk to him tomorrow on your walk?"

"I'll try to. Doesn't mean I'll manage to talk to him well."

Conner smiled at the thought. He wouldn't go over the top, but he wanted to at least try to fix things with her if she was willing to do so too.

By the time dinner had ended, they had learned that Aria was planning on going with Vanessa and Conner to look for ranunculus flowers the next day.

"What's the time, Cassie?" Katie asked her sister as she set her plate down in the sink.

"9:20." As she said this, Darius, Aria, Conner, and Vanessa set their plates down in the sink as well.

Everyone went off to bed rather early after consecutive showers, hoping to get some sleep in before their early trip that morning.

Conner stayed at the kitchen sink, washing the dishes.

Due to the number of pots, plates, and utensils he had to wash, he remained there for a little over an hour. Returning to his bed groggily, he lay in his bed with heavy eyelids.

Despite his fatigue, he struggled to sleep, stepping out of bed to turn the television off before realizing that Vanessa had her hands on the remote, and so he backed away as he headed back to his bed once more.

He turned to face the couch, seeing Vanessa gazing at him. "Tired?" she mouthed.

"No, not really" he said quietly.

"Wanna talk?"

"Yeah, sure."

Vanessa sat herself at the foot of his bed, blanket wrapped tightly around herself as she whispered. "Why do you need to talk?"

"Sorry about how that date went," Conner apologized. "I sorta wanted it to be special and a good time for us to hang out but I guess I ultimately failed." He looked to her as he wrapped blankets tighter around himself. "I heard you talking to Cassie about it at dinner."

"Oh…" She looked up at him. "It's not your fault, and I mean something good came out of it, remember? We found half the ingredients needed for that potion. And I'll admit, it wasn't the best date I've ever been on, but it wasn't the worst."

"That's reassuring." The words slipped from Conner's lips, but at this point, he was surely much too tired to care. "I messed up. But I get it."

"I guess that's at least a bit promising to hear," she concluded, her words encouraging yet bitter. "I had no problem with it, if that's what you're worrying about. The time was just inconvenient, so I didn't get the chance to really enjoy it."

To schedule another one was probably just inviting a repeat disaster, at least for the time being. To invite a girl on a date during a quest to save another missing girl was an embarrassing idea anyways, not to mention if it was truly moral.

He had no answer for her comment, so they sat in a silence for several awkward moments until he decided to change the subject. "I was thinking that we should start keeping track of Vitina and Andromeda," he ultimately suggested. "'Cause, I was reading the news today and it said that there was this group of black cloaks in a trial because they had tried to break into the Council of the Realm castle."

It took a few seconds for her to comprehend what he was saying, blinded by disbelief as tears were coming to her eyes. "When?"

"It was this morning."

Her eyes glossed over. What would they have done to her parents? What if they had succeeded? What if no one had caught them?

"Vanessa," Conner said. "Your parents are okay. I know you're worried about them, but remember, there's also more security around their castle, so it'll be harder for people like Vitina's army to break in."

"Yeah, yeah…" She sounded as if she was trying to tell herself this was true, so all Conner could do was try to believe that she was all right.

Conner beamed at her as she sniffled. "But back to what I was saying, how are we gonna keep tabs on her?"

"I don't know, but—" She stopped midsentence. "Do you have a camera that you can spare?"

"Uh, yeah, I have one in my backpack. Why?"

"What if, when we get to Rubidium, we place a camera in either Vitina or Andromeda's office?"

"But she'll probably hack it somehow and find a way to track us instead," Conner interrupted the thought.

"Oh, yeah, you're right."

She stayed silent for a moment; the subject had died out that fast, and they were left dry of things to talk to him about. Yet she still wanted to talk to him.

There was something on her mind, but could she really tell him that?

Was she really close enough with him yet to tell him? Could she still expect him to look to her the way he used to after she shared what was on her mind?

From the outside, Vanessa appeared extremely conflicted. Conner could ask her what was on her mind, but she seemed so unwilling to talk.

Maybe it'd be best to just talk to her in the morning.

Finally, she asked him, "Conner, can I ask you something?"

He stopped, processing her question for longer than he would've hoped, and nodded. "Sure, yeah."

"It's about my own magic," she clarified. "So, you know how all sorcerers from the Magic Realm can channel magic through solid objects other than their own wands?"

"Yeah. Why?"

She paused for a moment. Her demeanor showed a million thoughts, as if she was really thinking hard about what she would say next. She sighed, then looked away.

Then took in a really deep breath, preparing herself.

Maybe thinking, would he treat her any differently if she told him this now? Would he start patronizing her? Start thinking that she would be better off back home where she didn't hold them back with her limited magic?

"I can't."

"Can't? What'd you mean?"

Her face fell. Oh no. He would. She never should've said this. She never should've—

He asked her, quieter and sweeter this time, "What do you mean, Vanessa?"

"I mean that I can't channel magic. At least not the way everyone else can."

Conner silently, for a moment, looked at her and smiled. "Really?"

Why was he smiling? Was what she had predicted coming true?

Was he really going to start treating her differently?

"Really. They diagnosed me with a magical condition when I was younger that prevents me from being able to do it. My brain doesn't know how to harness the certain type of Resicus it needs to perform these types of spells, so I have to rely on my wand for magic."

Conner was still smiling, this time warmer and more caring than the grin he had worn previously. "Well, let me tell you a secret— I can't either."

There was a look of confusion and shock on her face.

She could barely comprehend what he said. "Really?"

"Yeah. If you didn't know already, I wasn't born here."

"You weren't born here!" Vanessa shouted, lowering her voice immediately as she whispered, "I didn't know. Why didn't you tell me?"

He blushed and looked down as he murmured, "Because I was scared it would mean you wouldn't accept a date from me. That you would see me as lesser."

"Conner, you idiot," she laughed. "Of course, I wouldn't. The last part I mean. You're an amazing friend and I don't give a crap if you came from a dimension across the entire universe. I would've accepted anyways."

"Really?" He looked up at her, his mind racing with the confirmation of her words.

"Yeah. Really."

He just looked at her for a long time, lost in the sight of her and how happy it made him. He wished he could feel this happy all the time. That he could stay in this moment forever.

And it also seemed as if, from the other side, Vanessa was enjoying herself as well.

An hour after their conversation ended, Vanessa was still feeling warm and jubilant from getting the chance to truly talk to him. Was she okay? Was something wrong?

Despite that feeling though, there was still a thought in the back of her head.

She was still having trouble telling herself that her magical condition was fine.

If she ever lost her wand, all she would have would be a charm. If she had an individual power of her own, not having her wand would have little to no effect on her, since individual powers came from the person, not magic cell towers.

If her power continued to go undiscovered and she broke her wand, she'd have to rely on a charm she'd gotten from her school, which she'd have to return eventually.

That would leave her with no magic at all. No reason to be here with them anymore.

"Get your head away from that," Vanessa whispered to herself. "Conner already told you your magic is completely fine. Your magic is fine. And Conner can't channel magic either. Doesn't that make you feel a little better?"

But as her mind pushed away the thought, she started thinking about something worse.

Conner.

Even though they had only known each other for a few days, knowing him made her happier than she'd ever been in school. She never remembered being close with anyone not the child of a Council member or borne of a kingdom's ruler. All those people only cared about her status as a princess, not about who she was as a person...

But Conner didn't.

Conner didn't care that she was princess of the most powerful kingdom in the Magic Realm. He cared about *her.*

Just her.

Not her status. Not her money. Not her family. He just cared about her.

Turning onto her stomach, she gazed at Conner across the room.

His eyes focused on the wall.

There was a rustle on Conner's bed, and he turned to see Vanessa staring at him. Holding his gaze, Vanessa was squirming. What was it about him that made her so nervous? She was never like this before! They weren't dating, right? What was she feeling?

A feeling she'd never experienced before.

A feeling she wished she'd felt that afternoon.

A feeling of love.

Oh, why'd her emotions have to be so out of place? If she had felt like this hours prior, she never would've been in that awkward position with Conner!

How could she tell him this? How could she tell him this when they weren't even that close? Her hands were clammy, sweat starting to build on her temples, and her stomach felt completely empty.

She'd just have to hide it from him for now. Wait until the right moment to tell him, which definitely couldn't be tonight.

He wouldn't mind her telling him that, wouldn't he? It seemed as if he liked her, at least a little, but did she like him? She felt like she did, but maybe it was because she was so tired from today that she wasn't thinking properly. Maybe she was just tired.

Maybe she just needed a good sleep.

***

That morning, a chill breeze brushed Vanessa's cheeks. After a breakfast of seasoned white rice with her friends, she'd expected to feel satisfied until their next meal, yet there was a growling in the pit of her stomach as they trekked.

She clutched her white faux fur coat around her chest even tighter, pulling over the white hood. Below the jacket, she wore her comfortable black turtleneck and thick, furry white pants, concealing brown snow boots. In her pocket, rested her twisted, wooden wand, which she ran the tips of her fingers over briefly.

On her right, Conner wore a deep brown parka, its black and beige fur tickling the skin on his forehead. Underneath, he nestled into a warm, flannel shirt lined with white mock fleece and a pair of thick black pants.

"God, it's cold," he shivered, watching a cloud escape from his lips at his words.

Vanessa crunched another few steps over the snow and replied, "I know. Too cold."

"So, did you fix things with him?" Aria whispered to Vanessa as she pulled down her sheepskin coat. A cold rushed through her legs, concealed by a thick pair of furry black pants. "It's so cold not even these pants can keep me warm."

"Yeah, I think we're fine for now," she breathed back, watching the sun illuminate a path before them. Around the clearing were lush green pine trees frosted with snow, guarding the footway as the trio walked down the path.

She turned to Aria. "Where'll we find the ranunculus flowers again?"

Pulling out a piece of parchment from her coat pocket, Aria examined the map, finding the right bottom corner decorated with mainly trees and a small city in the center.

Finding an area of crudely drawn pines, Aria stopped searching. "Just a couple minutes from here. We'll be there soon." She folded the map and shoved it back into her pocket, clutching a grass weaved basket in her freezing cold hands.

Their matching brown boots crunched inch on inch of snow.

They finally reached a clearing surrounded by looming pines. Above the trees congregated a band of blue jays, their group creating a canopy of blue.

Across the vast white and green space, white, pink, and yellow flowers decorated the ground, their petals only inches above the snow.

As Vanessa neared one, she glimpsed a blue jay eyeing her from a branch above.

"Why's that bird staring at me?" Vanessa questioned, turning from the patch of flowers.

"Don't know. Maybe it just doesn't want you to pick those flowers," Conner guessed. "Just pick it. It's not like it can do anything to you."

Carefully, Vanessa caressed the smooth bright green stem of a ghostly white flower, its petals curling in to create a rose-like appearance, eventually tightening her grip, about to pluck the flower.

The blue jay dipped in the air toward her in a flash of blue.

"No!" Vanessa shrieked over the howl of the wind, obviously in an unnecessarily difficult tug-of-war with the blue jay, its pitch-black beak clutching the petals. "I need this flower!"

The bird called on its friends in a high-pitched screech, a flurry of bright blue and white surging on Vanessa.

Conner dashed toward her, preparing to take the three of them away from the clearing, finally away from this persistent flock of birds.

Then the birds stopped.

"What's going on?" she asked, left disoriented from the events that had just occurred. "The birds just stopped."

With a high-pitched screech from the first blue jay, the birds erupted in a symphony of screams, high enough to alert the whole forest to their presence.

Conner slammed his hands over his ears. "We've gotta get out of here!"

Instantaneously, the trio dashed toward the path they'd taken into the clearing, the footway an arm's reach away.

A group of birds blocked the path, continuing to scream.

Frozen, the three stood, watching the birds open their mouths and release a shrill screech.

"Let's go the other way!" Aria yelled to the couple, leading them to the opposite side.

The birds blocked that path too, screeching as loud as they could.

Conner shut his eyes and thought of some sort of a solution.

How would they escape? They had become trapped, and even the birds knew that! There was no way to leave, they'd be stuck there...

"No," Conner thought aloud, an idea coming to his brain. "Our wands!"

He took out his own, his right ear aching from the deafening sound, the others following suit. Holding his crystal wand to the crowd of blue jays, he felt icy cold creeping along his skin, hand exposed to the painfully chilly temperatures. "Stupefaciunt exponentia!"

A blast of cyan blue light penetrated through the crowd of birds, their screeches ceasing…until they dove for Conner's wand.

"Stupefaciunt exponentia! Stupefaciunt exponentia! Stupefaciunt exponentia!" he repeated, his wand point facing crowds of them now as he shot a relentless series of magic.

As they continued to come, his chants became louder, the birds closing in on him until Vanessa and Aria, curled on the ground, couldn't tell the difference between the sounds coming from Conner or the blue jays.

Eventually, the birds stopped their attacks, flying toward the pines and perching on various branches as they glared down at them with their empty bird eyes.

Until the one that Vanessa recognized fluttered to the ground and stood beside her.

Vanessa braced for the auditory offense, so tired of everything to even start running away, only to find no sound coming from the bird. "Vanessa?" it said in a deep, naturally echoey sort of voice, its dark brown eyes cutting through her.

Vanessa stayed curled in her position, investigating eyes examining the bird, surprised the bird could even speak.

"Um, excuse me, Vanessa? Hello, I am Albion. Albion the blue jay," he cooed with a twitch of the feathers on his wings. "I already know you."

She gasped as she sat up and took him into her hands. "Albion, I haven't seen you in years! I've missed you so much!"

"I've missed you too, Ms. Caswell," he replied. "Let me recall." He paused, collecting his thoughts. "Ah, your parents are King Alistair Caswell and Queen Josephine Caswell. They kept me around the castle to keep you out of trouble; you were quite the odd child, indeed."

"But I stayed at your side and watched you grow up, until you left to go to Ivory Princeton High School," the bird remembered, happy like an old acquaintance meeting a long-lost friend. "Quite the student you are, yes ma'am, but I haven't come to revel in your intellect. I must inform you of a crisis in the Kingdom of Magic.

"It is threatening your parents."

"Oh yes," she said, dejected, "I've heard. There was a group of people in black cloaks who were trying to break into the ruler's castle."

"I see you know then. But it's much worse than you think."

"What else did the black cloaks do?" she inquired as Conner and Aria seated themselves beside her in the snow.

"I am sorry to say, madam, but several black-cloaked figures have been attacking your kingdom. They've looted the stores and attacked several of the royal guards. As we speak, they're planning to enter the ruler's castle, about to attack again.

"If this continues, your parents may already be hurt."

"Then I have to go home," she declared, about to stand up. "I have to help."

"Wait!" Conner stopped, taking her hand. He blushed at the contact but continued on saying, "You can't. What if they try to hurt you, too?"

"This young man is correct, Vanessa. To leave and probably get yourself hurt would do more harm than good, it's best you stay where you are now."

The bird looked at Conner. "What's your name, young sir?"

"Conner," he answered.

"It's best you stay with Conner for the time being, madam," the bird advised Vanessa.

She sat back down, hand still in Conner's as she let go, flustered.

As she put herself together again, she said formally, "Thank you for the information update, Albion. And so, from here on, you will give me daily updates on the state of my parents, kingdom, and the attackers. Understood?"

The blue jay nodded. "Understood, ma'am."

Vanessa glimpsed at the blue jay's friends, disseminated along the tops of the pine trees. "What about them?"

"They're my loyal group. We'll work for you, Princess Vanessa. They will help me to collect information on your desired subjects."

"Thank you, Albion." Vanessa set down her palms in the freezing snow, the thought of her hand in Conner's helping her to withstand the pain. "Come along now."

Hopping into her open palm, his small black toes feeling the smooth skin of her palms, he fluttered to the top of her head, setting himself down.

"I'm comfortable here, madam; is it all right?"

"Of course."

"What about my friends? Where will they stay?" Albion questioned, looking at the sad eyes of the birds surrounding him. "May they come too?"

"C'mon guys!" Vanessa directed to them, whilst Albion set himself on her right shoulder concealed by the faux fur white coat.

The flurry of birds flew around Vanessa and her friends, setting themselves on their heads, their shoulders, and everywhere possible to stay and keep warm. Once the birds were comfortable, they began their walk to another ranunculus flower clearing.

"Hey, Albion," Conner prompted, turning toward the bird on Vanessa's shoulder, "why couldn't Vanessa pick up that ranunculus flower?"

The bird turned to him with a perplexed look on his feathery face. "What do you mean?"

"I mean when Vanessa tried to pick the flower, you wouldn't let her; how come?"

"Oh, yes. I now understand what you're asking. Vanessa couldn't pick the flower because, as you may not have guessed, ranunculus flowers are notorious for being chemical tracking devices," Albion calmly explained.

"What? Tracking devices!" Conner turned to his sister and hissed, "Why did you tell us to look for them, then?"

"I didn't know they were tracking devices. Why would I lead you guys into a trap? I just thought they'd help us with the potion."

Albion nodded with understanding. "Ah yes, an invisibility potion."

Vanessa glanced at the bird on her right shoulder. "You know about those?"

"Why, of course, I do. I remember when you were younger—just nine years old to be exact—and you tried to sneak into the Royal Kitchen during your parents' meeting with Evelyn Remona. You made your own invisibility potion and tried to steal some of the leftover birthday cake from her birthday a few days prior.

"You always loved that type of magic."

"I remember that. I failed horribly and disrupted my parents' meeting. Evelyn was fine with it though and was about fourteen at the time and running a kingdom on her own. So I was able to become good friends with her a few years after."

Albion chuckled briefly at the memory, the sound traveling softly on the wind.

"How do you know how to make one?" Conner inquired.

"On school nights, I would hear Vanessa's mumbles about her Potions lessons back in grade school. They were simple potions you could create that didn't require any out-of-the-ordinary ingredients. Right now, you're looking for the ranunculus flower to add alongside glasswing butterflies, as their anti-glare coating can allow the potion to turn objects invisible."

"I only have one more question: how are ranunculus flowers tracking devices? How can an organic material activate a mechanical machine?"

"To answer your question, it's because of their chemical makeup. Ranunculus flowers, or buttercups as they're commonly known, contain slight hints of radon, a radioactive chemical that can stick to materials, but not enough to be harmful by themselves.

"This is activated the most during magical snowstorms. These storms involve chemically made ice that releases radon in these flowers. As radon is radioactive, when it comes in contact with, say, a chemical radar, the machine goes crazy.

"This can alert the user of someone's usage of a ranunculus flower, so anyone with a chemical radar has the ability to track you." He scratched his feathers with his black beak.

"But we need them for the potion, and people must be able to still use them if invisibility potions can still be used. Are there any exceptions? Is there any way we can still use them?"

"You can mash the flowers as soon as possible or wash them down. Either method will get rid of the radon. Yet, there's no water near here or object you can mash the flowers with."

"What'd you mean?" Conner said. "'Course there is. There are sticks all over this place. Let's just use one of those."

"That would be quite unwise," Albion reprimanded. "For instance, if you smash the flower and get radon on your hands, the chemical will stick to your hands until you can wash them." He stretched his thin, black legs, his white talons picking at Vanessa's coat.

"Hmm..." Conner pondered any possible solutions. "What if we find a nearby lake or river or something?"

"I guess that's a rather good idea, but we don't know where the nearest body of water is. We should try something different."

A lightbulb went off in Vanessa's head almost instantly. "Why don't we bury the flowers in the basket beneath snow? And when it melts, the flowers are already washed?

"Y'know, Albion," Conner breathed, "that's our best bet right now, it seems."

Albion yawned tiredly.

"That's a brilliant idea, Ms. Caswell!" Albion snuggled into a better sleeping position on Vanessa's coat and said quietly, "And after, it's best to leave as soon as possible."

"Leave?" Aria turned to Albion. "Why do we need to leave early?"

She received no answer as Albion, already looking tired, was immediately fast asleep, nestled in the fluff of Vanessa's coat, sitting upright with his face pointed to the ground.

She looked back at the path. "Guess we'll have to find out ourselves."

***

Back in the trailer, Cassie was just stirring from her sleep. Tugging at her dark purple sleeping shirt, she got up from her position groggily and stretched her arms above her head.

Before going on her phone, she noticed Darius sitting on the couch, looking out the window with a worried face as he watched a squirrel leap from branch to branch.

Soft snow fell from the leaves.

"What's wrong?" she inquired, walking toward the living room and rubbing sleep from her eyes. She watched as he continued to stare out the window, beige curtains now drawn back. "Is it our friends? Oh, don't worry; they'll be fine."

His expression faded away, and he looked up at her with a forced smile, almost as if he was faking it. Well, he was most definitely faking it. "Oh, it's not that. I was just thinking that we could maybe practice some spells."

She raised her eyebrows in shock and offense.

Did he truly think she'd fall for that?

"Yeah—sure. Once Katie wakes up. I promised that she could practice with me today, so I guess you could too."

"But I'm already awake," Katie said from behind her.

Cassie jumped at her sister's words and sighed deeply. "You already have a jacket?"

"Yeah." She handed a black parka to her sister. "And here's yours."

"Hey, Katie," Darius said from behind Cassie. "How would you feel if I joined you guys?"

"Oh, that's cool. Just make sure to bring a jacket. It's pretty chilly out there."

Cassie followed Katie out the van door, leaving Darius searching for a coat inside. He left with his wand in hand, joining the sisters in the snowy clearing surrounded by pine trees.

"All right. We've already learned a new way to make spells more powerful," Cassie explained.

"Circular spells?"

"You might think that," Katie said very professor like… "But… Oh, yeah, circular spells."

"Which spells have you already used?" he asked inquisitively.

"Attack, light, and force-field spells," Katie chirped. "We want to try a water spell today."

"A water spell, you say?" Darius pointed his wand at a tree. "Aqua exponentia!" With his wand lit, he drew the sign for a drop of water in the air and swiped at the light symbol.

Water doused every tree in his view as Cassie stared in awe and confusion.

"But that can't be a circular spell," she interjected, flipping vigorously through the pages. "What was that symbol for? Regular circular spells don't need that."

"I just performed an Elemental Spell, one of the hardest for a magic user to perform; it lets you control and produce the main four elements. Right now, there are four Elemental Spells, a water spell, fire spell, earth spell, and an air spell.

"Since they're different from other spells, they require a symbol to be drawn with light in order for the spell to actually work. These—"

Without another word from Darius, Katie cast, "Aqua exponentia!" yet her wand didn't light. "That's odd."

"If you'd let me finish," he said, rather passive-aggressively for a person of his demeanor. "You'd know that these spells require you to use a wand that has been used for magical purposes for a while. You both got your wands less than a week ago, so there isn't enough Resicus in your wands to perform these types of spells."

"So, the only reason you can do it is because you've been using your wand for a while?" Cassie noticed.

"Exactly. Although, I can't do any other Elemental Spells because those are much harder than Water Elementals and require a better knowledge of magic than what I have right now."

"So when will I be able to perform an Elemental?" Katie said, eyes twinkling with excitement.

"I can't tell you, because you can never really know," he admitted, disappointedly.

"Oh, dang it," she mumbled under her breath.

"But why don't we perform a spell that everyone can do?" Cassie insisted to Katie. "How about another defense spell?"

"A deflection spell?" Katie exclaimed, looking excited too.

"Yeah, we can do that."

"All right," Katie said, flipping pages in their spell book. "A deflection spell deflects any spell that a person tries to cast upon you, making it a great source of protection. The spell name is 'Claudicatio exponentia'."

Cassie held out her wand and placed her wand across her chest, directing to Darius, "Darius, you cast an attack spell so I can deflect it."

"Circular or regular?"

"Let's just go with the easiest for now."

He pointed his wand at Cassie, bellowing, 'Impetum exponentia!', a blast of light escaping from the tip of his wooden wand.

"Claudicatio exponentia!" Cassie yelled, Darius' spell flying off hers and nearly hitting his head before he ducked.

"That was close," he said, checking his hair for scorch marks. "But that was really good. It's a very risky spell, especially if you have a thin wand like yours and no aim practice."

"All right, let's try another!" Katie chirped over the out-of-place howl of the chill winter wind, skimming through the spell book once more. "Another defense spell would be good. How about a deviation spell? It says here that this type of spell moves the path of your attacker's spell. The words are 'Declinatio exponentia'.

"Cassie, how about you try it on me?"

With her wand pointed at her sister, Cassie cast, "Impetum exponentia" and watched as Katie's wand took control of the blast of light emitted from Cassie's own.

With a whip of wind from the swift movement of her wand, the light from Cassie's wand zipped toward a scrawny tree, splicing it in two.

"How many defense spells are there?" Cassie questioned after being handed the spell book by her sister. "There's gotta be at least ten, right?"

Katie peered over her sister's shoulder at the book, smiling and giddy as she continued, "Maybe even more…"

Chapter 16
The Infamous H.Q.

"WHAT THE IS *THAT*!" Conner exclaimed, pointing toward the morning sky.

Above them, the group glimpsed ginormous light-brown feathered wings attached to a hulking body. The lion, it seemed, had a furry mane of golden brown, its fur concealing its bulky frame from the cold.

"I think that's a type of amaratio," Vanessa piped. "They're these giant flying cat things. They're ferocious, but almost every magical leader has one. Great in battle, too." She frowned, Conner observing her face change. "Wish I had one."

He looked back at the amaratio and then to her, as if fighting the urge to say, "But why?"

"But anyway," Vanessa said. "We need to get going. Like somewhere where we're not exposed to the mystical creatures living in the woods."

"We'll be fine as long as we keep out of sight of the amarettos," Conner commented.

"Amaratios," she corrected immediately. "And it's better we take a safer route."

"You're just being paranoid."

"I'm just being safe. Unlike you."

"We stay on the path."

"We leave."

"No, we stay."

"No, we g—"

"Be quiet! Let's take this to an outside witness," Albion chided. "I normally don't raise my voice, but thanks to your bickering, I've been awoken from my nap!"

He turned to Aria. *"You'll* decide what we do."

Vanessa opened her mouth to speak.

"All right, should we leave or stay, Aria?"

Albion glared at Vanessa, then at Conner, the two people from whom he expected nothing but absolute maturity.

Both Conner and Vanessa looked right at Aria, giving her cold stares.

They were as if to say: *Pick my decision for me!*

"We'll..." She looked between her twin and Vanessa. "We shouldn't stay on this path. We'll leave and find another path where it's safer."

Vanessa pulled her fist back silently.

Conner continued, "But how would we do this exactly?"

It seemed as if he thought he had checkmated Aria, along with Vanessa as well, thwarting their original plan. But unexpectedly, Albion chirped up, "We'll take you."

Conner looked at the bird in disbelief. "How would you do that?"

The flock of birds clutched the group's arms and shoulders, their boots lifting higher and higher into the sky as the blue jays' wings flapped in a quiet symphony.

No, no, no, no, Conner's face showed! Appearing terrified, he was looking down as the ground moved farther and farther away. His wide-eyed, pallid face screamed silently, *I'm terrified of heights! What if I fall! What if they let go!*

What if an amaratio comes and hits me and I fall!

At his side, Vanessa was receiving his heavy breaths directly onto her cheek, his eyes now bulging out of obvious fear. "Don't you think we—"

Vanessa took clutched his hand, looking at him and smiling. "It'll be fine. Trust me."

Conner's panting subsided as he looked at her; he had just been holding her hand and not saying anything. Now, he seemed to realize it.

He drew his hand back swiftly as he hid his blushing face from her, hoping she wouldn't notice after he'd manage to make an absolute stubborn fool of himself in front of her.

Oh, definitely the fact that he'd made an absolute fool of himself.

After a while, Vanessa turned to look the sky ahead, flipping her head from side to side to check for any signs of any flying creatures. "Looks pretty safe from here."

She looked at her left side again, brown eyes widening at the sight she had just seen.

"Oh sh—"

The birds immediately dove downwards, avoiding the path of the creature, flying in random directions against the winter wind as they waited for Vanessa's instructions.

But it seemed she was too scared for her life to say anything more.

The blue jays eventually set off flying east, hoping to find a bit of cover in that spot of the forest. Higher and higher they flew, until the forest became a sea of green below their feet.

Despite this, the grove of trees toward which they flew were even taller than any others they had seen in the forest, their vast trunks at least forty feet in width, trunk bark peeling off toward the top.

At the sight of the tree, Vanessa seemed to break from her mindset of fear to see a looming opportunity.

"To the alcuses!" she yelled, the birds taking off at lightning speed.

Behind them, the amaratio approached even faster, glaring its glinting yellow teeth and flapping its wings intensely.

They slipped into the cover of the clouds near the top of the alcus, hidden in the cover of the dark green leaves, each at least a yard in width. Conner and Vanessa hung onto a branch while Aria hid in the cluster of leaves, breathing heavily under the weight of the situation.

"Conner," Vanessa breathed as she noticed him hoisting himself onto the branch they were hanging onto. "Help me up."

"Shhh!" he whispered once she was level with him, both watching the shadow of the amaratio stalking the branches beneath them.

It sniffed around the branch, searching for the cluster of birds it had just caught sight of, which, unbeknownst to it, hid throughout the tree. Its ears twitched, sensing something.

It looked up.

There in the darkness of the tree, it observed two blue eyes watching it…

…and fluttered toward them.

The animal watched them as they crouched on the branch, its fluttering the only thing breaking the still silence.

Conner watched it intently. "Can I—"

"ROAR!"

Vanessa shot Conner a piercing look, insinuating he should shut up.

And Conner, of course, would do whatever Vanessa wanted him to—so, he quickly did exactly that, clamping his lips as if not a word more would ever escape.

The amaratio looked at Vanessa, staring bright-eyed and confused, fluttering toward her inch by inch.

Moments later, its paws were on the branch they too were on, Vanessa backing away as it approached even closer.

What's it doing? her expression showed. *Is it gonna eat me? Will I—*

Her foot found nothing but air, making her slip, causing her to lose her footing on the branch. Conner caught her in his arm and watched as the amaratio looked over the edge at her, just hanging there. He was confused as to why she hadn't been mauled to pieces by now.

As Conner pulled her up, the amaratio licked the tips of her hair.

It was leaving the ends in disarray.

She took the pieces into her hands, inspecting the now watermelon smelling locks. "Why'd you…"

In front of her eyes, she watched the tips of her brown hair turning black at the tips.

Conner watched silently, continuing to stare into her eyes.

"Why are you staring at me?"

Conner opened his mouth to speak, making sure the lion beast thing didn't get to lick him too. "Your eyes..."

"What about my eyes?"

Conner continued to gawk at her. "They're... green."

"What'd you mean? They're brown?" she fretted. "My eyes are brown! You're kidding, right? I have brown hair and brown eyes. I always have."

"I'm not joking. They're green. Like vibrant green."

"How would they be green?"

He turned to the amaratio. "Did you have something to do with this?"

It answered in a series of meows and Conner sighed. "But we don't have time for this. We need to find some ranunculus flowers." He turned to the amaratio, sitting in front of them patiently. "You seem pretty nice for the most part. Could you help us find some?"

It meowed calmly, showing its back to them to indicate they get on it.

"Just give us a sec," Vanessa said, dragging Conner behind the trunk to where Aria hid.

"Aria," she whispered. "Hide the birds in your jacket—looks like we're taking an amaratio to find some flowers."

Stuffed inside every crevice and wrinkle in their coats were the birds, sitting in uncomfortable positions as they boarded the flying lion.

Vanessa sat at the front of the flying beast, her hands wrapped around its furry neck as she stroked its mane. Aria tried to keep herself from falling as she sat at the rear.

She clung tight, trying her hardest not to lean back.

Vanessa steered the flying lion east toward the sun, which had almost risen fully in the morning sky. "Smooth sailing from here," she announced nonchalantly. "We should be able to find some soon."

As they flew over a giant lake, Conner looked out at the forest so majestic and serene, like a scene from a painting. He searched the area for a clearing of flowers, finding one up ahead.

"We've finally done it!" he bellowed, loud enough for the entire forest to hear.

"Shut *up!*" Aria cried out, exasperated. "You could attract attention from other amaratios. Ones that may not be as nice as this. I thought *Vanessa* told you to shut up too!"

He looked away as she said this, shutting himself up yet again, embarrassed, mortified at her tone in the presence of Vanessa. He focused more on the clearing up ahead.

Anyways, his red face seemed to show. He disagreed.

Vanessa had *never* told him to shut up. She had only shot him a disapproving look.

After a few moments, Vanessa landed the amaratio in a large clearing littered with yellow flowers, their petals curling in like a rose.

It was just the way she had remembered the others doing as well.

The first to leap off of the animal—which was licking its paws with its stomach to the snow—Vanessa rushed to pick as many ranunculus flowers as possible.

They did this in quiet to draw little attention to themselves, but as time passed, the forest was losing its sound, becoming extremely still and silent.

Too quiet.

"Something feels off," Aria said, looking up from her flower picking after a quarter of an hour of silent picking had passed.

Past the clearing and into the covers of the woods were even more flowers, in the space where Conner was picking. He looked around the forest for a moment as if he'd heard something and stood up. What was that?

"What'd you mean?" Vanessa asked her.

"It feels too quiet here. The birds were chirping only a few seconds ago and now they're just…gone."

"I guess that would be something to worry about," she responded, getting up from her uncomfortable crouch. "We should get going then."

Vanessa looked over Aria's shoulder at Conner, something creeping up behind him.

At his back, an army of ten or fifteen—maybe even more—amaratios appeared behind him, each accompanied by a figure in a black cloak. Unlike the one accompanying them, these amaratios had a brownish-yellowish pelt spotted with deeper brown, just like a cheetah, with brown—almost black—wings splayed across the snow.

Vanessa froze in fear. Should she tell him? And if she did, what would they do to him? How would he get out?

"Aria," she whispered, heart pounding in her ears.

"Yeah?"

"Look behind you, now."

Aria too froze at the sight. "Oh God."

"Hey, guys!" Conner yelled, looking at the flowers he was still picking. He looked at the fear on their faces. "What's wrong? Is there something behind…"

He turned and saw the amaratios coming for him…

…and swore quietly.

At his words, the cheetahs began charging toward him, so he snatched up the flowers he'd picked and ran as fast as he could back to the clearing where his friends were.

When he arrived at the flying lion, Vanessa and Aria had already seated themselves on it, motioning their hands in a way to make him hurry up. As soon as he sat down, the creature took off, leaving the other amaratios on the ground, staring in awe.

Before anyone had a chance to say anything, the amaratios began soaring toward them, the hooded individuals riding them silently as their cloaks whipped back.

Their hoods continued to conceal their faces.

"Go faster! Now!" Vanessa commanded the lion, which increased its speed to the point where Aria looked as though she was going to fly away in the fierce wind.

In her view, she could see a stone cave beside a lake, toward which she directed the flying creature as soon as she saw the shimmering water.

As soon as they reached the mouth of the cave, they sprinted to hide, crouched behind a rock in a corner while their amaratio hid with them.

Vanessa watched intently as the group of cheetahs passed in front of them, hands over her mouth, appearing to pray that the amaratio wouldn't make a sound.

One cheetah threw a look at her, although it obviously couldn't see her in the dense darkness of the cave.

Then they all flew off.

"Coast looks clear now." She walked to the lake shore with a basketful of flowers in her hand. Sitting on her knees, she washed the flowers in the lake water the way Albion had instructed. "We can head home now," she said when she had finished. "Finally getting some well-deserved relaxation."

No one said anything as they recommenced flying over the water, noticing how it flowed through rivers and lakes, the occasional fish or duck appearing on its surface.

They sat in silence for a few seconds, just taking in all of the things that had happened in such a short span of time.

They continued along the path of the river for miles on end beside the banks of the forest.

The sun was already high in the sky by the time they started their flight downriver, but now it was almost noon, and their van was still nowhere in sight.

Against Vanessa's directions, the amaratio flew downwards toward the bank of the river sitting on the sun-drenched snow and lapping at the chill water.

"Are we lost?" Vanessa grumbled, leaning back against a tree trunk. "This morning has just been…" She let out a sigh of exhaustion. "…tiring…"

Aria pulled out the map she had been keeping in her pocket and spread it out on the ground. "Well, it's clear that we're somewhere in the woods, but I can't really give you a specific place. But I do know that the lake we started at, the one near the cave, connects to a river flowing through most of the kingdom."

"Most of the kingdom!" Conner choked, sitting up straight. "Finding the van is gonna take forever! Oh God…" And he lay back down again in the snow-tipped grass.

"Oh, what about this?" Vanessa pulled back the sleeve of her coat to reveal her charm bracelet.

"A charm? Like the one you told me about, right?" Aria asked, gazing at her reflection in the lapis lazuli gem.

"Yeah that one. I can't believe I didn't notice it until earlier." She took her wand out of her pocket and tapped it to her bracelet, while she said, "Albion. Track—um—my purse."

On command, the gem emitted a pale blue light into the air.

Zig-zagging white lines covered the circular screen, representing rivers and paths, and the image had two dots on it, one black and the other golden yellow.

To Vanessa's dismay, the yellow dot representing their destination was far from where they were. So far that the dot was almost unseeable from their location on the map.

Aria observed the screen coming from Vanessa's charm.

"So, how long will it take to get back?"

"Can't even tell, but definitely more than three hours. Maybe more than four." She looked up, the sun just barely at the top of the sky. "We should at least get home before evening."

A silent half-hour later, it was already noon, the bright sun shining down on the babbling river. Despite the sun's warmth, a sharp breeze would appear now and then, causing everyone to tuck themselves tighter into their coats in the wintery wood.

There was a ferocious rumble in Vanessa's stomach, causing her to stand up.

Both Aria and Conner had fallen asleep, along with their amaratio, which was purring on the river shore.

As Vanessa walked off, she pulled down her hood, heading off to find some berries or something.

She glanced at the map on her charm, showing that she was walking in the opposite direction of the yellow dot. Well, at least now, she knew which direction they'd be going in.

Since she had left the rest of the birds at the bank of the river, she had no way to travel other than by foot, nor anyone to talk to.

"Finally!" she cheered when she had found a blackberry bush.

She sat on a smooth rock while feasting upon the ten berries she had picked, the rumbling in her stomach calming down a bit.

Her face relaxed; she looked happy to have something to eat at last.

Without another thought, she tumbled backwards into a bush, disappearing with a rustle of leaves.

It appeared that she was in a large underground cave, the dirt floor covered in craters.

"I've gotta get out of here!" she thought aloud, frantically trying to find the entrance. There was a steep drop into the cave, and virtually no way to get herself out.

"You obviously don't care," a male voice said from behind her.

Spontaneously, she threw herself behind a group of stone stalagmites, slapping her hands over her mouth as she breathed heavily at the surprise sound.

"Look, I'm sorry about that," a younger female voice apologized. "I didn't mean to—"

"Oh, shut up," the male voice sneered. "I wouldn't give a *damn* if she killed you."

"I'm sorry, Leviathan. I—I didn't know."

"Of course, you didn't. Because you don't know anything. You never have!"

"Please just forgive me."

"I can't forgive you for what you did!"

As soon as she heard this, she caught sight of the black cloaks the two were wearing, hoods pulled over their faces.

"But it was an accident! I never meant to do any of that stuff. If you would've told me—"

"I can't tell someone as incompetent as you about a plan as important as this! You had one job! One simple job and you screwed it up. All you had to do was keep lookout, but apparently, you can't do that, either."

"We were gonna get caught anyways and if it wasn't for me—"

"You mean Morticia. Just face it, Hecate. There's no reason for you to be here! You're worthless! You're an idiot when it comes to magic! You—"

A slap rang throughout the cave, so sharp and loud that it hurt Vanessa's ears.

"Y—you *bimble!*" Leviathan bellowed, holding his searing cheek. He pulled out his crooked golden wand. "I should just kill you here myself! Get rid of this waste of air."

Hecate snatched the wand out of his hand, throwing it against the wall.

"WHAT THE HELL IS WRONG WITH YOU!" she screamed. "We used to be best friends! We did everything together and now you wanna kill me? After one stupid failed mission?"

"Yes, because that's what we were told to do. That's what we need to do."

"I can't believe you," Hecate spat. "This is what you wanna do? Be someone's henchman? Someone's slave?" She sighed, some anger leaving her voice as she did so.

"When we were kids, you told me you'd never give in to pressure. That you were your own person. That you would stand up for yourself. I never expected this. You choosing to kill your own friend for someone who doesn't care about you at all. Someone who wouldn't think twice about getting rid of you."

"But Hecate," Leviathan said, melancholia taking over his words. "You know that I don't want anything to happen to you, but I can't let Vitina become suspicious of us."

"Then let's just run away."

"But we can't! You know about the cloaking spell. If we escape, the cloaks will kill us. And you know for a fact that we can't get rid of 'em."

"But then—"

"There's no way for us to leave. We're stuck here until someone breaks us free."

"What about our families? Don't they know?"

"No, no one knows. I'm sorry, but—"

A painfully girly voice now came from around the corner, saying, "And I would've killed 'em all off if that bumbling numbskull hadn't been there."

"Hey, Domia," Hecate said, trying to sound as emotionless as possible.

"Don't talk to me," the girl snarled, people chuckling in her wake. "You were the reason the mission at the ruler's castle failed."

When the laughs had subsided, the girl and her followers walked down another tunnel in the cave, leaving Hecate and Leviathan alone.

Vanessa crouched, with time to think about what Leviathan had said.

Stuck here until someone would break them out? But how? How could she help them? They sounded genuinely afraid, genuinely scared. She shifted in her coat.

"What was that?" Hecate whispered, pulling out her wand. "I just heard something."

"Me too," Leviathan agreed. "I think it was behind that stalagmite."

Hecate approached the rock cautiously, leather boots soft against the cold, dusty stone of the cave. "Anyone there? Anyone?"

Vanessa held her breath and stayed silent—she couldn't risk being found.

Not in a place like this. Not now.

Hecate peered over the rock, seemingly unable to find anything, allowing Vanessa to let out a quiet sigh of relief.

"Let's just head back to the meeting then," Leviathan murmured.

With that, they walked off together.

Vanessa peeked over the rock, just the top of her hood visible over the stone.

Now how was she going to find a way out?

***

"Yes, yes, yes!" Vanessa cried out loud, nearing a light at the end of the cave tunnel.

Once she had crossed the barrier between where she'd formerly been and the outside, a deafening noise emitted from the cave's walls, metals spikes plummeting from above.

She looked dazed and confused amid the blaring noises and vibrant red lights as she narrowly avoided the metal spikes impaling her.

A dome of faint red was just about visible, forming around the cave.

Hidden by the protection of an alcus tree, she could hear the confusion in people's tones as they scrambled around within the cave.

She must have been hoping, praying, they wouldn't try to find the person responsible for the break-in. The clacking of their boots soothed her worry, giving her a moment to take in all the events that had happened so swiftly.

She had almost died, almost received a spike right through her body. She began running in the direction from which she'd come, finding a river toward the end of the forest.

She followed the water upstream, the trickle of the water faint. She caught sight of two people after a bit of running; they were sitting at the water's edge and discussing fervently.

It was Conner and Aria.

They were both sweating furiously, Conner more than his sister, seemingly worried about what may have happened to her.

"I thought a squadron had found you! Or maybe something even worse!" Conner said frantically.

"Where the did you go, Vanessa?" Aria shouted, more infuriated than worried, the exact opposite of her brother. "What happened?"

"I'll tell you guys later," Vanessa said, her tone more orderly and sterner, as if demanding them to follow suit as she boarded the amaratio that had now awoken.

"But we've gotta get out of here," she insisted.

As the amaratio took flight, the three of them atop it, Aria inquired, "Did you see something while you were gone?"

"Yeah, which is the reason we need to leave." She took a deep sigh as they flew over the water once more. "It was Vitina's army. Or at least a few members of it."

"Where?" Conner asked, not as surprised as seemed likely given the news. Perhaps he'd already had run-ins like this before.

"I was sitting on this stone a bit deeper on the edge of an entrance to this hidden underground cave. It seemed to be one of her headquarters. I found some people trying to break into the ruler's castle yesterday morning.

"I think their names were Leviathan and Hecate—and they wanted to leave. Like leave the army, but they couldn't. Because then, Vitina would kill them."

"Kill her own soldiers? Couldn't you help them somehow?" suggested Aria.

"I couldn't let myself get exposed, so I just let them leave. And then there was this person named Domia who showed up, who apparently hated Hecate, I guess.

"Although, I don't think that's important."

Aria and Conner seemed to be taking this news the same way she did; they looked confused and conflicted.

They were supposed to be the bad guys. But were they truly?

It had seemed to all of them before, that if you were part of Vitina's army, you were automatically evil. It had seemed Vitina's army had chosen that path.

Now, they knew that wasn't so.

It was easier to just separate those who had been forced to attend Rubidium from those in Vitina's army. But for some reason, for some ridiculously oblivious reason, none of them had realized that they were one and the same.

No one chose to go to Rubidium, and no one chose to be an army member.

It had never occurred to Vanessa that some people were there because if they chose to leave, they would have to sacrifice their lives.

They had no choice but to comply.

***

When Vanessa awoke from her late afternoon nap, she pulled her phone out of her purse and contacted her mom.

The phone dialed obnoxiously loud, but she was much too worried to concern herself with such a trivial thing and waited for her mom to pick up. Her voice eventually came through.

It was calming to hear her mother again; her tension relaxed, shoulders falling slightly.

"Vanessa? Oh, hi, darling! How are you doing today? Having fun on that trip with your friends?"

"Yeah, yeah; I'm totally fine, Mom," she said with a false sense of happiness to her words. "How're you doing?"

"I'm…" Her voice lost its cheeriness as she asked, "Can I be truthful with you?"

"Of course, Mom."

"I feel…stressed, Vanessa," she admitted. "Your father and I have been really worried about the kingdom lately and what happened yesterday morning. So, I was really happy when you told me you would be going with your friends on a trip since that way, you wouldn't be around in the kingdom during these attacks that have been happening."

"There have been attacks before?"

"Of course, there've been. Two important ones in particular. In the first, this group of almost fifty people showed up on castle grounds with torches and wands and weapons threatening to destroy the castle if they weren't able to take you."

"Why didn't you tell me about this, Mom!"

Her words felt accusatory, but as the princess of such an important kingdom, was she not entitled to knowing about important matters like this?

"Because it was when you were home for Christmas, and I didn't want you worried about people trying to take you during a time when everyone's supposed to be happy. Especially after what happened with your brother, Francis."

The name hit her like a blow to the head. Her eyes threatened tears. "Yeah, we wouldn't want something like that happening again," she was eventually able to answer.

"Then there was the second time where a smaller group of about six tried to break into the Princess Wing, where you were at the time, but the Royal Guard found them before they could reach you."

"I didn't know that they wanted me so badly there," she commented quietly. She wiped the tears surfacing in her eyes and took a quick breath of emotional regulation. "But there isn't time to ask those sorts of questions right now," she said, extremely quiet to ensure her mom couldn't hear her.

"I've been really worried about you, sweetie, but I do know that your friends are really sweet. And that they'll take good care of you. Is there anything that's been worrying you, though? Anything you wanna talk to me about?"

Vanessa pondered for a few moments.

What would happen if she told her everything? Would she force her daughter to come back home? Would she start believing that this trip was too dangerous for her now that she knew what was truly going on? But in the end, was she not going to tell her anyways?

So, what difference would it make to tell her now?

But no—she wouldn't risk this. Not after they'd come this far.

"Nope," she responded in her best lying voice, something she was praying her mom didn't see past. "I'm totally here."

Eventually, her mother hung up after telling her how some of her friends from school were doing and how she and her father were at home. She put the phone away.

Francis.

Her brother.

She clutched at her throat again, more tears coming to her eyes.

She would probably never see him again.

Chapter 17
Preparing for a Quest

"I NEED THE GLASSWINGS," Darius ordered, leaning over a large pot on the stove, holding a thick wood pestle in his right hand as he held the left out.

He turned to Aria, Vanessa, Conner, and Cassie shuffling around the trailer, looking for the butterflies and the various other things he said he needed.

"Here," Conner said, handing him two handfuls of butterfly wings.

"And these." Vanessa gave him another few handfuls. "That's all of them."

He sprinkled the butterflies into the boiling water, starting to mash them with a pestle and covering the pot with a lid.

Minutes later, a thick steam smelling of watermelon was filling the small kitchen.

"Why does the potion smell like watermelon?" Conner took in a whiff of the steam. "Is it because of the amaratio? Did he lick the ingredients?"

"Yes," Darius answered nonchalantly. "But it won't have any effect on the potion. Anyways, I need those ranunculus flowers." He turned to the pot again.

Aria handed him a basket of yellow flowers dripping water onto the floor.

He accepted them swiftly.

Grinding all the ingredients together in the boiling water, the potion continued releasing steam. Then he took a glimpse of the amaratio sitting on Katie's bed near the door, his head resting on one of her lavender pillows. Next to it, Katie stroked the creature, even though it was an animal fully capable of mauling her to death.

"So, what should I name him, guys?" she asked, still petting the amaratio as he purred, light brown feathers tucked in around him.

It seemed that the amaratio took over most of her bed, so she squeezed herself down next to the footboard separating her bed from Cassie's, to keep the animal comfortable.

She didn't seem to mind the discomfort.

"What about Steven?" Aria said, leaning against the wall as she peered over at Katie.

"Since he has wings, what about Winger?" Vanessa suggested, taking off her coat to reveal a simple black long-sleeved shirt and white pants. She set it on one of the booth seats. "I like the sound of that," she said.

"I think Maximillian would be nice," Conner chimed in.

"But none of those names feel... fitting." Katie turned to the creature. "What'd you think?

"I would like the name Maximillian," he said to her. "But want it to feel special. What about one like that bird, Albion?" The lion licked its paw. "Where is that bird anyway? Can I eat him?"

"No, you can't, you silly thing. He's a friend of Vanessa's, so he's our friend too. And you can't eat his bird friends either."

Ever since they'd returned from the Animal Kingdom Forest, Katie had been constantly telling everyone that she had communicated with the wolf she'd transformed into a butterfly.

Of course, no one believed she was an animal telepath, but now it was a fact that she was.

Either that or she was simply crazy.

"It's because the right part of Katie's brain discovered its ability to produce Resicus when she started using magic regularly, along with her being surrounded by the energy all the time.

"It seems that she found a way to discover the ability and has already gained control," Aria elaborated. "And since everyone ends up getting one…" She looked at Cassie. "You'll end up getting one, too."

Vanessa looked at her, seeming oddly excited about this news on Cassie's part.

"Have you been feeling any weird sensations lately? Like odd feelings you can't really explain?" Vanessa asked.

"Not really," answered. "I think I would've picked up on that by now."

Everyone was now staring at her, their attention removed from the potion and all eyes on her after the words escaped from her lips.

"What? What's wrong, guys?" she said. She lifted her hand, realizing the yellow hue that emitted from it and stumbled back. "So what? Is this my power? Being yellow?"

"Not exactly," Conner declared matter-of-factly, cutting his sister off before she was able to explain things like she usually did. "I've seen people with this power before. The color you're emitting depends upon the strong emotion that you're experiencing, granting you a certain power. It seems that right now, you're feeling extreme happiness. Which is the reason why you're emitting a yellow hue."

"So, if I'm sad, I can shoot water or something?"

"Pretty much. But it requires intense feeling, not just tints of emotion," Aria eventually got the chance to say.

Scrolling on her phone, Aria continued, "There've been a few reported cases of this individual power. And many of these people find it useful in life-threatening circumstances, apparently."

"Don't ya think it's great you've discovered yours before we have to leave for Rubidium!" Katie chirped, appearing at Cassie's feet. "Now we have an advantage over her!"

"Well, not really," Darius expressed as he toiled over the potion.

"What'd you mean? Vitina doesn't have one of these powers, does she?"

"Well, of course, she does," Darius began. "She may not have the ability to control it as well as, say, you, but she'll still have one. It's better that we prepare as much as we possibly can before we have to go since we don't know what she'll throw at us."

The excitement drained out of Katie's eyes as she looked back at the five of them, hoping to lift their spirits somehow, even though hers were rather low as well. "But I do have some great news though! I've come up with a name for the amaratio!"

"Well then what is it, Katie?" Cassie asked, trying to take part in the endeavor her sister had decided to take upon herself. "Was it one of the names that they came up with?"

She gestured to the friends around her.

"Actually, his name is Dillion! Do you like it, guys?"

"Yeah, it suits him," Conner remarked.

"Yeah," Vanessa agreed. "The name has a nice ring to it."

"Here, Dillion!" she called to him.

"Yes, Katie?" He stared up at her with his luminous, hazel eyes. "You woke me up from my nap, so this better be good."

"Good job, today, Dillion. Vanessa, Conner, and Aria are really grateful for what you did for them."

"Taking them out of danger? Oh, no problem. The real one was how lost they were."

Katie chuckled at this remark and allowed Dillion to walk off to continue with his nap.

When Darius had removed the lid from his potion, it bubbled a light shade of blue, every corner of the room touched with the gas as the steam rose.

Pointing his wooden wand at the center of the potion, he cast, "Potio inuisibilitas!"

Instantaneously, the steam turned dark blue, turning the room a shade of blue as a faceless voice rose over the chatter.

"An invisibility potion I am! Use me wisely, and you shall stand.

"Fail you in wisdom, and overuse, then the price you pay will harm you."

"*Huh*?" Conner said under his breath.

"Shut up, Conner!" his twin interrupted. "We might not be able to hear this again!"

The voice continued.

"The ingredients you collected will keep me working; and so, on your quest, you may continue lurking.

"Do not jump in water. These are the rules.

"If you do, you shall become a mule.

"Stuck as a beast, you'll continue to roam,

"Until the spell turns you to mere seafoam.

"After the six hours following these orders, continue your quest in the kingdom borders."

"What does it mean by the 'kingdom borders'?" Conner questioned as the steam subsided.

"I'm guessing it's giving us a clue about Rubidium," Vanessa opined. "Maybe it's on the border of the Kingdom of Sorcerers?"

"Could be, but why would the potion know that?" Aria asked. "It's just a potion, right?"

"Since I made the potion, it must have read my intentions of using it," suspected Darius.

Aria peered at the map pulled up on her phone. "Potion's right. Rubidium is on the border between the Kingdom of Sorcerers and the Land of Elves."

She put her phone away again.

When Darius had turned off the fire on the stove, she led them over to the dining table and spread out her parchment map, pointing to the bottom.

"Since we'll be going from here…" She pointed to the bottom left corner. "…to here…" She moved her finger to the line separating the Land of Elves and the Kingdom of Sorcerers. "… It'll take us two or three hours to get there." She checked her phone to ensure she was correct and nodded. "Yeah, two to three hours."

Conner flicked his eyes to his sister. "Do we need anything before we leave, like food or something?"

"Probably something that will allow us some energy. Something filling. I'll need you and Vanessa to look for that." She looked at Katie and Cassie. "And now, for you two, you can put your magic practice to use and find some medicinal plants in case anything bad happens to us. How does that sound?"

"Sounds like a plan," Katie agreed.

Putting on her white coat, Vanessa peered at the blue jays sitting on the couch. "Walking is just fine, right? As long as we get back by sunset?"

"I want you guys to be able to make it back in good time," Aria said. "So take Albion and his friends with you. I'll need them to tell me if something bad happens to you two."

When they had walked out of the door with the birds alongside them, Katie called over Dillion. He stood near her sister at the door.

As Dillion took off into the clouds, Katie stroked his soft fur. "Woo-hoo!" she cheered, hands caressing the clouds as they flew.

"Katie! You're gonna fall!"

"Oh yeah—right." She put her hands on Dillion's mane once more and smiled nervously. "That."

***

Now on the ground again, Vanessa clutched the black blanket she'd brought from the van, which she was planning to use to carry food in some sort of an efficient manner. She scanned over a parchment map she had and stopped walking. "Looks like there's some vegetables around here."

They continued walking for a few more minutes, finding themselves in an area they had never seen before. In the cover of edible celery stalk trees, their leaves covered in kale, they found small mushrooms poking out of the celery trunks. Sprouting from the grassy ground were small purple radishes, carrots with kale stems, and potatoes. Above their heads, flowers of purple and green broccoli decorated the tops of the celery in large bunches.

"What's this?" Conner picked at the trunk with his fingernail, releasing a stream of white ranch to drip down the trunk. "Is it edible?"

"Of course," she responded. "Right now, we're in the Elvin Forest of Vegetables as it's called. This is where the Elves get the majority of their food supply. Apparently, it continues to grow and regrow until the end of time, supplying anyone who finds it with food. It stretches from here to the border near the Animal Kingdom."

After ten minutes of picking the magic vegetables, Vanessa swung the blanket, which was tied at the ends, over her shoulder. She had directed the birds to start taking her and Conner back to their van when they began losing their grip on her.

And right now, their small claws were struggling to hold onto the fabrics of her coat as the blanket of food held them down…

And then they released her, unable to cling on anymore.

As she fell through the chilly air, she plummeted closer and closer to the ground. She looked around frantically for a way to get herself down safely but couldn't seem to find one.

She was reaching for her wand after adjusting the blanket holding food; Conner's arms were reaching for her as the birds flew him downward.

With horror and anxiety, he watched her descend. What if he couldn't make it in time? What if he was too late? What if he would have to watch her die right there in front of him?

His throat burned as tears were glossing his eyes over, his vision becoming blurry at the idea. Would he be able to?

His eyes locked with hers and he froze. His tears stopped, his breathing slowed.

And his heart pounded.

And he allowed the birds to let go.

As he fell, some odd state of mind seemed to come over him.

"My body is heating with every breath!" he gasped out, and it was a peculiar sensation indeed, as if something was erupting within him.

Before the birds could reach him, he let out a bellowing scream and Vanessa stared in shock as she watched him dive for her, a stream of white-hot fire left at his feet.

He held her tight in his arms, casting a force-field spell around the pair of them.

He was taking hard and shallow breaths, the strength he had mustered evidently wearing off as fast as it had appeared.

Inside of the invisible bubble, they fell, landing in a canopy of kale tree leaves.

"Conner?" Vanessa shook his back.

She received no response. No movement.

"CONNER!" she screeched, eyes welling up. "You've gotta be okay; you've gotta be!"

She sniffled as she stooped to check his heartbeat, pressing her ear against his chest.

There was nothing but silence.

"C-Conner? Are you…?" She was breaking down.

"Trespassers," a voice boomed, deafeningly loud, "WILL BE DENIED!"

Before she could even comprehend the things that had just occurred, the talking tree catapulted them up and into the atmosphere, Vanessa sobbing against Conner's touch as Dillion streamed through the air to catch them.

Unable to make it in time though, the amaratio watched with a strange, warped horror on its expression as they fell through the crisp winter air.

***

Freezing, Conner could taste garlic and chives in his mouth as he coughed, a taste that he slightly recognized. "Is this…" He tasted it again. "Ranch?"

He turned his head. Surrounding him was a sea of white ranch flecked with green chives, celery stalks sticking up out of the ranch lake.

He looked around for a moment, but no one was there.

Not even Vanessa.

He began paddling through the thick liquid, searching, yet there were not even any faint whispers of a voice on the wind.

"Vanessa! Vanessa!" He continued flipping his head left and right, whipping ranch from his hair. "Vanessa! Anyone!"

Not a single word.

How could he find her? How could he get back? Reflected in the body of ranch was the red and orange of an upcoming sunset, looking to be about six or so in the evening already.

In the middle of the lake, he just treaded water, appearing to be running over his thoughts.

***

As she sat beside Dillion, Vanessa looked at the washing shores of the ranch lake, behind her the vegetable forest. She was still crying uncontrollably and every time she looked at her hands, they were covered in tears.

She watched the sunset, hoping to somehow take her mind off what had happened with Conner. Dillion had rescued her from the air, it seemed, but he must have been unable to save Conner. But that wouldn't matter, would it?

All because Conner was…

She couldn't bear to think the sentence, let alone accept it.

There was a chance Conner might still be alive.

Maybe she should go out and look for him.

"I just need to know. I need to know for sure."

She said the words but to no one in particular.

"I should swim out there, shouldn't I?" She turned to Dillion, who just looked at her.

"Could you take me out there then?"

The lion yawned, a slight meow coming out of his mouth. He then allowed her onto his back, beginning to flap his light brown wings.

Dillion stepped on the ranch as if it was solid ground, with each step the water rippling beneath his giant paws like a wave of sound.

The idea that he could still be alive kept her from releasing tears. But as time passed, minute by minute, doubt was taking over.

She sighed. "Dillion…" The amaratio stopped and appeared to listen. "…maybe he really is dead. Maybe we can't save him."

She looked out, the ranch flowing around her as her nose stung and her eyes welled with tears, getting harder and harder to keep them at the edges of her eyelids.

She set her head against Dillion's mane, the fur engulfing her as she finally cried uncontrollably.

"Conner's dead. Conner's dead and I didn't help him. I didn't keep him safe. And I told myself I would. I told myself—"

There was a faint voice, and she raised her head, uncertain, frowning, screwing up her eyes in disbelief.

The tone of the small voice was familiar to everyone, warm and friendly. She smiled, appearing to know it too. It was the voice she'd worried she would never hear again.

It was Conner.

"Conner!" she cried happily, tears of joy streaming down her face as Dillion bounded toward him. "You're alive!"

When Conner held her hand tight, she pulled him in for a hug, breathing heavily and holding him close. "I'm so glad you're okay."

Conner was confused but allowed her to keep hugging him.

The warmth must have been nice after all.

So too, the butterflies.

"Do you remember what happened?" she asked him as she pulled away. "After the moment you caught me?"

"No. Not really," he answered. "But I did hear a voice when everything around me went black. It was pretty faint though"

"So, you weren't really dead?"

"I was dead!" He thought for a moment. "Then how am I here now?"

"Wait." Vanessa stopped and faced him, her eyes serious as she gazed back. "Conner, I think you've discovered your individual power."

"I understand that but what does it have to do with me coming back to life?" he said, immediately changing the subject to get his question answered.

"According to one of my professors, the human heart can stop for around ten minutes before saving becomes unachievable. Your power must be energy manipulation, which would explain the fire that came out of your feet when you rescued me.

"Since you can control and produce all types of energy, you must've used electrical energy in place of a defibrillator or something like that.

"And that's what brought you back to life!"

Conner looked stunned at the new discovery and seemed visibly excited to try using his power in a non-life-threatening way. "Can I control it?"

"I'm not sure really. That all depends on how your brain is producing the Resicus. But since you used it only during times you didn't expect it, and you've only used it once—probably not."

"So, any idea what happened when you were stuck in the lake?" Vanessa asked as she directed Dillion to start flying again.

"I remember that once I was drowning in this thick liquid, I tried to swim toward the surface but could feel something pulling me down. It must've been some seaweed thing because I was able to untie myself. But when I tried swimming up, I hit something, but couldn't see it. And with all the ranch in my eyes, I couldn't see anything around me, so was just blindly swimming with little air. Then I blacked out again."

"Do you remember how you were able to reach the surface again?"

"My coat must've acted like a life jacket I guess, because when I woke up, I was above the surface. Just coughing on all this ranch." He gestured to the liquid around them.

Vanessa thought about what he said for a moment, watching as Dillion flew higher and higher over the lake.

It was ginormous, stretching over such a large amount of land to the point where anyone could mistake it for a ranch ocean.

"So, where'd Albion and his friends go?" Conner asked. "I don't remember Dillion being here when we flew out to the Elvin Forest."

"They flew off to go alert the others because they couldn't save us in time, but I haven't seen them since then. But Dillion here found me and luckily was able to save me in time. Now, we're just gonna find Katie and Cassie so we can head back to the van."

"Find them? Where would they be?"

"Since Dillion was with them and was able to find us, I'm assuming they're somewhere around here."

"Well then," Conner said as the amaratio was reaching the top of the trees at this point. "Any idea what we'll be expecting tomorrow?"

"I don't know too much, but I do know a bit. Including that we'll need to save my older brother, Francis."

"Francis? The boy who…" He stopped short. "… I'm sorry that happened."

"I've been struggling with it but have been getting better. The important part is that he's alive and, hopefully, hasn't given in to the evil at that school. "

"I know that he's still the person he used to be," Vanessa stated wistfully.

"If I'm allowed to ask, what was he like?"

"An amazing brother with a really kind heart. I hated hanging out with him since he would pick on me so much. But when it mattered, he cared. The night before his eighteenth birthday was when the people in blue cloaks arrived though.

I had come back from school for a few days to watch him go off to his internship the next evening in a different kingdom. But after they stole him, they fled the castle while we were sleeping. Everyone, except… me.

I had to stand there and watch the whole thing. Watch as they stole my brother away from them. I knew I had to do something. I knew I had to save him."

Conner's breath stilled as he seemed to wait for her to continue.

"But I just stood there. Stood there in fear, so much so that, by the time they left, I was still frozen. I was eventually able to wake up my parents and tell them what had just happened. That they'd just taken him. Just chucked him in a burlap sack as he writhed and screamed with his mouth gagged. I was only thirteen."

Silence weighed on them for several moments as they flew, the atmosphere heavy over the whistle of the wind.

"And so, I wanna break him out. And Avery. I wish I could save everyone from that place. I really wish I could."

"Well, can't we?"

"What d'you mean? That's impossible for obvious reasons."

"Well, maybe not now, but one day. I just know it…" There was a hopeful twinkle in his eyes as he stared up into the sky. "We'll have to save two people first, but then…maybe one day…"

"…we'll save everyone else," Vanessa finished, perhaps indicating a hopeful trust in Conner's conviction.

One day, her look said as she gazed into the distance.

***

"All right Katie," Cassie said, crouching next to her sister. "Where are we?"

They crouched behind a bush in a grassy meadow, trees lining the area for miles.

"This place is the best spot to find aloe vera leaves." She set down their basket with elderberries and crenomoris flowers, a plant known throughout the Magic Realm that can help with magical pain and inflictions."

"But this place is crawling with Squadron drones. Katie, what were you thinking?"

"I was thinking," she said back, a tinge of annoyance in her voice, "that we need to complete the mission Aria assigned. And they're really only found here."

"Fine then," her sister grumbled. "What's the plan?"

"As you know, Squadrons use a sort of UFO-type system to take people, meaning we can't use a force-field spell or anything of the sort."

"So, we need to use attack spells?"

"Yes, basically. Impetum exponentia." When her wand illuminated, she drew a circle in the air, the disc moving with the wand's tip.

Cassie peered over the bush at a single Squadron, a red camera-esque light on its gray, metallic body scanning the grounds. She flicked her wand at the drone and a disc of golden light sliced it in half before it could react.

When the rest of the patrolling drones took notice of this, they investigated the bush where Katie and Cassie were hiding only moments ago.

Yet they had escaped just before anyone could find them.

Running in the cover of the forest, they shot attack spells at passing drones in the area.

By the time Katie caught sight of the cluster of aloe vera plants in the middle of the space, all of the Squadrons in their sight had been destroyed, broken metal littering the ground. She sprinted toward the plants with a basket in her hands, wind whipping back her ponytail.

"Here!" she said, accomplished, picking as many leaves as she could and putting them in her basket. "I think that—"

"Katie, watch out!" Cassie screamed, shoving her little sister out of the way of a blast of red light.

She ran alongside her into the cover of the forest, blasts of red light from a Squadron lighting the grass where they had just stepped with dancing flames.

"You are trespassing on property of Vitina's army," said the machine's robotic—rather feminine to be honest—voice. "Surrender or face punishment."

From behind the thick trunk of an alcus tree, Cassie and Katie simultaneously shot an attack spell at the drone, which dodged their magic with ease.

While they were running from their hiding spot, the drone recognized Katie and shot a beam of red-hued light at her, freezing her on the spot where she stood.

"Katie! NO!" Cassie shrieked as her sister floated in the air.

She kept her hands locked with Katie's, likely hoping she wouldn't begin flying as well.

With her feet firmly planted on the ground, she tugged at Katie's arm, but the pull of the light was too strong, sucking her along by its pull.

The drone began flying over the meadow, Katie and Cassie appearing terrified as they flew farther from the ground.

Was this how it was going to be for them from now on? Students in Vitina's miserable school, then members of her army without even a chance to save their sister?

Cassie put her wand into her pocket and scanned the space they were in. There had to be some way they could save themselves. Some way they could avoid capture…

"Impetum exponentia!" two comfortingly familiar voices shouted from afar, two discs of light splicing through the drone keeping them afloat.

Before they could even begin to fall, a hand caught Cassie, another gripping Katie, her chest rising and falling rapidly.

"Hey, you two. Seems you almost got yourselves caught, huh?" Conner hoisted Cassie onto Dillion.

"Thanks for saving us," Katie panted as she tried to balance on Dillion's back.

"No problem, we're just glad you two survived," Vanessa claimed, steering Dillion toward the van. "What happened? Why was that drone taking you?"

"Katie," Cassie breathed, exhausted, "you explain."

***

The group sat at the dining table, the sun already set as they feasted on a hearty meal of mashed potatoes and mushroom soup.

"I can't believe you guys were able to fight off all those Squadrons!" Aria said, clearly impressed, mouth stocked with food as she spoke. "Your spell practice really came in handy there, didn't it?"

"Well, I for one always believed you guys had magical prowess," Darius said in a formal dialect, directed at Aria.

"Why thank you," Cassie responded, playing along.

Dinner that night was an extremely enjoyable experience, despite them having to leave early the next morning—at four, to be exact.

From the looks on their faces and the happy chatter, they all enjoyed the time spent together but soon, they had to face true danger.

"Are you guys worried? Anyone need some spell practice?" said Katie frantically as everyone headed off to bed at about nine p.m.

"Katie, you'll barely get any sleep if you try to stay up tonight," Cassie berated, setting her plate down in the sink.

"I know," Katie mumbled as she headed off to bed. "'Night everyone."

"'Night," they all said back, lying down in their beds as they settled into their pillows.

***

Late into the night, Vanessa was struggling to sleep, tossing and turning on her couch bed in the dark silence. She was wriggling around as if feeling awfully nervous or excited.

There was a clear reason for her being excited: she would get to see her brother again.

But was there another reason, perhaps a less mature one?

Maybe one that had something to do with Conner, perhaps?

Good thing it was dark since otherwise, the glow of her cheeks could have been all too obvious.

Was she embarrassed by what she was thinking?

All manner of things were surely coming forth to occupy her mind, such as all the spells and maneuvers she was planning to use that morning.

But was there anything else floating around in her head, by any chance?

She ought to have been thinking of the water spell she could use to drown them out, but… Well, it was Vitina and Andromeda, after all.

They could easily defeat an amateur spell like that. Maybe she could use a slicing spell? Maybe she could slice one of their wands in half or something like that.

Still, she tossed and turned in her makeshift bed.

Something was disturbing her thoughts; that much was clear.

Perhaps it was the thought of an entire morning with Conner!

She smiled somewhat vacantly and looked across the sitting room at Conner already asleep. They had lately become close friends, so the moments around him now weren't as awkward compared to if she had already entered a romantic relationship.

She was just a girl secretly crushing on a good friend. It was obvious she loved her time with him since her features were noticeably aglow each time they had done something together. But otherwise, they were friends.

She enjoyed his company—that was all.

Anyways, maybe he did not really like her romantically.

It wouldn't have mattered to her. She liked the way she felt around him now and a trivial thing like that could never spoil her happiness.

This was what she continued to tell herself. Having a crush on a close friend could never tarnish the friendship, at least, most of the time.

He was fun to talk to and made her laugh and was just a good person overall.

Talking to him just came naturally for her, and it was probably the same for him as well. It was clear he really cared for her, so developing a liking toward him was normal and the regular order of things, wasn't it?

But what if, secretly, he did like her, and he was convinced that she was the one who didn't? What if he thought she hated him?

She sighed aloud. "Stop overthinking everything, Vanessa!" she chastised herself. She pulled the covers over her bare shoulder and settled down, finally ready for some sleep.

Chapter 18
The Break-In

"WE'VE GOT OUR INVISIBILITY suits, our wands, and the plan," Aria said, looking at her invisible team in the trailer, each holding their wands. "By the time they realize two students are gone…well, we'll be far away. Understand?"

"You and I stay here and watch for guards," Darius instructed, holding his wooden wand.

"Conner and I will look for my brother," Vanessa said, holding her wooden wand as Conner stood next to her with his crystal one that glinted in the moon's luminescence.

"And Katie and I will break Avery out," Cassie finished as moonlight streamed in through the window of the van in between the curtain fabrics.

"Seems you all have a handle on the plan," Aria ventured. "Meaning we go on three. One..."

Conner and Vanessa readied themselves, opening the trailer door to reveal a luscious clearing of grass, spread with moonlight, the black sky twinkling with stars.

"Two..."

Katie and Cassie stood behind them, both invisible like their friends, the tips of their wands shining.

"Three!"

The two duos took off onto Rubidium grounds, Conner and Vanessa going to the east part of the school, Katie and Cassie taking to the west.

As they ran through the dead school garden, Katie and Cassie struggled to keep from stepping on dead leaves, which crunched when stepped on during their rapid movement.

"Finally…we're here," Katie panted when they had reached the entrance door.

The stone castle was a gloomy black, its two spires towering into the dark sky. The few silver windows gleamed in the white light of the moon. Atop each spire was a black flag that waved in the gentle breeze, the left flag coming into view and reading:

Andromeda's Students

Whereas the second flag, on the right tower, read:
Vitina's Students

"Can't open it," Cassie said, rattling the gray lock on the door. "If only we could destroy it..." She lit her wand, which started to glow yellow.

"Wait," Katie interjected, putting her hand in front of her sister's wand. "That'll cause problems. There are obviously guards here, so we'll need some sort of distraction."

"Like what?"

"If you kick the door, the guards'll open the doors, and we can sneak in. While they're trying to find the culprit, we'll be able to get inside."

"You sure that'll work? They could just turn around and they'll know we're here."

"Definitely," she said cockily.

"Here we go." She steadied her balance to place her shoe at the door, sole only inches from the stone.

With a burst of energy and a loud thud, her shoe hit the stone, the gong-like sound ringing in their ears. Immediately after, they dove behind a nearby bush and watched as two blue-cloaked guards pushed the door open with their golden wands lit blood-red.

"Who's there!" one of the cloaks exclaimed in a gruff voice. "Show your cowardly self or face us!"

"Stupefaciunt exponentia!" Cassie and Katie shouted in unison, the blasts from the tips of their wand shooting for the guards.

The guards narrowly avoided their spells and charged toward the bush where the two sisters were hiding. They eluded the spells the guards were shooting while chasing them, eventually able to jump behind another bush to regain some composure.

Cassie watched intently as the two guards searched through the school garden within the stone gates, finding nothing but the occasional squirrel and bird.

"*Damn* it," the guard on the right sneered. "Where'd they go?"

"No idea," the monotone guard on the left mumbled. "Maybe we should search somewhere else, Damien."

"Sure, sure. Yeah…" Damien said skeptically as they turned their backs to search the back wall of the building.

"C'mon," Cassie whispered, leading her sister through the entrance doors.

In the darkness of the hallway, they could barely make out the golden-framed portraits of two school deans, Vitina and Andromeda.

The portrait nearest them was a painted picture of Dean Vitina Orbin, her tan skin pore-less and her dark brown hair curling down to her waist. She sat in a flowing dark purple halter dress that reached her ankles, the long dark purple gloves she was wearing clinging to her fingers as they rested in her lap. Despite her seemingly normal dean-like appearance, her smile was a look of deceit, evil, and undeniable wrath.

Her partner, the witch Andromeda, was attired in a light and airy black dress that reached below her knees, its trumpet sleeves obscuring pale white skin on her arms.

Andromeda's hair, a black bob, was in a style swept to the side, allowing her facial features to show. She had prominent cheekbones, slim black eyebrows and red, paper-thin lips curled into something of a slight smile, making it seem as if she despised life and everything in it. Her deep brown eyes shone through the darkness.

It was as if they were watching you wherever you went.

At the end of a corridor, they reached a staircase near Vitina's side of the school, spotting someone slinking through the hallway in a purple gown, her eyes sparkling with fear.

"Is that Vitina?" Katie whispered as they hid behind the stone stairs.

The figure watched the halls. "Come out," she whispered. "C'mon. She's not here."

"She?" Katie thought with a whisper. "Who's she?"

From the shadows, two beings emerged.

A male's burly build was obscured in a black suit, his deep brown hair parted to the side and his olive skin sweaty and scuffed. Beside him fluttered a woman in a black pantsuit. She had chestnut brown skin and curly hair in a tight bun, her black heels clinging to her small feet. Her electric blue wings buzzed as she watched the woman in a purple dress approach.

"Christina Robel, is it?" the woman in a purple dress said in a velvety voice. "Vitina Orbin. Pleasure to meet you."

"Thank you, Dean." Christina turned to the man. "This is my loyal guard and friend, Flynn Albecon. Best guard I know."

"Good to meet you," Vitina said, not looking at Flynn, but she quickly looked back at Christina. "But I must speak with you quickly, without Andromeda finding out."

Cassie and Katie exchanged a glance, then turned back to the conversation.

"About what? Those four treacherous fairies who manipulated me to steal my wand and frame my guards?" Christina scoffed. "We'll find those four and jail them for their crimes."

"Yes, yes, you told me this. But I have little time. Andromeda has been very suspicious of our school. She thinks that we've started teaching students who won't contribute to us in the end. After that group of students escaped the school last year, she's only been letting in the best of the best. But we have this new student, Avery, I believe, who seems excited to be here. Maybe too excited. Would you happen to have any information on her?"

"Not at all. But I came here to talk about those four, and you'd better let me, or our deal won't be made," Christina threatened, her obvious only intention and only goal to make Cassie and her friends face the consequences of what they'd done.

"Fine, fine. Tell me, who were they?"

"Katie Smith, Cassie Smith, Conner Thomas, and Aria Thomas. Do you know any of them?"

"I believe that Avery girl has mentioned the first two. Her sisters, she said. Odd, no? The suspicious girl related to the suspicious criminals."

"Not odd. Evidence. You should investigate that Avery. Might give me some information on her sisters."

"Yes," Vitina agreed. "But if you join me and my partner to help run this school, I promise to help you find Katie, Cassie, Conner, and Aria."

There was now worry in Katie's eyes at the mention of her and her friend's names.

"Is our deal made?" Vitina said, sticking out her hand.

"It is done." Christina shook her hand firmly.

Then they parted ways, Christina and Flynn taking off for the night sky out of a large window on an amaratio, too quick in their departure for either Katie or Cassie to decipher what type of amaratio it was.

The Dean walked away, back up the staircase behind which the two were hiding.

"She was our best ally, but now the President of the Animal Kingdom is against us, meaning the whole kingdom is against us," Katie whispered grimly. "And now that they're siding with Vitina and Andromeda, what are we supposed to do? We're running out of time. These kingdoms will track us down one by one until we can't even escape this place.

"We have to find Avery now. We have to get out of this dimension."

Katie looked full of anguish at the news.

What was even worse than the Animal Kingdom looking for them was Vitina, and what she would do if they didn't save her sister. She planned to use every weapon possible, every way feasible to interrogate Avery.

Even torture.

All because she wanted the Animal Kingdom on her side.

As soon as Dean Orbin had disappeared into her sleeping chamber, Katie gave her sister a worried look. "We need to get to Avery now."

"How?" Cassie whispered back.

"We'll need to find the girls' dorms, okay? Then from there, we'll look for Avery."

Still invisible, they climbed up the east staircase, passing stone walls with pictures of past and current students.

All the students, new and old, looked… miserable.

Their giant frowns and sunken eyes gave them a zombie-like appearance, as if they'd never lived a normal life, barely ever seen their families, never been close to anyone…

Cassie stopped.

"What?" Katie whispered, walking toward her sister. "What'd you see?"

Cassie stood stone-faced, starring at the reddish-brown rust growing on the border of a silver frame. The painting to which she flicked her eyes was of a girl with dark ginger hair, sunken, brown eyes, and a black pinafore with a white collar of a blouse beneath.

The peach-white skin on her collar bore a black scar on the left and purple on the right, thin as paper cuts.

"It's Avery," she whispered. "My sister... What are they doing to her?" She turned to her sister, shaking out of despair and fear. "Where'd those scars come from?"

"I don't know," Katie said, seeming to swallow her worry as she continued to walk. "But we're gonna get her out. And she's coming home."

Determination showed as her face turned serious. "With us."

Cassie clenched her fists and smiled with persistence against the tears that welled in her eyes. "Yes. We're bringing Avery back."

While they continued to walk, Katie caught sight of someone over the left railing in the hall below.

She was wearing a black pinafore with a white shirt beneath, her dark ginger hair swishing with each step she took. The girl looked up at the east staircase, observing the stairs for a while. She started to squint at the stairs, as if something were off about them.

The girl shrugged and continued to walk carefully through the halls, looking up at the staircase every now and then.

Katie locked eyes with the girl, stopping Cassie from continuing with her steps and pointing to the girl. "It's Avery!"

They smiled at each other and zoomed down the staircase as quiet as possible, meeting the girl at the base of the staircase and throwing their arms around her.

"What's going on? Get away from me!" the girl breathed, writhing in their invisible embrace. "What are you? Who are you?"

They backed away from her, allowing Cassie to whisper, "Your sisters, Cassie and Katie."

"But why can't I see you?" Avery said, searching for where the voice was coming from. "Did you use a spell?"

"Of course," chirped Katie happily. "We'd do anything we could to save you. And now, we're here with you!"

Avery's lips upturned into a bright smile for a couple moments, then frowned. "We've gotta get out of here." She looked at the corridor briefly. "If one of the deans find us, we're dead."

At her words, they began running back to the entrance of the school, Avery leading them because she knew the school layout all too well.

"There... are... guards... at the door," Cassie panted, sweating when the entrance door to the school was in view.

Since the guards stood on the inside of the entrance, they would have to be extra careful when they were to provide a distraction.

"I have an idea," Avery said as she watched the guards engage in a small conversation. "You guys need to wave your wands in the air like ghosts in front of the guards. When they don't fall for it, run to the west part of the school. Once you see the portraits of Vitina and Andromeda on the other side of the school building, stop and wait for the guards to leave, then come back to this entrance. I'll need you to meet me in the school garden. Clear?"

"Crystal," Katie and Cassie said simultaneously, heading in front of the guards.

"Oooooo," Katie said, elongating her vowels as her crystal blue wand was the only thing visible. "IIIII am a ghost frooom Vitina's paaaaast."

"And I am her sisteeer," Cassie added, holding up her wand as well. "If you don't listen to our message, we will kidnaaap your leeeaaadeeer."

The guard on the right snorted, glowering at the floating wands.

"You're no ghosts, you dumbass kids. And students aren't supposed to be outside of their dormitories at this hour." He lit up the tip of his wand. "If I need to give you another warning, I'll send you to the dungeon."

At his words, Katie and Cassie sprinted down the hall to the west corridor, the guards trailing behind them.

After they were out of sight, Avery pushed the stone doors open, revealing the moonlight clearing in front of the school. It stretched for a bit more than an acre, consisting of grasses, moonshade berry bushes, and the school's dead plant garden.

"What are those berries called again?" Avery asked herself, leaning against the stone wall near the door to the school. "Moonnight, moonrode, moon—moon—moonsh... moonshade!

"I swear, they were in my first book of Across the Universe! 'The bright blue berries are meant to look edible, trying to convince the brains of magic users to eat them.

"'However, ingest just one berry and instant paralysis in the legs will result. If the person does not get treatment after thirty minutes, the whole body will be paralyzed.

"'Without help within half an hour after that, the toxins of the berries will kill the victim through intense burning irritation.' See, I remember every word of it!"

She chuckled to herself, peering at the bushes surrounding the school.

This hellish place was full of horrible deadly berries. Fitting.

She looked over the school wall, seeing a beige trailer with two cherry red stripes.

Her mortified expression showed, *So, that's where they've been staying? A trailer? While I've been sleeping on a tattered blanket?*

As the doors thrust open, Avery began her run toward the trailer, hearing Katie and Cassie's heavy breaths from behind her.

The van was almost there. She was almost free. This was it.

She was getting out of here.

A woman appeared in front of her in a flash of purple with tan skin, long, dark-brown hair, and a flowing purple dress.

"Oh! Dean Orbin," Avery breathed, clutching at her gut as if nauseous all of a sudden.

"Yes," she said, caressing the wooden wand in gloved hands. "And you Avery Smith..." She glared at her with blank, emotionless eyes. "… will be coming with me."

"Will I be punished, Dean Orbin?" Avery questioned, throat dry with fear.

"Perhaps," Vitina said, looking back at her wand. "If you obey my orders, I may let you live. You're one of the best students at this school, anyways." She cryptically grinned at her. "Gives our school a good name."

Avery straightened her position, slightly raising her chin in defiance, clenching her fists. "And if I don't?"

"Why would you ask such a foolish thing like that? Don't you remember what happened to a student a year ago who tried to escape? That one by the name of Eda Anderton?

"I gave her a warning clear as day, but she didn't listen to me. So, I left her in the wrathful hands of Andromeda. Any idea what happened after?"

"Sh—she—"

"She died. That's what happened. That *is* what happens when you don't listen to your Dean. When you don't respect your Dean."

"But how do you know I'm alone? How do you know no one is here to attack you? That could easily happen." Avery kept her expression serious and firm, while Katie and Cassie, still invisible, hid their wands in their cloaks, tiptoeing behind the dean. "I'd recommend you don't try to kill me. I don't want my favorite dean dead."

"Don't flatter me, Smith," she said, frowning at the girl's disregard. "You're not that stupid as to try to assassinate a dean. An official dean. With connections to Andromeda."

"Yes, Dean." Avery stood beside Vitina, head down and lips curled in a frown, yet the glint in her bright eyes showed she was ecstatic.

It was their perfect chance. The perfect chance to destroy Vitina and get back to the Earth Realm. Back to her room, her old life, her friends.

And her parents.

Oh, how she missed her parents. She missed her mom's signature beef stew. Her gingery tea. Her warm, loving hugs and pep talks. And her dad who played tennis with her on the courts and helped her with her homework. If only she could see them again, if only.

A blast of blue hit Dean Orbin in the back of the head, knocking her to the ground.

"Let's go," Avery ordered, turning toward her sisters who had moved in from behind Vitina, to behind her. "Now we can leave…"

Katie and Cassie stayed silent, watching a shadow loom over Avery.

"Oh really," Vitina hissed, the tip of her wand digging into the back of the base of Avery's neck. "If you leave with that purple mark..." She pointed at the purple scar on Avery's collar. "... it'll shock you whenever I tell it to."

She laughed menacingly at the idea.

A bolt of purple electricity ran all the way down Avery's spine, causing smoke to escape from her head. Her spine felt as though fire was teasing it, and there was a sharp piercing sensation throughout her back.

"NO!" Cassie screamed, pointing her wand at Vitina's forehead. "You touch her again and I'll stun you! You touch her again and I'll kill you!"

"Oh, could you really?" the Dean smirked, shocking Avery again. "I can do whatever I want with this girl because she's in my custody. And I told her to listen to me, and she didn't. Don't listen to your elders and bad things happen. That's how it works."

"That's sadistic!" invisible Katie yelled, pointing her wand at Dean Orbin as well. *"You're* sadistic!"

"I know, right?" she giggled darkly. "Andromeda will be so proud of me. But you know you can't kill me anyways, kid. I'm Andromeda's partner. She has shared her lengthy lifespan with me. Like signing a deal with the devil himself."

Katie peered over Vitina's shoulder to see Conner and Vanessa together in a dorm room through a window, a shadow in the room with them. They were talking to the shadow, so it seemed, so that had to be Francis. All they needed was for them to come and they could outnumber Vitina and stun her long enough to escape!

"Are you plotting something, Katie Smith?" Vitina said, interrupting her thoughts. "You can't be saved, and you know that. If you didn't know, I can see you despite your pathetic invisibility potion. It's a bit worthless if you want to sneak around me."

Cassie blasted a ray of blue light at the Dean, who avoided it easily.

"Don't be stupid. A simple paralyzing spell like that has nothing on my powers. Especially my individual power. I can enhance my magic with my own personal power, allowing me to do magical things you couldn't even begin to fathom."

"Then why won't you?" Cassie tested her.

"Because I'll make you a deal. Your magic is pretty advanced, I must say, and Andromeda is recruiting new students. If you and the rest of your friends agree to attend my school, I'll let you live. My army could use your magic."

"Is that even a question? Of course, I won't join you!"

"You won't at least try to comply?" Dean Orbin smiled once more. "Then it is done."

She shot a ray of purple light at Avery, knocking her to the ground.

"YOU MONSTER!" Cassie shouted. "That's my sister! If she dies, I'll kill you! I'LL KILL YOU!"

"Damn teenagers," Vitina scoffed. "Your *meltdowns* won't do any good, you know? You still can't beat me, even with your fluctuating emotions. I can stun you too if you'd like."

"TRY! Try to stun me! I'll take a couple spells for my sister! Because I love her. Something you've probably never known… Love," Cassie remarked.

"You're just Andromeda's lackey!" Cassie went on. "By the time she has her army, she'll dump you. She'll dump you like the scum you are!"

"Don't talk to a dean like that!" Vitina screamed, Cassie's remarks finally getting to her, wand afire. She pointed it at Katie now, a tinge of insanity in her eyes as she screamed, "Just for the fun of it!"

A blast of purple hit Katie in the shoulder, knocking her to the ground, now limp and barely breathing.

Cassie could feel tears welling in her eyes.

Her two sisters were barely alive, and she couldn't fight Vitina, not with her spells. What was she gonna do? She had no plan, no advantage, no power.

Her power.

Her power to show emotions.

Why couldn't she have a more relevant one? To show Vitina her emotions would be stupid! Even as she said, her moods had no way to—

In that moment, she remembered what Conner had said, about how each emotion dictated a certain power.

What power would be the most helpful here? Sadness? Envy?

Anger.

That was the solution. If she mustered enough anger to produce fire from her hands, she could defeat Vitina, or, at least, knock her out. That was how it worked, right?

She had to believe that was how it worked.

She thought of the way Vitina had stunned Avery and Katie with no remorse. How she employed people to kidnap innocent kids. How she worked on the side of evil without a second thought. How she hurt people 'just for the fun of it'.

How she killed people.

Before Cassie could realize it, her palms were glowing bright red, the amount of light produced breaking the invisibility potion previously keeping her out of sight.

Her palms continued to emit bright red light, anger broiling inside her.

Her hands were so hot they lit aflame, yet she felt no pain at all.

An inferno of orange and red flames of anger and hate shot forth toward Dean Orbin, causing Vitina to fall to the ground in an obviously writhing, burning pain.

"Do you know how hard it is to kill me, you idiot?" the Dean breathed, standing up again. She was clearly much weaker after that, but she threw her gloves off her hands.

Her palms were turning light purple, dark purple smoke escaping from her fingers.

"You can't kill me..." She smiled darkly as the insanity Cassie had witnessed before engulfed her. "... But I can kill you."

As Vitina blasted purple light at Cassie, she countered with her inferno, the flames eating at Vitina's smoke.

"Looks like I'm beating a dean!" she provoked. "Guess you're rusty, eh?"

Vitina didn't answer, strengthening the smoke coming from her hands.

Cassie's own flames bent around her like a shield as her power struggled to defend her against Vitina's.

The flames licked at her skin, leaving searing marks that burned more as she persevered.

This was it. Her final moment in life, eaten by her own flames.

The fire radiated back in her face, surrounding her in painful heat. Was there any way to come back from this? Any way for her powers to defeat Vitina's?

Before she could even try, her flames engulfed her completely and she passed into unconsciousness.

***

"Little sis!" Francis said happily, hugging Vanessa. "Oh man, I missed you!"

"I missed you, too, Francis," Vanessa replied as she pulled away from her brother. "And this is my friend, Conner."

"Well, hi," Francis greeted.

"Hey," Conner said a bit awkwardly.

He looked from one to the other as though comparing their facial features. They were indeed similar; the same golden skin, the same rounded jaw, the same silky brown hair.

They stood in a small stone-floored dormitory where twenty eighteen-year-old boys slept in tattered blankets, heads laid on moth-eaten pillows. The boys plainly struggled to sleep in the chilly room, some tossing and turning on the hard floor.

"So, Francis," Vanessa said when they had exited the room and were heading for the east staircase. "How's this place been?"

"Awful. They teach the classes so horribly, so almost everyone ends up failing. And every question you get wrong is another thirty minutes you have to spend in detention—or the dungeon. Honestly depends on how the professor's feeling that day."

"A dungeon? What's there?"

"It's basically this place where you have to improve your military skills. It's run by Andromeda, and not the regular teachers, so whenever you mess up during the drills, she shocks you with a spell."

"Sounds horrible," Vanessa commented as they descended the stairs, watching for anyone. Although, she didn't look too shocked, probably having already known this school would be awful. "Well, it's good that we're getting you out of here. And did you hear what happened with Mom and Dad?"

"No, they don't allow electronics here. What happened with them?" he inquired.

Vanessa tensed up and looked from Conner to Francis; should she really tell him after how long he'd been gone?

"Long story short, there was an attack on the ruler's castle. It's been happening for a while now."

Francis looked appalled.

Chapter 19
The Answers

"**WHAT'S GOING ON?**" Cassie asked herself, noticing the drop in temperature. "Where am I?"

It seemed that her flames had disappeared. All she could see was a black room and a single pristine white door with a silver handle on the opposing wall.

Stepping toward the door, she set her hand on the knob, twisting it.

As she pulled it open, she walked into a white room where she found her friends standing in their black tunics and pants.

"You're all right!" she exclaimed, hurrying toward Katie and Avery.

She dived to embrace them in a hug…

…and fell flat on her face.

Rubbing her chin, she got up. Again, she tried to hug them, but ended up wrapping her arms around herself. "They're holograms?"

She tried to hug her other friends, all smiling in the same stance, but ended up unable to touch them as well. She stuck her hand through Katie, and began to glitch.

She leaned against a wall, crossing her arms over her chest.

All she wanted was to get home. Now, she had no idea where she was! Only days ago, she had been there with all her sisters and all the love she needed. But then it changed.

It had all changed when Avery disappeared into that portal.

But why *was* there a portal?

She had never stopped to think about it. Conner had said they appeared because they were attracted to strong magical energy. So then, why had it been their house in which a portal to another dimension appeared? Was one of them from here?

No, that couldn't be. The only reason they had magic was because of the wands. Because of the magical cell towers. But of course, they also had their own powers too…

But didn't everyone get those when they entered the Magic Realm?

"How do I get out!" Cassie belted out, but she received no answer. "I need to save Avery and Katie! I need to get them back to Earth where they're safe!"

For a moment, there was a still silence, then a woman appeared before her.

She had dark ginger hair and brown eyes like Cassie and her sisters, a black wrap dress and a pair of black high heels with a delighted smile on her face.

"Mom?" Cassie asked, eyes locked on the woman. "You're here? B—but how?"

"By the power of magic," she said. "Now give me a hug."

"You're really my mom?" Cassie interrogated, staying in her spot. "What's your name?"

"Trinity Smith."

"How many kids do you have?"

"Three: Cassie, age fifteen; Avery, twelve; Katie, ten."

"Who's your husband?"

"Micah Smith."

"You are Mom!" Cassie exclaimed, embracing her mother in a hug. "It's you, it's you, it's you! I've missed you so much, Mom! So much has happened! Avery was kidnapped and we found this lion that's now Katie's pet and we've almost died so many times…" She paused, backing away. "Why aren't you worried, Mom? Are you Vitina?"

"No, I'm not," said her mother sternly. "But that's who I need to speak with you about." She sighed before she continued, "Back before any of you were born, I used to be a sorcerer here in the Magic Realm. I used to work with the late Ruler Marjorie.

"She taught me spells and potions and Elemental Magic," she reminisced happily, lips turning to a frown almost immediately. "The day Vitina came, Ruler Marjorie told me to run.

"To run as far away from the Kingdom of Magic as I could, away from Andromeda and Vitina. But Vitina and Andromeda would stop at nothing to find me.

"If they found me, the reign of Ruler Marjorie would be completely over.

"And she could take over the Magic Realm.

"Yet on my getaway, I met your father who insisted that we go to a new dimension where Vitina and Andromeda couldn't go. Where they couldn't attack us. The Earth Realm. I didn't know how to get there, of course, but after trial and error, your father and I found a way.

"Opening the portal, we escaped through it, leaving the troubles of this world behind. And we started our life on Earth."

For the first time since she'd started speaking, she finally smiled. Genuinely smiled.

"And that's when we had you."

Cassie smiled, although her expression immediately turned puzzled. "Why is this important, Mom? Just because you know Vitina doesn't mean it's impor—"

She froze. "That's why she wanted Avery! Because she's the daughter of Ruler Marjorie's assistant! She must've known that somehow, someway she could be able to get to you if she was able to get to Avery. That's why she refused to let her leave, at least for the most part, right? So then, why was there a portal in the house?"

"Because the Magic Realm needed me to come back. To vanquish Vitina and Andromeda once and for all." She took a deep breath. "The realm opened the portal to tell me to come back. And apparently, the author of Avery's books knows of this place as well.

"Not sure how though. So, we need to meet the author of the Across the Universe series for answers. If we find them, they can give us insight into how to defeat Vitina and Andromeda."

"So, if the author lives in the Earth Realm, we have to get there then. That means we need to get to the author before Vitina does, or else we can't find a way to destroy her!" Cassie deciphered. "How would I beat Vitina though? My individual power is based on my emotions, but she beat me in a duel only five minutes ago.

"I don't have enough strength to defeat Vitina, let alone Andromeda."

"It's okay, Cassie," her mother reassured. "Because I do know a way you and your sisters can escape her for the time being." She gazed into her daughter's identical brown eyes as if gazing into her own, so happy to be with her again. "The answer lies in Crystalia."

"Crystalia?"

"Yes, Crystalia. There, you'll meet my best friend, Dalia Fulton, who can help you get out of the Magic Realm. She's a former teacher at one of the magic schools in Crystalia and a member of the Council of the Realm. She's also the mother of Stephanie Fulton at a magic school called Ivory Princeton High."

"Stephanie Fulton? I remember that name…" A thought popped into Cassie's head. "Her mother left her a note at school that said she can't go to Land of Elves.

"And then, when my friends and I had to pick up ingredients for a potion, we discovered a secret base for members of Vitina's army there!"

"You've already learned the connection between Rubidium and Vitina's army?"

"My new friend Conner explained it to me the other day. Vitina and Andromeda are taking kids to Rubidium to train them into soldiers for her army, which she's gonna use to take over the Magic Realm, I think. They're doing this to go undetected."

"Exactly! Which means we've got to defeat her before she hurts anyone else. My phone picks up on the news from here, and I've learned that she sent some of her army members to attack the ruler's castle in the Magic Realm. Luckily, the Royal Guards caught them.

"They want to defeat everyone standing in their way of getting power, which is why they're eliminating those with connections to the Council of the Realm or Ruler Marjorie, since they consider them their most powerful opponents."

"So that's how they'll conquer the realm. But what do they want with that power?"

Her mother sighed solemnly and answered, "I'm afraid they'll want to take over more dimensions. Including…" She gulped. "…ours."

"The Earth Realm! This is awful! We've gotta get to Dalia Fulton. And now that you're here we can find her together."

"Cassie," her mother began as she faded away in the white light. "I must leave, or the Hologram Room will trap me here. This temporary portal won't last long, you see.

"Goodbye Cassie; I love you so very much. Do what you need to get back home safe, okay? I believe in you!"

Then she was gone.

Cassie was still trapped in the white room and needed to find some way out. She needed to get out and tell her friends the plan. The plan to get to Dalia Fulton and meet the author of Across the Universe for answers.

"Anyone! How do I get out?"

No answer.

She tried to open the door to the black room that she had entered previously, but the door wouldn't budge.

That won't work. So maybe my powers will?

She focused on all the bad things Vitina had done, causing her body to start glowing red the same way it had when she'd fought her.

She continued feeding her anger and looked on as her hands caught aflame.

She blasted her flames at the walls in the room, yet nothing, rather unsurprisingly, happened.

What do I do? I can't burn this place down. Is there anything else I can try?

"No, Cassie," a deep voice said.

"Who said that?" she blurted, whipping her head around as she held out her wand. "Who's there!"

"Me," the voice said again. "The Hologram Room. I am the space where holographic interactions can be made. Here, and only here, may you see someone from a different dimension across the multiverse and speak with them as a solid being."

"How do I get out?" she asked the Hologram Room. "My powers don't seem to work."

"Of course, they don't. All powers are useless in the Hologram Room to prevent damage to this sacred location," the room explained. "But you *can* get out. To leave, you must destroy the things you love to prove you truly want to be freed from here."

"What am I…"

She stared at her hologram friends, still and glitching, and eyes widened with terror.

"I have to use my powers on them? My friends? Of course not!"

"You must prove you want to leave this place."

"But there's gotta be some better way," she breathed. "There's gotta be, right!"

"Do it!" it boomed. "Unless you choose to stay in this room for eternity."

She stopped for a few seconds, staring down at the ground in utter defeat. She wished there were some way around this.

She knew they weren't real, but could never fathom doing this. Not to her friends. Not to her sisters.

"Okay," she hissed, words harsh as she clenched her fists and ignited them aflame with bitterness and fury.

Not toward the Hologram Room though.

Toward herself.

She knew she had to get out of here but doing this felt wrong. It *was* wrong. It made her feel like a bad person. Like a traitor.

Like Vitina.

But before her flames could retreat at the harrowing thought, the painful comparison, her holographic friends had been scorched to a crisp.

They were falling to the ground in separate piles of ash.

She turned around, freezing up as her hands shook with guilt.

Her vision blurred at the sight.

"You've done it, Cassie Smith. You have proven you want to leave the Hologram Room. And now, you may."

It was sick. It was twisted what this room had made her do.

But the deed was already done.

And so, she disappeared in a puff of white smoke.

She was sick to her stomach, guilty and angry at herself as she shook with horror. It still weighed on her. Even if they weren't real.

But, in the very least, her questions had now been answered. The plan was clear.

Hopefully, this was enough to liberate her from the weighing guilt.

Chapter 20
Escaping a Sorceress

CASSIE AWOKE TO THE SOUND of crickets, her head pounding painfully. Standing up, she glimpsed a shadow carrying Avery and Katie over its shoulders like sacks of potatoes, and she felt the reoccurring anger toward Vitina again, coming over her like a wave she'd never experienced before.

"And where are *you* going?"

Vitina didn't turn back or answer, but continued to walk toward…

...the group's van.

Was Vitina going to attack it? Was she going to destroy it so that they couldn't escape?

Cassie sprinted toward her, hands outstretched to strike during her time of vulnerability.

She stopped.

The figure turned around, revealing it was only Conner with a smile on his face.

"Vanessa and I were able to stun her, by the way."

"Oh," Cassie realized embarrassingly, halting where she stood. "What about the guards? And where's everyone else?"

"Vanessa and I used a sleeping spell on them, so they won't be much of a problem. And as for the group, I told everyone to head back to the van where it's safe."

Walking toward the van, Cassie turned to where they were going with a straight face, not expressive enough for any sort of emotion to be picked up on.

"Y'know, one day, they'll find us. They'll track us down. And they won't stop at anything until they get what they want. Vitina and Andromeda want to get rid of every remnant of Ruler Marjorie's reign, including the people related to those on the Council of the Realm, families of the kingdom rulers, and her relatives."

"Like me…" He looked back at her. "So, then what'd we do?"

She was still facing the van but this time, there was a hint of hope on her face.

"I was able to contact my mom in this place called the Hologram Room when Vitina's spell knocked me out. She told me that we've gotta get out of this place. Out of this dimension. When we do, we'll actually be safe from Vitina."

"How'll we do that?"

"Oh that…" She smiled for the first time in a while. "… I've already got an idea."

***

After setting Katie and Avery down on Katie's bed, still unconscious, Conner sat at the dining table with Darius, Aria, Cassie, and Vanessa.

"Shouldn't we be leaving now?" He peered at the barely open window, the dark sky becoming a lighter gray as the stars were losing their shine. "That spell on the guards and Vitina will only last for one more hour. Probably even less."

"But we still need to know where we're going," Aria demanded. She looked at Cassie. "What were you saying again?"

"When I was fighting Vitina, her magic beat mine and I was knocked out. I was brought to a place called the Hologram Room where I was able to talk to my mom through a portal. She told me that she used to be Ruler Marjorie's assistant and how Vitina is looking for her. Since almost every one of us is related somehow related to Ruler Marjorie or one of the kingdom's rulers, she'll be looking for us too. So, we need to get to the Earth dimension before that happens."

"She talked about someone called Trinity Smith. Isn't that your mom?" Conner observed.

"Yeah, which is why my mom was able to leave before becoming a victim to her magic because of your grandmother's warning. I also learned that the author of the books that Avery's reading seems to know about this place somehow.

"And we have to meet that person for answers before Vitina does."

"But how do we get there?" Vanessa asked.

"We have to meet someone named Dalia Fulton who will be able to help us," Cassie answered.

"Another question. That portal in your house—how'd it open?" Aria investigated. "Don't those require strong magical energy?"

"It was because my mom needed to come back and defeat Vitina, so a strong magical energy was pulled to her, or at least that's what she said. Since we don't have a definite way of using that portal again, we'll have to meet Dalia Fulton who can help us get to Earth."

"Where does she live?" Conner questioned.

"Since news of the Kingdom of Magic attacks has started to spread, all the Kingdom of Magic officials and Council of the Realm members have moved to undisclosed locations.

"But before Grandma died, she told me that the Council of the Realm would have meetings in Crystalia," Aria responded.

"So, we just have to drive north," said Conner. "That'll be a couple of hours. But now we should find a forest far from here to stay in, far from Rubidium.

"So, we can rest up before we start driving again."

"That's only a few minutes of driving," Darius said, eyeing the towering alcus trees in the forest outside of the view of the school. "There's a forest to the east past the school wall."

Conner got up from his seat and sat himself in the driver's chair. Stepping on the gas, he rammed through a bush of moonshade berries, wiping bright blue goo on the windows.

"Can we eat those?" said Katie, finally awake and palms pressed against the chill glass. She looked at her friends at the table, then at Dillion, asleep on the couch.

"Definitely not," Avery said groggily. "I've learned that one berry can cause instant paralysis from the neck down. Without treatment, after a half-hour, your whole body's paralyzed. And in the next thirty minutes, the toxins kill you through intense irritation."

Katie felt petrified and gulped with fright. "Oh, all right then."

"Where's your brother?" Cassie inquired of Vanessa, looking around the room for the new person she'd seen before. "Haven't seen Francis anywhere."

"Taking his first bath in weeks. Smells like musty rotten egg," she answered, scrunching her nose. She saw everyone's look of disgust. "Because they don't have showers at Rubidium for obvious reasons."

"Well," Cassie said quickly. "The day's been long, I got little to no sleep, so I'm heading to bed. Goodnight—or good morning. I'm too tired to care."

Without even changing, she set herself down on her bed near the RV door.

In minutes, the faint sounds of her unconscious breaths were audible, blowing strands of dark ginger hair out of her face.

As everyone else peacefully went off to bed for a bit more sleep with the van parked in a much safer location, Vanessa sat in the dark at the dining table, everyone too tired to take notice of her absence or much too apathetic to ask after all that had happened.

Despite how tired he truly was, Conner struggled to finally sleep, coming up to her and sitting by her side at the dining table under the faint, soft light of the sun.

"Why're you up? You want at least a couple hours of sleep before the trip tomorrow, don't you?"

There was a soft tone to his voice, and her gaze drifted away for a few moments, mesmerized by it. She stared out blankly at the forest of trees. "I'm just missing my parents. Haven't seen them in a while, and y'know…" She looked back at him and grimaced. "…y'know what? Never mind, this—this is stupid."

"Wait," Conner stopped before she could rise from her seat. "Tell me."

She stared blankly at him for a moment.

He said, "If I've learned anything from all this time I've had to spend with my sister, talking about your problems is the best way to deal with them. Or at least face them."

She didn't say anything, prompting Conner to immediately respond to himself, "Or don't. I mean—if you don't want to, don't."

He was interrupted by a deep sigh from her, as she continued on, "I lived my whole life knowing that my parents were just a long walk away, but now all I can do is call or text them. And I know it sounds self-centered, considering the fact that the kids we had to see in Rubidium may never see their parents ever again, but…"

She gazed deeply into his blue eyes for a moment, then they flicked away almost as soon as she focused in on him.

"The looming threat of doom is scary, Conner. It terrifies me. And I'm afraid to admit it, but I'm scared. And I wanna go home. I wanna see my family again. But…"

"You can't," Conner admitted, speaking in a way directed more toward himself than Vanessa. "And I can't either. I've already committed myself to this. Committed myself to saving those kids and helping them to get somewhat better lives in the end.

"And I feel selfish for leaving them." He looked to the floor, then to her. "But now we can help all these people. And I met Katie, and Cassie, and Darius and…"

He smiled sweetly, lips upturning in a sort of way that Vanessa always enjoyed seeing him express. "… You. I'm so glad that I met you, Vanessa. Truly."

The moment they shared was melancholy, and bittersweet.

Her smile showed the words he was saying were right. She expressed that she felt selfish for leaving, especially when she'd discovered what was happening to her parents at home.

But even so, now they had the chance to try to give so many people better lives. And she wanted that. But additionally, the thing that made her smile so widely was the fact that she was able to be here with him.

"Vanessa?" Conner said, interrupting her thoughts. "Do you wanna go on a walk?"

"Um—well—sure."

To not wake the others, they crept through the van, grabbing their wands and fur-lined black cloaks. They silently snuck out of the van and cast a spell barrier around the trailer, walking off into the eerie stillness of the forest.

***

"It's beautiful up here, huh?" Vanessa asked Conner, arms wrapped around the thick trunk of an alcus tree as she watched the waters of a nearby lake lap the shore. "So calm, so still, y'know?"

"Y—yeah. That," he managed to respond, trembling. This was a scary place though, the branches holding onto all kinds of fearful things.

She stood for a few more seconds, taking deep breaths until she slowly pulled her arm from the trunk and started running in the opposing direction.

"WHAT THE HELL ARE YOU DOING!" he bellowed, the branch shaking with each step.

He gasped and flinched, watching her leap off the tip of the branch. He pulled out his wand, hissing a flurry of curses beneath his breath. "VOLANS—"

Rather loosely, her right hand gripped a branch just a jump away, and she nimbly hoisted herself over, looking back to Conner as she wiped a bead of sweat from her forehead.

"C'mon!" she screamed across. "You can make the jump!"

"What is she thinking?" he said to himself under his breath, half cursing her.

He slipped his wand back into his pocket, taking a deep breath as the world warped uneasily beneath his feet.

Determined, he closed his eyes, gaining strength, and now his feet were moving; he watched his step every now and then, whilst focusing on keeping the ground out of plain sight. And as he pushed off the tip of the wood, just like Vanessa had done, he landed…

…on the branch…

…his foot slipping.

Luckily, almost immediately, Vanessa caught his hand, pulling him up as she grinned and congratulated him.

"Was it difficult?" she eventually joked as his chest rose and fell dramatically.

"No, in fact," he said, sort of irritated as he spoke. "It wasn't difficult at all."

"Yeah, I know, right? So easy," she chuckled as she started to descend the thick trunk, branch by branch.

She descended with agility, as if she had loads of experience in comparison to Conner's nervous incompetent flailing of limbs.

Even if he felt somewhat irritated at the fact this girl could seemingly do everything, he couldn't help but smile, especially each time he heard the melody of her sweet chuckles.

Already far ahead of her, she had made her way to the grassy shore of a clear lake, a single willow tree rooted there; she couldn't help but lock her eyes onto it.

The light of the early morning sun sparkled on the water and there was a thick rope tied to a thick branch of the willow, implying someone was most likely here.

"Um, if someone's been here before," he pondered aloud, "this might be obvious, but shouldn't we be leaving? And Vanessa wouldn't be so stupid as to—"

Before he could even finish his internal sentence, Vanessa took off for the lake, removing her cloak and setting it at the base of the willow with urgency.

She backed away from the lake with the rope in her hand and kicked off her shoes, flying at the bark of the tree and snapping off a bit of it swiftly.

He witnessed her propelling herself through the air on the rope, then watched on as she let go and plunged into the water with an ice-cold watery explosion.

"Your turn," she said to Conner, wrapping the cloak around herself as she smiled in a fit of shivers. "Water's cold but could be worse, I guess."

He removed his cloak and shoes and jumped backwards with a firm grip on the rope, splashing the grass near Vanessa in more water than what was lapping at the calm shore.

He shivered as he emerged, dripping with freezing water.

He and Vanessa shared a fit of laughter.

When the mutual laughter had started to subside, Vanessa continued on again.

"It's calm out here. Peaceful." She cocked her head at him. "Is that what it's like in the Earth Realm? Like here, but just without magic?"

"Well, I spent most of my life there, so yeah, it is kinda like that." He rubbed his hands together, then tucked them back into his cloak. "There isn't any magic there, but the people never had it anyways. So, they never had to learn to live a life without it."

"Wonder what that's like," she pondered. "No Resicus. No wands. No…"

She gasped and looked at him with a scowl. "Don't tell me they don't have mythical creatures there!"

"No, sadly," Conner confirmed. "They don't. No amaratios…"

She let out a dramatic gasp, one that Conner was clearly picking up was ironic. "No ademonas!" She let out another. "And no remorias!"

She let out a belt of laughter at Conner's mediocre performance and fell to her back at his failed attempts to try and salvage it.

"That was..." She sighed to relieve her laughter. "…horrible, Conner. Truly, the worst performance I've ever witnessed."

"Never," he remarked. "You just can't admit that it was the best, clearly."

"No, Conner." She looked at him with a dead serious look in her eyes. "That was the worst performance I've ever seen."

He blinked a couple of times, watching as her grin started to appear and they both erupted into a fit of laughter once more.

The morning birds chirped as the chuckles died down, and Vanessa unknowingly leaned her head on Conner's shoulder nonchalantly. "Thanks for this, Conner. Genuinely."

"For what? Being an embarrassing dumbass?"

"Yes that." She grinned up at him, then back to the stillness of the forest. "But also taking me out here. It's helped take my mind off things. At least, for a good while."

She rose her head and met his eyes. "Hey, Conner."

Suddenly, though not exactly unpleasant, Conner pressed his lips to hers, both hands tilting her head toward him as she blushed wildly but couldn't help but subtly smile.

She didn't seem to mind but as he pulled away, he whispered beneath his breath, "Sorry."

"No, don't apologize," she said, starting to put on her shoes as she kissed his cheek. "Your gift…" She shifted her voice to a more proper manner of speaking. "…t'was much appreciated, good sir."

He smiled and began, "You're—"

"Wonderful? Impeccable? Amazing?" she joked cockily. "I know."

"Annoying," he finished.

"Yeah, but you still kissed me," she shot back.

"Oh, shut up."

Unlike other times before, this silence was nice. Comfortable. They felt as though they knew each other a lot better, and something about that kiss just made everything between them so much closer.

"Hey, what's that noise?" Vanessa inquired as she stood, pulling Conner up as well.

"What noise?" he inquired.

"Like a flapping noise. Like something flapping in the wind, y'know? It's…"

"W—where'd that thing come from?" she stammered, trembling as she pointed at the giant butterfly that loomed over Conner.

He turned to look at the creature, a lavender butterfly with a furry dark purple abdomen and head, wings flapping slowly as it bobbed in the air.

"I think I've seen one of these before actually."

"A rare lavender butterfly?" she said skeptically. "Where'd you find one?"

"It was in the Animal Kingdom. But this is a transformed wolf, I'm pretty sure…"

"Well, why's it here then? Why'd it fly all the way from another kingdom just to see you?"

"Well, maybe 'cause…" She glared at him as he was about to make a joke but stopped midsentence. "Never mind. I'm not really sure."

"So then, Conner. I'll ask you again," she declared demandingly. "Why did it follow you?"

"Well, I remember it from that night that it flew off after Katie talked to it, but it's not like I knew what it was saying. I can't have any way of knowing why it followed us, but Katie might," he explained. "She'll probably be able to give us a solid answer."

"Well, looks like we've gotta take this thing home then," she said, observing the butterfly for a moment then checking back at the lake to see if they'd forgotten anything.

Yet, in her peripheral vision, was a sight no one could imagine in their worst nightmares.

An army of navy-cloaked people marching in their direction, it seemed, a towering amaratio prowling alongside them with its golden-brown fur shining as it prowled. With a ferocious growl from its bristly muzzle, it locked eyes on Vanessa for a half-second, just when she hid Conner and herself in the cover of the willow.

"Vitina's guards," she breathed. "They're across the lake right now!"

Bolting for the forest behind the lake, the butterfly fluttered beside them, the amaratio belonging to the guards readying for flight.

"It's onto us! We've gotta—"

"Vanessa, I know! Now if you keep talking, you're gonna get us caught!"

Behind them, one cloaked figure boarded the lion, soaring across the lake at harrowing speed as the amaratio's hazel eyes tracked their movements.

"So, how're we supposed to hide from this thing, huh?" Vanessa panted as they crouched in the cover of the forests alcus trees.

"Deflect it off the path, obviously."

"And how do you presume we do that?"

"I don't—don't think I thought that far ahead," he panted, a hint of disappointment in his voice.

"Here," she whispered, putting a small stone in his hand as the amaratio plodded behind them. "Throw it, will ya? But be careful."

Aiming toward a bush several paces from the path, Conner watched as the stone whizzed through the air and fell into it, rustling in a way that imitated the presence of a person.

And as the creature ran directly toward the source of the sound, they took off in the opposite direction, so fast that at the speed they were running, they managed to make it to their van in merely a matter of minutes.

Vanessa immediately brought down the barrier that they had activated, hurrying into the van with the butterfly behind them. As soon as he entered, Conner threw himself into the driver's seat and started the trailer, smashing the bright red button beneath the steering wheel.

"Um—Cassie!" Avery said, as she gazed out the window. She could already see the branches of the ginormous alcus trees, the morning sun coming into view as they rose toward the sky. "What's happen—"

And with a rumble of fire, the van took off for the sky, fluffy white clouds obscuring them from view as they rocketed away.

Vanessa exchanged a nervous glance with Conner in the driver's seat mirror, then glanced back at her friends who were looking for some sort of answers. "Vitina's guards found us."

Chapter 21
The Return of Flynn

"THEY COULDN'T HAVE!" Cassie shouted, distressed. "How'd they even find us?"

"We saw them across the lake in the forest. A whole army of guards," Vanessa added, sitting down at the booth table. "In case any of you spot them, tell us. If they find us, they could destroy the protective barrier around the trailer and destroy it, giving them the chance to destroy us."

"Look at little sis," said a deep voice from the sitting room. "Spoken like a future queen." He shared a laugh with himself.

Sitting across from his sister, Francis gave Vanessa a smile and smoothed his curly brown hair back. He yawned as he walked toward the table, hands in the pockets of the wrinkled jeans he'd borrowed and in which he slept soundly.

Vanessa mocked his smile. "Don't forget, I'm the one who save you from them and I'd be happy to give you back."

"What a horrible thing to say to your brother! After all I've been through," he tsked. "Mom would be so—"

"Hey, Francis." There was a sternness to her voice. "Don't bring Mom into this. Please."

His eyes stayed on her for few moments, although he'd already understood immediately what she'd said. "Okay," he agreed. "I get it."

***

"Nothing but the occasional bird," Cassie reported as she watched the windows. "We should be fine for now."

Seated at her bed, she noticed Avery's grim expression, staring down at the ground. "Avery…" Her younger sister looked up at her. "…are you all right?"

"Of course I am, Cass. It's just that, I kinda thought this world would be more…fantastical, y'know? I did all this. Scared all these people. Scared Mom. And Dad. And—and…" She gazed up into hazel eyes. "…and you." She looked back at the ground once more. "I'm sorry that I did this to you. And I'm sorry that I was so stupid and so—"

"Stop," Cassie said sternly.

"What'd you mean 'stop'? Stop what? Telling the truth about me? About what I did?"

"Y'know, Avery, being honest with you, I kinda thought that too. That you disappearing into that portal was one of the worst things that ever could've happened…"

"Because it was, Cassie. You admit it, don't you?"

"Never," Cassie contradicted. "I'd never say that about you. What I'm trying to say…" She took a deep sigh. "…is I've matured out of that mindset, Avery. All the good people we've met and all the good things that we've done for people never would've been if not for you. And even if you think it was just a stupid mistake, and nothing more, it resulted in a lot of good things happening." She could feel her eyes welling up over as she took Avery in her arms. "And Avery…" She could feel her voice start to waver. "…I'm so sorry that you had to suffer through so much. You are so amazing and so strong and…just know I love you, ok?"

Avery smiled. "You're getting good at these pep talks."

"I know, right?" Cassie admitted, wiping tears from her eyes as she beamed at her.

Just then something hit the van.

As everyone was tossed to the side, the thud of metal reverberated painfully in their ears.

"They've destroyed the barrier!" Vanessa shouted, holding onto the booth seat and removing her wand as everyone else did the same.

Before anyone could get up, three more thuds came, throwing the RV from side to side. And with one last thud, the van stopped in midair, no longer moving.

And in a way that felt unreal, they began plummeting to the ground.

In the driver's seat, Conner desperately tried to lift the van again by punching at the red button repeatedly, yet to no avail.

"Get your stuff!" Vanessa ordered as they crawled around for their belongings. "And get ready for this crash!"

With their bags at their sides, they all covered the backs of their necks with their fingers intertwined, the ground coming ever nearer. Watching to see everyone was in a safe position, Vanessa grabbed her wooden wand and pointed it at the ground.

"Nubes exponentia!" she chanted, beginning to lift from the ground as she flew with the pull of gravity.

As the small cloud beneath the van formed, it sputtered and strived to expand even as they were only a few feet off the ground.

In a puff of fluffy white, the van stopped falling.

Opening the door, Vanessa took notice of the ginormous, pillowy cloud beneath them, and as she stepped out, she looked at the back of the van; it was dented quite badly.

Luckily, not so much that it would affect them a lot.

She observed the front of the van, scanning the entire hood compartment, closely inspecting the engine.

"G—guys," she stammered, a sense of shock and overwhelming worry in her words, "the front compartment's fried."

Everyone stepped outside to see the disastrous sight, eyes widened in recognition they couldn't fix it. Sure enough…

"And we can't fix it," Cassie admitted, dejected. "No tools."

"There isn't a repair spell?" Avery suggested desperately. "There must be, right?"

"There is, but it's not like there are enough magic cell towers around for that."

"So, we're living off the land again," Conner sulked. "And there's an army of guards chasing us on top of that."

"Your boyfriend's kind of a downer, sis," Francis whispered to his little sister, in an attempt to bug her somehow.

"Oh, shut it," she hissed at him. "At least I'm dating someone." She raised her voice to speak to the rest of them, ignoring him as she paced forward. "But, yeah, until we find Dalia Fulton, looks like we're living in the forest as fugitives for the time being."

They took hold of their belongings and bags from the wrecked van, including their tied bag of food from the Elvin Forest of Vegetables.

"We'll be eating these for a while then," Aria said as she held the blanket. "And we'll need a fort by sundown."

"Or we could stay in a cave," Katie insisted. "Would be more spacious and roomier than a fort, don't ya say?"

"We'll need to find one then," Vanessa said, leading the group from the sight of the crash. "And stay there to rest for the trip to Crystalia."

"Which'll be a day's walk at least," Conner added. "It's a good thing those guards haven't found us though."

Everyone nodded in agreement, their moods improving, at least a little bit.

After a few minutes of walking, they came across a large cave, its entrance hole concealed by a curtain of leafy, emerald vines. As they shuffled through, they found the inside to be a large space, the walls, floor, and ceiling lined with soft, green moss, several basketball-sized holes along the cave walls allowing sunlight in.

"Isn't this space convenient?" Francis said, happily, sitting down at the back wall. "Glad we get to stay here for the night."

"I know, right?" Katie chirped, setting her backpack on a stone near the right wall. "Last time, we had to build a place to stay. And that was…" She looked up and grinned sadly. "…that was a lot."

"Wasn't really that bad," Conner stated, sitting down against a rock near the left wall. "Until those wolves came, of course."

"But for now," Vanessa began, grabbing the bag of vegetables from Aria, "we're eating breakfast. And there's no need to worry about stuff like wolves, especially out here in the actual forest."

She set the blanket down on the floor, then collected potatoes, celery, mushrooms, and a variety of other vegetables rolling out of place along the blanketed patches of grass.

Katie seized a stalk of celery and began chewing, the bland juice of the vegetable trickling down her throat, refreshing but lacking in appeal.

"Needs flavor," she said and grimaced, taking another slow bite.

"Better than nothing though," Avery said, glancing at her black pinafore, with a celery stalk in her hand. "Back at Rubidium, they fed us nothing but sloppy gruel. Or we just didn't eat at all. At least this is actual food."

Aria glanced around the room for a moment, then caught sight of Vanessa talking to Albion. "What's the matter, Vanessa?"

"Albion's insisting he goes to the Kingdom of Magic to tell my parents what's happened."

Aria walked over to her and sat down beside her and the blue jay.

"I say you should let him go. Vitina and Andromeda probably don't know about them, so they won't be able to interrogate him, right?"

"Yeah…" she said worriedly. "But what if he gets hurt on the way though?"

"I'm sure that Albion knows his way around this place. And he has his friends on top of that as well."

"Why can't I just call my parents? That way, Albion can stay here."

"But what if the call is hacked and someone finds out about our plan? If Vitina knows what we're up to, we won't have any advantage on her. For information as discreet as this, the best way to communicate is in a way that no one who is possibly our enemy can pick up info on us. And if Albion is willing to do it, and his friends are too, then why not?"

"When you put it like that, I guess so," Vanessa finally said.

Aria pulled out her map and pointed at the corner of the map marked 'Crystalia', finding a large, clear mountain with a roughly sketched cottage on it. "I've been to the house before, and it's basically used as a safe house during times like this. Just tell your parents we'll be going there and that we'll be safe. They should believe one of your friends, right?"

Vanessa turned back to Albion with a melancholy smile. She clearly didn't want to lose him again. But this was something they could do to help her parents. They deserved it.

"All right," she said to him. "I want you and your friends to find my parents, wherever they may be, and tell them that we'll be going to the Earth Realm.

"And that I'll be safe for now, so they aren't worried. We'll be going to a safe house in Crystalia; tell them that, all right?"

The bird nodded at her instructions.

"By my, Princess Vanessa Caswell's, orders, you will perform this task. Understood?" Vanessa commanded, regal in her princess-like tone.

"Understood, Princess Vanessa."

In a cloud of blue, black, and white feathers, the birds flew away from the cave and high into the sky, a cluster of alcus trees obstructing them from view as they soared in the cool air.

Aria sighed deeply as she looked at the grassy ground. Looking around at everyone sitting in a relaxed position, she saw Dillion in the corner of the room as he paced in a circle.

Was he bored?

"Could I take Dillion out for a flight?" she asked Katie.

"Sure," Katie whispered groggily, eyes closed as she spoke. "But it's best you go with someone. May be dangerous out there in the forest."

Darius awoke from his light nap and yawned. "Could I come?" he asked as he scratched his scalp. "Some fresh air would be nice after all this sitting inside."

Aria grinned happily at him. "Sure, nothing's going on right now anyways. And Dillion seems free." She gestured toward the pacing amaratio circling around the grass as if there were some invisible thing to run rings around.

They walked out of the cave curtain with their coats and wands in their pockets, Aria walking alongside Dillion.

She pulled her black sheepskin coat around herself as a brisk wind blew at her hair, Darius climbing atop Dillion first. He had wrapped his dark blue windbreaker tightly around his torso. He was stroking the amaratio's fur as Aria climbed aboard.

"I would've loved to have an amaratio as a kid," he said. "I had always wanted a big, sweet pet. Or maybe an ademona. I'd always loved those as a kid."

As they took off, Dillion's wings flapping and raising them farther from the ground, Aria added, "Ademonas—like those big lizard creatures?"

"Salamander—but yes. Have you ever seen one?"

"I think I've seen one at a market in one kingdom. I was a baby, so it was only as big as me, but it had brilliant blue eyes and red skin striped with blue I remember."

"Have you ever seen one use its power?"

"I saw the vendor telling it to move a puddle from the ground to a pool. It took a while for it to do so, but after, it squeaked in triumph."

"That's so cute," he sang as Dillion's flying leveled out and he started gaining speed.

He looked below him at the sea of pine green, the wind blowing through his hair swiftly. Being this high above the ground on such a mystical and majestic creature was invigorating, an experience sure to let him set aside all tension and fear.

"So where are we going?" Aria asked him as they soared through a cloud, its untouchable fluff opening to allow them to soar through seamlessly. "A lake? A clearing?"

"Since we can't really go anywhere, we're just gonna take a flight near the cave," he responded. "Like I said before, just something for some fresh air."

Aria didn't say anything back as she stared into the distance.

Darius looked back at her bulging eyes, then forward again. "What is it?"

"A train."

"A train!"

"Yeah, look!"

She pointed to a wood building in the distance that sat upon a hardwood platform. Beside the platform was a solid black steam train with two bright red stripes on either side, standing atop wooden train tracks, thick and dark gray smoke escaping from its chimney.

"That'll take us to Crystalia!" he realized triumphantly as he directed Dillion toward a clearing a good distance from the train station.

He directed Dillion toward a clearing near the station and got off of the amaratio.

"What are you doing?" Aria inquired.

"You should go get the others, then I'll send a blast of water into the air, so you know where the train is," Darius directed.

"But what about those guards?"

"I'll be fine, really. Just go, all right?"

"All right," she said after a moment. "Dillion, let's go back to the cave." Aboard the amaratio, she soared off into the sky, leaving Darius behind on the ground.

A few minutes after she left, he pointed his wand to the sky and chanted, "Aqua exponentia!"

With the tip of his wand lit, he drew a large circle in the air surrounding the symbol of a drop of water.

He flicked his wrist, causing a jet of water to continuously stream out of his wand.

He tried to keep his eyes opened as the water drenched his coat, eventually put out of his misery when his friends appeared in a rather speedy manner.

***

While everyone was checking that they had everything at the train station, Katie, to the incredulous sight of many surrounding passengers, was communicating with the lavender butterfly. "What did you need to tell me?" she communicated to it silently, via telepathy.

"I have very valuable information for you about Vitina's army, but you must do something for me after."

"Of course, just tell me," Katie thought to the creature.

"If you ever encounter Vitina, Andromeda, or their army, make sure your friends activate an invisible force field."

"How come?"

"Vitina and Andromeda have started using a new sort of spells that can be invisible. From water to fire, the spells are completely unseen. Therefore, whenever they're around, always keep your force field up."

"I wonder when they were able to do this? But thanks for telling me. Now, what do you need me to do for you?"

"Could you turn me into a wolf again?"

"Of course, that won't be a problem."

She took her crystal blue wand out of her bag and pointed it at the large lavender butterfly. She closed her eyes and pictured a gray wolf striped with streaks of dull black, and her wand set off glowing blue. She stayed focused on the spell despite the few people whispering around her, allowing her to say the incantation.

The light hit the butterfly, causing it to become a swirling ball of sky blue, flipping and spinning around. When the spinning had stopped, the ball of magic reached the ground, a gray wolf left in its place, eyes full of gratitude as it gazed up at the girl.

"AH! IT'S A WOLF!" screamed someone on the other side of the platform, hiding behind their bags.

No one seemed to care that the woman in a red suit had exclaimed this, and most people continued with their normal business.

"What's with people and thinking we just attack randomly? But anyways, Katie, thank you," rang the wolf's voice in her head. Without another word, it trotted off into the woods.

"Here's your ticket, Katie," Cassie said, handing her sister a golden strip of paper that the young girl crumpled in her grip.

She followed her friends with her bags to a line where a few people were boarding a compartment at the front of the train.

Standing at the door was a brunette-haired man with peach skin and a navy suit, golden tassels on its shoulders.

"Why, hello there," the man greeted cheerfully. "May I have your tickets?"

Each person handed their tickets to the man, who handed them the ticket back when he had finished examining it. "Please refrain from using magic on board. We don't want any destruction on the train, you see."

"Yes, will do," Vanessa said, leading her friends into the front compartment.

Inside, the floor had a mahogany red carpet and on both sides of the cabin were mahogany booth seats lined with gold. In between the seats rested brown wood tables, a white lily flower centerpiece within a glass vase positioned on each.

"Where are all the passengers?" Katie asked as she looked around the empty cabin.

"Maybe they're in the next car," Aria suggested, walking to it through a tall, oak door.

The cabin was the same design as the previous one, yet it was packed with passengers reading books and newspapers, using their devices, or simply sleeping.

Back in the previous cabin, the group sat at two booth tables across the aisle from each other. "At least now, we don't have to worry about someone overhearing our plan. So. where's the train's—"

Conner was interrupted by a voice over the speaker in the train.

"Hello there, passengers," the speaker began in the conductor's warm and friendly tones. "This train will be stopping in three hours at the Crystalia Train Station, a bustling mansion where hundreds upon hundreds of trains end and begin their journeys across the Magic Realm. The mansion is near the base of the glorious Crystal Mountain, the tallest landform in the whole kingdom of Crystalia. For a sightseeing tour of the mountain, please speak to an employee at the Crystalia Train Station. All tours will be shown to you at said train station. Thank you for listening, passengers, and enjoy your onward trip."

The train gained speed as Avery looked out the window, the forest of pine trees and alcuses blurring past.

Before Cassie could take out her phone, Avery stopped her.

"Could I have the second 'Across the Universe' book, sis? I need to read up before we meet the author, y'know? Gotta make a good impression on one of my favorite people."

"Here." Cassie handed her the brown book with two small wooden wands on the cover.

"Hmmm," Avery pondered as she ran her fingers over the covers of the book. "Never noticed these wands on the cover. But they look kinda familiar."

She glanced at her wand. "So, what do they mean?"

"Two wands would probably represent two magic users. What're the books about so far?" hinted Katie.

"They follow the stories of these two best friends named Jane and Lilith, magical ones I mean. And adventures they take as friends and stuff."

"I've never heard those names before," Cassie said, a hint of disbelief to her voice. "But if Mom said something about them, they've gotta have something important about 'em, right?"

"Right..." Avery opened to the page she was on. "Maybe reading further will—"

"Oh, but there's something I wanna show you."

Cassie took out one of the later books in the series out of her bag. "This has a staff on it, but haven't we seen it before?" She showed them a twisted wooden staff, its top wider than the bottom, a glowing purple crystal in its grasp.

"Oh wait!" Katie realized with triumph. "I've seen that staff before! In the attic of our house! Mom keeps it there as a 'prop', but what if it's there to be kept from Vitina? We've gotta make sure it's safe!"

"Seems your mom was smart to do that," Conner said from across the aisle. "After Ruler Marjorie died, Vitina searched the castle for her staff. But in the end, she never found it."

"Legend says the Staff of Infinite Power, they call it, can destroy whole dimensions with its power," Aria mentioned, the gravity of the situation weighing down on them. She continued uninterrupted. "If Vitina and Andromeda get their hands on it, they'll have the power to do anything they want. And after that…" She gave a sigh of apprehension, and admitted, "…I'm scared of what'll happen next."

It was silent in the car for several minutes, nothing but the rumble of the train tracks and the whistle of the wind. It was ominous. Eerie even.

Unsettling, to be honest.

Without another moment to contemplate the challenges they would face, a man in a black suit appeared before them, black hair pushed to the side in a somewhat familiar way.

Beads of sweat rolled down his olive skin, panting ringing in the quiet space as everyone's breaths stilled and their muscles tensed.

It was as though they'd seen him before, somewhere in a nightmarish trance.

Yet as soon as he spoke, Katie was the first to remember this man.

"I've finally found you," he chuckled, an insanity to his foreboding words. "I've finally found you…"

No one spoke in response to his words, too terrified to move, and much too frightened to make a sound.

"Don't you remember me?" he asked, words desperate, yet still managing to raise the hairs on the backs of their necks. "I'm President Christina Robel's bodyguard, Flynn, remember? You took her wand, all of you." He stood up straighter and smoothed down the body of his suit with his hands. "That's a serious crime, but that's not all that you did, in fact.

"In addition, you were all at the scene of the crime when the President's new allies, Dean Vitina Orbin of the Rubidium School of Magic, meaning you eight tried to kill her, hmm?"

"Well, can I add something?" Francis added as he stood.

"What are you thinking?" Vanessa asked as her eyes bored into his. She could tell he could see her through his peripheral vision; he'd also always told her that he could.

She couldn't have him taken again. Not after they just got him back.

But somehow, she managed to trust him. If Francis had made it this far at Rubidium without retaining permanent injury, or somehow getting himself killed, then he had to know what he was doing.

Right?

He backed from them toward the door of the car, wand pointed to the ceiling of the train car. "Ignis exponentia!" he bellowed as his wand went alight.

He drew a symbol of the fire in the air.

A sudden swipe of his wand sliced the symbol in half, the ceiling catching aflame before their eyes. Almost immediately, the flames began to wisp with smoke, filling their nostrils as it burned and expanded in a conquering cloud.

Immediately, luggage in hand, they ran to the conductor's compartment, bursting the door open to yell, "There's a fire in cabin one!"

The train came to a slow stop at this news, stopping completely at the base of a bridge that fell away into a large river. The conductor gripped a small speaker in his hands.

"Everyone, evacuate the train now! There is a fire in compartment one! I repeat, a fire in compartment one! Evacuate with your belongings and important luggage as quickly and calmly as possible! All doors are opening now!"

Hurrying out at these words in a flurry of panicked screams and stampeding feet, the passengers and conductor watched as the first compartment's flames devoured the train.

In only a few moments, this whole train is done for, a voice in Cassie's head said frantically. *What am I supposed to do?*

I don't think my magic can really…

Vanessa's eyes were welling up too, most likely at her own incompetence. At her own inability to take care of everyone. She didn't know what to do.

Aria, too, looked lost and helpless, rubbing her nose and eyes as the smoke overtook her.

"Why can't I just be useful for once!" they moaned beneath their breaths, simultaneous to the point that it appeared they could all hear each other's thoughts.

Yet, in reality, they were all struggling with the same thing.

For what was their worth in the world if not to lead? If not to be the shoulder to cry? If not to know exactly what to do all the time?

They took notice of each other, each unable to really speak, yet their eyes said it all.

They understood each other.

Almost as if they had formulated a plan aloud, Cassie held out her hands as Aria and Vanessa pointed their wands at different points of the fire.

They couldn't do this alone. They couldn't handle such a daunting task as only one person. But with some support…some other people there to help…

Maybe. Just maybe.

On Cassie's side, all the emotions she'd been bottling up this whole time spilled forth. All the tears she'd refused to cry to be strong for Katie and Avery. All the crying she'd wanted to do before it shifted and shaped into fury.

Just pure sadness.

For the first time in a while, she finally let herself feel.

A dark blue hue illuminated her skin as the bottled-up feelings came out.

As she did so, the fire was going out in ferocious hisses, Vanessa and Aria letting out a jet stream of water that ensured that the job was complete.

"You did it, guys!" Katie cheered as she tackled the three girls in a hug.

"Awesome job," Conner's voice said, soft in way that made Vanessa appear to crumble with joy in his warm embrace.

He turned to his sister. "And you too, Aria. Thank you. Genuinely."

Francis stood by as they all embraced each other, not exactly feeling left out but simply basking in fatherly pride toward his younger sister.

She deserved the praise after all that she'd done in her short life. For all the horrors she faced and things she'd had to face alone, all by herself without him there.

"Yeah, awesome job, Vanessa," he finally said quietly to himself.

He was the first to turn and see the conductor standing on a stone at the edge of the forest, calling for the attention of the confused and astonished crowd of passengers.

"As you can see, the fire's been put out," he started, "and compartments one, two, three, and four are officially out. Thanks to the help of…"

He looked to Cassie, Vanessa and Aria, whispering, "…your names?"

"Cassie."

"Vanessa."

"Aria."

"Thanks to the bravery and strength of Cassie, Vanessa, and Aria, we can now safely continue our journey to the Crystalia Train Station.

"Now everyone, aboard the train once again."

It was shocking to see that their compartment still looked rather the same.

Although there were scorch marks on the leather of the booth seats and parts of the wood table had crumbled to dust, it was nothing that they couldn't fix with a repair spell…

…although they didn't have one.

Katie, last to enter, immediately took notice of the dripping water on the seat beneath her, the wood table crisp as it still wisped with smoke.

Although, their seats had been moved; toward the back of the compartment, things looked burned to nothing but a crisp, smoke wisping from the piles of ash.

This forced them to slightly open up the windows of the train car.

"I'm still confused about how that guy was able to find us," Avery commented. "Because even if he did know your names—"

"It was because we made the stupid mistake of telling his boss, the President of the Animal Kingdom, our full names, so they probably used some sort of spell to find us," Cassie elucidated.

"Wait, hold on." Vanessa stopped her before she could continue. "Who was that guy? And what do you mean he 'knows' Vitina?'

"Yeah," Darius agreed. "I don't remember you guys mentioning that guy."

"When we were looking for Avery in Rubidium, we saw Vitina, the President of the Animal Kingdom, and that guard in a conversation. They were talking about how the President wanted to find us, meaning me, Katie, Conner, and Aria, because we had to use her wand for the Seeing Portal spell." She looked to her sister. "The one we used to find you."

"Anyways, they'll help each other as long as they can possibly stand each other—which I'm hoping isn't for too long—to find and get more information on us. As well as info on Avery. And that's when Katie and I knew that we really had to get you out of—"

"What's going on with her?" Darius asked, a tinge of worry in his usual calm words.

"What'd you—"

At her side, she watched as Avery convulsed with purple electricity, like she had before Cassie's duel with Vitina. Was this because of her purple scar? Was this what Vitina had meant? That as long as that mark was there, she could still be electrocuted?

Well, of course it is, Cassie thought.

Katie, in a desperate attempt to somehow help her, seemed to concentrate, perhaps racking her brain for ways to treat those who fell to electrocution, attempting to keep herself from breaking into a fit of crying as the shocking continued.

In that moment, Avery collapsed, falling onto the mahogany carpet of the train car as Cassie kneeled over her sister on the floor.

Holding back the tears, she cried out, "Oh God, oh God, oh God…" She put her ear to her sister's chest, trying to hear some sort of heartbeat

Nothing.

Nothing.

Nothing.

Then she heard a single beat. Then another. Then another.

Cassie sighed with relief and addressed to her friends crowded around her. "She's okay. But we should try to get to Mrs. Fulton's house as soon as possible."

She returned to her seat, sitting beside an unconscious Avery and watching to make sure she was breathing every now and then in the apprehensive stillness of their compartment.

For the rest of the three-hour trip, Darius, Vanessa, and Francis couldn't stop asking Conner and Aria about what life in the Earth Realm would be like.

They sought to somehow uplift the mood, although Avery's state was still the object of focus whenever the forced conversation was dying down.

Meanwhile, Katie focused on writing down all the questions she wanted to ask her mom once they had returned home, such as "Did you develop any new spells?" or "What was Ruler Marjorie like?" or "Have you ever used the Staff of Infinite Power?"

As she recorded these questions, she would look outside at the majestic mountains behind the groves of alcus trees and the flowing rivers and streams that ran through the forest.

In the light blue sky patterned with fluffy, white clouds, black birds flew in triangular flocks, soaring through the sky.

She focused on them, attempting not to look at poor Avery.

When they had finally reached the mansion, Katie's eyes stayed locked on the height of the structure. It was divided into two compartments, a large and wide building in the front, and an even taller hotel in the back. There was also a white marble, shaded patio at the front of the main building, large pillars supporting the roof.

Connecting the two buildings in the back was a golden sign lined with scarlet that said CRYSTALIA TRAIN STATION in bronze lettering.

The mansion was beside a wide forest where deer and squirrels ran around freely among the alcus and rainbow eucalyptus trees, their bark flaking off in vibrant neon orange, bright pink, orange, and grayish-blue chips that littered the emerald-green grass.

"I've heard it's common to find ademonas here," Aria said excitedly. "I've been really hoping that I'll find one."

Over the speaker, the conductor declared, "Thank you for riding with this train today. Thanks especially to Ms. Cassie, Vanessa, and Aria for putting out the fire; your bravery and strength are appreciated, and I would be pleased to journey with you all again someday."

Outside of the train, the group was left alone as the other passengers headed into the train station with their belongings. Passersby stared intently at Dillion, some children asking their parents if they could pet the creature as their eyes lit up.

The day was rather busy, and a large crowd was gathering in the middle of the white-tiled space in front of the main mansion.

"What are they looking at?" Aria asked, looking over the crowd at the towering stone fountain, its water spraying into a ginormous pool below with a relaxing trickle.

Yet, as she stopped at the fountain, she couldn't help but smile.

"What's that?" Darius asked, peering over the crowd at what was in the fountain.

There was a blue-skinned salamander roughly the size of Avery. Its moist skin was striped with purple, and it had shining purple eyes that bored into the audience of people.

From its wide mouth came a squeaking noise, exposing sharp teeth to the crowd, who responded with 'ohs!' and 'ahs!' of amazement and intrigue.

"It is really cute," Darius said, leaning at the edge of the gray stone fountain to lock eyes with the ademona. "Hey there, little guy." He waved his hand at the creature.

With a squinting of its eyes, the creature moved some water from the pool into the shape of an orb, the fluid levitating right above most of the crowd.

The ademona released the water by blinking, raining fountain water atop the crowd. Most of the crowd laughed and proceeded to walk off as Darius and Aria stayed behind, drops of fountain water catching in their hair as they crouched closer to the rim of the fountain bowl.

"Well, that's a shame," Aria said, twisting the water out of her locks. "I really thought I could adopt this ademona." She waved the thought away, shrugged her shoulders as she eventually stood up. "I don't think I'd ever get one anyway though. So, I think for now…"

She took notice of the glassy mountain looming over them to the west. "…I should start focusing on getting us up there."

They returned to their friend's sides silently, walking together as they silently took in the marvelous sight of the mountain.

It seemed constructed of diamonds, reflecting light from the sun across their vision as it glossed over with impeccable luster. On a large ledge halfway up the mountain, somewhat obscured from view, was a small, white stone cottage with a dark tiled roof.

Surrounding the house was a garden full of lavender wisteria, walling the house into a haven of natural protection, flowers draping over the garden's wall.

Aside from the wisterias that danced in the gentle wind, there were also bunches of red and pink begonias, such a large number that they were easy to see from where they stood toward the base of the mountain. Tall sunflower stalks grew there too, their flowers facing toward the ground as they danced heedlessly close to a drop in the mountain.

"It looks… amazing…" Cassie said in awe. "It's so beautiful, but…" She looked to Aria. "Why would that be the safe house?"

"It's where Mrs. Fulton must've been living for a while. And as the only house she's had for at least a year, she must've wanted to make it at least a bit homey, y'know?"

A safe house, a home? I kinda like that idea. It's nice and makes me wonder, what'll this Mrs. Fulton be like?

Chapter 22
The Potion Maker

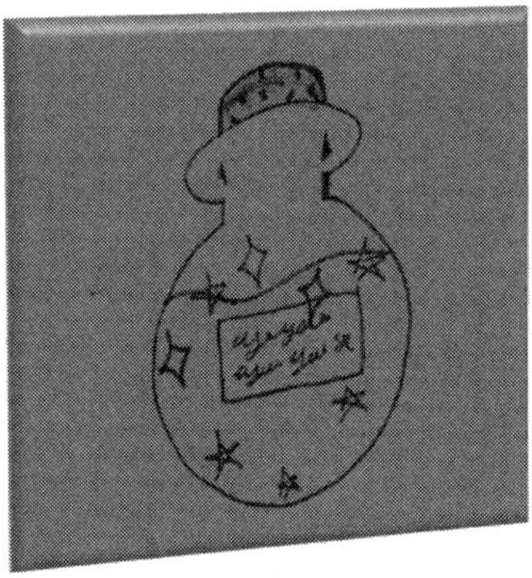

AFTER A TIRING CLIMB HALFWAY up the mountain, Katie was relieved to have finally arrived as she kicked out her legs and sat on the warm diamond crystal, smoothed to appear rather glass-like. "We've made it!" she celebrated, looking at Cassie. "Aren't you excited to see Mom and Dad again? I can't wait to hug them after all this time!"

Until now, Cassie had never truly taken a moment to think about how Katie felt about all this. And, in retrospect, she was feeling bad for all that she'd had to go through with this.

But she was proud of her for managing to stick it out for this long. Even if she never needed to. Even if most kids her age would've given up.

She had managed to persevere. And for that she had to be proud.

"Yeah, that'll be really wonderful, Katie." She beamed down at her.

The group of friends followed a waving stone path lined with pebbles to the cottage, Katie beginning to run toward the door halfway.

"Oh my God, Katie…" Cassie shook her head as her sister was repelled back a few feet from the cottage, rubbing her head as she sat astonished on the ground.

"Looks like she needs to know we're the ones at the door," Aria said from behind.

"Yeah, we know," Conner interrupted before she could go on any farther. "Just hold up for a minute before you go off on another tangent for— like—the fourth time today."

Aria whispered a curse beneath her breath as Conner cockily took his crystal blue wand out of his backpack and pointed it at the force field.

And just as the first word of the spell was about to leave his lips, Aria shouted in retaliation, "Make sure not to mess it up, dear brother!"

"Shut up!" he yelled back, something in his voice telling her that she might as well continue if this was the reaction she was getting.

After all this time, she was finally able to get to him.

"Disputatio—"

"Don't screw it up, Conner!"

His wand fell into the soft garden grass as he approached his sister, all sense of joking having evaporated with his clear sense of frustration.

"I swear to God, Aria, if you don't shut th—"

"Hey!" Francis stopped him, gesturing toward Katie. "Don't curse in front of kids, all right?"

Before Conner had the chance to even continue, Vanessa handed him his wand.

"Shut up, will ya? We don't have time for you to pull this type of crap right now. Once we get to Earth, argue as much as you want, okay?" She glared at the both of them, eyes locking on Conner for a few extra moments. "Then after that, I don't care whatever you do."

She wasn't exactly annoyed, but there was irritation to her words.

It was just like when Aria would try to speak to him after she'd pulled an all-nighter or when he'd managed to break one of her things again.

But something about it seemed comforting, somehow. It was visible in his smile.

He stood as if pondering for a few seconds.

But then the silence was disturbed, a deafening boom ringing though the mountain as everyone slammed their hands against their ears.

"What'd the spell do?" Cassie questioned as she stood from the ground. "And what was with it being so loud?"

"It had to break the soundproof barrier on the force field, so we can talk to her without having her take down the force field. It ensures the protection of the person inside, and—yeah—I know that I could just remove the spell myself but we still wanna make a good impression on her, right?" Vanessa insisted.

Francis stepped forward toward the invisible field, being the first to ensure their safety at the moment. "It's good!" he said from before them. "Now say what it is you wanted to say."

"Mrs. Fulton," Conner said through the field.

At her name, a woman with caramel brown skin and dark brown eyes peeked out of the door, her black locks resting on her shoulders as she locked eyes with the random boy who stood there. "Who are you?"

Conner gestured Cassie to the shield and instructed her, "Tell her who your mom is."

"I'm Trinity Smith's daughter," she said back. "These are my friends."

She showed her Avery's limp body on her shoulders. "And I need you to help my sister. If you can, of course."

"Oh God." Dalia quickly brought down the force field, letting the group inside.

She brought it up once more with a wave of her wand as she inspected outside the door for a few moments before eventually closing it.

She led them toward the wood door, opening it to reveal the quaint living space inside. "Come in, come in, please."

Within the one-floor cottage was a small living room with a mahogany couch, flatscreen TV, two light-brown, velvety soft side chairs on either side, and a sanded brown coffee table atop a fluffy white carpet. At the back of the space was a small walk-in kitchen equipped with a shining metal microwave, dishwasher, and oven.

Next to an obsidian black burner atop the oven was a white granite counter below white cabinets where she kept her bowls and paper towels.

"You guys stay here while I fix you some tea," Dalia said, walking off to the kitchen.

Cassie watched Avery for a moment, checked her heartbeat—almost steady, but a bit slow—and sat her back down next to her on the couch.

"Here you go," Dalia said, handing everyone a small teacup full of tea. "One spoon of sugar for each if that's all right." She took her own cup in her hands as she sat down last. "Now, what's going on with your sister?"

"Well, have you heard of Vitina?" Cassie started.

"Oh…" Dalia stayed quiet for a few seconds. "Yes. Yes, I have. She was the reason I have to leave here now. Why I have to go away from my daughter, Stephanie."

The melancholy in her words was undeniable.

"Well, ma'am, if it's any consolation, your daughter is safe at school and is doing just fine," Vanessa added.

"Thank you for saying that. Ms. Vanessa, I believe? Stephanie talks quite a lot about you after her lessons. Says you're an excellent student and an incredibly good friend…"

She looked back at Cassie. "But I'm getting off track. What did Vitina do to your sister? It must have been some sort of magic, right?"

"She was taken to Rubidium, which is one of the reasons we came here because we know that if anyone can save her, you can. But the problem is that there also this mark on her collar that Vitina's been using to electrocute her. It just happened a couple of hours ago.

"And you need me to find a way to remove the mark?"

"If you could, please. But if you can't, I just need you to help my sister regain some sort of consciousness."

"All right then," Dalia said, finishing the last of her tea and setting the cup on the coffee table. "Come along with me. I'll show you where I can help her."

***

They were inside a small, dark room lit with only white and black lamps hanging on the high ceiling. In the middle of the room was a long oak table with a black cauldron atop a ginormous stove, and the entire room walls comprises tiny wood shelves holding glass mason jars filled with potion ingredients.

"A healing potion, right?" Dalia said as she was searching for ingredients on her shelf.

"Yes, but why can't we just use a healing spell?" Cassie commented. "That would be the faster option, right?"

"Yes, it would be a lot quicker, but it wouldn't be as strong as a potion, so it won't be able to heal your sister to the fullest extent. I also might be able to remove those marks."

"What about mine?" Francis said, pointing to the purple and black scars on his collar.

"Oh!" Mrs. Fulton exclaimed. "Both of you were taken to Rubidium?"

Francis nodded. "But luckily, I haven't been shocked yet; there's a chance Vitina hasn't noticed I'm gone."

"So that's a healing potion and one to remove those marks. That's going to take quite a long time…" She set down the notepad on which she had been scribbling. "But I should be able to do it."

She hurried to a wall lined with scrolls of parchment, each one labeled with the potion name and the ingredients it needed. She stopped at a list that rea.

On the opposing side of the room, she pulled out a round vial containing a neon green liquid, the small vial titled *Magical Mark Removal.*

She sat the unconscious Avery down in a small rocking chair, holding the vial in her other hand as she shifted Avery's head to the side, leaving the mark exposed.

"All I have to do is put a drop of this potion on each mark and they should disappear in a few seconds." She looked to Cassie for confirmation. "Is that okay with you?"

She nodded eagerly as she said, "As long as it helps her get better."

Carefully, she put a single droplet of potion on Avery's purple scar.

She then dropped another on the black mark on the other side of her collar almost immediately after, covering the vial after.

The potion bubbled at her skin, a green steam wisping into the air as the scar was eaten up by the magical concoction.

"Doesn't that hurt?" Francis questioned. "Sounds kinda painful."

"No, it's more of a warm feeling against your skin. And it only lasts for a few seconds, probably a minute at most, truly."

In a few more seconds, the marks faded.

Cassie smiled as Mrs. Fulton retrieved the vial's cap.

"Thank you so much for this, Mrs. Fulton," Cassie thanked, lips upturned in a beaming grin. "Genuinely, thank you for this."

"Oh, don't thank me yet. I still have to help her because of the electrocution. It'll leave a couple of marks too." She glanced at Francis. "Please sit here."

"All right…"

Francis appeared very skeptical of the potion as she placed a drop on each mark. Before he could question the concoction, the same result ensued and the marks started to fade away.

"Oh wow, it really did work," Francis realized, tapping the place where the scars once lay; the area now bore his own new skin.

At the moment of witnessing it, he couldn't help but start crying with joy.

He hadn't felt so free… So free to live, in such a long time.

With the scars gone, he never had to worry about receiving electrocution whenever he felt he'd done anything wrong. He didn't have to fear death by shock at any point in time.

Now, he was finally free.

Free from the death and fear that had loomed over him from such a young age.

"It really worked!" he cheered as he hugged his sister and Dalia. "Thank you so much, Mrs. Fulton! I'm finally…" He took a deep breath as he freed the women from his tight grasp. "Thank you, Mrs. Fulton. Thank you so much for this."

"No problem," she breathed. "I am a certified potion maker, after all."

Vanessa grinned up at her brother as his lips stayed upturned in a smile.

"What is it?" he interrogated her immediately, seeing her eyes on him. "Does it look off? Yeah, I know. It'll be like that for me too for a while."

"No, it's nothing. It's just that I'm glad you're finally getting this," she explained. "The chance to finally not have to deal with Vitina's crap anymore, I mean."

"Three years…" He smiled again, eyes bright with genuine excitement. "Three whole years! It's over! Finally!"

He trapped her in another tight hug again, and Vanessa smiled as she embraced him back. She seemed to have missed seeing him smile like this.

And she must've missed hearing the chirp to his words when he was speaking.

In other words, she had surely missed having her brother.

As Dalia insisted on letting everyone besides the three sisters leave the potions room, Francis trailed along with his little sister, obviously with the intention to catch up on all the 'big brother' moments he'd never gotten to experience with her.

As Dalia whipped up the healing potion from the ingredients on her shelf, checking the scroll for the correct measurements every now and then, she began stirring the cauldron.

She poured the thin, water-like liquid into several round-bottomed vials with corks for caps as she packaged them away, placing them on one of her shelves, also handing one to Katie and another to Cassie.

"I'm going to need each of you to get her to swallow it. All of it. Or else she'll still experience the effects of the electrocution."

Cassie, the first to give her the potion, tilted her head back and slipped the liquid down her throat. Following after, Katie did the same.

Watching intently, they noticed her fingers begin to twitch, eyes opening groggily as she looked up at the two of them.

"Katie? Cassie?" she said, looking at her sisters as they stared down at her. She must have caught sight of Dalia Fulton as well, putting healing potion vials on the shelves.

"Who's that?"

"Dalia Fulton. A friend of Mom's." Cassie beamed down at her. "She helped you get rid of those collar marks and is gonna help us get to Earth."

"Really?" she shouted happily. "They're really gone? Are you serious"

"Yes, Avery," Dalia said, turning around. "And—"

"Thank you, Mrs. Fulton!" she shouted as she wrapped the woman in a hug.

It was odd from Dalia's perspective, this child she barely knew hugging her like this. But she did remind her a lot of Trinity. So affectionate and sweet all the time.

Yet at the same time, she had gone through so much.

***

After a filling lunch that Dalia had insisted on serving the eight of them, she scrawled a list of ingredients for an interdimensional potion down on the table with the three sisters in the potion room, each of them gawking at the collection of words.

"All of this?" Katie groaned. "Seriously?"

"Yes, and I believe that I have all the ingredients…" She paused at the last and examined her shelf from afar. "Except for this one."

"'Bark of the rainbow eucalyptus tree'," Cassie read. "Isn't that at the base of the mountain? We could go collect that now."

"No way!" Dalia reprimanded, wincing at the way she rose her voice so suddenly. "Sorry about that, Cassie. It's just that the forest is covered in clear crystals that can pose a threat to those who dare to step foot there. That's why the train station is so far from the growing sites of those crystals."

"What's wrong with them?" Avery questioned. "Seem like normal crystals to me, from what I've learned."

"These are special crystals. These rocks can manifest into the most terrifying predator, at least in your opinion, as soon as you catch sight of them."

"Can they actually hurt you?" Katie inquired.

"Yes." There was a sense of immediate apprehension in her words as she answered.

Cassie deflected her eyes from Dalia's as she questioned, "So, what do we do then?"

"Someone could take Dillion," Katie insisted. "Even though you can see them, they can't attack you if you're out of reach, right?"

"That's solid logic," Dalia insisted. "But the best bark of the tree is always close to the ground, meaning the predators could reach you anyways."

"We'll have to be fast then," Katie said as she adjusted her coat, Avery piping up as she jumped from her chair, "Could I come?"

"Avery, you just recovered from being electrocuted," Cassie dismissed. "It's best you stay here. It'll let you get to know everyone better, too."

"But I want to be a true member of the team, Cass!" she argued. "You guys have done all of this just for me. All because I decided to be an absolute idiot and do something that could've killed me. *Would've* killed me if not for you guys."

She sighed as she looked down. "I just wanna prove my worth. Somehow. Just wanna prove that saving me was truly worth it."

"Trinity used to speak like that," Dalia reminisced softly, somewhat hidden in the light of the faint lamps. "Used to put herself down all the time. Saying that she had to prove herself to Ruler Marjorie. To Micah. Even to me."

"Mom?" Avery softly said. "Really?"

"But truthfully…" Dalia wrapped her arms around Avery the way that Avery's mother would. "…she never did. She was always worthy of the love from others. Always deserved the good things she got. And you, Avery. You remind me of her, y'know?"

She paused, Avery absorbing the stillness of the moment. "So wonderful and amazing and full of potential. You're incredible, Avery. Please realize that. I know that this advice seems quite cookie cutter and—"

"I miss her," Avery managed to say through the choking tears. "I miss my mom. She was amazing. And why would she ever put herself down? Someone as amazing as her? Why?"

"That's what I'd like to ask you, Avery. But like your mother, realize how amazing you are. Not ridiculing. Realizing. Embracing. Do that for me, for your mom, okay?"

Avery nodded excitedly as she pulled away from the hug. "I will. Thank you…again, Mrs. Fulton."

"All right then," Dalia said, clasping her hands together. "Avery and Katie, you two will be collecting the tree bark. Quick tip by the way: make sure to collect as much as you possibly can. Try to get the bark toward the base of the trunk, but if you can't, don't sweat it. Just stay safe, all right?"

Leading the three of them toward the door to her cottage, Avery buttoned her cloak around herself as Dalia led them through her garden, Dillion prowling right after them.

"Stay safe out there. I'm sure that Trinity can't wait to see you guys again. So, let's get you home!" she cheered.

Dillion's wing flapped as he took off, leaving a worried Cassie and a proud Dalia witnessing as they departed.

***

"So, you can talk to animals?" Avery questioned, seated behind her.

"Yeah, exactly that. Not aloud though."

"How come? And why can't Cassie or Mrs. Fulton or me?"

"Every human has a specific part of their brain that can control their use of magic. Everyone can perform spells because of this, or at least that's how Conner and Aria explained this stuff to us," Katie elaborated. "When it comes to everyone's individual power—like mine is to talk to animals—a part of their brain goes off because they've already started using magical abilities. That's why I was able to access mine when I started using magic the first night we were here."

They were flying over the Crystalia Train Station Hotel when Avery asked, "Can you predict what type of power you'll have then?"

"I'd like to think so, but I'm not really sure, in fact. An interesting question though."

"So, if you like animals, then there's a chance you'll have an animal communication power, right? So, it has to do with special interests?

"Like I said before, not sure, but I guess that would make some sense. I don't think that you can genuinely predict these sorts of things."

Avery thought about this for a moment then the Rainbow Forest came into view. "She wasn't kidding," she said, observing the ten-foot trees. "They are close to the ground."

A few trees were rather tall, but they were in close proximity to towering crystals, and Katie and Avery weren't going to take that risky chance to manifest a gigantic predator.

They scanned the ground.

The trees looked as if someone had torn away their bark crudely, leaving the vibrant neon green and hot pink bark marks in its place.

Katie swerved Dillion toward a clearing where two rather short, rainbow eucalyptuses stood, the space barren of crystals.

They hovered near the top of the eucalyptus tree and ripped strips of bark off of its trunk, throwing the pieces into the basket.

As they worked, they tried their hardest to not to look at the crystals in the forest, hoping and praying they wouldn't accidentally flick their eyes that way.

"Why don't these crystals attack the train station?" Avery asked again.

"Might be because no one ever looks at them, so they can't attack them. But just because I've been in this place for a while doesn't mean I really know everything about it, y'know?"

"I know that, but you're managing to answer these questions pretty well, right? So then, as long as no one can see the animal, it doesn't exist?"

"Or *probably* not. It might be that when they manifest, the being is already created and can't just disappear."

"That means one wrong look and we're done for," Avery said grimly, now aware she couldn't risk screwing this up, not after what she'd promised back at the cottage.

They had finished collecting the bark once they started their flight up the mountain. Avery looked down at the ground as they took off, making the biggest mistake possible.

She looked at a crystal.

Before she even had the chance to look away, the crystal morphed into a lengthy aquamarine shape, the creature's ginormous scaled wings flapping as it neared them.

The resultant dragon had long sharp horns and was breathing steam from its long snout with each breath, acrid smoke that filled the air and stung their noses.

Katie's immediate response when she heard it roar was to fly as far from Dalia's cottage and the train station as possible.

Even if they got lost, if they could somehow get the creature off their tail, it'd be worth it.

"Seems they don't disappear if you look away," Avery said regretfully, a sense of joking to her voice that made Katie believe she was trying to lighten the mood.

"No not really!" she agreed, irritated, instructing Dillion to gain speed, leaning forward as she tried to keep herself from getting blown back.

Avery kept watch of the dragon as they flew, telling Katie when to deviate from the path of the flames as they narrowly avoided trees simultaneously.

"Left!" she said as the fire seared the air on the right of them.

The dragon was beginning to lose its speed as they flew, allowing them to hide in a small stone cave beneath a ledge, overlooking a babbling brook in the light of the afternoon sun.

"Oh shoot, Katie, I'm really sorry…" Avery said frantically.

"Look, it's fine." Katie was watching as Dillion sat at the river for a small drink. "Since the dragon isn't on our trail anymore, we can head back to Dalia's place now."

They had only just started flying again when the dragon that had been chasing them caught sight of them, hot on their trail once more.

"Not again…" Avery groaned, looking back at the dragon. "This thing has to let up sometime soon."

Avery watched as it slithered in the air, trying to gain speed on them in order to flame them alive from the front; that way, they could barely escape.

Dillion and the dragon were in a race to see who could fly the fastest, the dragon inching on Dillion's advantage as they eyed each other face to face.

The amaratio ducked and flew under a canopy of trees in the forest, giving them a few seconds to breathe as the dragon searched for them. When this method didn't work, it seared the forest with its fiery breath, causing them to soar away from the path of fire behind them.

They were back over the forest again, the dragon creature beginning tire once more.

"Can't you talk to it?" Avery asked as she looked over her shoulder.

"I have to get close to it to do that!"

Avery was examining the creature even more, trying to find a way to get rid of it.

It wasn't as if she had a power. She couldn't have one unless…

…but she had used magic before.

Even if it was magic taught to her by Vitina or Andromeda, it was still magic.

That meant that she could access her power, right? At least if she tried hard enough. If she focused hard enough.

Any power would be useful right now.

Without a second thought, she thrust her hands at the dragon, hoping for something to happen.

It stopped short in flight.

"Dillion, stop flying," Katie instructed.

As they hovered in the sky, Avery moved both of her hands up, causing the frozen dragon to move up as well.

So, that was her power. Telekinesis, it seemed.

"Yes!" she cheered. "Now all I have to do is levitate it somewhere far from here."

She stretched her arms as high as she could, placing the dragon a few feet below a large cloud. Avery thrust her hands upwards as forcefully as possible, causing the dragon to be pushed through the clouds and out of their view.

"Well," Avery chuckled, happy yet awkward. "Looks like I have a power, too, huh?"

***

"A dash of windleweed," Dalia said, adding flakes of a dark-green weeds to the potion. "And a stock of the krintle mushroom."

She dropped thick sunset-colored mushroom into the watery violet potion.

"Is that everything on the list?" Darius asked, looking at the parchment.

"Yes," Dalia answered as she stirred it. "Now all I need is the rainbow eucalyptus bark."

"What does the bark do for the potion?" Cassie asked, observing mauve smoke escaping from the boiling cauldron.

"The rainbow eucalyptus tree is one of the most mystical and majestic plants on Earth. Not only is it beautiful, but it also has magical properties. When added to any potion at all, it gives it an extreme degree of power. Because the rainbow eucalyptus is one of the most magical plants in the Earth Realm, it can allow this interdimensional potion to get you to Earth." She backed away from the boiling cauldron and sat in the rocking chair in the corner of the room. "As we wait for your sisters to arrive, you guys can just relax."

"It's been more than an hour and I wanted them back early," Cassie said, rather perturbed as she leaned against a wall. "Not to mention that Flynn knows we're here, too."

"Flynn? Who's that?" questioned Mrs. Fulton. "Seems awfully suspicious for all of you to want to look out for him."

"Flynn's the guard for Christina Robel, the President of the Animal Kingdom. We found out that she's working with Vitina, so Flynn and all the other President's guards are working for her, too. On the train here, Flynn heard us talking about coming here.

"So now he knows where to find us."

"That's rather worrisome," Dalia sighed, glancing back at the simmering potion. She eyed the group's gloomy faces. "But not to worry though, everyone! This strong force field will keep myself and this cottage safe." She froze. "As long as they don't decipher the counter potion, of course."

"What'd you mean?" Vanessa inquired. "This is one of the strongest spells in the history of magical spellcasting, or at least that's what my professor taught us. How in the world would they manage to find out that?"

"Indeed, it is, but long ago, a sorceress by the name of Lilliana Orbin developed a potent potion that could disintegrate any spell's Resicus," Dalia said. "But the potion's unstable power meant destroying the recipe for good so it didn't fall into the wrong hands. But..."

"...it was created by an ancestor of Vitina," Conner continued.

"Yes, which means if Vitina finds some way to dig into her family past, she could decipher what the potion is."

"So, she could have the Staff of Infinite Power and a potion that can defeat any spell we throw at her?" Cassie hesitated, questioning herself. "But how would she uncover her family's past anyways if she doesn't know already?"

"If there are magic cell towers in the area, an event can be recorded without a spell. With the correct spell for looking into the past and by knowing the time when the event happened, the spellcaster can view the scene. But of course, since there weren't many magic cell towers built back then, the picture would be fuzzy or difficult to see at all," Aria explained.

"But in the instance that she can read it, we're toast," Francis said, distraught as he fiddled nervously with his fingers in his pocket.

"But no one knows the incantation for the spell, right?" Cassie said, trying to be optimistic.

"Well, some people, people like me and the Council of the Realm members, have made a pact to not tell anyone about this."

"So, she could find a way to get it out of someone?" Darius inquired. "Just like that? Really?"

"Yes," admitted Dalia somberly. "Yes, she could, in fact."

They all sat in silence for a moment, the gravity of the situation weighing down on them. There was a whole array of bad things that could happen to them.

"Hello!" a happy muffled voice said from outside the barrier. "We need to get in!"

"They're back!" Dalia shouted, mood shifting almost immediately as she sprinted for the door with her crystal wand in hand, Cassie following tightly behind her.

Katie, Avery, and Dillion were outside with a basket full of indigo, neon green, and hot pink bark. After bringing down her barrier and letting them into the house, and bringing up the force field once more, Dalia led Avery and Katie toward her potions room.

They ventured through a mahogany hallway.

"And now for the bark…" Dalia said, sprinkling half of it into the cauldron. As she stirred it, she told Avery and Katie, "Thank you for collecting these for me, you two."

She watched everyone lean in as the potion gradually changed color from violet, to magenta, to chartreuse green.

"Now everyone, think about the realm you want to transport to. Really think hard about it. And if you've never been to Earth, just think about the word, all right?"

As they followed her instructions, Dalia prepared eight syringes for each of them, extracting the exact amount of the chartreuse potion into each.

"Here you go," she said, handing one to each of them. "Keep your thoughts on Earth, everyone."

"Now on the count of three, each eject the potion into your mouths, okay?"

They all nodded yes and placed the full syringe over their open mouths.

"One..."

Avery visibly tensed up.

"Two..."

There was a clattering in the kitchen.

"Three!"

Each squirted the chartreuse potion into their mouths, all except for Avery. It went down their throats like a thick smoothie, bitter and sweet at the same time, warm yet cold, so contradictory yet so simple in a way.

"Avery, go on. Take your potion," Dalia instructed, observing the seven chartreuse portals slowly gaining in size in front of Francis, Vanessa, Conner, Aria, Cassie, Darius, and Katie.

"I heard something clatter in the kitchen," she said, glancing at the hallway leading to the potion room.

"What'd you mean, Avery? I didn't hear anything."

"But I definitely heard something. We need to go check it out, Dalia," she insisted, walking down the hallway before Dalia even got a moment to agree.

"Y'know your mother always had a knack for this type of stuff. Always the cautious one, wasn't she," Dalia said as they walked down the hallway. "Not surprised that you do too." She looked at the group and, more than halfway down the hallway, she mentioned to them, "Check the rest of the cottage everyone!"

Avery followed Dalia to the force field, somewhat trying to take charge of this odd search for the source of this 'sound'.

"Looks fine," she said, Avery opening her mouth to argue. "We should—"

"Hey, guys!" Conner shouted from within the cottage. "You'd better see this!"

They all rushed to the guest bathroom beside the kitchen, finding a cracked window, the sink and toilet covered in shattered glass.

"Someone broke in..." Dalia said, breathless. "How! How in the world could someone break in!"

"Maybe when you were bringing down the force field at some point. But where is this person?" Francis added. "And who are they?"

"I don't know, but I'd have to suspect it's Flynn," answered Aria. "So, until we find him and get him out, we're staying here."

"But maybe Dillion could sniff him out," Katie suggested.

Katie looked the amaratio straight in the eye. "All right, Dillion, could you find any unknown heat signature perhaps? Or just follow any unknown scent that you're not picking up from us?" she sent telepathically to him.

"Of course, Katie," Dillion's deep voice said.

He turned his golden-brown face to the door and led everyone to Dalia's bedroom.

"Go on Dillion, lead us to him."

Following the winged lion through Dalia's bedroom and to her white marble bathroom, Dillion began growling excessively.

"I've found an odd scent here," Dillion thought to Katie as he waded to the right corner of her walk-in closet on the left side of the bathroom.

Dalia pointed her crystal wand at the hanging shirts on hooks, yet she couldn't find anyone.

"Dillion," Katie thought to her amaratio. "Any signs?"

"No, but someone was just here." He seized a white sheet of paper in his mouth and laid it in Katie's hands.

Unraveling the note, Katie gasped in astonishment.

> Vitina's on your trail, you fugitives. I could've killed your precious Mrs. Fulton if I wanted to. Coulda killed all of you.
>
> But I want to bring your hopes up, so when they fall, it's just that much sweeter.
>
> You might as well just quit while I'm ahead. I know your plan. Vitina knows your plan. Andromeda knows your plan.
>
> In the end, you'll always know you're criminals, even if you think you're doing the right thing. I work under the President of the Animal Kingdom, and if she says something's right, it's right without question.
>
> If she works with Vitina, she saw something special in her, something good in her. If you can't see why you're doing the wrong thing, there's no helping you.
>
> You're lost causes. The whole horrid lot of you. When we find you and all the others fighting against us, they'll lead us straight to your beloved Trinity Smith.
>
> We'll find you,
> Flynn.

Chapter 23
Finally! Out of the Magic Realm

"**WE HAVE TO FIND A WAY** out of here," Conner said, worry increasing as they all rejoined in the potions room after reading Flynn's note.

"I know just the solution," Dalia said. "But it won't allow us to save everyone."

Inside, the portals had expanded to a size they could step through.

She told Avery to take her syringe.

"I've had a lot of free time without as many Council of the Realm duties, so I've been studying some powerful spells. And with all this time I've been having, I discovered one known as the Black Hole."

"Like the ones in space?" Avery questioned. "The ones that can eat up entire planets?"

"In a way I guess, yet it's a ginormous portal that can transport entire structures into different dimensions. I won't tell you the incantation for fear that Flynn may be listening, but it's important you all take that portal to Earth first."

Everyone checked they had everything they had beforehand, then each gave a farewell hug to Dalia and thanked her for her help. Francis was the most grateful of all of them.

"Thank you so much for this, Mrs. Fulton!" he choked through his happy tears.

His death grip was strong, but she managed to escape and said, "Don't worry about thanking me, Francis. I'm just happy that you're okay now."

As everyone disappeared into the swirling chartreuse light of the portal, they disappeared with a whoosh, the last to leave being Dillion, who followed Katie into her portal.

"Okay then," muttered Dalia to herself. "Now I've just gotta perform that spell.

"And I'm out of here.

"I'm leaving the Magic Realm."

It was clearly an unsettling thought. To leave the world behind that had changed so much since Vitina's reign. She'd miss those memories.

But now, she'd finally get the chance to see Trinity again.

She must have missed seeing her.

But she was also leaving this place in its time of need. As a member of the Council, she should have known better, right?

"I'm going there to make people's lives here better. To find a way to finally defeat Vitina and Andromeda. To finally free this world from them.

"For good."

And with a deep breath, she raised her wand in the air.

"Cavum exponentia! Cavum exponentia! Cavum exponentia!" she cast, her wand alight as she drew a ginormous circle in the space between her kitchen and living room.

"To Earth!" she shouted, tapping the center of the circle with the tip of her wand.

She looked down at the ground, a black void rapidly swirling.

"It's working," she mused happily.

As if something was sucking her into the drain of a sink, it stretched her until she was floating in an empty, quiet space. When the weightlessness had worn off, something was pulling, pulling… taking her to the ground as if by a rope, only that there wasn't one.

Closing her eyes, she let the spell do its work, her surrounding space becoming colder and colder until she seemed to be stuck in a frozen tundra, only her dress as a source of warmth.

"I'm almost there," she said to distract herself from the piercing cold. "Almost to Earth, almost to Earth."

By the time she opened her eyes again, there was a large circular sphere colored with blue, green, and white clouds.

She seemed to be flying toward the planet at top speed, a black space filled with bits of light that blurred around her.

She closed her eyes again, awaking in her house. She was hungry.

She quickly looked out of her window, finding not a single person without a wand.

She had done it. She'd truly done it.

She was finally here.

She was finally on Earth.

Acknowledgements

There are just so many people to acknowledge who made this book go from a dream to a reality.

To my editor, Annie Jenkinson, who validated my writing ability, and believed that I had phenomenal talents for a 12-year-old. Thank you for being my second eye, encouraging me, and making this book the best that it could be.

To my parents, Isaac and Lucy, who worked long hours to format the specifics of this book so that it could become what it is.

To my siblings, Tammy and Tuana who cheered me along during the writing process and gave me the encouragement to write.

To my cover page artist Emma, who helped turn my thoughts to reality with my imagination brought to life.

To Barnes and Nobles, which, although a little odd, inspired my love of reading with all of the fantasy books galore. (And not to mention the amazing coffee, by the way)

To my elementary school reading and writing teachers who believed in my ability to write and express my creativity.

And finally, to the many authors whom I have indulged with their countless books since I was 3 years old. They made me love and cherish reading so much. I derive most of my best childhood memories from renowned authors.

Without these people, this book would've never been a reality, and for that, I am forever grateful.

ABOUT THE AUTHOR

Taylor Gitonga is a twelve-year-old author starting her new book series in the fantasy genre. She considers reading and writing a relaxing pastime and enjoys indulging in a variety of works of literature. This book will be the first in the new Portal in the Pantry series and she is extremely excited about what this series will, hopefully, become in the near future. "Writing this story was an adventure in itself of self-discovery, bettering myself, and development as a new up-and-coming author that I was grateful I got the opportunity to embark upon. Taylor lives with her family in the United States of America.

Made in the USA
Columbia, SC
01 October 2022

68335216R00198